With a sound of frustration, he swept her up in his arms and strode into the hall with her.

"What are you doing?" Francine squeaked. "Put me down this instant!"

Ignoring her, he kept walking.

A flutter of unease curled in her stomach. "Garrick," she hissed, "put me down or I'll scream and wake everyone up!"

"Go right ahead," he said. "It will only prove my point."

"And your point is?"

He stopped and looked down at her, his jaw tight, his eyes dark.

"You will learn that I am lord and master here, that I can do whatever I want, whenever I want, and no one will stop me."

She cleared her throat. "Garrick . . ."

His mouth closed over hers, cutting her off. . . .

A $\mathcal{K}$NIGHT
TO *C*HERISH

Angie Ray

JOVE BOOKS, NEW YORK

TIME PASSAGES is a registered trademark of Penguin Putnam Inc.

A KNIGHT TO CHERISH

A Jove Book / published by arrangement with
the author

PRINTING HISTORY
Jove edition / September 1999

All rights reserved.
Copyright © 1999 by Angela Ray.
Excerpt from *The More I See You* copyright © 1999 by Lynn Curland.
This book may not be reproduced in whole or part,
by mimeograph or any other means, without permission.
For information address: The Berkley Publishing Group,
a division of Penguin Putnam Inc.,
375 Hudson Street, New York, New York 10014.

The Penguin Putnam Inc. World Wide Web site address is
http://www.penguinputnam.com

ISBN: 0-515-12567-9

A JOVE BOOK®
Jove Books are published by The Berkley Publishing Group,
a division of Penguin Putnam Inc.,
375 Hudson Street, New York, New York 10014.
JOVE and the "J" design
are trademarks belonging to Penguin Putnam Inc.

PRINTED IN THE UNITED STATES OF AMERICA
10 9 8 7 6 5 4 3 2 1

For Kristen

My undying gratitude to two great writers:
Sandra (Paul) Chvostal and Barbara Benedict

And special thanks to
Denise Silvestro

Prologue

W ITH A SCOWL on his face, the tall, dark-haired knight strode through the hall where the servants, laughing and chattering, were setting up the trestle tables for the midday meal.

"Out of my way!" he snarled at one unfortunate enough to be in his path.

The room grew silent. Ducking his head, the servant murmured an apology and stepped back, as did the others. They watched without speaking as their lord and master stalked the length of the room and disappeared up the stairs at the far end of the hall.

The servants exchanged knowing glances, then went about their work, speaking in low whispers now.

"Did he try . . . ?"

"Who was he with?"

"Grace, the village laundress. . . ."

" 'Tis a terrible shame. . . ."

In a shadowed corner, a minstrel leaned toward the ebony-haired lady seated next to him and said mockingly, "A laundress? This grows pitiful, indeed. You must lift the spell, Anne."

The lady's lips tightened and her dark eyes flashed in the

way the minstrel knew so well. "I will not. He is only being stubborn. Like all men."

The minstrel sighed, half in exasperation, half in amusement. "You've paraded every woman in the kingdom before him. Not one of them inspired this grand passion you're so intent upon. Although personally, I think he had quite a passion for Lady Violet and Lady Yolande—"

"Bah! You know nothing of love."

"Not as you define it, obviously. And neither does Sir Garrick. Or any other man. I don't believe it exists."

"You're wrong, Rafael! It does exist!"

"Does it?" He stroked his thin, black moustache. "I'll believe that when I see it."

Rafael strolled away, plucking at his lute, and Anne stared after him in a fury. How could he see anything when he was so blind? What a lackwit! She would prove to him that real love existed—she *would*. Even if it took a hundred years.

Unfortunately, at the rate she was going, it might very well take a thousand years.

She left the hall and made her way to her stillroom, thinking hard. The minstrel was right about one thing. Her protégé *had* met nearly every eligible maiden in the kingdom, and none of them had been exactly right for him. Well, she would just have to look farther afield.

Anne entered the stillroom and carefully shut the door. She walked over to the worktable and sat on a high stool. Before her were bunches of sweet-smelling herbs and an earthen bowl of water. She looked down into its depths.

Slowly, a picture formed. Hazy at first, the blurry colors gradually cleared and sharpened into the image of a blond, rather prim-looking young woman in a strange room full of books.

Anne studied the woman for a moment, then smiled.

"Ah, yes," she breathed. "She'll be perfect. . . ."

Chapter 1

FRANCINE PEABODY WIPED her moist palms on the skirt of her navy-blue suit and glanced cautiously to the left, then to the right.

The long library aisle was deserted. Furtively, almost reluctantly, she scanned the titles on the shelf in front of her.

The Visual Dictionary of Sex. The Art of Sexual Ecstasy. Everything You Always Wanted to Know About Sex But Were Afraid to Ask.

The titles dismayed her. Did they have to be so . . . so *crude*? She was half tempted to forget the whole thing and just go back home. It would be embarrassing to check out one of these books. What if someone she knew saw her—someone from work or one of her neighbors? What would they think? They would probably think she was a twenty-five-year-old virgin who had to read a book to find out about sex.

And they would be right.

Although not for much longer, she comforted herself. In three months she would be a married woman, and then she would find out about sex firsthand. With Stuart.

Stuart. Butterflies fluttered in her stomach at the thought of him and what they would do on their wedding night. Finally, after five long years, they would consummate their re-lationship. The thought was exciting. Thrilling. And maybe just a little bit frightening. After all, when it came right down to it, she really didn't know all that much about sex.

She almost wished that she hadn't been quite so insistent that they wait.

"It will make our wedding night much more special," she'd told him after he'd proposed and tried to prolong a kiss. "I don't want to cheapen our relationship that way."

He'd instantly agreed with her and begged her pardon, telling her how much he admired her principles. They had both agreed to control any untoward impulses. Firmly.

The only problem was that now, after controlling them so firmly for so long, the thought of having to unleash them made Francine a bit uneasy.

Being a logical person, she'd immediately tried to think of some way to alleviate her uneasiness. Remembering Grandma Peabody's axiom that fear is caused by ignorance, she'd decided that the obvious solution was to increase her knowledge of sex.

Hence her trip to the library.

She just hadn't expected to feel so self-conscious. She hitched her purse strap higher on her shoulder. What would the librarian think when Francine checked out the book? Probably that Francine was some kind of pervert. A sex maniac. That she got her kicks reading books that—

Oh, for heaven's sake. She was being stupid. It didn't matter what the librarian thought. Or anyone else, either.

Just pick out a book and go, she told herself.

Taking a deep breath, she reached out toward the shelf. But just as her fingers touched the spine of a book, she saw a flash of motion at the end of the aisle. Instinctively, her fingers flew to the adjoining shelf and grabbed a book from there instead.

From the corner of her eye, she saw a man, short and pot-bellied, stroll down the aisle, perusing the titles. Francine buried her nose in the book she'd grabbed and waited for him to pass by.

To her dismay, he stopped next to her and studied the

books on the shelf intently. Then, without the least sign of embarrassment, he took down *The Visual Dictionary of Sex* and opened it. He flipped through the pages, stopping whenever he came to a picture.

What a pervert, Francine thought. Then, hastily, she corrected herself. Maybe the man wasn't a pervert. Maybe he was a virgin. Or maybe he suffered from some sexual problem.

Or maybe he's just a pervert.

Hunching her shoulders, Francine turned her back to him. She found it a bit unsettling to be standing next to a complete stranger while he ogled pictures of naked women.

Again, she was tempted to flee, but she couldn't leave yet. She was going to have to make love with Stuart soon, and she was determined not to goof it up when she did. Besides, every time she'd come to the library the last three Saturdays, she'd chickened out. At this rate, it would be her wedding night and she still wouldn't know anything about sex.

The potbellied man finally left, *The Visual Dictionary of Sex* tucked under his arm.

How could he seem so casual? she wondered, watching him stroll away. It must be because he was a man. Men were not as easily embarrassed as women.

Francine set down the book she was holding and turned back to the shelf of sex manuals, but before she could take one, someone else turned down the aisle. Hastily, she grabbed the book she'd just put down.

She stepped closer to the shelf to let the elderly woman pass by. The woman glanced at Francine's book and smiled.

"Are you expecting?" she asked.

Francine froze. Was it so obvious? "Expecting what?"

"A baby." The old woman nodded toward the book. "I bought that book for my granddaughter just a few weeks ago—she's expecting her first child."

"Oh." Francine looked at the book in her hands. *Joy of Pregnancy.* "Uh, yes," she lied.

"Congratulations, dear." The elderly woman proceeded to turn to the shelf of sex books and scanned the titles. She took out *Joy of Sex.*

Good heavens! Francine would have thought the woman was much too old to be interested in sex. Wasn't she worried about having a heart attack?

The woman must have seen Francine's stare, because she winked and said, "It never hurts to take a little refresher course."

"Oh . . . oh, yes," Francine stammered.

The woman left, and Francine stared after her, envying the woman's poise. But of course, the woman was older. Francine couldn't expect to have that sort of aplomb.

A girl of maybe thirteen or fourteen wearing a Catholic girls' school uniform turned down the aisle.

Popping her gum, the teenager sauntered up and with complete nonchalance took down *Everything You Always Wanted to Know About Sex*, and then left without even glancing at Francine.

Francine gaped after her. Then she squared her shoulders. If a *teenager* could check out a book on sex, then certainly *she*, a mature woman, could. Without looking at the title, Francine grabbed one of the sex books from the shelf and marched to the check-out desk.

Her bravado faded a bit as she put the book down on the counter and she saw the title in gargantuan print: *Sex for Dummies.* In slightly smaller letters the book promised: *Learn How to Change Yourself from a Lousy Lover to a Great One!*

Mortified, Francine tried to snatch the book back, but too late—the librarian had already picked it up.

The librarian glanced at the title. Her expression growing very blank, she stamped the book and held it out to Francine.

Before she could stop herself, Francine blurted out, "A friend asked me to check this out for her. She's bedridden."

The librarian's blankness slipped a little. *Yeah, right,* her expression said.

Her cheeks burning, Francine took the book and her library card and fled.

Francine still felt warm half an hour later when she got off the elevator and walked down the corridor leading to her apartment. But she really did not have time to wallow in her embarrassment. All her waffling at the library had made her late. She had to take a shower and change, and she wanted to glance through the book before Stuart arrived in less than an hour.

Holding the book tightly against her chest, she rounded the corner, then stopped, seeing her elderly neighbor, Mrs. Rappaport, talking to a silver-haired man.

"This is ridiculous," Francine heard the man say as she started forward again. "You must come home, Annie."

Mrs. Rappaport's dark eyes flashed. "You forget, you have no right to tell me what to do. This isn't the Middle Ages, you know—" She broke off, smiling as she saw Francine. "Ah, hello, dear!"

"Hello, Mrs. Rappaport." Francine glanced at the man. He had a thin, white moustache and his shoulders were slightly stooped, but his blue eyes were sharp and compelling in spite of his age. He was holding Mrs. Rappaport's wrist in a tight grip, Francine saw. "Is this man bothering you?"

"Yes, he is," Mrs. Rappaport said, her wrinkled face sad and helpless. "Will you call the police, dear?"

The man released her and stepped back. "Very well, Annie. Play your games if you must. The result will still be the same." He reached for a cane by the doorjamb and, using it to guide himself, tap-tapped his way down the corridor.

A soft exclamation escaped Francine. "He's blind!"

"Yes, dear, but don't let that fool you." Mrs. Rappaport smoothed the floral print of her dress and patted her gray hair. "Ray Guise is a dangerous man. Thank you for coming to my rescue."

Francine glanced at the older woman doubtfully. "You're welcome." She found it hard to believe that a blind old man could be very dangerous. But then, Mrs. Rappaport was a bit eccentric. Francine had realized that soon after the old woman moved in three months ago.

Still, the woman was very sweet, and Francine, who had been a bit surprised by her congeniality—most of the tenants in the apartment building kept strictly to themselves—

had become friends with her. Mrs. Rappaport had a habit of popping in at odd moments—and even appeared in Francine's dreams.

In fact, all last week Francine had dreamed about Mrs. Rappaport. In the dreams, the old woman talked to her in not one but *two* strange languages, and Francine could understand and even speak them. She'd been puzzled by the recurring dream at first, but finally decided that in some symbolic way the old woman must remind her of Grandma Peabody. After Francine's mother's death, Grandma Peabody had raised her. Although Grandma lived several hours away, Francine still talked to her on the telephone almost daily and visited her frequently.

Francine glanced at her watch. "Oh, my! Please excuse me, Mrs. Rappaport, but I have an important date."

"You do?" Mrs. Rappaport's dark gaze drifted to the book Francine held. Her eyebrows rose.

Blushing a little, Francine shifted her arm so the book's title was covered. "Stuart and I are going to a matinee and then out to dinner. I must hurry. Goodbye!"

"Goodbye, dear."

The old woman was frowning, but Francine barely noticed as she unlocked her door and hurried inside. She set the book on the kitchen counter and pulled a can opener from a drawer. She opened a can of tuna and emptied it into a bowl. Out on the balcony she heard a plaintive meow.

"Just a minute, Bentley," she called. She went outside, catching a glimpse of orange and white disappearing over the edge of the balcony as she did so. But then she felt something soft rubbing against her legs. Looking down, she saw Bentley.

Francine bent down and stroked his sleek, black fur. He purred in ecstasy.

"Hello, Bentley," Francine said, setting down the bowl. "You seem like you're in a good mood. You haven't been chasing that calico tabby from across the street, have you?"

Bentley looked up from his bowl, his whiskers quivering indignantly.

"I know you would never do anything ungentlemanly," Francine said. "But males are sometimes tempted."

Bentley returned his attention to his food.

Although it was October, the hot southern California sun beat down on the balcony, making Francine feel uncomfortably warm. She patted Bentley one last time, then hurried back inside to the blessed coolness of her apartment. She liked to keep the temperature a constant seventy-two degrees year-round and, thanks to central air-conditioning and heating, she rarely had to expose herself to unpleasant fluctuations in temperature.

Francine picked up the book, went into her bedroom, and set the volume on her nightstand. Slowly, methodically, she took off her clothes. She brushed the jacket and skirt and hung them in the closet. She inspected her blouse for stains and sniffed the underarms. There were no spots and no perspiration odor, but she did detect a faint scent from her deodorant. She tossed the blouse in the laundry basket.

She took a quick shower, blow-dried her hair, and set it in hot rollers. She removed the rollers a few minutes later, applied a generous amount of hairspray, and shook her head experimentally. A curl flopped onto her forehead. Frowning, she smoothed the curl back into place and sprayed again.

She applied a light touch of makeup, then pulled a cream linen skirt and fresh white blouse from her closet. She put them on and inspected herself in the mirror.

Hmm. Did she look a trifle . . . prim? Maybe a little. But Stuart liked her skirts and blouses. He said she always looked very ladylike in them. Unlike Susie Howlick, he'd muttered once.

Susie Howlick was the bookkeeper in the cubicle next to Francine's who always wore extremely tight, brightly colored dresses that clashed horribly with her dyed red hair. Her books never balanced, but for some reason she never got fired. Francine didn't really care for her, but Susie was very popular with all the men in the office. Except for Stuart.

Dear, sweet Stuart. When he'd been hired by her department five years ago, she'd known almost immediately that he wasn't like other men. She'd been assigned to take him around, and when she'd introduced him to Susie, the woman had taken one look at his polka-dot bow tie and horn-rimmed glasses and snickered out loud.

Stuart had flushed painfully, and Francine—who'd been the target of more than a few of Susie's snickers herself—had felt an instant affinity with him.

They had quickly become friends, and their brown-bag lunches together had soon become dinners, then dates to the movies, and even an outing to a play once. One night, after they'd been dating for three years, he'd taken her to dinner and proposed.

She'd said yes immediately. But not wanting to rush into things, she'd asked for a long engagement; he'd agreed that waiting would be sensible.

Stuart had been quiet on the ride home that night, but she'd been too distracted to pay much attention. He was probably thinking deep thoughts behind those thick glasses. Maybe, like her, he'd been thinking about their future together.

She knew exactly what the rest of their lives would be like. There would be a house in the suburbs. Two children, a boy and a girl. She would quit work after they were born. Stuart would come home and tell her about his day at work; she would tell him about their son's Little League game and their daughter's Girl Scout meeting. Then they would spend the rest of the evening watching TV. . . .

At that point, sitting next to Stuart in the car driving home, Francine had felt her throat constrict. For an instant she couldn't breathe; she'd felt as though she were suffocating. But then the car had gone over a speed bump, jarring her out of her reverie and releasing the tightness in her throat.

Staring at the book on her bedside table, Francine felt a sudden, similar tightness now.

She wasn't quite sure why. This was what she wanted. Stuart was what she wanted. She would have security and contentment, both of which were very important to her. She might *think* about doing something exciting once in a while, but the truth of the matter was, she didn't actually want to *do* anything too adventurous. Adventures meant taking risks. And being uncomfortable.

Sex was a perfect example. In just three months Stuart and she would be married. Forever. And as part of that commitment, she would make love with him. Although part of her was curious, another part of her dreaded it. Just thinking about it made her palms sweat.

What would it be like? Would it hurt? Would it be messy? From everything she'd heard and read, the act of sex was hot and sweaty.

She didn't like hot and sweaty. She liked being calm and cool in all situations.

She chewed on her lip and glanced at the top of her dresser where Stuart's face smiled at her from a framed picture. Taking a deep breath, she slowly walked to the bed, sat down, picked up the book, and opened it at random.

A photograph of a woman with heavily made-up eyes and pouting lips stared up at her. She was dressed in a black leather corset and collar, five-inch heels, black hose and a garter belt, and not much else. Except for the whip in her hand. Underneath was the title "Sex Cults and Sex Games."

Francine stared at the picture for several seconds before coming to her senses and hastily turning to the front of the book. No need to read *that* chapter.

She scanned the table of contents, skimming over such topics as "Sexual Dysfunction" and "Role Playing." She was about to go to the chapter "How to be a Great Lover" when another title caught her eye—"101 Different Positions."

One hundred and one? Impossible, Francine thought.

She glanced again at Stuart's picture. She rose to her feet and put the photograph in the bottom drawer, underneath her sweaters. Sitting down, she picked up the book again. Quickly, she flipped to page 223.

She gulped a little when she saw the illustrations. She turned the pages, and her eyes grew rounder and rounder. Naked men and women with their arms and legs entwined, twisted, contorted; with their hands and mouths . . . good heavens! Would Stuart expect her to do these things with him?

She turned another page and stared at the couple pictured there. No, she assured herself faintly, Stuart would never want to try this. He was much too dignified. He would be shocked by the very idea, she was sure. As shocked as she was. Did people really do these things? How on earth could anyone get their legs up that high? The woman must be an acrobat. Francine looked at the caption below the photo.

"This position may require some practice," she read out loud.

Francine paused, an unladylike impulse rising within her. She hesitated a moment, glancing at the dresser again. Reassured, she lifted her foot and tried to put it behind her head.

She had just managed to get her toe by her ear when the doorbell rang.

Startled, she let go of her leg. It thumped down, hitting the bedside table with painful force.

"Ouch!" Rubbing her shin, she glanced at her watch. It was only two o'clock. Stuart was early. With an exclamation, she thrust the book under her pillow and limped to the door. She paused there a moment, gathering her composure. Then, putting a welcoming smile on her face, she opened the door.

But in place of the tall, bony figure she expected, she found the short, rounded silhouette of Mrs. Rappaport.

"My dear, I wondered if I might ask a small favor of you." The old woman's forehead was creased and her dark eyes worried.

"Of course, Mrs. Rappaport," Francine said automatically. "What is it? Has that man come back?"

"No, no. But could you please come to my apartment for a few minutes?" the old woman asked.

Francine glanced at her watch again. Stuart wasn't due for another half hour, but she wanted to read more of *Sex for Dummies*. Looking at Mrs. Rappaport's pleading face, however, Francine found she couldn't refuse.

She followed the old woman into the apartment across the

hall, wondering what Mrs. Rappaport wanted and hoping it wouldn't take too long. Usually the old woman's tasks were simple—like reaching a book on a top shelf or reading the fine print on a label. Once, however, Francine had spent over an hour helping Mrs. Rappaport rearrange her crystals to precise specifications to "improve the energy flow" in the room.

"Sit down, dear," Mrs. Rappaport said, heading for the kitchen. "I'll be right back."

Sit down where? Francine wondered. Old books were piled on the sofa and just about everywhere else in the tiny living room. Dusty glass bottles with labels lined the shelves on the walls. A spinning wheel sat in one corner, and the crystals were arranged at various points in the room, including a pink one on the chair closest to her. She knew better than to move it.

She saw a flash of green on one cluttered shelf, and stepped over a stack of books on the floor to get a closer look.

It was a new crystal, one she hadn't seen before. The stone, attached to a gold chain, glowed a deep, rich green. Francine stared at it, half mesmerized. She reached out and picked it up, almost unconsciously.

"Beautiful, isn't it?"

Startled, Francine turned to see that Mrs. Rappaport had returned from the kitchen, a large heart-shaped box in her hands.

Hastily, Francine put down the necklace. "I'm sorry. I know better than to touch your crystals."

"It's all right, dear. It's not one of my crystals, it's just an emerald necklace. Why don't you try it on?"

"Oh, no, I couldn't!" Francine was aghast. The huge emerald must be worth a fortune. "You shouldn't leave it lying around, Mrs. Rappaport. It could get stolen."

The old woman laughed. "I don't think so. Please put it on. I want to see how it looks on you."

After a moment's hesitation, Francine put it on. "Is this why you wanted me to come over? So you could see how the necklace looked on somebody?"

"No, no, dear. I asked you over for another reason entirely." She shoved a pile of books from the sofa onto the floor. "Sit here."

Francine complied. "I really can't stay very long. I'm expecting company—"

"Yes, dear, that's what you said earlier. Your fiancé, right?"

"Yes. Although he won't be my fiancé for much longer."

Mrs. Rappaport's face brightened. "You're going to break up with him?"

Francine laughed. "No, of course not. I just meant that we're getting married soon. Then he'll be my husband."

The glow on Mrs. Rappaport's face dimmed. "I will definitely have to speed things up here," she muttered.

"I beg your pardon?"

"Nothing, dear." The old woman took the lid off the heart-shaped box. "Would you like a chocolate?"

Francine hesitated. Stuart had gently suggested a week ago that she might want to try to lose the few extra inches on her hips before her upcoming fitting for her wedding dress. Embarrassed, she'd resolved immediately to cut out sweets from her diet.

"Go ahead, dear."

Well, one won't hurt, Francine thought. She took a piece and nibbled at a corner. The sweet, slightly bitter taste of dark chocolate sang on her taste buds.

Mrs. Rappaport sat down on the bench of the spinning wheel, holding the box of chocolates on her lap. "I hope you won't think my request strange."

"I'm sure I won't, Mrs. Rappaport." Francine popped the candy into her mouth and sucked on it, allowing it to melt a little.

The old woman beamed. "You are such a sweet child. I noticed that immediately when I moved here. And I thought, 'Here is the perfect girl for the task.'"

"What task?" Francine mumbled around the chocolate. She bit down and the intense sweetness of maple cream exploded on her tongue. A small sigh of pleasure escaped her.

"The task of civilizing mankind."

Francine choked a little on the maple cream. "Civilizing mankind?" she croaked.

"Well, *men*, really. I've figured out the perfect time and place. England. 1214. Take another chocolate, dear."

Francine automatically complied. "You want me to go to England at twelve-fourteen to civilize the men there?" she repeated.

"No, no, dear. I want you to go to England in the *year* 1214 and civilize the men there."

Francine stared at the old woman's sweet smile. Slowly, she put the piece of chocolate down on a nearby napkin. Poor Mrs. Rappaport. Poor, poor Mrs. Rappaport. "Of course I'll help you," she said gently. "Can you tell me the name of your physician?"

"My physician? I don't have one. I don't believe in doctors. They're all idiots." She paused a moment, then looked directly at Francine, her ebony eyes gleaming. "I'm not senile, my dear."

"No, no, of course not," Francine said hastily. "It's just that . . . well, I think it would be kind of difficult to go to England in the year 1214."

"It won't be difficult at all." Mrs. Rappaport ate her own piece of chocolate. "The emerald will take you there."

"Oh, really?" Francine said faintly.

"Yes, indeed." The elderly woman licked her fingers daintily. "So, what do you say, my dear? Will you do it?"

Francine hesitated, unsure whether or not she should humor the old woman.

Mrs. Rappaport looked at her with a pleading gaze. "Please, Francine."

"I wish I could," Francine said, trying to evade the question. "But I wouldn't know what to do."

"It will be obvious once you're there. Please say you will do it."

"I really don't think I can." Francine tried to make a joke of it. "I don't think the year 1214 would suit me at all."

"I believe you'll be surprised, dear," Mrs. Rappaport said. "But if you don't like it, you don't have to stay. Once you've completed your task, you need only return to the fairy circle and the emerald will bring you home."

Fairy circle? As kindly as she could, Francine said, "I'm sorry, Mrs. Rappaport."

The old woman's face crumpled. "Please don't say no, Francine. I need your help desperately. Please, *please* say you'll go."

Francine looked at her helplessly. How could she say no when the poor old dear looked so upset? "Of course I'd love to go to the year 1214," she said soothingly. "I would be delighted to help civilize mankind—"

Francine never finished her sentence.

The emerald grew warm against the hollow of her throat. She glanced down and saw it glowing with a pure, bright-green light. A strange sucking sensation suddenly jerked her backwards. Flashes of light exploded around her and a metallic, smoky smell made her cough. As if through a long tunnel, she saw Mrs. Rappaport, smiling, growing smaller and smaller and smaller. Francine opened her mouth, tried to say something, and tasted cold, biting slivers of ice on her tongue. The tunnel started to turn and she spun around and around until dizziness overcame her, and she had to close her eyes as she was pulled back, back, back. . . .

Chapter 2

SHE LANDED WITH a thump on her derriere.

For a moment, Francine didn't move. She sat completely still, waiting for the dizziness to subside. When the whirling in her head had stopped, she opened her eyes.

Blinking, she looked around in confusion. Instead of Mrs. Rappaport's apartment, she saw a misty lake on the edge of a dark, ominous-looking forest. Francine closed her eyes and shook her head before opening them a second time, but the scene didn't change. She was sitting on a rock underneath a willow tree within a circle of mushrooms, out in the middle of nowhere.

Dazed, she stared at the mushrooms, her brain unable to make sense of what she was seeing. What on earth had happened? One moment she'd been sitting in Mrs. Rappaport's living room, the next she was . . . where?

She looked up again at the dark, twisted trees of the forest, just as two shadowy figures emerged into the mist. Furtively, the figures—two men, she realized—drew nearer.

Francine stood up slowly, her gaze not wavering from the strangers. They were dressed in rags, with hoods pulled forward over their heads. What little she could see of their faces was covered with dirt and straggly beards. The sun glinted on an object in the shorter one's hand.

A knife.

Her heart began to pound. She had to be dreaming. She must have dozed off on Mrs. Rappaport's couch. That knife could not possibly be real.

But it sure *looked* real.

"Wake up," she murmured to herself. And then, a little louder. *"Wake up."*

The taller man was only a few yards away now. She could see open sores on his filth-encrusted hands and arms.

"WAKE UP!" she screamed.

The man didn't disappear. Instead, he grinned, revealing blackened, broken teeth.

Francine turned on her heel and ran.

At least, she tried to. Her pumps stuck in the soft mud. She kicked them off. Sharp rocks and pebbles hidden in the grass bruised and scratched her feet, but the evil laughter behind her kept her stumbling forward.

A hand grabbed her sleeve, ripping it from its seam. Another hand wrenched her fingers, then snatched at her throat. The man gabbled in an incomprehensible language. Metal cut into her throat. *The knife,* she thought, but then saw the shorter man lift the blade in a high arc. It started to descend.

Her scream was echoed by a shout.

The man lowered his knife, his head jerking around to stare in the direction of the forest. Francine looked up just in time to see an apparition burst out of the trees.

Riding on a great black horse, the man wore chain mail and a helmet, and carried a shield and sword. With another shout, he lifted his sword aloft and charged.

A *knight?*

Abruptly, the two men released her and ran in the opposite direction.

With pounding hooves and a whoosh of wind, the knight passed by Francine in pursuit. She stared after them, watching as the two men disappeared into the fog. She expected the knight to do the same. But instead, he wheeled his horse around and returned to where she stood trembling, her teeth chattering.

Her confused brain couldn't determine whether he was real or just a dream. But one thing was clear—this man had saved her. Her heart swelled. "Th-thank you!" she choked out. "Thank you!"

He didn't speak or lift his helmet as he dismounted and removed a cloak from his saddlebag. Gently, he wrapped it around her and lifted her onto his horse. He mounted behind her, adjusting her onto his lap so that they both fit in the saddle. She leaned back against his broad chest, and his forearm came around her waist, holding her securely.

For the next several minutes, as they rode through the fog, Francine clung to him. She knew this all must be a dream, but, oh, what a wonderful turn it had taken! She'd never felt so safe, so protected as she did in this dream man's arms. She felt light-headed, giddy, in love. He was brave. Strong. But kind and gentle, also. He was her hero.

Even if he did smell.

Just a little. Well, okay, a lot. But he probably hadn't had a chance to bathe today, since he was out rescuing damsels in distress.

She closed her eyes. She didn't care how he smelled. He had saved her. She loved him, and if she didn't wake up too soon, she would marry him. Just as soon as he took a bath.

She didn't open her eyes again until the horse stopped and the knight lifted her down. She gazed around at oddly dressed people scurrying in and out of strange buildings with thatched roofs. Behind them rose high stone walls with scaffolding and ladders attached and above those, tall, slit-windowed towers. A discordant clatter of shouting, hammering, sawing, dogs barking, bells pealing, and other unidentifiable sounds assaulted her ears. And good heavens, what was that terrible stench?

Her giddiness faded. The logical part of her brain, a bit battered by all the shocks it had received, started to function again. Surely it was unusual for a dream to smell quite so pungently? And surely it was unusual for a dream to be so loud that it hurt her ears?

But this couldn't be real. Could it? No, of course not. Yet she felt awfully wide awake for a dream. She stared up at the knight standing next to her. In his chain-link shirt and boxy helmet, he looked like he'd just ridden off the pages of a King Arthur story. If this wasn't a dream, then who was this guy? Where was she and how had she gotten here?

The knight shouted and several boys scurried forward and took his horse. Then he grabbed her wrist and tugged her toward one of the thatched buildings—a long, tall one.

She went along with him willingly enough, half trotting to keep up with his long stride. "Excuse me, Mr. Knight," she said, rather tentatively. "I'm a little bit confused. Could you please tell me where I am? And how I got here? I'm not dreaming, am I? Is this a movie set? Or a reenactment? Or—"

She stopped talking when they entered the building. Cold and murky, the huge room smelled worse than outside. A fire blazed in the middle of the floor; the smoke made her cough and her eyes water. Heads of dead animals hung on the walls, staring sightlessly down at the laughing, chattering men in smocks and tights who were setting up tables and benches and making an enormous racket as they did so. But as the men noticed the knight, the noise lessened and then ceased altogether. The men stood silently in the huge room.

Without speaking, the knight led Francine across the mats on the floor toward a doorway and a narrow staircase. She tripped along after him, wondering why everyone was staring. She was about to ask, but then stepped on something sharp. Wincing, she glanced over her shoulder and saw several bones on the floor.

Francine grew more confused. This couldn't be a dream. Everything was too real. But it couldn't be a movie set either—it smelled too bad. Was it some sort of weird commune?

The knight led her up the stairs to a dark tower room. Iron bars crisscrossed the small, glassless window, and piles of ashes filled the open stone fireplace. In the middle of the room stood a huge bed covered with furs.

Francine looked at the bed uncertainly. She was tired, yes.

The shocks of the last hour or so had definitely taken their toll. But she couldn't sleep until she had some answers.

She cleared her throat and tried once more.

"I must thank you again. I really appreciate your help. But . . ."

Her voice trailed off as the knight suddenly took off his helmet and she saw his face for the first time.

It wasn't a particularly attractive face. Too hairy for that, she thought, noting the thick black beard that covered its bottom half. His nose was too big, his light-gray eyes too hard and cold.

She shivered a little, seeing those eyes. Their expression was not what she'd expected from her gallant savior. But perhaps it was only the poor light that made them seem that way. As for his homely face—well, she really couldn't expect him to be noble *and* handsome.

She continued her sentence. "But I'm fine now, and I really must be getting home. Could you please tell me where I am?"

He didn't return her tentative smile; he removed his gloves and said a few unintelligible words.

Francine stared at him blankly. He spoke the same strange language as the two thieves. Something was vaguely familiar about it, although she couldn't quite place—

The dreams! It was one of the languages Mrs. Rappaport had spoken in the dreams, and Francine had been able to speak it also. Could she now?

She thought for a moment. Yes, she could. How weird. But she would have to puzzle over how that was possible later—right now she needed to communicate with this man. "Greetings," she said a trifle haltingly, using the foreign language. "Forgive my rudeness, but I must ask you some questions."

He uttered a string of words, far too rapid for her to comprehend.

"I beg your pardon," she said. "What did you say?"

He folded his arms across his chest, his gaze never wavering from her face. He spoke slowly and clearly, enunciating each word.

"Take off your clothes."

Chapter 3

FRANCINE STARED AT him, disbelief and unease warring within her. She must have misunderstood. This was the kind and gentle knight who had saved her from those ruffians. He was her savior. Her hero.

"Take off your clothes," he repeated, unbuckling his sword belt and leaning it against the wall.

There could be no mistaking his meaning, but she still couldn't believe what she was hearing. "No," she replied.

His face hardened. "Take off your clothes or I will take them off myself."

She clutched his cloak around herself. "No," she said again, her voice a little louder.

He stepped to her side and yanked the cloak from her grasping fingers. Then he grabbed her already torn blouse and ripped it right off her.

With a screech, Francine swung at him.

Her open palm connected with his cheek, the sound of the slap ringing throughout the room. He grunted and wrapped his arm around her, lifting her right off her feet and pressing her against his chain mail. Feeling him yank at her bra, she kicked frantically, but to no avail. The front catch broke, and the two pieces of material sprang apart.

She bit his hand—hard.

He swore again, then lifted her and threw her on the bed. Before she could move, he seized her wrists, holding them with one hand and resting partially on top of her as he unbuttoned and unzipped her skirt.

She bucked wildly, twisting and turning against his hold. The chain mail dug into her skin, as cold and hard and unrelenting as its wearer. With one mighty yank, he pulled her skirt, panty hose, and underwear down her legs.

Cold air struck her heated skin. A scream burned in her chest. It expanded, pressing against her rib cage. She opened her mouth, but her throat was so constricted, only a tiny, croaking sob came out. Oh, dear God, she didn't have a chance. He was too strong—terribly strong. She couldn't fight him. But she couldn't give in, either. She had to think. If she couldn't fight him, she had to outwit him. She had to make him think she'd given in. Then, at exactly the right moment, she would bring up her knee as hard as she could. . . .

Her breath scraped along her throat, her body shook uncontrollably. Closing her eyes, she forced herself to lie limply as he pulled off the tangle of clothes. Her nerves shrieking, she fought the nearly overwhelming urge to try to cover herself. Deep shudders wracked her as she waited for his attack.

An eternity passed—or was it only seconds?—and everything was quiet and still.

Fearfully, hesitantly, she opened her eyes.

He stood by the bed, staring down at her body. She tensed, and his gaze moved up to meet hers. The gray of his eyes had darkened, and his mouth was tight and pinched.

Without a word, he picked up her clothes and strode from the room.

Garrick stalked down the stairs and through the hall where the servants were now laying cloths on the tables. They grew silent when he appeared, but as he went out the door, he heard an excited burst of chatter.

Fury churning within him, he strode across the courtyard.

The week had been one disaster after another: first that damned laundry maid; then the delivery of a load of underweight stones that had to be sent back to the quarry, delaying work on the east wall by two days; and then ten men had quit because one had a dream that the castle was struck by lightning and they were certain it was an omen. But none of those problems compared with this new disaster—this *woman*. She was the final straw.

Garrick strode through a flock of geese, ignoring the angry flapping of their wings and their outraged honking. He'd known, of course, as soon as he'd had a clear look at her—the revealing clothes, the way she'd clung to him on his horse, curling against his thighs like a lover; her willingness to go to his chamber—it had been only too obvious.

Arriving at the small building behind the kitchen gardens, he thrust open the door, banging it against the wall.

The ebony-eyed woman seated at a worktable looked up. Her dark gaze swept over him, lingering on the ball of clothes under his arm.

"What did you do?" she asked. "Rip the clothes off her?"

He threw the garments on the table. "Yes."

The woman made a soft exclamation. "She must be frightened to death! She'll think you a barbarian."

"It matters not what she thinks, Lady Anne," he growled, prowling around the room. The room was really too small to prowl in, but he made do. "I'll have no more of your interference in my life."

Anne sprinkled a few herbs into the bowl before her. "I know not what you mean."

"Do you not?" He laughed sardonically. "'Tis amazing how every time you visit here, a woman appears within a fortnight, swooning by the castle gate."

Anne drew herself up. "Are you saying you would prefer that I not visit you?"

Garrick sighed in exasperation. "Do not try to change the subject. I will not fall for your tricks. And I will not play your game—"

"You speak in riddles," she said. But her next words proclaimed her guilt all too plainly. "Tell me, what do you think of her?"

"I have no thoughts about her one way or another."

He gave her a hard stare. She met it for a long moment, before she lowered her gaze to the mortar and pestle.

"Perhaps she is the one you have been waiting for," she said mildly.

He snorted. "I've told you before, I'm not waiting for anyone. Besides, she is an ugly thing. Her hair is short and coarse."

But even as he spoke, an image rose in his mind of how she'd looked lying naked on his bed, her eyes closed, her rasping breath lifting the curves of her breasts, the softly curling hair between her thighs. . . .

He dismissed the memory that belied his words and returned his attention to Anne. "Get rid of her."

"But—"

"I mean it. I want her gone before supper."

"But—"

But she was speaking to thin air. He had gone.

Francine sat on the bed, her heart still pounding, one of the heavy furs draped around her shoulders, her hand clutching the hilt of the Beast's massive sword. After he'd stalked out of the room, she's retrieved the weapon from beside the door where he'd so carelessly left it. She wasn't sure why he'd suddenly abandoned her mid-rape, but she was prepared to defend herself when he returned.

The minutes ticked by, however, and neither the Beast nor anyone else came to disturb her solitude. Her heart rate slowed, and she waited with nothing to do but wonder what was going on.

She had definitely ruled out that all this could be a dream, a movie set, or a reenactment. But then who on earth was that lunatic, and why had he locked her, naked, here in this room? There was only one logical explanation.

This must be some weird sex cult and the Beast intended to turn her into a sex slave.

The pieces were all falling into place. She remembered

the picture of the black-leather-clad woman in *Sex for Dummies* and the heading "Sex Cults and Sex Games"—she wished now that she had read the chapter. It might have given her some clue as to what these perverts were planning to do with her. But even without reading the chapter, she could guess some of it. Sweet, elderly Mrs. Rappaport had deceived her. The chocolates must have been drugged. While unconscious, Francine had been brought to the place by the lake and left there. The "rescue" had probably been engineered as part of the game. No doubt the Beast would return soon, dressed in a dog collar and black-leather-loincloth and pick up where he'd left off—

The latch to the door lifted.

So did the hair at the nape of her neck. She scrambled to her feet, fear pumping through her, and clutched the fur tightly with one hand while trying to lift the sword with the other. She'd managed to raise it an inch or two off the ground when a woman of about thirty entered, carrying a bundle in her arms.

Relief that it wasn't the Beast swept through Francine. She let the tip of the sword clank back to the floor, but still wary, she gave the woman a hostile stare.

The woman paused a few feet away. "Oh, my dear child, did he frighten you?"

The woman wore a tightly fitting black gown and white linen wrapped around her head and throat with a small round white hat perched on top. The outfit gave her a nun-like appearance. Her dark eyes sparkled and she sounded friendly, but Francine wasn't about to fall for the same trick twice. The woman spoke in the strange language, so Francine automatically did the same.

"I demand that you release me at once! I will not join your . . ." Francine searched for an appropriate word, but there seemed to be no translation. Determined to have her say, however, she kept talking, using English words when she couldn't come up with an alternative. "I will not join your . . . perverted cult! Nor will I ever agree to be that beast's . . . sex slave!"

"Perverted cult? Sex slave? What are those?"

Francine didn't respond. She just looked at the woman suspiciously.

The woman shook her head. "Never mind. Come, put down the sword. No one will hurt you. Especially not Garrick."

"Then why did he tear off my clothes?"

"He meant no harm. He's just a trifle thoughtless at times."

Francine stared at the woman incredulously. *A trifle thoughtless?* The man was obviously a depraved lunatic! He should be in jail. Francine had every intention of contacting the police—as soon as she got out of this place. "Where am I?" she demanded. "And who are you?"

"I'm Lady Anne," the dark-haired woman said, ignoring the first question. "What is your name?"

Francine hesitated, but could think of no reason not to tell the woman her name. "Francine Peabody. If you let me go now, I won't report you to the police."

Anne looked mildly surprised. "You're free to leave any time you choose, but you can't go like that. I have brought you some clothes. Put down the sword and I will help you dress."

Francine clutched the sword more tightly. She wasn't about to trust this woman.

"Come, Lady Francine. I promise no one will harm you."

The woman's voice was very soothing, very reassuring. And her eyes—they were almost hypnotic. Without meaning to, Francine released her grip on the sword. It crashed onto the floor.

The sound startled her. She looked away from Anne's mesmerizing gaze and glanced down at the sword. She should pick it back up, she thought a little hazily. But really, what was the point? She could barely lift the leaden weapon. She'd rather have the protection of clothes.

"I can dress myself." Somehow, her fear had disappeared, but her modesty hadn't, and there was no way she was going to stand naked in front of this woman. Not even Grandma Peabody had ever seen her naked.

"The ties can be tricky," Lady Anne said, displaying the crisscrossing strings on the old-fashioned, dark-blue dress.

"You expect me to wear *that*?" Francine asked in disbelief. "Don't you have a skirt and blouse?"

Lady Anne's eyebrows rose. "This is all we have."

Francine hesitated. She wanted to refuse, but under the woman's matter-of-fact gaze, she couldn't get the words out. The fur followed the sword to the floor.

With businesslike efficiency, Anne helped her dress. In spite of her modesty, Francine was soon glad for the woman's help; she never would have figured out how to put on the garments otherwise. The clothes were very odd. First came a chemise—a slip of sorts. Then came a cote and surcote. The two dresses had no buttons or zippers, only laces at the sides. Anne also provided a silver-and-blue embroidered belt, hose, garters, and pointy-toed shoes—but no underwear. In spite of the layers of clothes, Francine felt naked without underwear.

Anne tied the last lace, then inspected her handiwork. "The color matches your eyes." She sighed a little as her glance fell on Francine's hair. "Sir Garrick was right. Your hair will present a problem."

Francine stiffened. "Did he say that?"

"Don't worry. It will grow."

"I don't want my hair to grow." Francine raised her hands protectively to her head. "I just want to go home."

Anne didn't respond immediately. But then she said, "If that is what you wish. The emerald you wear should pay the cost of your travel."

Francine's fingers flew to the necklace around her throat. She'd forgotten about it. A slight, stinging abrasion encircled her neck where the chain had cut when the two men had tried to yank it off her. Her engagement ring was gone—Stuart was going to be terribly upset!—so the necklace was the only thing of value she had. She was surprised the brutish knight hadn't tried to steal it along with her clothes.

"Where am I?" she asked Anne. "What is this place, and why is everyone dressed in costume?"

Anne hesitated. "This is Pelsworth Castle, home of Sir

Garrick," she said finally. "Don't you know why you are here?"

"No, I don't. The last thing I remember is sitting in Mrs. Rappaport's living room eating chocolates."

"Were you not conversing with her?"

"Yes, of course. She asked me to do a favor for her—"

She broke off, remembering exactly what that favor had been.

"Yes?" Anne said. "What favor?"

To go to England in the year 1214 and help civilize mankind.

Francine couldn't say the words out loud. They sounded too insane. Instead, she glanced at the primitive bed, the sword on the floor. She thought of the knight's armor, the way the people were dressed, and the strange language that she was somehow able to speak and understand. Her fingers tightened around the emerald. She remembered how it had glowed and the strange sucking sensation she'd felt. . . .

"What year is this?" she blurted out.

Anne's brows lifted. "'Tis the fifteenth year of the reign of King John."

King John? Francine swallowed. "No, I mean what year. Like the year 2000. Or the year 1850."

Anne frowned. "Let me see. The priest deals more often in such numbers. But I believe it is the year one thousand, two hundred, fourteen."

One thousand, two hundred, fourteen—*1214.*

Francine sank down onto the bed. She felt hot, then cold. "I don't feel so good," she said, a trifle thickly.

Anne sat next to her and chafed her hands. "Dear child, what is wrong?"

Francine could only shake her head. This was impossible. She could *not* have gone back in time to the year 1214. There must be some other explanation. But she couldn't think of one.

She shuddered. *Please God, don't let this be happening to me.*

"I'm not supposed to be here," she said weakly to Anne.

Anne stared at her intently. "Yes, you are, my dear. You—"

Before she could finish, the door flew open. The tall, black-bearded knight stood in the doorway, glowering.

For a moment, Francine shrank away. But then she straightened her spine and glowered back. She didn't know if she had really traveled through time, but she knew one thing—she would never let this . . . this *savage* see her fear.

He turned to Anne. "Why is she still here?" he asked coldly.

"Please, Garrick, don't be so rude. Her name is Lady Francine and 'tis impossible for her to leave."

"Why?"

"She has come from the fairy world."

Francine gaped at her.

"Lady Anne, do not try to befuddle the issue with your nonsense," Sir Garrick warned.

Anne's eyes sparkled. "Did you or did you not find her in a fairy circle?"

He hesitated. "There was a circle of mushrooms, yes, but—"

Francine made a small gasping noise, but the two combatants ignored her.

"And did Samuel Cheney, or did he not," Anne demanded, "say that he saw fairies dancing in the woods last night by the light of the moon?"

"He did," Garrick answered through gritted teeth. "If you believe in that sort of thing—"

"Then the matter is clear," Anne said firmly. "She is here for some important purpose. If you make her leave, it will bring down the curse of the fairies on us."

Francine closed her eyes for a moment. Traveling through time. Fairies. What next?

"Lady Anne, you try my patience with this talk," the knight said.

Anne shrugged. "You may not believe it, but you know the others will."

Garrick's eyes grew narrow and mean. His lips twisted and the portion of his face visible above the beard flushed dark red. He appeared to struggle inwardly for several moments.

"How long?" he finally asked.

"Three months," Anne said. "And then the choice is up to you."

"Very well," he said, his voice a snarl. "She may stay. But keep her out of my way." His cold gaze traveled over her. "Make certain she washes her hair. It stinks."

He left, slamming the door.

Francine gaped after him. "*I* stink? Why, that big, smelly, overgrown ape. . . ."

Anne laughed. "Do not judge him too harshly. There are, ah, circumstances that make him so ill-humored. In truth, he is a good man." She sniffed the air delicately. "Your hair does smell a trifle odd."

"Maybe it does," Francine admitted, remembering the hairspray she'd liberally applied earlier. "But *he* has no business pointing it out. Why did you say I am a fairy?"

"So he won't send you away. The castle folk are very superstitious."

"I see," Francine said, although she really didn't. But the conversation about fairies and fairy circles had triggered a memory. What was it Mrs. Rappaport had said?

You need only return to the fairy circle and the emerald will bring you home.

Francine sighed in relief. If she *had* gone back in time—something she still had trouble believing even in spite of all the evidence—then she should be able to go home if she returned to the circle of mushrooms.

"We really must do something about your hair if you're going to be here three months," Anne said, interrupting Francine's thoughts. "I know just the thing. Wait here. I'll be back anon."

Three months! Francine was horrified. No way was she staying here that long. She was getting married in three months, and Stuart would be—

Stuart! In all the turmoil, she'd forgotten about their date. He would be at her apartment, wondering where she was. Oh, she had to get home right away!

She waited for several minutes after Anne left, then carefully tried the door. It was unlocked.

Releasing the breath she hadn't even been aware she was holding, she eased open the door. No one was outside. She crept down the stairs, trying not to touch the damp stone walls.

As she entered the hall the first person she saw was Garrick. She immediately drew back into the shadows, but it was too late. He had seen her.

With purposeful strides, he approached. "What are you doing?" he asked.

She quaked inside at his scowl. Although Anne had assured her that he would not hurt her, the knight still made Francine nervous. What kind of animal ripped the clothes off a woman?

In spite of her apprehension, she lifted her chin. "I need to go back to the lake."

His scowl deepened. "You are not going anywhere. Get back upstairs and stay out of trouble."

Her chin trembled a little, but she kept it high. "I'm sorry if I've caused you any trouble, but I must go back to the fairy circle. I'm, um, supposed to meet friends there who will take me home."

He stared at her with narrowed eyes. "And you would leave without what you came for?"

She wasn't sure what he was talking about, but she didn't want to ask, so she just nodded.

Abruptly, he grabbed her arm and began dragging her toward the door.

"Hey!" she squeaked, her facade of fearlessness cracking. "What are you doing?"

"Taking you to the lake. That's where you said your friends would meet you, correct?"

"Yes, but . . . but you don't need to come."

"You'll never find your way alone."

Francine dug in her heels. "I'm not going anywhere with you after what you did."

He stopped and looked at her blankly. "What did I do?"

She quivered with indignation. "You tore off my clothes!"

"That was for your own protection. Your clothes made you appear a whore."

"A whore!" She'd never been called such a thing in her entire life. "What I was wearing was perfectly respectable!"

"Perhaps where you're from, but not here."

Francine was stunned. Incredible as it seemed, she supposed to a Medieval person her outfit might have seemed indecent. But that still didn't excuse his actions.

She burned with embarrassment at the memory of how his hands had touched her legs and hips and breasts while she'd struggled against him. He had pressed his chest and his thighs against her bare skin. And then he had stood up and *stared* at her naked body. His gaze had traveled up and down over every curve—missing no detail, she was sure.

She wanted to get as far away from him as possible. Preferably several centuries away. Now.

But the only way to accomplish that was to go with him.

She shuddered. Reluctantly, she trailed after him, weaving her way through the carts filling the courtyard. A barrel had fallen off of one of them and split open, spilling dried fish into the dirt. Recognizing the source of the smell she'd noticed earlier, Francine looked in amazement at the carts that were filled with hundreds of barrels. What were the people here going to do with all that fish?

She forgot about the fish, however, when Garrick stopped at the stable and ordered two horses to be saddled. Swallowing her misgivings—and her pride—she told him in a small voice that she didn't know how to ride. He looked disgusted, but not surprised.

"You will have to ride with me, then," he said.

Francine's fingers curled into her skirt. "Couldn't we walk?"

"It will take too long," was his terse reply. He mounted and held out his hand to her.

Francine stared at the large, gloved hand, then up at the bristling black beard, fierce beetling brows, and cold gray eyes. He had frightened, humiliated, and insulted her. Although his explanation had somewhat alleviated her fear of him, she couldn't forgive his barbaric behavior so easily.

She disliked him more than any person she'd ever met. She wished desperately that she didn't need his help.

But she did.

Reluctantly, she put her hand in his and allowed him to pull her up behind him on the rear of the horse. Her skirts bunched up around her thighs. Quickly she pressed the folds of material between her legs to prevent her buttocks—and other more tender parts!—from coming into contact with the horse's hindquarters.

This ride was very different than the earlier one. She held on to the cantle of his saddle, determined to minimize all contact with the brute in front of her. But without even stirrups to prevent her from sliding around, she was bounced mercilessly and would have fallen off if she hadn't grabbed Garrick around the waist. The links of his chain mail were warm from the heat of his body, and she almost snatched her hands back, but another bump made her clutch him all the more tightly.

She was relieved when they arrived at the willow tree and the fairy circle. Eagerly, Francine slid off the horse and ran to the middle of the ring. Turning her back so that Garrick couldn't see what she was doing, she pulled the emerald out from where it lay concealed beneath her dress and whispered, "Take me home."

Nothing happened. Frowning, she looked around the circle, then seated herself on the rock. Holding the emerald, she said in a firm voice, "Take me home!"

Still nothing happened.

A tiny dart of fear pricked her. Clutching the emerald, she screwed her eyes shut, and with every ounce of her being, willed herself to go home. "Take me home!" she repeated, the intensity of her voice vibrating in her ears.

She opened one eyelid a crack and saw Garrick standing before her, watching with cool mockery in his eyes.

"You said someone would meet you," he said.

"I guess I was mistaken." Trying not to panic, she released the emerald and turned away. What had gone wrong? Did she have to stand in a certain spot? Did it have to be a certain time of day? What exactly had Mrs. Rappaport said?

Francine grew still as she remembered.

The emerald will bring you home . . . once you complete your task.

Her task. Oh, dear Lord.

She looked at Garrick's knotted beard, smelled the odor of dirt and sweat. She heard him swearing in his rude, primitive language.

The enormity of her situation finally sank in.

She had traveled back in time to the year 1214 and she couldn't go home until she'd "civilized mankind."

And, judging from the specimen in front of her, that was going to take a long, long, *long* time.

Chapter 4

SEATED BEHIND GARRICK on his horse, Francine was silent on the ride back to the castle. Tears stung her eyes. She couldn't believe this was happening to her. She couldn't stay here. "Civilizing mankind"—whatever that was supposed to mean!—would take an eternity. She would have to miss work—she couldn't do that. Who would feed Bentley? What would Grandma Peabody think when Francine didn't call her? And what about her wedding? There were a million arrangements to be made. Stuart would be very unhappy if everything wasn't just right.

Poor Stuart! What had he thought when he'd come to her apartment and she wasn't there? He'd probably believed she'd stood him up. He was probably hurt and angry. Would he ever forgive her?

The tears welled up, and she sniffled. Would he cancel the wedding? No. Surely not. Stuart would have faith in her. He would know that she had somehow been unavoidably detained. He was so good. So trustworthy. So *civilized*. How she wished she were with him right now. . . .

Sniffle. Sniffle. Snif—

"It will not work."

Francine stared at the back of Sir Garrick's head, uncertain if she'd heard correctly. She wiped her eyes on the sleeve of her dress. "I beg your pardon?"

"It will not work." He slowed his horse to a walk and glanced over his shoulder at her. "The tears. The innocent face. I am not deceived—I know what you are about. But I warn you right now, nothing will deter me from my course. So you see, your tricks to win my affection and induce me to marry you are useless."

"Marry you!" Francine didn't know whether to laugh or be insulted. "I have absolutely no intention of marrying you. I'm engaged to someone else."

"Oh?" he said skeptically. "Then why have you come here? Why aren't you at home with your betrothed?"

"I have come to . . . to perform a task of great importance to mankind," she said with as much dignity as she could.

"You expect me to believe that you are not part of Anne's plot to marry me off?"

"I know nothing of any plot," Francine said equally coldly. "I assure you, I have no interest—*no interest at all*—in you."

He snorted, his disbelief very obvious, and nudged the horse to a canter.

Francine glared at his broad back in futile fury. What a jackass! Did he think that every woman who came to his home wanted to marry him? Well, she had news for him—a woman would have to be insane to want to marry a hairy, primitive, malodorous boor like him. She could actually smell *sweat* on him. She'd been willing to forgive it earlier—when he'd been busy saving her from those thieves—but he could have washed up while he was at the castle. If she was going to civilize these people, the first thing she would do would be to get them to take baths.

If she was going to civilize these people. Did she have a choice? If she wanted to go home, she apparently had to complete the task assigned to her. Which left her with a huge problem: How could she ever hope to achieve such an impossible goal? Baths aside, where was she even supposed to begin?

She pressed a hand to her forehead. Her brain was begin-

ning to ache, but she ignored the pain as best she could. She
had to *think*. What could she do?

Long shadows were falling and a chilly breeze blowing
when they reached the castle gate, and still no brilliant answer had occurred to her.

Perhaps she should spend the rest of the evening observ-
ing the situation, she thought rather desperately. Maybe then
the answer would come to her.

Garrick left her in the stables, striding away without so
much as a nod. She grimaced at his retreating back. Whatever she had to do to get back home, she was going to make
sure that she accomplished it as far away from *him* as possible. He was rude and unbelievably conceited. Did the jerk
really think that *she* would ever be interested in a half-
human gorilla like him?

Still annoyed by his arrogance, she made her way back to
the hall where the servants were now setting the tables and
lighting candelabra. Anne, who was talking to a dark-haired
man with a lute, glanced up, met her gaze, and immediately
rushed to her side.

"There you are!" Anne said a bit anxiously. "Where did
you go?"

"Sir Garrick took me to the fairy circle. I was supposed to
meet friends," she added glibly, "but they weren't there."

"Sir Garrick took you to the fairy circle?" Anne sounded
astonished.

Francine nodded. "He was eager to get rid of me. He
seems to think I'm here because of some plot of yours to
marry him off."

"What nonsense," Anne said, an innocent look on her
face.

"That's what I said, but I don't think he believed me."

"Hmm." Anne looked at her rather thoughtfully, but all
she said was, "Come back upstairs. I have found just the
thing for your hair."

Reluctantly, Francine allowed herself to be led back up to
Garrick's room where Anne presented her find—a nun's veil
and hat exactly like the one Anne wore.

"We'll have to wait 'til morning to wash your hair," Anne

explained. "It would take too long to heat the water, and 'tis nearly suppertime. But the wimple will do very nicely."

Anne arranged the wimple, completely covering Francine's hair and throat. There was no mirror, and Francine was glad. She suspected she looked like an escapee from a convent.

She thought longingly of the tailored suits in her closet. If only she were home right now. She and Stuart would be watching the matinee movie. Stuart might even be reaching over to hold her hand. . . .

She took a deep breath. She couldn't allow herself to think about Stuart. She might start crying again if she did and she couldn't waste time on tears right now. She had to go down the stairs, observe the primitive people there, and see if she could figure out what she needed to do to get home.

Taking another deep breath, she adjusted her wimple and followed Anne out of Garrick's room, down the stairs, and into the hall. Then she stopped. She stared. Her mouth dropped open.

Through the smoke from the fire, she saw men seated at rows of tables gnawing on huge shanks of meat and guzzling down the free-flowing beer. They talked and laughed boisterously, spitting inedible bits of food onto the table and throwing bones over their shoulders. Mangy dogs and cats hovered, waiting for the scraps.

She was supposed to make something civilized out of all this?

Anne beckoned Francine to sit at Garrick's left after a whispered argument with him. She did so reluctantly, wrinkling her nose at the rancid smoke rising from the branch of candles in front of her. On her left squatted a creature with greasy hair, a matted beard, and a face covered with grime. His clothes were stained with food and sweat. His teeth—what few there were—appeared never to have been brushed. Wiping his nose on his sleeve, he stared at her in apparent awe for several minutes, then forgot about her as he began to eat. From the corner of her eye, Francine watched as the man hunched over his plate, his beard trailing in his food.

He ate with his fingers, stopping every few minutes to belch or flatulate.

Others around the table were similarly uninhibited.

Shock gradually gave way to disgust. These men made the teenage boys in the frat-house flick she'd accidentally turned on a few weeks ago look like graduates from the Emily Post Academy of Good Manners.

What was she going to do? she wondered for about the thousandth time. Why hadn't Mrs. Rappaport been more specific about exactly how she was supposed to accomplish this miracle?

It will be obvious what you need to do, Mrs. Rappaport had said.

Well it wasn't, Francine thought, half peevishly and half despairingly.

When they saw her, most of the diners quieted some, staring furtively and whispering to each other. The rowdiest group, however, appeared oblivious to her presence. As her gaze fell on the men, three of them stood up and swaggered over to the fire in the middle of the room. They peed into the flames, then laughed uproariously as if they had performed some exceedingly clever act.

Francine stiffened as a sharp ammonia smell filled the room. The only thing obvious was that these men needed to take a course in etiquette.

She frowned. Etiquette was definitely a mark of civilization. But would teaching manners to the men here at this one place be considered "civilizing mankind"?

She wasn't sure. But she had no other ideas of what to do, so she might as well try it. After dinner she could just tell everyone a few rules of etiquette and talk about bathing and that would be that. Then surely she could go home. Tonight.

If it worked.

It had to work. It *would* work, she told herself firmly. She wouldn't allow herself even to think of failure. It would be easy.

She glanced at Garrick.

On the other hand . . .

It was obviously useless even to try to teach him anything. He'd changed into a white shirt and a black leather vest, but the clothes did nothing to improve him. Miraculously, there was no food in his beard, but she was sure it was only a matter of time. He was a rude, dirty, smelly, repulsive animal.

But she didn't need to include him. In fact, she probably didn't even need to include everyone in the hall. All she needed was a small select group. Once she'd taught them the basics, she would go home, leaving them to spread the word on the wonder of table manners.

She looked around the room, and her gaze fell upon the men peeing in the fire.

Perfect.

Now all she had to do was arrange to talk to them. She glanced at Garrick again, considered asking him about the men. Then, shaking her head, she hunched her shoulder and turned to the man on her other side.

"Hello," she said politely. "I'm Francine Peabody. What's your name?"

The man stared at her, his mouth hanging open to reveal chewed-up food on his tongue. Raising her gaze to his forehead, she waited for a response, but he said nothing.

"This is all very new to me," she finally said. "I've never been in a castle before. Have you lived here long?"

Still the man stared at her, not responding.

"You're wasting your time," a hateful voice said from her other side. "Maynard is deaf and mute."

"Oh!" Francine glanced at the man in pity. "Was he born that way?"

Garrick shook his head. "He was injured during a tournament. He ran out to rescue his fallen master. A horse kicked him in the head and addled his wits. He hasn't been able to hear or speak since."

"That's terrible. I hope the man he rescued appreciates what Maynard did."

"He didn't," Garrick said rather curtly. "He deemed Maynard useless and bade him find other employment."

Francine was shocked at this further evidence of the barbarity of this place. She started to turn away from Garrick, but then remembered she needed to find out who the men peeing in the fire were. Reluctantly, she turned back to him.

"Who are those men, er, by the fire?"

He glanced up briefly. "Those are the men-at-arms."

"What are their names?"

Tossing a bone over his shoulder, he looked at her. "Why do you want to know?"

Distracted by the sound of two dogs snarling behind her as they fought over the bone, she hesitated a moment, wondering how to phrase her intent to transform his men into civilized human beings in an hour or less. "I thought that after supper they might enjoy learning some of the ways of my village."

"Oh?" He threw another bone. "And what ways are these?"

"Well . . ." The bones cracked and crunched as the dogs chewed. Francine tried to think of a tactful way to tell Garrick that everyone in the room—including him—needed a bath. None occurred to her. She decided to start with an improvement a little less personal. "In my village, it's customary to eat with forks."

"Forks? What are those?"

"Utensils to eat with," she explained patiently. "So that you won't get your fingers dirty."

"But the forks would get dirty."

"Yes, but they can be washed."

"So can fingers."

Francine frowned. "It's not the same."

He snorted. "True. Someone would have to wash all these forks. Are you volunteering for the position?"

Francine looked around the crowded hall. There were at least a hundred people there. She had a sudden nightmarish vision of being stuck in the Middle Ages for years, supporting herself as the castle fork washer. "Perhaps the forks can wait," she said. "But what about—"

"My lady," he interrupted, turning to fix an inimical stare on her. "I have no choice but to keep you here as a guest. But everyone is very busy, and I forbid you to interfere with their work. That is my final word on the subject. Now be silent and let me eat in peace."

She opened her mouth to protest, but meeting his hard stare, she meekly closed it again, fuming inwardly. The arrogant brute! He was the most obnoxious man she'd ever met.

Well, she didn't care what Garrick said. She could talk to the men without his help. She would just have to find out their names and their whereabouts herself after supper.

Broodingly, she picked at her food for the rest of the meal. She ate a piece of melon, but not much else. Certainly not the unrecognizable meat, which had been prepared under heaven only knew what unsanitary conditions. She refused the beer that everyone else was guzzling down and cautiously sipped the water. To her relief, it tasted clear and fresh. That was good—the last thing she wanted was a case of "Medieval England's Revenge."

She was glad when the meal was finally over. She was eager to find the men-at-arms and talk to them.

But she didn't get a chance to talk to anyone. It was dark outside now, and everyone left the tables in a shoving, quarreling, smelly mass of humanity. Adding to the confusion, the servants bustled about, clearing the tables and disassembling them. Before Francine could locate the men-at-arms, Anne came to her side, carrying a candle.

"Sir Garrick," the older woman called out just as he was about to go up the stairs that led to his bedroom. "Where will Lady Francine sleep?"

Garrick paused on the bottom step. Without turning around, he said, "She can sleep with the servants." He stomped off up the stairs and Anne let out a sigh.

"Stubborn mule," Francine thought she heard Anne mutter. But then Anne turned to Francine and smiled brightly. "Come, I will show you where you may sleep."

Francine shook her head. "I need to talk to the men-at-arms first. Could you tell me where to find them?"

Anne's eyebrows rose. "They are all preparing for bed. You can speak to them in the morning."

"But—" Francine closed her mouth tightly, realizing suddenly that it would do her no good to protest. Night had fallen, and even if she talked to the men, she still had to get to the fairy circle. Although she'd observed the way carefully when Garrick had taken her there earlier, she would never find it in the dark. She would have to spend the night here.

Oh, dear God.

"Do you wish to use the garderobe before you retire?" Anne asked.

That must be the bathroom, Francine realized. "Yes, please."

Anne led her to an evil-smelling closet. Inside was a stone bench with a hole in it and a pile of hay on the floor. Francine closed her eyes for a second. But she truly needed to go, so she wiped off the bench with some of the hay, then hiked up her skirts and gingerly sat down. Stifling a small shriek as her bare buttocks came into contact with the cold stone, she did her business as fast as she could.

When she came back out, Anne was waiting. Anne led her to a basin to wash her hands and gave her a twig to clean her teeth. It was like using a toothpick to brush. Carefully, Francine scraped every millimeter of every tooth with the twig.

"The servants should be finished clearing the hall and setting up the beds," Anne said when Francine had finished.

With growing unease, Francine followed Anne back to the hall where beds with curtains had been set up around the perimeter of the room. Her heart sank as Anne led her toward one near the stairway. Wasn't she even going to have a bedroom?

Anne stopped by a tiny, hunched old woman who was standing next to a bed. "Edith, will you share your bed with our guest?"

Share a *bed*? Francine knew these people were primitive, but really. . . .

The old woman looked at Francine fearfully. "Will she put a fairy curse on me?"

Anne frowned. "Hush! You must not speak of such things. Do you wish her to burn at the stake?"

Burn at the stake? Francine swallowed. This was getting worse and worse.

"She won't hurt you," Anne continued. "Will you, Lady Francine?"

"Er, no," Francine said, smiling weakly.

Edith didn't look entirely convinced, but she nodded. Smiling in satisfaction, Anne continued on her way.

Desperately, Francine glanced around the hall, searching for some alternative sleeping spot. People climbed into the other beds by twos, threes, and even fours. Others perched on benches less than a foot wide. Still others wrapped themselves in their cloaks and lay down on the filthy, trash-strewn floor.

Shuddering, she took off her wimple.

The old woman stared at Francine's hair. "How do you make your hair stick out like that?" She reached out to touch it, and her eyes widened. "Your hair is hard. 'Tis like a halo of wood. Are you truly a fairy?"

"No, of course not," Francine said. "It's only hairspray."

"Hairspray? I've never heard of such a thing. Is that what makes it reek so?"

Francine stiffened, but all she said was, "It's very common in my country." Turning her back to the woman, she looked at the narrow mattress in dismay. She'd never shared a bed in her life, let alone such a small one.

She glanced around the hall one final time, then climbed into the bed. Without removing her dress, she crawled under the blanket.

Edith took off her surcote, blew out her candle, pulled a curtain around the bed, and climbed in next to Francine. Within seconds, the old woman was asleep.

The room grew darker and darker as other candles were snuffed.

Scooting to the very edge of the mattress, Francine turned on her side, facing away from the old woman. The mattress had a horsey straw smell, and it barely disguised the hardness of the board underneath. Edith kept pulling on the thin blanket, poking Francine with her skinny elbows every time she turned over. And Francine's stomach was growling due to her reluctance to eat anything at supper.

She lay stiffly, afraid to move. A sense of unreality gripped her. How could this be happening? How could she be lying here in this strange place, in this strange time? What would happen to her tomorrow? What if her plan didn't work? What if she was stuck here . . . forever?

Her throat tightened. She felt terribly small. And terribly powerless. And completely, utterly alone.

Her eyes wide open, she stared into the pitch blackness, trying to see something. Anything.

An image rose before her, of when she'd been a child—perhaps three years old. Her mother had taken her to Grandma Peabody's big, old Victorian house. She had left her there and driven away. Grandma Peabody, smelling of medicine and mothballs, had talked to her, but Francine couldn't understand most of what the woman was saying. She'd waited for her mother to come back, but it had grown dark and Grandma Peabody had fed her supper, then led her upstairs to a strange room. There'd been no crib, no night-light. Francine had lain in bed, in the dark room, her eyes wide open. . . .

Francine closed her eyes. How foolish to be remembering such a thing now. She'd been a child then. A timid, easily frightened child. The situation here was not at all the same. She was a grown woman. She could take care of herself now.

She couldn't lay here feeling sorry for herself. She needed to save all her energy for the task at hand—civilizing the men-at-arms. She had to think positively. She could handle these people. Of course she could. After all, she had more than 750 years of knowledge at her disposal. Freud, Jung, Machiavelli, Dear Abby—she'd read them all.

The constriction in Francine's throat eased, and she took a deep breath.

What she should be doing now was making plans for tomorrow. First thing in the morning, she would get up and find the men-at-arms. She would teach them as much as she could, then go straight to the fairy circle. By noon tomorrow, she would be back home in her nice, clean apartment and all of this would seem like nothing but a bad dream.

What exactly should she teach the men? To use forks. To take baths. And what else?

Maybe more than teaching them what *to* do, she needed to teach them what *not* to do. Not to spit. Not to urinate in the fire. . . .

A loud noise erupted from somewhere in the room.

Not to flatulate in public. . . .

From the bed next to her, she heard a soft moaning, and the crackling of straw as the mattress moved. The moans grew louder. And louder.

Fear rushed through her. She sat up, hugging the blanket to her chest. What were those horrible noises? Was someone being attacked? Was someone ill? Should she go and try to help?

"Yes, there," a female voice panted. "Right there. Oh, yes, yes, *ye-e-e-e-sss*!"

Realization struck Francine. Heat warming her face, she lay back down. Had these people no modesty at all?

Trying to ignore the sounds, she concentrated on her list, but the noise went on and on. And on. In spite of herself, she tensed as the sounds from the next bed grew quicker and more intense. Francine put her pillow over her head, trying to block out the intimate sounds, but to no avail.

"AAAAAAHHHHHHH!" a feminine voice cried. A hoarse masculine groan followed. Then silence.

"Finally," Francine muttered, her cheeks burning. Now perhaps she could get some sleep.

She closed her eyes. She was just drifting off when she heard another moan from the next bed.

"Again, Warren?" the soft voice asked.

Again? Francine thought incredulously.

"Again, sweeting," Warren replied.

The moans started up again.

Staring up into the darkness above her, Francine added one more item to her list of things to teach these people not to do.

Chapter 5

FRANCINE AWOKE THE next morning to the tolling of bells. Disoriented, she sat up and looked blankly around at the sheetlike curtains encircling the bed. An old woman stuck her head into the tentlike space.

"Time to get up, Lady Francine," Edith said.

Memory of yesterday's events returned. Groaning, Francine fought an urge to bury her head under her pillow and pretend none of this had happened. But make-believe was impossible when her eyes burned from lack of sleep, her throat was clogged from inhaling smoke, bruises screamed at her from every nook and cranny of her body, and her ankles itched unrelentingly—

"Oh, dear heaven!" she screamed, leaping out of bed and brushing at her dress frantically.

Edith stared at her as she hopped around. "Is aught wrong, Lady Francine?"

"There are fleas in that bed!"

"There are?" Edith's small, wizened face didn't show much surprise.

"That mattress and those sheets need to be thoroughly cleaned!"

Now Edith appeared surprised. "If that is your wish, I can

give them to the village laundresses. Come now. Mog and Nancy have been carrying buckets up to the solar all through morning prayers. Your bath should be ready."

All through morning prayers? Her skin still crawling at the thought of the insects inhabiting the mattress she'd slept on, Francine shook her head in disbelief. No sunlight peeked through the cracks of the shutters covering the windows. Except for a few candles, the room was dark. It had to be about four in the morning—what time did these people get up?

Eager—no, *desperate*—to take a bath, Francine followed the old woman until they reached the stairs that led to Garrick's room. "Why are we going up there?" she asked.

"Sir Garrick has given permission for you to bathe in the solar."

"I'll bet he has," Francine muttered. In a louder voice, she asked, "And just where is Sir Garrick now?"

Edith's brow wrinkled in confusion at Francine's sarcastic tone. "He is outside, with the men working on the castle."

"Oh." Feeling a little ridiculous at her suspiciousness, Francine followed the older woman up the stairs to where the bath was waiting. The two girls, Nancy and Mog, stood by the wooden tub expectantly.

Realizing they expected to stay in the room while she bathed, Francine firmly shooed them out the door. "I want you to make sure no one interrupts me," she said.

She struggled out of the unfamiliar clothes, gasping when she saw her bare flesh. Angry purplish-blue spots covered her left side from shoulder to thigh. It looked like she'd been bruised by a fishnet—or chain mail, she thought, remembering Garrick lying half on top of her, his armor pressing into her skin.

The brute, she thought angrily.

Naked now except for the emerald necklace, she fingered the jewel consideringly. Better leave it on, she decided. It was her only way home, and she couldn't risk it getting lost or stolen.

She stepped into the tub. The water was lukewarm and the wood smelled slightly rotted, but at this point she didn't care. She scrubbed every inch of her skin with the soap and sponge Edith had provided.

Feeling blessedly clean again, Francine was pulling the cote over her chemise when there was a tap at the door. Edith entered, holding a tray with a heel of bread and a cup of water.

"In case you are feeling a trifle hungry," the older woman said. "Dinner is not until sext bells."

Francine, nearly starving after her meager meal of the night before, devoured the bread while Edith helped her dress. "When is sext bells?"

"Three hours after tierce bells," the woman replied.

"Is that before or after noon?"

"Before."

Francine vowed to be long gone by then.

"I'm going to the village to use Joan the Weaver's loom," the old woman said. "Would you like to come? You can bring your spinning or sewing."

Francine didn't have the first idea how to spin or sew. Shaking her head, she said, "Thank you, but I need to speak to the men-at-arms. Do you have any idea where they'd be at this time?"

"They might be in the courtyard, helping unload the barrels," Edith said. "If they're not there, then they would most likely be in the field at the back of the castle."

"Oh." Francine looked at the woman curiously. "What *is* all that fish for?"

Edith looked surprised. "For Advent and Lent, of course. It's best to buy it now, at a reasonable price, than to wait and have to pay a fortune. Have you not found it so?"

"Oh, yes, of course," Francine said hastily, then quickly left the room.

Shivering in the cold, wet fog, she peered through the near-darkness, searching for the men-at-arms. There was no sign of them, nor of the barrels that had filled the courtyard yesterday. The fish odor had abated, but now she could smell hay, manure, and livestock, which was almost as bad.

Already men were working, the racket of hammers and saws increasing by the moment. Francine marched toward the field at the back of the castle where Edith had said the men-at-arms would be, more determined than ever not to waste a single minute in doing her task and returning home.

When she reached the field, however, she froze, terrified by what she saw. In the dim gray light of early dawn, two men in chain mail and helmets were fighting with swords in their hands. A circle of men, also in chain mail, stood around the combatants, egging them on.

As Francine watched, one of the swords slipped past the other's guard and struck. The man staggered under the force of the blow.

Francine screamed. She started forward, afraid the man would be killed right before her eyes. Yelling, "Stop! Stop!" she ran to the circle of men and shoved at them in her efforts to get to the combatants. The watchers moved aside readily enough, staring at her in some confusion, but she didn't halt until she was in the middle of the circle.

"Stop!" she shouted.

One of the combatants glanced in her direction. The other immediately took advantage and struck a blow to the man's shoulder. The taller man sank to the ground amongst cheers and groans.

The man on the ground pulled off his helmet, revealing a youthful, freckled face and sweat-soaked red hair. Glaring at her, he demanded, "Why did you do that?"

Another man, older than the others, with a protruding gut and short, skinny legs, strode over to the one sitting and cuffed him in the head. "Show some respect to the lady, Angus," he ordered.

"Sorry, Captain," Angus muttered. "Beg pardon, my lady."

"I . . . I'm sorry," Francine stammered, caught off guard by his sullenness. "I thought you were going to be killed. Are you all right?"

"Of course!" Angus responded rather scornfully. "It was the merest tap."

The captain interjected, "The edges of the swords are blunted, my lady. It would be very difficult to kill anyone."

"Oh," she said blankly. "But . . . why were they fighting?"

The captain looked at her strangely. "They were practicing, lady. For war."

"Oh," she said again. Recovering a little from her shock, she said, "They shouldn't be practicing on each other! One of them could have been seriously injured!"

There was a silence.

Francine looked around at the circle of faces. Most of the men were looking her way as though she were insane. A few darted nervous glances at her and made the sign of the cross.

Feeling foolish and awkward, Francine cleared her throat, and tried to salvage the situation. "Well, never mind that," she said, addressing the men-at-arms. "The reason I came out here was to tell all of you that I'm going to be giving a class on manners. Everyone is welcome to come."

No one spoke. They all continued to stare.

"The class is free of charge," she added brightly. "It will start in a few minutes in the hall, and it's limited to the first seven people who register."

Still no response.

Francine kept smiling with an effort. "Good manners will help you improve your social skills, and . . . and . . . help you win the lady of your choice."

Finally one of the men spoke. "Hey, Orson, you should go. Maybe Mog would be willing to part her thighs for you!"

The other men burst into roars of laughter.

Orson, a slightly beefy young man with brown hair and eyes, flushed dark red, then launched himself at the jokester. Soon the men were all rolling on the ground punching each other.

"Aren't you going to stop them?" she asked the captain.

"No." He shrugged. "A little brawling never hurt anyone. Besides, to be ready for war, a man must have seen his blood flow and had his teeth crackle a few times from the blow of a sword."

Francine shuddered. "But I want them to come to my class."

The captain shook his head. "I'm sorry, my lady, but they're training. Sir Garrick would have to give permission for them to go to any class."

"Oh." Dread filled Francine's stomach. She'd hoped to teach the men and leave without having to see the Beast again. Knowing that he'd seen her naked made her squirm. Even Stuart had never seen her without her clothes. It was unbearable to think that *that man*, that complete stranger, had greater knowledge of her body than her own fiancé.

She hated the idea of having to appeal to him. But once again, it seemed she had no choice.

"I suppose I will have to ask him, then," she said without enthusiasm. "Do you know where he'd be right now?"

"Probably with Thomas the Engineer, my lady, somewhere in the inner ward." The captain turned back to the men. "Hey, Ivo! Are you going to take that? Keep your defenses up, man, your defenses up!"

Francine watched the fight for a few seconds more. Then, straightening her spine, she turned and headed toward the front of the castle, telling herself that she would conduct herself in the manner Grandma Peabody had always insisted upon: calm, cool, and—no matter what—dignified.

The nearly finished castle loomed in the morning mist, the gray stone towers reaching toward the brightening sky. Engineers consulted their plans; masons measured and cut the stone; mortar makers, diggers, carpenters, and blacksmiths all busily plied their trades. Men nimbly traversed the ramps erected on scaffolding against the walls, dragging loads of rubble, mortar, and stone. The scents of metal scraping against stone and wood, chalk being burned for mortar, and smoke from the blacksmith's fire filled the air. The noise of chipping stones, hammering, and sawing was nearly deafening.

Garrick stood in the center of the inner ward, silently appraising the progress being made. Three of the inner curtain walls were finished, and battlements were being added to the fourth. The northeast tower was only half completed, but the southern ones were finished and the northwest tower roof was being covered with slate. Work had begun on the new barracks and hall, but the new kitchen and living quarters were still only marks in the dirt.

In three, perhaps four months the outer walls and towers would be finished. Once completed, there would be no finer castle in England, of that Garrick was certain. He'd designed much of it himself, basing it on the castles he'd seen in the Middle East, while on crusade. There was no keep, as in the old-fashioned castles, where the defenders would withdraw to make their final stand. Instead, the castle walls formed two circles, one within the other, each part protecting and protected by another part. There was no weak spot. If the outer wall was breached, the attackers would find no cover in the bailey, leaving them defenseless against the counterattack of Garrick's men.

Yes, the castle was fine indeed. King John would be able to find no fault; he would have no reason to renege on the half-promise he'd made to approve a marriage between his ward and Garrick once the castle was done. The marriage would bring much to Garrick—manors, property and, most important of all, power. Power, he had learned, was the most important thing a man could possess.

In just a few more months, it would be his . . . unless some catastrophe occurred—such as if a new war broke out and the king summoned all his knights. Or if the quarry sent inferior stone again, causing more delays, or some other calamity prevented the men from working. . . .

Garrick's gaze fell on Thomas, the master mason and builder, standing near the empty space where the living quarters would be built. A group of laborers were gathered around him, their faces and movements agitated as they spoke passionately on some subject. Thomas nodded, his expression solemn, then shook his head and gestured toward the unfinished tower. The men hesitated, then sullenly dispersed.

Frowning, Garrick caught the mason's eye and made an almost imperceptible gesture. Instantly, the older man hurried to his side.

"My lord!" Thomas shifted the iron compass he held under one arm. "Good morning. Is aught wrong?"

Garrick studied the slight twitching of Thomas's eye. "I was about to ask the same of you. Is there trouble with the men?"

The compass slipped from under Thomas's arm. Quickly, he bent over and picked it up. "Not exactly. That is, they have heard that a fairy is staying in the castle, and they are . . . er, concerned."

Garrick watched him carefully clean the mud off the compass. "What are they concerned about?"

"Apparently several of them have had bad experiences with fairies."

Garrick's lips tightened. "What experiences?"

"Matthew of Stourhead says a fairy once put pixie dust in his ale that made him oversleep and be late for Mass the next day. John the Mortarmaker says a fairy cast a spell on him that made his mind wander, thus causing him to put too much lime in the mortar and ruin the whole batch. Rufus Wilkins says he was bewitched by a fairy, causing him to be unfaithful to his wife. And Charles the Digger says—"

"Enough," Garrick said curtly. "I do not have time to listen to every nonsensical fantasy these men have created in their heads. Tell them if they cannot do their work, they will be fired."

"As you wish, my lord." Thomas shifted the compass back under his arm. "However, we are already shorthanded. If too many leave, it will slow completion of the castle."

Garrick swore under his breath. It appeared he could not win either way—the men would be frightened if the "fairy" stayed, and they would be frightened of her "curse" if she were made to leave. He should never have brought her to the castle. He'd known from the first moment he'd set eyes on her that she was trouble. But stupidly, he had ignored the warning voice in his head.

After her first pitiful attempts to attract him while riding with him had failed, she'd quickly acquired a most unpleasant manner. No man would want a woman with a prudish air like hers. When they'd ridden back to the fairy circle, he'd noticed how she'd tried to avoid putting her arms around his waist until she almost fell off the horse; and the way she tried to keep her breasts from brushing against his back. Had she been trying to impress him with her newly found modesty?

Or could the woman be telling the truth—that she did not wish to marry him at all? 'Twas possible, he supposed. Anne was becoming much more sly, that much was certain. No doubt she hoped this woman would breach his defenses by making him remember things he had banished from his mind.

But Anne had truly missed the mark this time. He was not so weak-willed. And besides, did she really think that a plain, smelly-headed wench with superior airs would appeal to him?

For an instant, a memory flashed into his mind of the ride to the castle after he'd rescued the woman—and of how her rounded hips had fit between his thighs. He tried to squash the thought, but it lingered stubbornly.

It had been so damn long.

Anne and her spells, he thought bitterly.

Obviously she'd cast another one to make him want this woman. And although in the normal course of things he was certain he wouldn't have wanted her at all, in his current situation, he found he could not control the reactions of his body quite so easily.

Garrick gritted his teeth and forced the images from his head. So perhaps part of him responded to the woman. Still, it was only that one part. It didn't change his mind. He'd done without a woman for this long—with so much at stake, he must endure a few months more. Once his betrothal to Lady Odelia was announced, Anne would have to concede that he wasn't going to fall in with her plans, and that he wasn't going to allow this Lady Francine or anyone else to sway him from his course. The sooner Anne—and the wench, whether she was innocent of the plot or not—realized that, the better.

"Do what you can to ensure work on the castle is not interrupted," Garrick said to Thomas. "And in the meantime, hire more men. If anyone leaves, at least the work won't be slowed."

"Very well," Thomas said, nodding. "I will send word to the city that we are looking for additional labor. Is there aught else, my—"

Thomas stopped, an almost comical look of horror on his face as he stared at something behind Garrick.

Garrick turned slowly, a certain tensing of his muscles warning him what he would see.

Approaching was a woman. A woman with a bright, determined smile on her face.

Garrick did not return her smile.

'Twas the troublemaking fairy herself.

Garrick's gaze was not welcoming, but Francine pretended not to notice.

Calm, cool, and dignified, she reminded herself.

"Good morning," she said with a polite smile, raising her voice to be heard over the construction racket.

He didn't bother with the courtesy of smiling back. Instead, he looked her over from head to toe and asked in a hateful tone, "Falling in with Anne's plans after all?"

Francine's teeth clenched together, but she kept the smile on her face. "Are you referring to your wild accusation that Anne brought me here to trap you into marriage?"

His only response was the cynical arch of one brow.

Francine breathed in deeply. She curled her toes. She counted to ten.

He's a barbarian, she told herself silently. *You must make allowances for him.*

She forced herself to laugh. "How amusing you are. Ha, ha. But all joking aside, I wanted to thank you for letting me stay here. I hope it won't inconvenience you."

"It will not inconvenience me at all," he said, turning to watch a wooden apparatus with ropes and pulleys lift a large stone block from the ground. "I have no intention of entertaining you."

Could this man possibly be any ruder? Francine wondered. She forced herself to say pleasantly, "I wouldn't dream of taking up your valuable time. No, I intend to make myself useful for the short while I am here."

He cast a sharp glance at her. "And how do you intend to do that?"

"I believe I mentioned last night that I was willing to share some of the ways of my village with your men-at-arms. I spoke to them this morning and offered to have a small class, and they seemed, um, eager to attend."

She had his full attention now. "Eager, you say?"

"Um, yes."

"You astonish me. How did you accomplish this miracle?"

"I told them the class would help improve their social skills and win the lady of their choice."

"Oh?" For an instant she thought she saw a gleam in his eyes. "You're very inventive, Lady Francine."

"Mmm. Well, so, anyway, I was wondering if they could take off a few hours from their training today to come to my class." Earnestly, she added, "It will benefit them enormously."

The gleam in his eyes faded. "No."

Francine blinked. "I beg your pardon?"

"I said, no." He turned his back to her and shouted at the men working the apparatus that was now swinging the block into place. "Not so fast! Mortarmen, get ready!"

Francine stared at his back. That was it? No explanation, no discussion, nothing? She set her chin. She didn't like being dismissed. Especially not when her entire future was at stake. "Then I'll stay and tell *you* about our ways," she said. "Starting with *manners*. In my village, it's considered very rude to turn your back on someone."

Still ignoring her, Garrick strode over to the wall where a small group of men stood whispering near several blocks of stone. Francine followed, only to hear him say to the workers in a menacing tone, "Is there a problem here?"

"N-n-no, your lordship," one of the men stammered. The others slunk away.

"I don't pay you to stand around and gossip. If you cannot work when you are supposed to, then perhaps you should find other employment."

"Yes, your lordship—"

"Now, wait a minute here," Francine interrupted, disliking both Garrick's heavy-handed threats and the worker's trembling fright. "Perhaps this man has a reason for talking. Perhaps he was exchanging vital information necessary for him to continue."

Garrick gave her a searing glance, then turned his gaze back to the man. "Well? Is that what you were doing?" he asked, his voice needlessly sarcastic, Francine thought.

"No, your lordship," the man whispered, his wide eyes darting between Garrick and Francine. "I beg your pardon. It won't happen again."

Francine frowned at him. "You shouldn't give in so quickly. You may have a legitimate grievance here. I'll bet you don't get rest periods. I'll bet your pay is miserable. I'll bet—"

"My lord!" the man interrupted, his voice panic-stricken. "Please believe me—I never said naught about any of those matters, I swear! Indeed, I am most happy here! My lord is a most kind and generous master! I swear I will work harder than ever if you will keep me on!"

"Very well," Garrick said. "You may return to your work."

The man practically flew up the ladder to where the stone was now in place and workers were scrambling to tie it with weighted ropes. Francine stared after him in astonishment.

"Well!" she said. "It's obvious the workers here are frightened to death of you!"

Thomas, who had been hovering nearby, spoke up. "Beggin' your pardon, my lady, but 'tis more likely they are afraid of you."

"Me!" she gasped. "Why would they be afraid of me?"

"Several of them believe you're a fairy. They fear you might put a curse on them."

"Oh, how foolish!" she exclaimed. "I would never . . . even if I could . . . which I can't. . . ."

Seeing Garrick's malicious enjoyment of her discomfort,

she stopped, biting her lip. After a moment she said to him with as much dignity as possible, "I still think you didn't need to be so rude. In my village, anyone who spoke to an employee like that would risk being sued—"

"I have no interest in the customs of your village, and I would prefer not to hear about them. In fact, I would prefer that you not speak about your village or the customs thereof at all."

Francine stiffened. "What possible objection can you have to hearing what I have to say? You might learn something."

"There is nothing I need to learn."

"You're greatly mistaken! If nothing else, you need to learn that it's extremely rude to tear someone's clothes off!"

Hearing a gasp, she glanced over to see Thomas and another man, who was approaching, goggle at her. Francine felt her face turn bright red.

Garrick made a noise suspiciously like a laugh, but when she looked at him, he'd turned his back on her to speak to the stranger.

She fumed silently while the two spoke. The barbarian was impossible! He was ignorant and obviously preferred to stay that way.

Staring blindly down at the hieroglyphiclike markings on a stone block, she took several deep, calming breaths. She couldn't give up. She had to think of a way to get him to agree to let the men come to her class. She must stay calm.

Fixing her smile back in place, she turned her attention to Garrick again only to see he was reading a scroll of some sort. Curious, she stood on her tiptoes and tried to read over his shoulder.

She had barely caught a glimpse of indecipherable writing when abruptly he rolled the parchment back up.

"Is it polite where you come from to be so prying?" he asked sharply.

"I'm sorry," she said, hastily stepping back. "I was just curious—"

"Your curiosity could cause you trouble if you do not take care."

Burning with embarrassment, she waited while he gave the messenger several coins and spoke to Thomas.

"Hold off on sending an inquiry to the city. It will be faster if I go myself and hire the men. I'll make certain not to hire anyone who's *superstitious*." He stared pointedly at Francine as he said this, though she pretended not to notice.

"You should hire someone to build bathrooms," she said.

"Bathrooms?" said Thomas. "What are those?"

"Rooms where you take baths and, um, relieve yourself. Water comes through pipes to fill the bathtub and washes away the waste from the, um, garderobe."

"An interesting idea," said the engineer. "I have seen a similar device, with a cistern and pipes leading to a basin where one may wash one's hands, but I have never heard of anything on the scale you mention."

"And I see no reason for this castle to be the first," Garrick said. "I want the castle finished as soon as possible. We do not have the time for such luxuries."

The engineer nodded and went back to work, but Francine continued to argue with Garrick.

"You really must do something about the bathing situation here. Everyone should take a bath at least once a day."

"Everyone does, lady. Sponge baths, to be precise."

"Sponge baths are not the same. They don't get rid of the . . . odor."

"If you're too fastidious to smell a little honest sweat, 'tis your problem, not mine," Garrick said.

She pursed her lips. "You also must resolve the issue of the sleeping arrangements. I hope you are planning bedrooms for your castle."

"Bedrooms?"

"Rooms for beds. Everyone ought to have his or her own room, so that people may have at least a modicum of privacy. I could not believe the noises I heard last night—"

"What noises?"

Suddenly remembering who she was speaking to, Francine said, "Uh, snoring."

"You should have ignored the snoring and gone to sleep."

"Sleep! It was impossible! The people next to me, er,

snored very loudly! And they weren't the only ones! The, um, snoring went on all night long from every corner of the room. It was shocking. Utterly shocking—"

"The snoring shocked you?"

Francine closed her mouth abruptly. "Um, yes. In my village, people are more restrained about their snoring."

He studied her a moment. "Does snoring perhaps have a different meaning in your village than it does here?"

"N-no. . . ."

"Oh. It sounded as if you were speaking of the noise people make when they are coupling."

"No, I wasn't!" Her cheeks burned fiery hot.

"Your guilty expression indicates otherwise. Now *I* am shocked. Here, the subject of lying together is not considered a fit topic of conversation between man and maid."

"I told you, I was *not* talking about . . . lying together. I was only talking about snoring."

"I am relieved. I would find this discussion very embarrassing otherwise. But as far as the snoring goes, there is nothing I can do—unless you wish to sleep with me. I do not snore." His gaze swept over her. "I am willing to share my bed."

"No, thank you," she said, averting her gaze. Obviously, it had been a waste of time to talk to him about anything— his pealike Neanderthal brain couldn't comprehend the importance of what she was trying to accomplish. She would find someone else to help her. "Please excuse me. I . . . I just remembered something I must do."

Burningly aware of the mocking smile on his lips, she rushed off, putting as much distance as possible between her and the Barbarian of Pelsworth Castle.

Chapter 6

FRANCINE HURRIED AWAY from Garrick, half running. The brute. The rude, impossible brute. He was laughing at her, she was sure of it. To suggest that she share his bed! She would drown herself in the river like a swooning Victorian heroine before she would do any such thing.

He was obviously going to be no help at all. What was she going to do now?

She stopped at the castle wall and looked around uncertainly. Everyone hurried about as if they had some purpose, somewhere to go or someone to see. Workers climbed and descended ladders; they rushed to and fro with chisels, axes, and trowels. Men shoveled at a large hole against one wall, and others loaded and unloaded the carts that constantly lumbered in and out of the gate. Boys rushed across the courtyard with buckets of water and bundles of wood and baskets of vegetables.

For an awkward moment, she stood there, feeling foolish and uncertain. She had nowhere to go, nowhere she could be alone to brood. People brushed past her, eyeing her warily or ignoring her completely. She'd never felt so alone, so *alien* in her life.

Except, perhaps, in high school.

Because she had skipped kindergarten, she'd been younger than most of the kids in her class. She'd always done well academically, but socially she'd been a bit of a misfit. Shy and awkward, she'd acquired the nickname Francine the Queen Bean.

She gave herself a mental shake. That had all been long ago. Her dismal high school years had no bearing on her current situation. She had to get to work.

Since Garrick wouldn't cooperate, she needed to find someone else to help her.

Anne seemed the logical choice.

Francine asked a boy for directions, then headed for the small cottage near an herb garden behind the kitchen. Anne smiled when she answered the door.

"Good morning, Lady Francine. Do come in."

Francine entered, glad to be out of the cold, only to pause as she saw a tall, dark-haired man with a thin, black moustache lounging against a wall. He wore a scarlet tunic and yellow hose and had bright blue eyes that looked at her with gleaming good humor.

"Oh, I'm sorry," she said to Anne. "I didn't know you were busy."

"No, not at all," Anne replied. " 'Tis just Rafael. He was just leaving. Weren't you, Rafael?"

Francine glanced at Anne, surprised by the sharpness of her tone.

"If that is your wish, sweet Anne," Rafael said in a deep, melodic voice. With a bow, he strolled out of the cottage.

Francine stared after him, a frown knitting her brow. There was something vaguely familiar about the man. . . .

"Come sit down, Lady Francine. You must tell me how you are faring."

"Well enough." Shrugging off the faint sense of recognition, Francine looked around the small, pleasant room. Dried herbs hung from the ceiling, rows of small jars lined the walls, and everything was spotless. "How pleasant it is in here!" she exclaimed. "And how clean!"

"The herbal potions I make require very pure ingredients.

In order to do my work when I visit here, I must have my own place."

"You don't live here all the time?" Francine asked, confused. "Are you related somehow to Garrick?"

Anne shook her head. "I was a friend of his mother."

"Oh," Francine said, more confused than ever. She had thought Anne was younger than Garrick.

"She was a very fine lady," Anne continued. " 'Tis a shame there isn't someone like her here. The place needs a lady's influence. Perhaps when Garrick takes a wife . . ." She smiled at Francine.

Francine politely smiled back. She doubted such an event would happen any time soon—who would have the brute? "Why aren't there any women here?" she asked.

"There are a few—Edith, the cook Gunilda, and the kitchen maids, Nancy and Mog. But most of the village women avoid this place—the men can be a trifle rough."

A trifle rough! That was the understatement of the year, Francine thought. But Anne's words reminded her of her task. "Lady Anne, I wanted to ask you—do the men-at-arms have any free time? Time when they can do whatever they want?"

Anne frowned. "Very little. A short while before they go to the training field, I suppose. Sir Garrick and Captain Fletcher keep them very busy so they won't get into trouble."

Francine's heart sank. Apparently, she'd already missed her chance for today. Which meant that in all likelihood she would have to spend another night here. The thought made her feel ill. She would probably miss work tomorrow. What on earth would her supervisor say? And what about Bentley? Her poor baby must be starving! He was probably sitting on the balcony right now, meowing piteously. . . .

"Are you all right?" Anne asked. "You look pale."

"I'm fine," Francine said, trying to smile. "I'm just worried about my cat—I hope someone is feeding him."

"Surely he can find food himself?"

"Maybe," Francine said, thinking of the trash bins behind her apartment. But she hated to think of Bentley having to stoop so low. "There's also my work; and my grandmother;

and Stuart, my fiancé. They must be wondering where I am. I really need to get home right away."

"Mmmm," Anne murmured, not seeming very interested in her plight. "Tell me about your betrothed."

"About Stuart? Stuart is . . . Stuart is wonderful. He's an accountant in the office where I work. He works very hard. He's very considerate and punctual and steady. Everything a woman could want in a husband."

"But is he everything you could want in a man?"

Francine looked at her blankly. "I beg your pardon?"

"Is he everything you could want in a man?" Anne repeated, leaning forward in her seat. "Is he passionate, exciting? Does your heart beat faster when you see him?"

Francine hesitated a moment. "Yes, of course. We're in love."

"Ahhh." Anne leaned back. "How fortunate you are. Most people here don't understand about love—even Garrick. Once he finishes building the castle, he plans to marry the king's ward in order to advance his own position."

"Why, that's terrible!" Francine exclaimed. "The poor girl! The poor, poor, *poor* girl."

Anne frowned a little. "You needn't feel sorry for her— she's quite eager for the match. Garrick is, after all, the kind of man that would make any woman's heart beat faster. . . ."

From fear, most likely, Francine thought.

"He's so brave, so handsome. . . ."

Handsome? Well, Grandma Peabody always said that beauty is in the eye of the beholder. . . .

"He is high in the king's favor," Anne continued. "With the fortune he brought back from the Crusades, he bought this land from King John and gained a knighthood. What more could a woman want?"

Someone whose knuckles don't drag on the ground, Francine thought. Out loud she said, "You seem very close to Garrick . . . is there any chance you could convince him to allow the men to come to my class today?"

Anne frowned. "I have very little influence with Garrick. But you might try. I am sure he admires you."

Francine coughed a little. Was the woman blind? Couldn't

she see how much Garrick detested Francine? "I think you are mistaken. Tell me more about the men-at-arms."

"They are all second sons without land. Garrick has very kindly taken them in and agreed to train them."

"Are they fast learners?"

"No, they are a bunch of blockheads . . . unlike Garrick. He learns very quickly indeed. He can read and write and cipher. . . ."

"Uh, that's really great," Francine murmured. Why did the woman keep harping on about Garrick? She'd thought Garrick's idea that Anne was matchmaking was ridiculous, but she was beginning to wonder. . . .

"Garrick will make some fortunate woman a wonderful husband." Anne smiled at Francine. "Tell me, what do you think of him?"

Francine choked. "I, um, really don't know." She started edging toward the door. "I don't know him very well. He seems very busy."

Anne frowned. "That's true. You need to spend more time with him. Perhaps I should talk to him. You are a guest, after all—"

"Oh, no!" Francine shook her head vigorously. "No, thank you! I don't want to bother him. In fact, I'd better be going now. Thanks for your help, Lady Anne!"

Before Anne could say another word, Francine fled.

Early the next morning, Francine stood shivering in a corner of the hall, looking down at a dirty bowl of water in disgust. "You expect me to wash in this?" she asked Edith.

Edith looked surprised. "Everyone else did."

"Yes, I can tell," Francine said. "Isn't there any clean water?"

"I can draw some more from the well, if you like."

The water was only half the problem, Francine thought. "But where am I supposed to wash?"

"Right here."

"But people—including men—are constantly walking through here!"

"If you're modest, you can leave your dress on," Edith said. "Wait here, and I will bring fresh water."

Edith scurried away. Francine sat on a bench and pressed her fingers between her eyebrows, massaging the ache there. She wanted to argue with Edith over the bath, but she had an uneasy feeling she wasn't going to win. She'd already lost one battle to the tiny old woman—Edith had refused to order a tub of hot water for her. Garrick hadn't authorized it; therefore it couldn't be done.

Francine was tempted to seek the tyrant out and tell him what she thought of his chintzy hospitality, but after the scene in the inner ward yesterday, she was less eager than ever to speak to him.

She wondered if the older woman had had to get his permission for the laundresses to air out the straw mattress and change the sheets yesterday. She supposed she should just be grateful that the bed had been clean last night—at least she didn't have any new bites this morning.

But she still needed a bath. Perhaps she could make do with a sponge bath, but at the very least she needed a place where she could take off her clothes. . . .

"I have good news!" Raindrops dotted Edith's clothing when she returned a short while later. "Lady Anne said that you may use the solar to take your sponge bath!"

"The solar? You mean Sir Garrick's room?"

Edith nodded. "Yes. You will have complete privacy—he never goes there during the day."

Francine hesitated. After everything the Beast had said and done, the idea of being in his room was not appealing. Especially without her clothes. "Isn't there someplace else I could go? The stillroom, perhaps?"

"You *could*," Edith said doubtfully. "But Lady Anne has people visiting at all hours for illnesses. No one goes to the solar."

"I see," Francine said. She'd never really appreciated what a precious commodity privacy was. "I suppose I'll have to make do with the solar, then." She turned toward the stairs.

"Wait!" Edith cried.

Francine glanced over her shoulder.

"If you will do the same for me, I will comb your hair and check it for nits every morning."

Francine felt the blood drain from her face. *Lice.* Oh, God, please, no.

She wanted to refuse, but the thought of bugs in her hair compelled her to accept.

To her relief, neither she nor the old woman found any "nits." With a silent prayer of thanks, she went up the stairs to the solar.

In spite of Edith's words, Francine still feared Garrick might come into the tower room. Keeping a wary eye on the door, she left her chemise on and, shivering from the cold wet air that blew through the window, did her best to wash herself. The results were less than satisfactory.

The castle needed plumbing, no doubt about it.

Baths and manners, she thought as she dressed then went back down to the hall to where she was to meet the men-at-arms. More than anything else, she would drum those two things into her pupils' heads.

In the hall, the windows were all covered by leather hides, making the room dark. Francine peered through the gloom at the steady stream of rain-drenched people entering and leaving the hall. They were mostly men, wearing coarse brown smocks and heavy boots, hats clutched in their fists. They trekked over to speak to a man sitting at a table near the fire. The man either nodded or shook his head after talking to each person and made a note on the scroll stretched out before him. No men-at-arms came in, though.

Francine had trailed after them throughout most of the afternoon yesterday, hoping to find a time when she could speak to them. But Anne had been right—Captain Fletcher kept the men very busy. They never stopped working except for meals.

Although she hadn't been able to speak to the men, she did manage to ask Captain Fletcher to remind them that the class would be today after morning prayers. He'd promised to pass the message along.

So where were they?

Seeing some benches along the wall, Francine dragged

several of them over by a window and arranged them in rows. Then she removed two of the leather hides covering the window. The smell of rain and mud blew in her face as pale morning light and cold, foggy air crept into the hall. She moved the benches a little farther from the window. Satisfied with the arrangement, she glanced toward the door. Still no sign of the men.

She sat on one of the benches and, while she waited, mentally reviewed what she would teach them. To the list she'd made the night before last, she added "don't keep people waiting."

What time was it? she wondered. She looked around the walls, seeking a clock, even though she knew she wouldn't find one. She guessed it was about seven A.M. Hopefully the men would come soon. She rose to her feet and looked out the window to see if any of them were approaching. Through the rain, she saw pigs and geese and carts and servants coming and going through the castle gate, but not a single man-at-arms.

The smell of meat cooking wafted to her nose and her stomach growled. She was hungry. Apparently Medieval people believed in only two meals a day—"dinner" in the morning and "supper" at around four P.M. Still suspicious of the meat, she'd eaten very little at either meal yesterday. She couldn't wait to get home and eat a nice, germ-free, microwave dinner.

Where were those men?

Ignoring the cold, wet weather, she leaned out over the waist-high sill of the window to see more of the courtyard and finally caught a glimpse of a familiar face—Garrick's.

She ducked back, but she was too late—he'd seen her. He approached the window and looked up at her.

"What are you doing?" he asked, suspicion in his voice.

She brushed a raindrop off the end of her nose. "Nothing," she said airily, glad of the two-foot height advantage her position gave her. It was nice to look down on him for a change. "Merely enjoying the view. What are *you* doing?"

"I am on my way to speak to Anne—not that it's any of

your business." His cold gaze wandered over her. "You were looking for someone. Who?"

She eyed him, wondering whether he would be annoyed by what she had planned. The man was dripping wet—and she doubted the cold had done anything to improve his temper. But he would probably find out sooner or later, so she decided she might as well tell him now. "I invited the men-at-arms to attend my class. I was just looking to see if any of them were on their way yet."

Garrick stared at her for a moment, then burst into laughter.

The bustle of the courtyard slowed and came to a halt as people stopped and stared.

Not sure why they were staring, but feeling self-conscious anyway, Francine glared at him. "What's so funny?"

Garrick wiped his eyes. "The men-at-arms have all gone out hunting."

"Oh." Francine's heart dropped. "Maybe Captain Fletcher forgot to remind them about it."

"He likely didn't bother. You really expect the men to come and sit through some foolish class?"

Francine bristled. "I thought they seemed very interested when I told them about it yesterday."

"Mmm-hmm," he said. "I'll bet they laughed themselves silly."

Unable to deny it, Francine flounced away. She heard Garrick chuckle and then his footsteps squelching away from the window.

Francine spent several minutes calling him the worst names she could think of, but once her anger had spent itself, the import of Garrick's words sank in. Slowly, she sank onto the bench, feeling hollow inside. If the men were out hunting, she wouldn't be able to talk to them until tomorrow. But even worse, she had an uneasy suspicion that Garrick was right—the men weren't going to come to her class tomorrow or any other day.

What in heaven's name was she going to do?

She must find a way to convince them to come to her class. But how?

Anne would not be any help—she only seemed interested in finding some poor sucker to marry Garrick. Francine didn't think she could endure listening to more stories about how wonderful Garrick was.

She could ask Captain Fletcher to order the men to her class. But she doubted he would agree, even if he had the authority to do so.

She could ask Garrick . . . no. That idea wouldn't bear even the smallest consideration.

Who else? she thought. Who else might be able to influence the men?

Their wives.

The answer came to her in a flash of inspiration. Or if not their wives, then their girlfriends.

What was it Anne had told her yesterday? That most of the women lived in the village, but that a couple worked in the kitchen? With so few women here, they probably had great influence with the men. If the women asked the men to go to her class, they would probably fall all over themselves to comply.

Francine set off for the kitchen.

Ducking her head against the rain, she dashed across the courtyard to the other building. Outside the door, a pen contained some chickens and geese, and a scrawny goat was tethered to the fence. She patted the wet goat, then entered the kitchen, only to stop, gulping a little at the scene before her. The large room was warm and smokey; people ran about in all directions. Dogs lay in the corners licking platters. Greasy pots stood on tables and cupboards while lettuce leaves and melon rinds littered the floor. Nancy and Mog, with aprons and white caps, were chopping vegetables; some barefoot boys were taking loaves of bread out of ovens with long, wooden paddles. Still more boys were chopping up huge slabs of red, bloody meat. The smell of onions, smoke, bread, and spices filled the air, along with an underlying stench of rotten vegetables and spoiled meat. Francine made a silent vow not to eat for the rest of the time she was here.

As they became aware of her presence, everyone stopped working and stared at her. Their gazes were not particularly friendly, Francine noticed. She cleared her throat. "Good morning."

"What do you want?" a fat woman with a dirty apron demanded, her long, wooden spoon held at a menacing angle. "We're busy."

"You must be Gunilda," Francine said, trying to sound friendly. "I . . . I thought I might help."

Gunilda looked her up and down, then, with lightning speed, she turned and rapped her wooden spoon across the knuckles of a boy who was reaching into the stewpot. The boy yelped and hastily withdrew. The cook turned back to Francine and ordered, "Hold out your hands."

Afraid she was about to receive the same treatment as the boy, Francine hesitantly complied. The woman took Francine's hands and stared at them. Francine stared, too, rather shocked by the difference between their hands. Hers—clean, soft, with polished oval nails. And the cook's—callused, scarred with burns, with dirty ragged nails. Mog, looking from behind, gasped.

"I ain't never seen such hands," she whispered.

"Pretty, yes, but useless, I would say." Gunilda dropped Francine's hands and looked at her with a hostile expression. "What can you do?"

Francine clasped her hands tightly together. She could calculate a tax return and balance a set of books faster than anyone else in her office; she knew DOS, three word-processing programs, and five different spreadsheets. But she doubted the cook would be impressed by any of those skills. Francine tried to think of her domestic talents. Cooking was not her strong point. She could make bread—but only with her automatic bread machine.

"I know a recipe for Chicken Flambé," she finally said.

The cook snorted. "Is that one of those fancy French dishes? I have no use for them. But if you want to help, you can start with this."

She thrust something at Francine, who automatically took the soft, white bundle. She looked down at it and saw glassy red eyes staring up at her.

"Aaaaaaaaaaaaahhh!" she screamed, dropping the dead chicken onto the floor.

A dog immediately ran over and snatched it up.

Chaos ensued, with the cook and the kitchen maids and cookboys all chasing the mangy animal.

One of the boys managed to grab the dog. The cook wrenched the chicken—now filthy and covered with straw—from the dog's jaws and thrust it at a small boy, before turning to Francine in a fury.

"What is the matter with you? Are you trying to ruin our dinner?"

"I . . . I'm sorry," Francine stammered. "I . . . I was just a little startled. I'm not used to seeing dead chickens. Perhaps . . . perhaps I could help in some other way?"

"Fine," the cook grumbled and handed her a mortar and pestle. "Grind these mustard seeds."

Francine, averting her gaze from the boy who was now plucking the chicken, moved next to the two girls at the table. Her hands trembling a bit from the shock of the dead chicken, she picked up the pestle and started grinding.

Nancy, a pretty girl with light-brown hair, nodded and smiled shyly. "Good morrow, Lady Francine," she said in a sweet voice.

"Good morning, Nancy. Mog." Francine managed to smile at them. They both wore aprons knotted on their hips over simple brown dresses with pinned-up hems—apparently so their skirts wouldn't trail on the dirty floor.

Mog had dirty reddish-blond hair, and a dirtier face and apron. Her brown eyes looked at Francine with suspicion. "Are you a fairy?"

"No, of course not," Francine said.

"Hmmph." Mog glanced at her concealing wimple, then chopped an onion in two. "I saw your hair yesterday morning. Why did you cut it? Did you have a fever?"

"No, it's the style in the village where I live."

"It's hideous." Mog diced the onion into tiny bits. "I would not like to live in your village."

"You have beautiful hands," Nancy said hastily. "I have

never seen such hands—not even on fine ladies. They're so . . . so *clean*."

Francine, recognizing the opportunity she'd been waiting for, said, "In my village everyone takes a bath every day—in a bathtub. It keeps our entire bodies very clean."

"I'm surprised you haven't all caught your deaths of cold!" Nancy exclaimed.

Mog looked skeptical. "Who carries all the water?"

"It's piped in," Francine told her. "Hot and cold water both."

"How amazing!" said Nancy. "I've never heard of such a thing!"

"That's because such a thing doesn't exist," said Mog. "It's impossible."

"No," Francine insisted. She coughed a little as a boy applied bellows to the fire, causing a huge plume of smoke to fill the kitchen. "It's true. The men are very clean also. And they have excellent manners. In fact, I am giving a class for the men-at-arms to teach them about the ways of my village."

"Why would they want to learn the ways of your village?" Mog growled. "Your village sounds very silly to me."

"I think it might be nice for a man to be clean," Nancy said rather wistfully. "But I don't think any of them will agree to take a bath every day."

"Perhaps you could talk to them about coming to my class?" Francine said.

"I doubt they would listen to me," Nancy demurred.

"Bah!" Mog said. "I like Pascal just the way he is."

Surprised, Francine stopped grinding the mustard seeds and glanced up. "Pascal . . . he's the man-at-arms with black, curly hair and an audacious manner, isn't he? Is he your husband?"

Mog flushed a little. "No . . . but I'm sure he will propose soon."

Francine stared at her defensive face. A case of unrequited love? she wondered. Unwilling sympathy for the unpleasant girl rose in her. She remembered very well what it was like to be ignored by all the boys. "You're welcome to come to the class also if you like," she offered impulsively.

"Me!" Mog drew back and her face whitened under the smudges on her cheeks. "Why would I want to go to your stupid class?"

Belatedly realizing how tactless she'd been, Francine tried to backtrack. "I just thought you might be interested . . . that is, it might help you with Pascal. . . ."

Mog gripped her knife, her stare hostile. "Why have you come here? To mock us with your silly stories and ways?"

"No!" Francine was appalled at the antagonism she'd raised so inadvertently. "I've come here to help you."

Mog burst into an ugly laugh. "How can you help us when you can't do anything—not even pluck a chicken? Why should we listen to an old maid like you?"

It was Francine's turn to flush. "I'm not an old maid. I'm engaged."

"If you are getting married, then why are you here? Where is your betrothed?"

"I, um, was on my way to meet him," Francine improvised. "But I was attacked by bandits and separated from my party."

"How awful!" Nancy said sympathetically. "You're lucky Sir Garrick was there. He is very brave. He went to the Holy Land on a Crusade and killed a thousand infidels."

Francine shuddered. Garrick had actually *killed* people. Allowing for some exaggeration on Nancy's part, he'd still probably killed hundreds. The man truly was a barbarian.

Glancing at Mog's still-angry expression, Francine went along with the change of subject, hoping the girl would calm down. "I'm very grateful to him for saving me from those two vagrants."

"I'll wager you're grateful," Mog said.

The girl's sarcastic inflection made Francine pause. "What do you mean?"

"*I* know why you're here—I have eyes in my head." Mog faced her, hands on her hips. "Since your own betrothed won't wed you, you've decided to try to trap Sir Garrick into marriage."

Francine choked. What was it with everyone thinking she

wanted to marry Garrick? "I do *not* want to marry Sir Garrick."

Mog looked at her disbelievingly. "It's fortunate that you don't—because he's going to marry the king's ward as soon as he finishes the castle."

"I feel sorry for the girl," Francine said honestly. "I wouldn't want to marry such a bad-tempered brute."

"Ha!" Mog sneered.

"Ignore her," Nancy said, rushing to Francine's defense. "She's just angry because she tried to get into his bed once and he kicked her out."

Mog flushed and said, "He didn't kick me out—I could have had him if I wanted him. It's only because of his problem with—"

"Mog!" the cook roared, making all three of them jump and turn. "Your idle wagging tongue will be the death of you! Come over here and turn the spit."

Sullenly Mog complied.

Francine stared after her in confusion, then turned back to Nancy. "What problem?"

Nancy kept her eyes on the onion. "Er, I don't know exactly. I only know it makes him ill-humored at times. I believe it is an old leg injury he has. Sometimes it cramps very badly and keeps him awake all night. He ought to consult a physician. Or an astrologer. But he refuses to see either."

The astrologer would probably be just as good as a Medieval physician, Francine thought. "An old injury is no excuse. Personally, I think he's just a mean, nasty, foul-tempered brute."

Francine's words fell into a sudden silence. She glanced up and noticed that everyone in the kitchen was staring at a point behind her.

Glancing over her shoulder, she saw Garrick standing in the doorway.

Oh, dear heaven, she thought, turning back to the mustard seeds and grinding frantically. What was he doing here? Had he heard her? She risked a peek at his face.

His expression was cold and hard—no different than usual, really. He didn't *look* angry.

Someone behind him moved forward. It was Anne, smiling pleasantly as usual.

"Good morning, Lady Francine! Just the person we were looking for! Would you come outside, please?"

Trying to subdue her nervousness, Francine put down the pestle and followed them out into the cold, foggy courtyard. A furious burst of chatter echoed from the kitchen as soon as the three left the building.

Handing Francine a cloak, Anne said brightly, "Garrick is going to town to hire some workers today, and he thought you might like to go along."

Gratefully wrapping the thick, soft cloak around herself, Francine cast a sideways glance at Garrick. His face impassive, he gazed off toward the castle wall. "Uh, that's very kind of you, Sir Garrick, but I prefer to stay here."

"I prefer that you come with me."

Francine, busy tying the strings of the cloak to keep out the cold, looked at him again, surprised by his words. She would have thought he wanted her company about as little as she wanted his. But he must not have heard what she'd said about him in the kitchen.

Why the invitation, though? Francine glanced at Anne. The older woman must have spoken to Garrick about his duties toward his guest. Francine had to give him credit for at least making an effort. "I'm afraid I'm very busy," she said, softening her refusal with a slight smile. "Thank you for the invitation, though."

"You misunderstand." He turned his gaze from the wall and looked at her with gray eyes that would have made a blizzard seem warm. "You *will* come with me whether you want to or not."

Francine stiffened, realizing her mistake in trying to give him credit for anything. She opened her mouth, but he continued before she could speak.

"And unless you want to find out exactly how mean, nasty, and foul-tempered I really am," he said in a low growl that only she could hear, "I suggest you don't argue."

Chapter 7

FRANCINE'S INITIAL SQUIRMING embarrassment was swept away by outrage. How dare he tell her she would come with him whether she wanted to or not? Just who did he think he was? She would rather pluck chickens than allow him to dictate to her! She would rather wash forks for a thousand men-at-arms than allow him to get away with talking to her like that! She would rather sleep in a flea-infested bed for a hundred years than go anywhere with him!

But in spite of her indignation, she found herself trailing him meekly across the courtyard to the stables, not quite daring to say the rebellious thoughts out loud.

The sight of his horse saddled and waiting, however, was more than she could bear. "This is ridiculous!" she exclaimed. "Don't you have some sort of vehicle we can travel in?"

"The wagon would be too slow."

"I absolutely refuse to ride on that horse with you again!"

He looked at her with an implacable gaze.

She bit her lip. "Don't you have some other horse I could ride? An older, gentler one?"

He stared at her for several long moments. "Perhaps we do. Nutekin, saddle Bathsheba."

Nutekin, a wiry boy with dirty, blond hair, appeared to hesitate, then ran to do Garrick's bidding. A few minutes later he returned, leading a donkey.

Francine stared at the animal. It was blind in one eye, its gray hide mangy, its mane and tail patchy. It let out a loud bray, blasting her with its sour breath from ten feet away. "Surely you don't expect me to ride on that?"

"It's the only suitable mount we have for you," Garrick said.

The stableboys snickered.

Francine looked at Garrick suspiciously, but his expression remained bland.

"You may ride behind me on my palfrey if you choose," he said in a bored voice.

"I'll take the donkey," she said with ill grace. "I suppose I'd rather ride *on* an ass than *behind* one," she muttered.

"What did you say?" he asked, frowning.

"Nothing." She mounted the donkey with a little help from Nutekin. Head held high, she followed Garrick out through the castle gate.

But an hour later, her chin was drooping down on her chest.

Cold and wet, she bounced along the narrow, rutted lane, wondering how much longer she could endure the torture. Fog rolled around her, condensing on her face and dripping off the end of her nose.

She glared at Garrick's back, barely visible through the heavy mist. He hadn't even bothered to look back to make sure she was still following. The taciturn devil had barely spoken two words to her.

A man in a cart, singing in a slightly off-key baritone, had waved cheerfully as he drove by; several riders carrying on a lively conversation had greeted them enthusiastically. A man praying at a wayside shrine had blessed them and wished them Godspeed.

Garrick had returned these salutations and others politely, even stopping to speak for a few minutes to a farmer leading a cow down the path.

But to her, he said nothing.

Then again, perhaps he had reason, she thought, a twinge of guilt assailing her. She wouldn't be feeling any too friendly toward someone who'd bad-mouthed her behind her back. Especially if that person was someone whom she'd rescued from robbers and allowed to be a guest in her home.

Biting her lip, she stared at the straight, proud back riding in front of her. Yes, she'd definitely behaved very badly. She owed him an apology, she knew. Even if he refused to accept it, she had to offer it all the same.

She kicked her donkey. The animal let out a muffled snort, but didn't increase its pace. She kicked it, harder, and the animal suddenly took off at a bone-jarring trot. She felt herself sliding sideways, and hastily grabbed on to the high ridge of the saddle and pulled back on the reins. The animal slowed just as she caught up to Garrick.

He stared straight ahead.

It was harder than she'd expected to say the words. She tried to ease into it. "Nice day, isn't it?" she said, watching beads of mist form in his beard.

"Umph," he grunted.

"I'm looking forward to seeing the town," she said. "Will there be many people there?"

"Likely."

"Do you think you'll be able to hire all the men you need?"

"Perhaps."

Obviously he wasn't going to make this any easier for her. She took a deep breath, then said in a rush, "I want to apologize for what I said in the kitchen. It was wrong of me. Speaking before I think is one of my worst faults. Grandma Peabody warned me against it often, but sometimes I still say things I shouldn't."

He made no response.

His silence made it clear that she was not forgiven. Ducking her head, she started to drop back again. But then, to her surprise, he looked over his shoulder and said, "Keep up or you will be left behind. I cannot afford further delay."

A few hours ago the harsh words would have infuriated

her. Now she realized they were the height of affability for Garrick. Relieved, she urged the donkey forward again.

They rode quietly, but after a while, she could no longer restrain the question that had been hovering on her lips for some time.

"If you're in a hurry, why did you insist I come along?"

"As Anne pointed out, I dared not leave you behind. God only knows what trouble you could stir up in my absence."

Francine's lips tightened. She kicked her donkey again. The animal brayed in protest, but quickened its pace.

"Can't you slow down a bit?" she asked as she bounced in the saddle. "I thought knights were supposed to be chivalrous."

"You've been listening to too many troubadours' tales of King Arthur and Sir Lancelot. Knights are warriors—we have little time for chivalry."

"Does that mean you have to be rude? Just think—if everyone were polite and courteous you might not have to fight wars anymore."

He turned his head to look down at her. "And then what would men do?"

"They could get jobs. And start families."

"That's supposed to be an inducement?"

Francine frowned. "Don't you want to get married and have a family?"

"Of course."

"Oh, yes," she said, remembering what Anne had told her. "You plan to marry the king's ward. For self-advancement." She shook her head in disapproval. "How can you marry someone you don't love?"

"What does love have to do with marriage?"

Her mouth fell open in horror. "It has *everything* to do with marriage. My fiancé and I are deeply in love."

"Your fiancé." He studied her with inscrutable eyes. "Tell me about him."

"Stuart?" The request caught her off guard. "Well . . . he's an accountant in the same office where I work."

"A steward?"

"Sort of. He's very steady. He never gets angry. He listens to me when I talk."

"What do you talk about?"

"What do we talk about?" Francine parroted inanely. She tried to remember exactly what she and Stuart had talked about. She really couldn't remember anything specific. Actually, Stuart was rather quiet. They often ate in silence. But it was a *comfortable* silence, Francine reminded herself.

"Accounting, mostly," she finally said. "And about family and friends."

"Doesn't he tell you how beautiful you are? Doesn't he talk of coupling with you?"

"No! Certainly not! That wouldn't be . . . respectful. He is perfectly happy to wait until after the wedding."

"Hmm. So to you love is speaking of numbers to a silent man who has no physical interest in you."

"No . . . of course he has a physical interest . . . oh, for heaven's sake, that's not what it's like at all." Francine shifted in her saddle. "Haven't you ever been in love?"

He didn't answer immediately. For a few moments, all was quiet except for the clip-clopping of the horses' hooves, the creak of the saddle leather, and the sound of birdsong in the forest.

His expression was unreadable, but his silence made Francine think that he had indeed been in love once—and that the experience had not been pleasant.

"Tell me," she said quietly.

He shot a glance at her, then looked straight ahead again. "I was in the army. I was just fourteen. A woman rode by our camp. An incredibly beautiful woman."

"Yes?" Francine encouraged softly.

"She had eyes of emerald, skin whiter than finest linen, hair like blackest jet. Her brow was wide, her chin small, her lips plump and red. She wore a silken gown that matched her eyes, and she rode with indescribable grace. Rings sparkled on every finger of her dainty hands."

Francine immediately guessed what had happened. The haughty, beautiful woman. The poor, homely boy. The woman laughing scornfully at his avowal of love. The boy, his pride and his heart crushed, swearing never to love again. . . .

Tears pricked at her eyes. Poor Garrick. No wonder he was so cold and hard. No wonder he didn't believe in love.

Reaching up, she put her hand on his knee. "Tell me what happened," she said gently, blinking back her tears.

Garrick's gaze traveled from Francine's face to her hand on his knee and back to her face. "She bent over and her dress gaped away and I saw her breasts."

Francine waited, but he said nothing more. "And then what happened?" she urged him on.

"Nothing. That's it."

"That's it?" She withdrew her hand from his knee. "*That's* what made you fall in love with her? She didn't talk to you? Or do something kind?"

"Er . . . no."

Francine was so disgusted she could hardly speak. "Men! I can't believe how juvenile you are. I suppose if I bent over and you saw my breasts you would instantly be in love with me—"

She stopped abruptly, suddenly remembering that he *had* seen her breasts—and obviously hadn't fallen in love with her either.

"It depends," he said gravely, "on your breasts. The lady's were *very* nice." He looked her over. "To tell you the truth, I've forgotten what yours look like. If you'd like to show them to me . . ."

"You're disgusting." She turned away, trying to hide her heated face. "You'd better concentrate on the road. There are a lot of ruts."

"You're certain you don't want to show me your breasts?"

"Yes."

"I will give you my expert opinion—"

"Sir Garrick!"

He laughed. He actually had the gall to laugh.

He was hopeless, Francine thought, gritting her teeth. Absolutely hopeless.

*   *   *

Francine heard the town before she saw it—bells pealing nonstop. Clamoring pedestrians, riders, and carts clogged every road and lane, reminding her of rush-hour traffic back home. She steered her donkey close to Garrick's side, afraid she might lose him in the crush as they inched forward.

The fog had cleared, and Francine stared in fascination as they rode closer to the sprawling market. Merchants plied their wares from booths of rough-sawn pine hung with elaborately painted signs of yellow, red, blue, and green. People in coarse but colorful clothes crammed the narrow lanes, pushing and elbowing good-naturedly in their efforts to get through the throng. Ragged beggars held out beseeching hands to the passersby. There was the ever-present smell of smoke and manure, but these were overlaid by more pleasant scents—those of baking bread and roasting meat.

Garrick did not dismount, however. He skirted the edge of the fair until he came to a less crowded area, stopping at a barn where the smell of straw and manure was stronger. Horse sellers made their pitches to men in rough, woolen smocks and fine velvet capes alike. Off to one side stood men holding various implements—apparently, the tools of their trades.

Garrick dismounted, and Francine slid off her donkey hastily, before he could offer to help her. She stumbled a little, her lower half one big ache. Resisting the urge to rub her bruised posterior, Francine craned her neck to see the market.

Finished haggling with the stableboys, Garrick came to her side. Her looked at her thoughtfully.

"Anne asked me to buy a special herb for her. Would you discharge this duty while I am interviewing these men?"

Francine nodded. She would be glad to be spared his company for as long as possible—and the fair beckoned irresistibly. Although the lanes looked crowded and dirty, shopping *was* shopping.

Garrick removed a purse from his belt and flipped a small silver coin into the cup of a blind man being led by a dog.

"God bless you, milord," the man said and continued on his way.

Garrick handed the purse to Francine. "The herb is wild arrach, and Anne said it must be purchased from a woman named Riva Arber. Do not buy from anyone else and be sure to mention Anne's name."

"Very well," Francine said, taking hold of the purse.

Garrick didn't release it immediately. He stared down at her, a slight frown on his face. "You will be safe enough—but watch out for cutpurses."

"I will," she said, tugging on the purse.

He released it. "You may spend whatever is left over after you buy the herbs—but you must return here by the time the sun reaches its zenith."

"I will. Thank you," she added a trifle belatedly. She didn't quite know what to make of his generosity with his money. With a nod, she turned and headed toward the booths with a wobbly, bowlegged gait.

She paused as she was about to enter a crowded lane and glanced over her shoulder toward the workmen.

To her surprise, she saw no sign of Garrick. She glanced at the barn, just in time to see him go around the back corner and disappear from sight.

How odd, she thought. But then she shrugged and plunged into the crowd.

"Worcestershire salt! Worcestershire salt!" called one merchant.

"Rushes, fair and green!"

"Fine and strong Sussex iron; Sussex iron, strong and fine!"

Francine walked down a narrow lane where one man was showing animal pelts to a customer, another was deftly stitching a dress, and still another was cutting leather. The smell of pastries in one stall made her mouth water, but she couldn't buy anything until she found Riva Arber.

She searched for the herbalist's booth, but finally had to ask for directions. After several tries, she found someone who told her to go to the far edge of the fair.

The booth was smaller than most of the ones Francine had seen, and there was no sign. But spread out on planks were herbs tied in bundles along with several mortars and pestles.

Seated on a low stool, an old woman with a deeply wrinkled face and gnarled hands slowly sorted and tied more bundles.

"Are you Riva Arber?" Francine asked.

The woman looked up with eyes nearly as dark as Anne's. "Who wants to know?"

"My name is Francine Peabody. I'm here on behalf of Lady Anne, who wishes to purchase some herbs."

"Ahh." A bit of sparkle entered the woman's eyes and she rose to her feet with surprising quickness. Reaching up, she grasped Francine's face with a clawlike hand and studied her intently.

Surprised, Francine tried to draw back, but the woman's hold was unexpectedly strong.

Then, as suddenly as the woman had grabbed her, she released her and sat back down. "Yes, I'm Riva Arber. What herbs do you need?"

"Something called wild arrach." Francine rubbed her jaw, eyeing the woman warily. Riva hadn't scratched her, but Francine felt as though her bones had been crushed. How could such tiny, gnarled hands be so strong? Francine wondered.

"I thought so." Riva withdrew a small packet from her dress and held it out to Francine.

Francine took it rather gingerly, careful to avoid contact in case the woman grabbed her again. "Thank you." She reached for the purse Garrick had given her. "How much do I owe you?"

Riva shook her head. "No charge for Lady Anne and her friends. But take care not to speak of this herb to anyone." The old woman looked up from under thick gray brows. "You do understand that it is useful only as a method of prevention, *not* termination, don't you? I don't hold with turning half-baked buns out of the oven."

Prevention? Half-baked buns? What was the woman babbling about?

Francine gasped as she realized the answer—and the implication of the woman's words. "This herb isn't for me . . . I'm not . . ."

She broke off, biting her lip. "Thank you," she said with all the dignity she could muster. "But I must be going now."

"Give Anne my blessing," Riva said. "And fare thee well."

Francine nodded and hurried away, half embarrassed, half intrigued in spite of herself. Birth control! Who would have thought such a thing existed in this primitive time? But judging from the woman's warning to keep quiet about it, the herb's properties weren't common knowledge.

Francine stared at the small packet. Lifting it up to her nose, she sniffed. Her nose wrinkling, she quickly tucked the small packet into Garrick's purse. The herb smelled like rotten fish.

She walked along, the herb's odor quickly supplanted by more pleasant scents—roasting chicken, apple pie, sausage. . . .

Her stomach growled.

No, she told herself firmly. Heaven only knew what conditions this food had been prepared under. The idea of eating any of it was totally repulsive.

Her stomach growled again. And she was terribly thirsty.

She stopped and looked longingly at a loaf of bread being removed from an oven. Her mouth watered.

"Fresh bread!" the baker cried. "Fresh bread and mead, half a penny!"

She had to eat and drink *something*, Francine thought. She ate bread at the castle; surely it would be okay to eat it here. And mead sounded harmless enough.

She stepped up to the counter and handed the baker one of the small silver coins from Garrick's purse. The baker gave her a thick slice of bread and a jug of mead. Then, to Francine's surprise, the man cut the coin in two and gave half back to her.

Francine sniffed the contents of the jug. It smelled like apples and cinnamon. With the edge of her sleeve, she carefully wiped the rim of the jug, then sipped cautiously. To her relief, the drink was sweet, tasting of honey and spices. She tilted the mug up again, drinking thirstily. She paused to catch her breath, then gulped the rest down quickly.

She held out the jug to the proprietor, and turned to continue on her way. For an instant, the fair spun crazily, and Francine had to grab the stall post to keep from keeling over.

The spinning stopped quickly enough, and feeling curiously light-headed, she continued on her way, tearing off bits of bread and eating them as she walked.

Once she'd finished that, she stopped at a booth selling drumsticks from some bird. She dimly remembered there was some reason she shouldn't buy one, but the smell was so tempting, she went ahead. It tasted absolutely heavenly.

Tossing the bone aside, she licked the grease from her fingers and inspected the wares of the other shops.

She bought pine-scented candles for the garderobe and peach-scented soap for herself. She also bought a new white silk veil—to wear on special occasions.

She bought a crabcake, but then threw it away when the sight of a man in another booth yanking a tooth from a customer's head effectively killed her appetite. Gagging, she headed back toward where she was supposed to meet Garrick. She was almost there when she felt a need to go to the bathroom.

She sidled up to a woman selling cider in one of the booths. "Can you tell me where the garderobe is?"

The woman raised her brows. "The privy is at the edge of the fair—over yon."

Francine looked over and saw a line of women waiting to use the small shacklike facilities a short distance from the barn where Garrick had stabled the horse and donkey. Some of the euphoria that had enveloped Francine since drinking the mead faded. She thanked the woman, and with a sigh, walked over to get in line. No matter what century she was in, she hated public rest rooms. She'd always avoided them as much as possible. But the alternative—crouching behind a bush—was too appalling to consider.

Two women in patched skirts with shawls wrapped around their heads got into line behind her. "Did you hear what happened, Marge? A bird flew thrice around our house. My Daisy saw it with her very own eyes. I'm certain it is a good omen."

"Perhaps, Beth." Marge, a tall, thin woman with harsh lines in her face, spoke cautiously. "What kind of bird was it? If it was a raven or a crow, it could be a sign of ill to come."

"Daisy said it was a bluebird," the much shorter, rounder Beth replied. "There can be nothing ill-omened about a bluebird."

"Unless it was a jay. It might have been a warning that Daisy is growing lazy and her chatter idle."

Beth's plump face crumpled with worry. "I had not thought of that. Oh dear, oh dear. I will speak to Daisy as soon as I get home."

"Very wise," Marge said. "Oh, look! There's the fishmonger!"

Francine followed the direction of the woman's pointing finger only to see a man on a sledlike conveyance, his wrists and ankles bound and a dead fish tied around his neck.

"Ha!" Marge snorted in satisfaction. "I suspected he was selling putrid fish. He'll have to spend at least a day in the pillory. Let's go see when we're done here."

"Very well," said Beth, although she didn't look nearly as enthusiastic as her companion.

Francine reached the front of the line. She could already smell the foul odor from the privy. Taking a deep breath, she dashed inside.

The inside was dim, the light from a high window barely illuminating the hole in the ground and a stick lying next to it. But Francine didn't especially want to see anything. She wanted to do her business and get out as fast as possible before she ran out of breath and had to inhale.

Tucking her bundle of purchases under her arm, she was about to yank up her skirts and crouch over the hole, when she realized . . . there was no straw or leaves.

How like a public rest room!

Almost blue from lack of oxygen, she pulled open the door and inhaled a great ragged breath. She looked at Marge, waiting in line. "I'm sorry to bother you, but there's no straw in here. . . ."

Marge looked past her. "The communal stick is right there," she said rather impatiently.

"The communal . . ." Francine's voice trailed off as she realized what the stick next to the hole was for. "You mean . . . everyone *shares* that stick?" she asked in disbelief.

Marge stared at her as if to say, "Of course, you dummy."

The last vestiges of Francine's earlier euphoria vanished, leaving her feeling sick. She left the privy, saying in a thick voice, "I can wait."

For a short while she'd forgotten where she was—how primitive and disgusting this place was. She remembered now. Longingly, she thought of her apartment and her bathroom and her pine-scented air freshener—how she wished she were home right now! She hated this place.

Still nauseous, she glanced up to see Garrick behind the barn, talking to a red-bearded man. The man appeared to be arguing, waving his hands as he tried to convince Garrick of something. Garrick, his face expressionless, kept shaking his head.

Unwilling to face Garrick when she was feeling so nauseous, Francine tottered up to the area where the workmen were. She leaned against a fence and closed her eyes, taking deep breaths.

"Are you all right?" a rather high-pitched voice inquired.

Francine opened her eyes to see a scrawny man several inches shorter than she standing before her. He was eyeing her anxiously, and Francine forced herself to give him a faint smile. "I'm fine."

"Oh, good." He paused a moment, then said, "Do you need a genealogist, my lady? I can trace your family tree back to our Savior, or even to Adam and Eve if you like."

"No, thank you," she said.

The slight spark in his eyes faded away, leaving a curiously flat expression. He bowed and turned away.

Her gaze followed him, and she noticed again how thin he was. She'd thought the workers at the castle were poorly dressed, but this man's clothes were nothing but rags and he didn't even have shoes. She felt sick again, but for a different reason this time.

"Did you talk to Sir Garrick—the tall gentleman with the black beard?" she asked.

Turning back to her, the little man shook his head, his eyes resigned. "I spoke to him, but he had no use for me. I don't have any building experience."

"Oh. That's a shame. Is there a great demand for genealogists?"

He shook his head again. "It's not easy to get established."

She hesitated. "When did you last eat?"

"A few days ago."

"A few *days*?" Francine swallowed, thinking of the crabcake she'd thrown away. "What will you do if no one hires you?"

"I don't know," he said.

She was about to ask him another question, when Garrick came up.

"It's time to go," he said abruptly. "Are those your purchases? Give them to me and I will put them in my saddlebag."

Francine gave him the bundle. Glancing at the genealogist once more, she followed Garrick to the barn. "Did you hire the men?"

"Yes," he said.

Francine looked around, half expecting to see a huddle of men following them, but there was no one. "How will they get to the castle?"

"They will walk, of course." He flipped a couple of coins to the boys who brought their mounts. "I gave them directions and told them to be at Pelsworth by tomorrow," he said as he put her bundle into his saddlebag.

"Oh," Francine said. She turned away and started to clamber onto the donkey.

"Wait," Garrick said. "Have you used the privy?"

"Uh . . . no," she replied.

"You'd best do so before we leave. I don't want to have to stop on the way."

"I don't need to go," she said.

"Are you certain?"

"Positive," she assured him.

"Very well."

Before Francine could get into the donkey's saddle by her-self, Garrick put his hands on her waist and swung her up.

Her waist burned from the touch of his hands. "Thank you," she said as calmly as she could.

He nodded and mounted his own horse. They set off in the direction of the road.

As they passed the area where the workmen were, Francine's gaze fell once more on the genealogist. She pulled back on her reins, bringing Bathsheba to a halt.

Garrick looked at her questioningly.

"I think you should hire that man over there by the fence," she said.

The leather of his saddle creaking, Garrick turned to look. "The genealogist?" He snorted. "I need a castle built—not a family tree."

"Perhaps he could help with the building," she said in a low voice. "There must be some simple job he could do."

"He looks too weak. I doubt he'll be able to do much. And I've already hired enough."

"He needs the work. Can't you just give him a chance?"

He stared at her, his brow knit. "Why do you care? There are hundreds more just like him."

Francine bit her lip. "I don't know. I think it's his eyes. They look so . . . hopeless."

Garrick stared at her for a long time. Her heart began to sink. She knew it had been foolish to ask. She doubted this man had ever felt compassion for anyone.

"Very well," Garrick said abruptly. "But if the man can't do his fair share, he will be fired."

For a few seconds, Francine was speechless with surprise. Then she smiled her first real smile since arriving in the Middle Ages. "Oh, thank you!" she exclaimed.

He grew still, staring at her, and her smile faltered. "What's wrong?" she asked.

"Nothing." His expression shuttered, he rode over to the man and spoke a few curt words.

The blank eyes lit up. "Oh, thank you, milord," Francine heard the man repeat over and over. "I will work hard, you may be sure." He looked across the short distance to Francine. "And bless you, milady," he called, "for your kindness."

Francine blushed a little at the fervency of his words. She waved to the man as Garrick rode back to her, looking impatient.

"May we go now? Unless you want to ride home in the dark, at the mercy of every robber and vagrant in the shire."

Much in charity with him, Francine rode along at his side. Garrick was silent, as usual, but she didn't complain. She was too happy that he'd hired the genealogist.

Perhaps there was a flicker of humanity in him after all, she thought. She decided to reward him by trying to engage him in conversation. "How many men did you hire?"

"Ten. Eleven counting the genealogist."

"Did you hire that man you were talking to behind the barn?"

His hands tightened on the reins, and his horse side-stepped uneasily. "What man?"

"The red-bearded one that looked like he was trying to sell you London Bridge. You kept shaking your head. What was he trying to get you to do?"

He stared at her with an inimical gaze. "You are the nosiest female it's ever been my misfortune to meet."

"I was just curious—"

"Curiosity in women is a great sin. I suggest you cure yourself of it."

"There's no need to be so grouchy. I was just trying to make conversation."

"Then direct your conversation elsewhere."

"Okay, okay," she muttered. They'd entered a forest a short while ago, and the carpet of leaves muffled the clopping of hooves as she tried to think of some other topic. "Actually, I did want to talk to you some more about the etiquette class—"

"That again?" he interrupted.

In spite of his discouraging tone, she plunged ahead. "As I told you before, I would like the men-at-arms to attend."

"They are welcome to do so—as long as it doesn't interfere with their training."

"Yes, well . . ." Francine pushed aside a branch that was threatening to slap her in the face. "So far none of them have come."

"I can't imagine why."

"I can't, either," she said, ignoring the dryness of his voice. She fixed her gaze on a point between the donkey's ears. "Perhaps you could order them to attend."

She glanced at him quickly, to see his reaction.

He was staring at her, his brows nearly reaching the thick fringe of his hair. "Why would I want to do that?"

"So they will learn how to behave like men rather than animals," she said earnestly.

"You think *you* can teach them to behave like men?" Garrick shook his head. "Only the master-at-arms can do that."

"I'm not talking about fighting. I'm talking about improving themselves."

Garrick's face hardened. "The only area they need improving in is their fighting skills."

"So you're saying you won't order them?"

"No, Lady Francine, I will not."

"Won't you at least consider it?"

"Why should I?" he growled.

Francine tried to think of a reason. "Perhaps we could make an exchange."

His face took on a still, watchful look. "What kind of exchange?"

"Maybe I could help you with something—oh, I know! I'll help you with your problem!"

"Problem?" he said, his voice sounding strangely constricted.

"The girls in the kitchen mentioned it—and that you were thinking of visiting an astrologer or physician for a remedy. But I'll bet I know more than they would—"

Francine stopped abruptly as Garrick grabbed the donkey's bridle and yanked it to a halt. He leaned down, his angry face with its bristling black beard thrust close to hers. Startled, she stared into flaming gray eyes.

"Never," he snarled between clenched teeth, "never men-

tion my problem again. I have no problem. Do you understand?"

"Yes." Her voice came out a squeak.

Without another word, he released her donkey and cantered ahead, leaving her to trail behind him.

Francine clutched the reins tightly, trying to still the trembling of her fingers. What on earth was the matter with the
man?

He must be extremely sensitive about his leg injury to
react so strongly. Probably in this primitive time, any weakness was considered unmanly. How silly! And how unfortunate that she'd once again antagonized him. She doubted he
would help her now.

Well, she was just going to have to find some other way
to get the men to come to her class. She wasn't about to ask
the irrational beast for any more favors.

They rode in complete silence for about half an hour before Francine became aware of a problem of her own. A very
urgent problem.

As the donkey jiggled and bounced, the problem became
more and more acute. She shifted in the saddle, wishing she
hadn't drunk that whole jug of mead.

"Sir Garrick," she called to the man twenty feet ahead of
her.

He didn't appear to hear her.

"Sir Garrick!" she called more loudly.

He didn't turn or even slow down.

"Sir Garrick!" she shouted.

She saw his back stiffen. She thought he was going to ignore her, but then, slowly, he reined in his horse and waited
for her to catch up.

"What is it?" he asked harshly.

"I was wondering . . ."

"Yes?"

Francine swallowed a little. "I was wondering . . . if there
is a cottage near here where I could stop and, um, use the
garderobe."

He looked at her with narrowed eyes. "You told me you
didn't need to use the privy."

"I . . . I didn't. But now I do."

For a second she thought he was going to say something nasty. But instead he nodded curtly. "Very well. You may go."

She glanced around at the thick forest. "Go where?"

"Behind whichever bush or tree you choose."

She stiffened. "You expect me to go out in the open?"

"No," he said slowly, as if speaking to a child. "In the forest. We do not have time to search for a cottage. 'Tis growing dark, and unless you want to travel at night, easy prey for every thief and robber, we must not delay."

"But . . . but what if someone sees me?"

"There's nothing around here except deer and squirrels. And I'm certain they won't mind."

"You can't be serious."

"We can continue on if that is what you prefer."

Fury churned through Francine at his lack of consideration. She clenched her fingers tightly around the donkey's reins, fighting an urge to ride up to him and beat upon his leg—the only part of him she could reach at the moment. Controlling the insane impulse, she dismounted, grabbed a handful of leaves, and stomped behind a tree.

How could he be so inconsiderate? she fumed silently as she hitched up her skirts. And how much lower could she sink than having to squat behind a tree in full view of anyone who happened to pass by?

That particular disaster didn't occur, but as she remounted her donkey, all her earlier kind thoughts about Garrick were gone.

As far as she was concerned, they'd come full circle from where they'd started this morning—he was nothing but a mean, nasty, foul-tempered brute, and she couldn't wait to get out of this hellish place and return to the sanitized life she led in the twentieth century.

In the meantime, until she returned home, she was going to make sure she spent as little time in his company as possible.

Chapter 8

FRANCINE REMINDED THE men-at-arms frequently about her class over the next several days. Every morning she waited in the hall, hoping against hope that some of the men would show up.

She was beginning to get a sick, panicky feeling that she would never return home, when, to her relief and delight, one of the men-at-arms walked in one morning and said he was there for the etiquette class. "I want to learn how to win the affection of a woman," he said woodenly.

Francine surveyed the brawny young man, trying to stifle a twinge of doubt. She recognized him from the fight in the yard—the others had called him Orson. He reeked of onions, and judging from the severe case of acne and the greasy strands of hair hanging about his face, she doubted he'd ever taken a bath in his life. She could actually see bugs in his wispy beard.

She restrained a shudder. How could she ever transform this poor man into one a woman would even tolerate, let alone feel affection for? But she couldn't let him see her revulsion. She didn't want to hurt his feelings. Besides, this was exactly the kind of man she needed to civilize. If she did a good job with him, then maybe he would recommend her to the others.

She smiled at him brightly. "Very well, the first thing we will talk about is personal hygiene." She gestured toward the benches she always optimistically set up by the window.

A sullen expression on his face, he stomped over and sat down. "What's that?"

"Personal cleanliness," she said, wondering why he looked so sullen. "You must sponge yourself thoroughly with soap and water every day, wash your hair at least once a week, keep it combed neatly, wash your clothes on a regular basis, clean your teeth after every meal. . . ."

Furtively he made the sign of the cross, as if she'd suggested something profane. "How is this going to help me win a woman?" he growled.

"It will, believe me," Francine said fervently. "But it's just the first step. Once you're clean, then you must learn to carry on a conversation with the lady of your choice."

"You mean *talk* to her?"

"Yes," Francine said, ignoring his look of horror. "Women like to talk."

"What am I supposed to talk about?"

"Why, um, whatever you like, I suppose," she said. "The events of the day, books, music, art . . ."

"Art?" he choked out.

She heard a loud rustling noise and some snorting sounds from outside the window. The swineherder must be allowing the pigs to root in the courtyard, she thought with some distaste. In the last week, she had learned that the animals could be obnoxiously loud. She hoped the noise didn't interrupt her lesson.

"Well, perhaps not art," Francine conceded. "What does your lady friend like to talk about?"

Orson turned bright red. "I don't have a lady friend."

The grunting sounds outside the window increased in volume.

"Oh," she said, a bit distracted by the noise the pigs were making. "Is there someone you are interested in?" She remembered hearing the men mention Mog. "Mog, the kitchen maid, perhaps?"

A roar of laughter erupted from outside the window.

Orson, his face dark red and his teeth clenched, rose to his feet and ran over to the window, drawing his sword from its scabbard.

"See if you can laugh with my sword down your gullets, you poltroons!" he shouted, then jumped out the window.

Stunned, Francine ran to the window and looked out.

There, rolling in the dirt laughing, were the men-at-arms. A few, tears of laughter running down their faces, were clumsily trying to deflect Orson's blows with their own blades.

"What the hell is going on here?" a commanding voice snapped through the ruckus.

The laughter stopped immediately. They jumped to their feet and stood at attention as Garrick glared at them. "What do you men think you're doing?"

"Er, the lady offered to give lessons in etiquette," Pascal, one of the bolder ones, said. "Orson took her up on her offer."

Garrick eyed Orson's sullen face. "And what made you decide you need to improve your manners?"

"The short straw," Orson muttered.

"I see," Garrick said, his face stern. "I'm glad you all have time to entertain yourselves with these little pranks. Since you have nothing else to do, you can help the stable-master cart manure out of the stalls. There's enough there to keep you busy for a few hours at least."

A quickly suppressed groan rose from the group, before they scuttled away. Once they were gone, Garrick turned to look up at Francine standing in the window embrasure. "Why is it that you are always at the center of some trouble, Lady Francine?"

Francine was trembling a little from the shock of discovering that she had been the butt of a joke on the part of the men-at-arms, but she lifted her chin as she stared down at Garrick from the window.

"I was merely trying to help," she said.

"Do me a favor," he said. "Don't."

Feeling safe from her vantage point, she said, "I'll do as I like."

His eyes narrowed. "I think not." Swiftly, before she could retreat, he stepped forward and reached upward. Taking hold of her by the waist, he swung her out of the window.

He set her down, his hard hands still holding her. "I am lord and master here, and it's time you learned that. When I tell you something, I expect to be obeyed. Understood?"

He was leaning over her, a dark frown on his face, his voice harsh.

"I understand you perfectly—I'm not deaf, you know. There's no need to shout and glare in that ridiculous way." This was perhaps a trifle unfair, since he hadn't raised his voice at all, but she was getting a little tired of his oblique threats.

His frown deepened. "God's throat, you are the most irrepressible wench I've ever met. You do not seem to understand that this castle could be attacked at any time. The men have no time for foolishness—they must be trained. I've warned you before not to cause trouble, but so far you've frightened the workers, stirred up the kitchen staff, and interfered with the men-at-arms' training. So I tell you now—cause any more trouble amongst the people here, male or female, and I myself will boot you out of this castle right on your pretty arse. Do I make myself clear?"

He made himself very clear indeed. A shaft of fear pierced through Francine. What would happen to her if he forced her to leave? Where would she go? Shrinking inside, but trying to hide it, she said, "L-Lady Anne wouldn't allow you—"

"You overestimate Anne's influence. Occupy yourself with some women's work if you are bored, but do not cause any more trouble."

He turned and stalked away.

Francine stayed where she was, shivering.

The next week did not go well for Francine. She continued trying to civilize everyone, but it seemed hopeless. Afraid to ask the men to come to her class, she talked to them individually, but they stared at her uncomprehendingly when she suggested that they wash themselves and refrain from belching and passing gas at the dinner table.

She urged Gunilda, the cook, to clean up the kitchen, but the woman snapped at her that she was welcome to take on the chore if she was so concerned about it and Francine had retreated, not wanting to cause trouble.

She tried to ask the blacksmith to make forks for her, but he was a big, beefy man, with arms and a neck bigger than her thighs. He had small eyes that were further obscured by a heavy ridge of eyebrow. One glare and she'd scurried off.

Her days went from bad to worse. She put the pine-scented candles she'd bought at the fair in the garderobe, and nearly set the castle on fire when a spark fell into the straw. She used the peach-scented soap in her daily sponge baths in Garrick's room, but the odors of the castle and its inhabitants decreased as her nose adjusted to the smells, making her fear that she too might have begun to stink, and she didn't even know it.

She was forced to lower her standards in other ways, too. After feeling light-headed and almost passing out one day, she realized she had to start eating more or she would make herself sick. Reminding herself that she'd suffered no ill effects from her gluttony at the fair, she began eating meat and drinking beer and tried not to think about the kitchen and its filthy state.

The sense of urgency to get home increased daily. She worried about how they were doing without her and what they thought of her disappearance. She worried about her job, and her bills piling up unpaid, and her library book that was now overdue. Thoughts of Stuart and Grandma Peabody and Bentley plagued her constantly. The date of her wedding was still more than two months away, but she was supposed to have a fitting for her dress at the end of the week. The bridal shop might cancel her order if she didn't show up. She had to get home. Soon. Before . . .

She kept the terrible thought at bay, unable to bear putting it into words.

Despair sometimes threatened to overwhelm her. The situation was hopeless. She was making no progress. And she was cold all the time. The lack of privacy and the constant noise of the castle set her nerves on edge. She often felt like she was living in an ant colony—yet she felt isolated and alone.

Her loneliness increased when Anne left to visit some baron or other, cheerfully informing Francine that she would return in a month or two.

Francine felt abandoned. Anne and Edith were the closest thing to women friends she had, even though they both suffered the same fault—hero worship of Garrick. Sometimes Francine thought that if she had to listen to one more story about his heroism, his bravery, or his wonderfulness, she would jump out the tower window.

Edith did introduce Francine to a few of the village women. They tried to teach her to sew and spin and weave, but they giggled at both her clumsy efforts and her ideas of improving village life.

Nancy was kind, but busy, and Francine was afraid of Gunilda. Mog would barely say two words to her—especially after an incident that happened toward the end of the week.

Walking back from the fairy circle one morning—she went every day just in case the emerald suddenly decided to transport her home—Francine was approaching the castle gate when she heard Pascal laugh and say, "You're wasting your time, Mog. Why would I be interested in an ugly little shrew like you? When I marry, I'm going to choose a pretty wife with a dowry and some status—someone like Nancy."

"All the men-at-arms want to marry Nancy," Mog sneered. "What makes you think she'll look at you?"

Pascal laughed. "Oh, she'll look, all right."

Entering the gate a few seconds later, Francine saw Pascal strolling away, whistling an airy tune. There was no sign of Mog, however.

Francine was about to continue on her way when she heard a sniffle from behind a pile of stone blocks. Peeking around the corner, she saw Mog sitting on one of the stones, her head on her knees.

Francine hesitated. She wasn't feeling too kindly toward Mog—the girl never missed an opportunity to make a nasty remark—but Francine could not quite bring herself to ignore the other's misery.

"Mog . . . ," she said, tentatively.

The girl leapt to her feet as if a bee had stung her. Tears stained her dirty cheeks, and she wore a scowl that rivaled Garrick's for fierceness.

"What do you want?" the girl hissed.

"I . . . nothing. I just . . ." Francine searched for the right words to say. "I heard Pascal. . . ."

Under the dirt, Mog's face flushed bright red. "Don't look at me like that—I don't need your pity. Why don't you go back where you came from?" Without another word, she turned and stalked away, her thin shoulders held straight and proud.

Francine hadn't tried to talk to Mog again. The whole incident was typical of the way the castle people seemed to regard Francine. Even when she tried to be nice, they regarded her with suspicion or downright fear. Or, in the case of Garrick, with a complete lack of interest.

She found this extremely annoying. *She* had planned to avoid *him*. It was very irritating to find it unnecessary.

She found herself watching him from a distance, with a sort of brooding fixation. He always seemed to be in motion. If he wasn't monitoring the builders and the progress of the castle, then he was talking to Thomas the Engineer, Clifford the Steward, or some messenger.

The whole situation would have been intolerable if it wasn't for one person—the genealogist, Harvey.

He was Francine's one true friend, the only one she could talk to freely. But he had not fared too well, either. He had worked for several days with the mortar makers, but could not seem to get the hang of it. So he had been sent to help in the stables. Unfortunately, he was terrified of horses. Finally, he was assigned to herd the geese back and forth from the castle to the fields each day. So far he'd had some luck with this job, and Francine sometimes accompanied him when he went.

After one particularly horrible day, she walked with Harvey down the path to the village, complaining bitterly. "No one listens to me. I could not believe it when everyone started booing that poor juggler last night."

"He was terrible," Harvey said. Neatly dressed in a new light-brown tunic and darker hood that covered his gray-peppered hair, he'd gained a little weight and his hazel eyes had lost that flat, hopeless look. Using his staff, he herded a rebel goose back onto the path.

"Yes, but did he deserve to have food thrown at him?" She raised her voice to be heard over the goose's loud protests. "That mutton bone cut his cheek. What if he'd lost an eye?"

"It would be God's punishment for choosing an inappropriate profession."

"God's punishment!" Francine stepped sideways to avoid trampling a gosling. "Do you really think God is so spiteful?"

"Spite has nothing to do with it. God has put us on earth to fulfill a particular purpose. It is the cloud's purpose to give rain, the peasant's purpose to grow food, and the knight's purpose to fight."

"And what if someone doesn't know their purpose?"

"Then one must search for it. I, myself, have tried several different professions."

Francine bit back a sharp reply to this nonsensical philosophy. She'd been feeling a trifle testy the last few days, but she didn't want to take her ill temper out on someone as kind as Harvey. "Another thing . . . I cannot believe the lack of hygiene here. I told Ivo, one of the men-at-arms, that he needed to take a bath, and you know what he said? That he'd just taken one . . . a month ago! Can you believe that? There needs to be some kind of bathroom facilities here."

"When I was in Spain, I saw many Turkish steam baths." Harvey glared at the goose that refused to stay on the path. The goose hissed.

"A steam bath," Francine said thoughtfully. "That might work. It would definitely be easier than installing plumbing. Although plumbing is definitely needed. I told the men yesterday not to urinate in the fire, and what do you think happened at dinner? Not one, not two, but all seven of them did so! I think they did it on purpose to annoy me."

Harvey shook his staff at the goose. "The men here are very uncouth, I agree. The men in the household where I last served were much more discreet—they relieved themselves in a corner."

Several of the other geese began hissing in sympathy for their comrade.

"Mmm," Francine said noncommittally. Then, in a burst of frustration, she cried out, "Oh, I just *have* to be gone from here by the end of the week. I *have* to!"

"Why?"

"Because . . . oh, just because," she said as the geese started honking loudly, preventing further conversation.

As Harvey tried to get the geese under control, Francine walked silently, wondering if she dared approach Garrick about the steam bath. So far he hadn't agreed to any of her ideas. She decided to try to talk to him tomorrow—she was in no mood to try to be pleasant today.

She took an unwary step and stumbled. With an exclamation, she glared down at her feet. The ill-fitting shoes pinched her toes unbearably, and the rutted path didn't help matters. She limped along, thinking gloomily that it would be a miracle if she wasn't lame when she returned home.

If she returned home. . . .

They rounded a corner and the village came into sight. She stopped suddenly, causing Harvey to bump into her. "What's wrong?" he asked.

"Oh!" she cried, her hand flying to her mouth as she stared at a gibbet about one hundred feet in front of her. Two men carried a long object that looked disturbingly like a body wrapped in canvas toward a wagon. As she watched, the men swung the body three times and then threw it into the wagon next to another wrapped corpse. It hit the wooden boards with a thud.

For a second Francine thought she was going to be sick. But then, as she averted her gaze from the wagon, she saw Garrick sitting on his horse near the reeve's house, talking to the reeve. The stocky, bearded man gestured toward Francine, and Garrick turned in the saddle to look at her.

Garrick appeared to hesitate a moment, then wheeled his horse about and rode toward her.

Wearing his heavy chain mail and coif and sitting on his huge black horse, Garrick looked large and threatening. Francine stifled an impulse to run.

He stopped at her side. Harvey, discreetly pretending to tend to the geese, moved a short distance away.

Garrick dismounted and nodded toward the bodies. "The two vagrants who attacked you have been punished. Although there was no sign of your ring, at least you need not fear them again."

"Those were the two men who robbed me?" She swayed a little. "You killed them?"

Garrick nodded, his face hard. "I don't allow criminals on my land."

Francine felt sick. In her own time, she'd always favored the death penalty. But actually seeing the results of it made her cringe. Especially since these two men had died because of *her*. Logically, she knew it wasn't her fault—but still, she felt as though she were personally responsible for their deaths. It was not a pleasant feeling. "Did they have a trial?"

Garrick shook his head. "They could provide no friends to swear to their innocence. Since they had robbed and killed several people, and many were able to identify them, they chose to be given the ordeal by fire."

The knowledge that the men had robbed and killed others made Francine feel a little better. "Ordeal by fire?"

"They each had to lift a red-hot iron and carry it three paces. After three days, their hands were examined. Their palms had blistered, proclaiming their guilt for all to see."

Francine swallowed. "That's barbaric. They should have had a trial. There might have been extenuating circumstances. Perhaps they had difficult childhoods. Maybe they couldn't find jobs. Maybe they had low self-esteem."

"Low self-esteem?" Garrick repeated. "That is the stupidest thing I ever heard."

"I'm sure *you* would think so," Francine replied, unable

to stop herself even though she knew she was being foolish. "But it happens to be a fact that criminals are often people who were mistreated as children and as a result have low self-esteem."

"I don't care about self-esteem. I only care about justice."

"Justice? You executed them without giving them a chance to defend themselves!" She hugged her arms to her chest.

"They had no defense."

"Oh? Maybe they just wanted to steal my clothes. Maybe they were no different than *you*."

His mouth, barely visible through his beard and moustache, took on a tight, pinched look. "I did not steal your clothes."

"No? What would you call it, then?"

"I already told you, I took them for your own protection."

"Next time you decide to 'protect' me, I would appreciate it if you would allow me to decide whether or not I want it."

"Very well," he said coldly. He remounted his horse and, scattering Harvey's geese as he rode, thundered back to the reeve. Francine could not hear what Garrick said, but she saw the anger in his face and the way the reeve shrank away.

Trembling, she turned to Harvey, who approached her after Garrick left. "I can't believe what a tyrant that man is!" she cried, feeling strangely on the verge of tears.

Harvey, ignoring his scattered geese, cast a worried glance at her. "You should not speak so to him. He might have your tongue cut out."

"Hmmph." Hiding the dart of fear Harvey's words engendered, Francine stuck her nose in the air. "I'd like to see him try."

Garrick growled at Adam Reeve, but his mind was on the woman he had just left. He'd never met a more bothersome, meddlesome, contrary wench in his life. He ought to have her tongue cut out.

Enough was enough. He'd been more than patient with her. The woman was going to have to leave, no matter what he had promised Anne. Three months was too long to endure. She was bossy, rude, and a royal pain in the arse.

She rarely seemed to think before she acted. Witness her defense of the castle workers, her insistence on hiring the genealogist, and her concern over two convicts—men who had attacked her! She was foolishly generous. She had no sense of how the world worked. She tried to change things that could never be changed.

She was a strange woman, full of odd humors. Her stubbornness and contrary ways made him want to beat her; but just when he was angriest with her, she would say something that made him want to laugh.

And as if all of that wasn't bad enough, there was his body's reaction to her.

He was certain a new spell of Anne's had caused his desire, and he was determined not to succumb to it. And yet, with every passing day, it seemed he became more aware of every part of Francine—the deep blue of her eyes, the pearly whiteness of her teeth, the unblemished smoothness of her complexion. . . .

He'd tried to ignore her effect on him. But the desire was growing more acute, not less. The smallest thing could set him off—the touch of her hand on his thigh on the trip to the market; her smile when he'd agreed to hire the genealogist; the sweet peach scent of her skin. Even her natural perversity had a strange effect on him. When she argued boldly with him as she'd just done, heat flowed through him, so hot and so violent, it made him want to drag her to the tower chamber—whether to beat her or bed her, he wasn't sure.

Garrick shook his head. It was obviously another of Anne's spells. But he would *not* succumb to this one, on that point he was determined. He was going to marry the king's ward. He was *not* going to become involved with this woman who could bring him no power—only problems.

"Is there aught else, my lord?" the reeve asked.

"No . . . yes. Have those bodies buried immediately."

"Yes, milord."

Finished with his business in the village, Garrick rode toward the castle, only to rein in his horse when he saw Harvey, running in a crouched position, hands extended, trying to catch one of the scattered geese. There was no sign of Francine.

"Hey, genealogist," he hailed the man. "Where is Lady Francine?"

The genealogist stopped chasing the goose and turned to face Garrick. "She went back to the castle," he panted, sweat glistening on his forehead.

Garrick's annoyance increased. Hadn't the fool woman learned that she shouldn't be walking alone?

Leaving Harvey to his task, Garrick spurred his horse forward and rode along the path, silently rehearsing the tongue-lashing he intended to give Francine.

He reined in his horse as he came to the end of the woods, and looked ahead to where the path wound up to the castle. There was no sign of Francine.

She could not possibly have reached the castle so quickly. So where was she?

He wheeled his horse about and rode back down the dark, narrow path, cursing himself for not ordering the trees cut back.

He watched the path and the surrounding trees carefully for any sign of her. He listened, but he could only hear the birds and the rustling of the wind through the branches.

A cold sweat broke out on his brow. Had she been set upon again? Had she hurt herself?

He was about to return to the castle and call out a search party when he saw a broken branch on a bush and faint footprints in the soggy, leaf-covered ground. The underbrush grew too thick for him to follow on horseback, so he dismounted, tied his horse to a tree, and headed toward the lake.

He found her sitting in the middle of the fairy circle, her wimple, shoes, and hose in a pile beside her, her short golden curls tousled, her skirts bunched up around her knees.

She was crying.

Fear swept through him once again. What had happened?

Had she been injured? Raped? He would kill with his bare hands anyone who'd harmed her. . . .

Quietly, he moved forward and gently laid a hand on her shoulder.

"Oh!" She jumped and turned. "Oh, it's you." Hastily, she pushed her skirts down.

His gaze ran over her, searching for injuries. "Francine . . . are you hurt?"

"No." She scrambled to her feet, avoiding his eyes. "That is . . . I'm fine."

He stared at her averted, red-rimmed eyes. She wasn't telling him the truth, he could tell. "Then why are you crying?"

"I'm not crying—"

"Did someone attack you?"

"No—"

"Did something happen?"

"It's nothing!"

"It can't be nothing. If someone has hurt you, I must know."

"No one hurt me. I only hoped that my friends would be here. I hoped they would take me home before . . ."

"Before what?"

"Never mind. Just go away so I can put my shoes and stockings back on."

"Why did you take them off?"

She bit her lip. "I . . . I have a blister."

He didn't believe her. She was hiding something, he was certain. Squatting down, he grabbed her ankle and started pushing up her skirt.

"What are you . . . hey! Stop that!" Frantically she tried to hold her skirts down.

Inexorably he pushed them up, ignoring her squawking protests.

Holding a fistful of material at her knees, he stared at her legs, searching for injuries. There was nothing—nothing except shapely knees, softly curved calves, and finely turned ankles.

His throat grew dry.

She stopped struggling. Tearing his gaze away from her legs, he glanced up and saw that her expression was half resigned, half tragic. A single tear traced down her cheek.

"What?" he demanded fiercely. "What's wrong?"

"Don't you see?"

Thoroughly confused, he said, "See what?"

"My legs . . . they . . . they're *hairy!*"

He looked back at her legs and saw a fine sprinkling of light hair covering her shapely calves. "Yes?"

"It . . . it's under my arms, too!"

"You want me to look at that also?"

She stared at him suspiciously. Garrick tried not to smile, but his expression must have given him away because she glared at him and yanked her ankle and skirts away from his loosened grasp. "Oh! You don't understand. Where I come from it's considered very unfeminine. We always shave our legs and under our arms."

He straightened slowly. "It's considered feminine to look like a child?"

"No, of course not!"

"Children are the only ones I know of who don't have hair in those places."

"Oh, for heaven's sake, never mind!" She glared at him. "You obviously don't understand."

"You're not explaining yourself very well."

"What is there to explain? I'm stuck in this horrible place, my cat is likely starving, my grandmother must think I've been abducted, and my fiancé probably thinks I've abandoned him." Tears welled in her eyes again. "I was supposed to have a fitting for my wedding dress today."

Garrick stared at her, his brow knit, trying to figure out what the hell was the matter with her. Although he could see she might be upset by the things she'd mentioned, none of them were new. She seemed overwrought. He hadn't seen a woman so testy since Lady Mary of York had taken a knife to him. . . .

His brow cleared. *"Oh."*

She stiffened at that, her tears disappearing. "What's *that* supposed to mean?"

"Nothing."

"Don't give me that—you obviously meant something. I insist that you tell me."

Bluntly, he said, "I know women are often emotional and ill-humored prior to their monthly flows."

Her mouth dropped open, affording him a glimpse of white teeth and pink tongue. A flush rose in her cheeks. "You . . . you sexist, macho pig!"

"I beg your pardon?"

"I can't believe such prejudice exists even now!" she railed.

"Prejudice?" he repeated, watching the color in her face deepen.

"About women being emotional and bad-tempered during . . . at certain times of the month! As if you had to humor us and condescend to us because of a few hormones. Well, let me tell you, buster, that my mood has *nothing* to do with . . . with anything like *that.* . . ."

"What am I supposed to think when I find you sitting here, crying over nothing?"

"I'm *not* crying over nothing. I'm crying because . . . because I miss my fiancé."

Garrick found it difficult to believe that she missed the weakling she'd described to him on the way to the market, but all he said was, "If you say so."

"I do say so," she snapped. With a flounce, she sat back down and pulled on her stockings and shoes. Crumpling her hat and wimple under her arm, she stood up again and took a step toward the path.

Seeing her favoring the foot with the blister, Garrick said, "I will give you a ride back to the castle."

"No, thank you," she said haughtily.

"I insist," he said. "These woods are dangerous and I can't take the time to rescue you *again.*"

She glared at him, but didn't argue as she followed him back to his horse. A short while later they were cantering back toward the castle.

He had his arm around her waist, but she sat stiffly. She felt thinner, more fragile than the last time he'd held her.

Was she trying to starve herself? Garrick wondered. He would not be surprised. She was full of odd notions.

This new fixation of hers was a perfect example. She was an idiot to want to look like a child. She was a fool to want to change her shapely legs in the smallest way.

A strand of her hair—soft, not stiff and smelly like it had been last time—blew against his mouth, and suddenly, just like that, he was hard as a rock. He'd been half aroused ever since he'd looked at her legs, but his worry had distracted him. Now desire pulsed through him, an ache, a hunger so strong that he wanted to pull her off the horse, lay her down in the soft leaves beneath the trees, and thrust himself deep inside her. . . .

His arm tightened around her.

She pulled away immediately. "What are you doing, you pervert? Let go of me."

He loosened his grip instantly. "I assure you I have no interest, perverse or otherwise, in you," he said coldly.

"Hah! That's what they all say."

The heat that had gathered in his groin and addled his wits quickly dissipated. In six more months—three, if he was lucky—he would finish the castle and be married to the king's ward.

He had no intention of allowing this strange woman from the fairy world to affect his plans.

No matter how she affected his body.

Chapter 9

HAVING A MENSTRUAL period in Medieval times was as miserable as Francine had thought it would be. She'd never appreciated twentieth-century women's sanitary products as much as she did during the next several days.

Products she feared she would never use again.

She was sitting at the supper table on the last day of her period when she realized the terrible, horrible truth. She wasn't going home. Not ever.

Looking around the dirty, smokey room at the loud, crude men, Francine felt her heart sink all the way down to the points of her ill-fitting shoes. There was no way she could ever civilize anyone here. She'd been deceiving herself to think that she could. The men had no interest in her classes. She'd been wasting her time trying to get them to come. They were all animals. Especially Garrick.

He sat next to her, ignoring her completely as he ate meat speared on the end of his knife.

She hated him, she thought, staring down at the eels on her trencher. She hated him more than she'd ever hated anyone in her whole entire life. It wasn't bad enough that she had to suffer the terrible indignities of living in the Middle Ages—no, he had to be there to witness her degradation, or even cause it. He'd embarrassed her and humiliated her from the day she'd arrived here. He'd stripped her and stared at her naked body. He'd laughed at her attempts to civilize the men. He'd spoken to her of intimate, personal things that should never be discussed between a man and a woman unless they were married—and probably not even then. She couldn't imagine Stuart being so crass as to make her pee behind a tree or to mention her period.

Stuart. She would never see him again. She would never go to another matinee with him or eat another Early Bird Special at Lou's Chinese Cafe. She would never find out what it was like to make love.

What must he be thinking? That she was dead, probably. He would be heartbroken. She only hoped that it didn't ruin the rest of his life. She hoped he found someone else to love. But knowing Stuart, she feared it was more likely that he would grieve for her until his dying day. As would she. . . .

The meal ended and Francine, still brooding, was on her way to clean her teeth and use the garderobe when she heard a voice hiss, "Lady Francine! Psst! Lady Francine!"

Turning, she saw Orson standing in the small alcove of the window embrasure.

"Yes, Orson?" she said.

He shifted his weight from one foot to the other. "I was wondering . . . um, that is, I wanted to ask you if . . . if you would be willing to teach me those etiquette things you spoke of."

Francine stared at him. "You want to come to the etiquette class?"

"Um, well . . ." He shifted his weight again. "I was wondering if we could do it . . . privately. I don't want Pascal or any of the others to find out."

"What made you change your mind?" she asked, wondering if this was another joke.

His face turned beet red. "Well . . . to tell you the truth, I . . . I want to win Nancy, but she doesn't seem to know I'm alive."

"I see," Francine said calmly enough, but inwardly she was practically bursting with excitement. Her first student!

Perhaps her situation wasn't as hopeless as she'd thought. She was sure she could train this man. She would civilize him, and maybe that would be enough to get her home. . . .

"Very well," she told him. "I will help you."

He smiled, revealing food-encrusted teeth. "Thank you, Lady Francine. And may God bless you for the rest of your days!"

Lying in bed later that evening, Francine tried to think of a location where she could give Orson the lessons. She couldn't have him go to the hall—not without everyone finding out. She could have him come to the fairy circle, but that was one of the few places she could have a bit of privacy. She liked to go there just to get away from the racket and constant flood of people that seemed to surround her all the time.

No, she didn't want Orson invading her small bit of space. But then, where?

It seemed there was nowhere they could be alone. But Francine didn't give up. She was determined to figure out a way around the problem. Orson was her best chance of getting home—and of never having to see Garrick again.

It wasn't until the next morning that an idea on where to hold the lessons occurred to her. She washed and dressed quickly and went down to the village to Joan the Weaver's cottage.

"Good morning, my lady." The woman had a squarish face and bright, curious eyes. "You're up and about early."

"Yes. I have lots to do today, and I wanted to ask you a favor."

Joan checked the baby sleeping in a cradle by the fire. "If 'tis within my power, I will be glad to help, my lady."

"I was wondering if you would be willing for Orson and me to come and sit in your cottage for a short while every morning."

"Why, certainly, my lady. I would be glad of the company." Joan returned to her loom, her glance turning sly. "Is he courting you?"

"Good heavens, no! I'm merely going to teach him a few

manners. I don't want you to talk about this to anyone, though."

Joan tossed the shuttle through the separated threads of the loom. "Of course not, my lady. My lips are sealed, I assure you!"

So it was that the lessons commenced at Joan's cottage.

"You must clean your teeth every morning and evening," Francine told Orson.

"Why?" he asked.

"For several reasons," Francine explained patiently. "Number one, it will help keep your teeth healthy—you will be less likely to lose them as you get older."

"Does it prevent tooth worms?"

"Tooth worms?" Francine repeated, a bit faintly. What new Medieval horror was this? "What are those?"

"The worms that eat holes in your teeth. They're very tiny—I've never actually seen one—but the tooth-drawer had to pull two of my teeth because of them."

Francine breathed a little easier, realizing that the "tooth worm" was just a bit of Medieval folk myth. "Some very learned men in my village say that the holes are caused by the food decaying and causing the tooth to rot. This decay is part of what makes someone's breath smell bad—clean teeth will make you much more attractive to a woman. . . ."

Francine noticed that Joan's motions with the shuttle grew slower and slower, until they finally stopped, and she sat listening unabashedly.

Francine didn't think too much about it, but the next morning when she entered the cottage she found not only Joan and Orson, but also Sarah the Spinster, there.

"Sarah came to spin and keep me company while I weave," Joan said.

"Good morning, Sarah." Francine nodded and smiled to the thin woman with the long nose, then began her lesson.

"It is very important to wash your hands with soap and water after you use the garderobe. Doing this will help prevent illnesses. . . ."

* * *

A few days later, Francine was returning from the morning lessons when she stopped to watch a wall being built. She saw Harvey walking around offering the working men drinks of water from a bucket and dipper. Upon seeing her, he smiled and waved. "Good morning!"

"Good morning," she said, falling into step beside him. "You have a new job, I see."

"Yes. being a gooseherd really did not suit me very well. The geese took an unaccountable dislike to me and kept pecking and honking loudly at me whenever I tried to drive them to the fields. Many of the villagers were complaining about the racket. I offered to help with the cooking, but Gunilda said that I was ill-omened and refused to have me in her kitchen."

"Hmm." She eyed him a little curiously as they climbed up to the battlements. "You said once that you've tried many professions. Did none of them appeal to you?"

He gave a dipperful of water to a guard. "I liked being a barber. Unfortunately, my clients had a lamentable tendency to die right after I tended them. I, um, had to leave several places in a hurry."

The guard choked on his water. Hastily, he handed the dipper back to Harvey and stepped away.

Francine couldn't blame him. "Your clients died after you cut their hair?" she asked in disbelief.

"Oh, no." Harvey continued along the battlements. "My clients died when I attempted to bleed them. I never could quite tell how much blood needed to be drained to balance the humors. I never cared much for that part of the job. What I liked was cutting hair and shaving the men—I was always good at that. Unfortunately there's not much demand for those services."

"Hmm," Francine replied. A few weeks ago she would have been shocked by his explanation of Medieval medical practices, but she was becoming inured to barbarities. "The men here could use a good shave and haircut."

"Yes," Harvey agreed, looking rather wistful. "Now there

is something I would enjoy. I wielded the razor with unparalleled skill."

"Perhaps you could set yourself up as the castle barber," Francine said.

"I doubt anyone would avail themselves of my services," Harvey said. "Men tend to be possessive about their beards."

"I'll bet Orson would do it," Francine said.

"Why do you say that?"

"Because he would do anything to win Nancy's favor. I've been giving him lessons in manners the last week to help him. But don't tell anyone. He wants to keep it a secret."

"I'm afraid his secret is out," Harvey said. "I've heard several people talking about the lessons."

Francine frowned. "Oh, dear. I hope he's not upset. Although I suppose it was bound to happen. Almost all the women in the village have been coming to the classes also—the cottage is so crowded, they have to stand outside the door and windows. Do the other men-at-arms know?"

"No, although I did hear one of them—that Pascal—telling Orson that he was as sweet-smelling as a lady's herb garden—and as clean as a newly baptized infant."

"Oh, dear," Francine said again.

"Orson bore it stoically," Harvey said. "But he may not wish to lay himself open to more teasing by shaving."

"Hmm. You may be right. Why are they being so stupid? They would look so much better without the beards—and they wouldn't have trouble with dried bits of food always being stuck in their whiskers. They should recognize what a *privilege* it is to be able to shave. Why, I would *love* to be able to shave."

"No, I don't think you need to." Harvey peered at her face. "Although the peach fuzz above your upper lip is a bit thick. It's not bad, but perhaps I could—"

"No! That's not what I meant." Self-consciously, she rubbed her finger across her upper lip. "I meant I would like to shave my legs."

"Shave your legs?" he asked incredulously. "But why?"

"For my self-respect," she answered. "Could you lend me your razor?"

"No, no, you cannot be serious. To shave the legs is not natural."

"It is where I come from."

"My lady, it's not an easy matter to shave the skin—you could easily cut yourself."

That gave her pause. The idea of handling a naked blade made her uneasy. What if she did accidentally slice open a vein or something? There was no doctor worthy of the name within seven hundred-plus years of this place. She could very well bleed to death.

"You could do it for me," she said.

As soon as the impulsive words came out of her mouth, Francine had second thoughts. Shaving one's legs was rather a private thing. It would be embarrassing to have even someone as harmless as Harvey do it for her.

She opened her mouth to take back the words, but Harvey spoke before she had a chance.

"No, my lady, I couldn't do that. Sir Garrick wouldn't like it."

"Sir Garrick! What does he have to do with it? It's none of his business what I do with my legs."

Harvey eyed her doubtfully. "Still, I think it might be wise to get his permission first."

"You must be joking." All thought of taking back her words was forgotten in her determination to make her point. "I don't have to ask his permission. He doesn't own me."

"My lady, you cannot have considered the matter carefully. Surely you do not want to have your legs shaved in the courtyard in full view of anyone who might walk by? Even in the hall, you would be exposing your lower limbs to the gazes of many."

"I want to be shaved only up to my knees. You worry too much. Besides, we don't have to do it in the courtyard or hall—we can go to Garrick's room."

"His room!" Harvey's eyes bulged from his head. "If he caught us in there he would likely have us executed."

"Nonsense. I wash in there every morning."

"He allows you the use of his room? That proves it—he *does* have an interest in you."

"Don't be silly. He doesn't even know I go in there."

Harvey stared at her. "Aren't you frightened he will catch you?"

"No. Edith assured me he never goes in there during the day. And he never has, in all the times I've been here. So you see, you have nothing to worry about."

He still looked doubtful, but she could see he was wavering.

"Please, Harvey," she said. "You don't know what it's like for me. I've endured so much. If I could just have this one little thing, I'll at least be able to hold my head up."

Harvey swished the dipper in the bucket of water. "Very well," he said unhappily. "I cannot refuse you when you have done so much for me."

"Thank you, Harvey!" Francine practically danced along the battlements, too delighted to pay attention to his gloomy face. "Go get your razor and other supplies, and I'll get some soap and a bucket of hot water. I'll meet you in Garrick's room."

Fortunately Gunilda had some water boiling over the hearth, and although she grumbled, she allowed Francine to take what she needed. Francine thanked her and hurried back to the hall, almost bumping into Rafael as she entered.

"Oh, I'm sorry!" Francine said to the scarlet- and yellow-clad minstrel.

"'Twas entirely my fault, my lady!" he said with a charming smile. Stepping aside, he gave her a sweeping bow. "Please go ahead."

Francine thanked him and went inside. Harvey was hovering near the hearth. He was looking doubtful again.

"Lady Francine, are you certain . . . ?"

"Yes, yes. Please don't argue, Harvey. I *need* this."

Taking the bucket, he sighed deeply. "Very well, my lady. But let us hurry and be done with it. And please don't ever tell Sir Garrick that I did this."

"Don't worry, I won't." She retrieved the peach soap she'd bought in town from the small chest that Edith allowed her to share. At the stairs, she paused and glanced over her shoulder just to make sure Garrick wasn't lurking somewhere. Although he'd never come to his room while she was there, she usually didn't go so late in the day.

The hall was relatively empty—although she caught a glimpse of bright color over by the doorway. But even as she glanced at him, Rafael stepped outside. The coast clear, she led Harvey up to the solar.

She sat on the chair next to the table, then hesitated, a sudden uneasiness trickling through her. Perhaps this wasn't such a good idea after all.

But how pleasant it would be to have smooth, silky legs again; to have that small reminder that she was still a civilized woman; to have that secret reassurance of her own twentieth-century superiority. . . .

She pulled her skirts up to just above her knees. Stretching out one leg, she rested her ankle on the edge of the bucket.

Harvey stared at her leg as though it were a rattlesnake that would turn around and bite him. He gingerly picked up the razor.

His worried expression faded, however, as he began stropping the blade on a leather strap. With an air of deep concentration, he soaped her leg thoroughly then scraped away the lather with his razor. A smooth, bare patch of skin appeared.

Briskly and efficiently, he continued the process until the leg was hairless from ankle to knee. Finished with her right leg, he admired his handiwork for a moment before starting on her left. He was working up the lather when the door suddenly opened.

"What, may I ask," Garrick said in a very soft voice, "is going on in here?"

For a moment Francine couldn't move. Harvey seemed likewise affected. Garrick stood in the doorway, his broad shoulders preventing any attempts at escape. With his black leather jerkin, black knee-high boots, and bristling black beard, he looked like a cross between a pirate and a Hell's Angel—only much more menacing.

Harvey dropped Francine's leg like a hot log and jumped to his feet, trembling and stammering in an effort to explain.

"Nothing, my lord, I assure you! That is . . . her ladyship

had a fancy to have her legs shaved, and I didn't . . . she
didn't . . . we didn't . . ."

Garrick fingered the knife in his belt.

Harvey fell to his knees in front of Garrick. "Oh, forgive
me, my lord! I am truly sorry! Please, please spare my life! I
knew . . . that is, I tried to explain to her . . ."

Garrick stared at him a moment, then moved aside and almost imperceptibly jerked his head toward the door.

Bowing and scraping, Harvey backed out of the room.
"Oh, thank you, my lord! God bless you, my lord! May all
the saints in heaven give you good fortune, my—"

Garrick shut the door, cutting off the barber's babbling.
Leaning back against it, he stared at Francine steadily.

She didn't like the way he looked at her, although she
couldn't have said exactly why. He wasn't frowning or
scowling. He wasn't yelling. He really didn't look angry. He
looked . . . bland.

She swallowed a little. "Are you upset? I'm sorry, I suppose I should have asked permission to use your room.
Please don't blame Harvey—it was all my idea. I didn't think
you would mind—"

"I don't mind at all," he said pleasantly, making her even
more nervous. He stripped off his gloves and tossed them on
the bed, then strolled forward and knelt beside her. Picking
up her leg by the ankle, he began splashing water on her,
rinsing off the soap.

She jumped a little in her chair. "Hey, stop that," she said,
trying to pull her leg away. "Harvey's not finished."

His hold, although gentle, was unbreakable. "Harvey is
gone. And the soap will burn your skin if it's not washed off."

She supposed he was right. In spite of its pleasant peach
scent, the soap *was* very strong. His hand moved rhythmi-
cally up and down her calf. She watched, half mesmerized by
the motion. His fingers circled up to the back of her knee,
tickling the sensitive skin there, then swept to her ankle and
back up again.

"I can rinse my own leg. . . ."

"It is only right that I perform this service for you, since
apparently it was I who frightened away Harvey." He pushed

her skirts out of the way, farther up her leg. His fingers seemed to linger just above her knee.

She was suddenly burningly aware of the fact that she had no underwear on. She could feel the roughness of the calluses on his palm against the smoothness of her skin on her inner thigh.

"I . . . really. I'd rather do it myself," she insisted.

"Why? You were willing to have Harvey do this for you. Why not me?"

She couldn't think of an answer. Shivers coursed up and down her leg as he smoothed away the soap. She sat there helplessly, breathlessly aware that with each sweep of his hand his fingers reached a little higher, and a little higher. . . .

"Stop that!" She yanked her leg from his grasp and jumped to her feet, trembling and blushing all over. Her skin burned everywhere he'd touched, from her ankle to her knee to almost the very top of her thigh—and it wasn't because of the soap. "Get out of here, before I scream!"

His brows lifting, he rose to his feet. "It would appear you have forgotten something. This is my room. I thought you were extending an invitation."

"An invitation! I never . . . I wouldn't . . . that is, I would never invite you to . . . oh, never mind." Embarrassed and flustered, she hurried toward the door.

"Francine . . ."

She paused in the doorway, looking over her shoulder.

"I suggest you stay out of my room. Unless you want to find yourself on your back in my bed."

Heat flooded her face. She opened her mouth, then shut it again.

Without a word, she fled.

The racket in Joan the Weaver's cottage was nearly unbearable. Usually Francine was tolerant of the noise and interruptions—babies wailing or smacking their lips at their mothers' breasts; children, chickens, and geese wandering in and out of the cottage—but this morning it increased the ache in her head tenfold.

She wished to high heaven that she had some aspirin—but

even aspirin wouldn't wipe out the events of the previous day.

"It's important to keep your bed and sheets clean," she told the class.

Garrick couldn't have been serious, she was sure. He was teasing. Or bluffing. Or trying to scare her. Of all the possibilities, there was only one she was certain didn't apply. She was certain he didn't want her. Not any more than she wanted him. . . .

"If you can't wash every day, then you should at least air out your dirty linens."

Those strange sensations that had spiked up and down her leg as he had stroked it . . . they didn't mean anything. She was ticklish, that was all. It was no wonder she'd felt certain sensations. They'd had nothing to do with him personally. . . .

"Fresh air is preferable."

He'd been rude and obnoxious as usual—refusing to let Harvey finish the job. And now look—she had one leg shaved and one not! It felt very odd. Every time her right leg brushed against the left and she felt the hairiness of one and the smoothness of the other, she was reminded of everything he'd said. Could it be possible he really did want to have sex with her?

"Doing this will help keep your bed free of unwanted pests."

No, she was sure he didn't. But even if he did want to, she didn't think he would stoop to rape. No matter how barbaric he was, surely he would draw the line there. More likely he would try to seduce her.

Seduce her. As if a hairy brute like him could ever seduce *her*. The idea was laughable. "Ha, ha! Ha, ha!"

"Lady Francine, are you all right?"

Startled, Francine looked up and saw that everyone had grown quiet and was gawking at her. Even the infants, their eyes wide and round, seemed to be staring at her. Joan was watching her with a worried frown. "Yes, of course, Joan," Francine said automatically. "Why do you ask?"

"You were making such a terrible noise."

Francine stiffened. "I was *laughing*."

"Oh!" Joan looked doubtful. "Are you sure? You sounded as though you were in pain."

"I'm fine," Francine insisted.

"Then tell us—what was so amusing? We would enjoy a good story."

Francine glanced around at the curious faces. "Nothing," she mumbled. "It was just a private thought."

She certainly didn't want to tell anyone what she found so funny. They might not realize what a joke it was.

"That's it for today, class. See you tomorrow."

Whispering and casting curious glances at her, they all crowded out of the cottage, heading toward the well where they could gossip unrestrainedly and get their morning water. Even Orson gave her a look of concern.

Hoping to sneak away to the fairy circle and have a few minutes of peace and quiet, Francine waited until everyone had left the cottage before she started for the door. But before she could escape, a surly, dirty-faced girl appeared in the entryway—Mog.

Francine lowered her gaze and edged toward the door, hoping to avoid the acrimonious remarks she and Mog always seemed to exchange.

"Good morning, Lady Francine," Mog said sullenly.

Francine stopped, her jaw dropping at the girl's greeting, sour though it was. "Er, good morning, Mog." And then, when the girl continued to block the doorway, she added, "Um, is there something I can do for you?"

Mog's lower lip thrust out farther. "My mother made me come."

"She did?" Comprehension dawned in Francine. "You want to come to the class?"

Mog nodded stiffly.

"I see." Francine studied the girl. Her hair was full of rattails, every inch of her seemed to be covered with dirt, and her face was twisted into what seemed a permanent scowl. But behind the scowl and the dirt and the hair, Francine caught a glimpse of the misery she'd seen once before in Mog's eyes.

Francine hesitated, sympathy and dislike warring within her. Sympathy won out. "Of course, you may come."

The stiff set of Mog's shoulders eased a trifle. "Can we do it now?"

"Oh, no," Francine said. "The class is over for the day. You may come tomorrow, though."

Mog's narrow shoulders tensed again and her scowl deepened. "I don't want to come with *them*." Her voice tightened. "They'll just laugh at me."

"Hmm." Francine suspected Mog was right—the girl didn't seem to have many friends. "Could I come to your house? Tomorrow?"

Mog scuffled her feet on the floor. "Very well," she muttered.

So the next morning, before going to Joan's cottage, Francine hiked to the far end of the village. There, some distance from the other houses, stood a small, shacklike edifice. From inside, Francine could hear the plaintive wail of a baby.

She knocked on the door tentatively. It was answered by a slovenly woman who reeked of alcohol. An equally dirty infant was attached to her breast. "Who are you?" she demanded.

"I . . . I'm Francine Peabody, from the castle," she said, taken aback. "I'm here to give lessons to Mog."

"What lessons?"

Before Francine could answer, Mog came to the door, two children hanging on to her skirts. "Oh, it's you," she said ungraciously. "Well, I've changed my mind. I don't want to take any lessons."

She lifted her chin.

Francine stared at the girl's tight lips, the proud tilt of her head. Quietly, she said, "May I speak to you outside?"

Mog hesitated a moment, then nodded. Detaching herself from the children's clinging fingers, she came outside and shut the door behind her. She faced Francine, her arms folded across her chest.

"What do you want?" she asked, her voice full of familiar antagonism.

"Mog . . . ," Francine paused, trying to think of a way to

reach the hostile girl. Nothing occurred to her, forcing her to plunge ahead awkwardly. "If you want to take the lessons, I'm willing to teach you."

Mog's thin face was tight and pinched. "I can't. I don't know what I was thinking yesterday. It's just that Nancy told me that Orson asked to walk her to church on Sunday, and I thought . . ."

Mog bit her lip and stopped, but Francine didn't need her to go on. She remembered the girl's effort to attract Pascal's attention.

"Come to the lessons, Mog," Francine said, "We can meet at . . ."—she hesitated the briefest moment before continuing—"at the fairy circle. No one will disturb us there. With a bath and a new dress, I'm sure any number of men would be interested in you."

Mog shook her head. "It's impossible. Look at me. Pascal said—"

"You're too good for Pascal," Francine said fiercely. "Let me help you, and you will find someone better, I promise you."

Mog looked at her, her face a mixture of hope and despair. "Very well. I suppose it can't hurt. . . ."

On Sunday, Francine was at Nancy's cottage, helping her and Mog with the final touches to their dresses.

Nancy, looking very pretty in a blue gown that matched her eyes, peeked out the window.

"Orson is here," she said. "But I'm not ready yet. Will you go tell him I'll be out in a moment?"

"Of course," Francine said. She turned to Mog and said, "You come out right after Nancy, okay?"

Mog hesitated, looking scared. Francine took her hands and said, "You can do this. You've done very well this week. Everyone will be impressed."

"You think so?"

"I know so." Francine smiled at her reassuringly, then went outside to talk to Orson.

He stood by the well, stoically ignoring the taunts of the men-at-arms standing in a circle around him.

"Oooh, Orson!" Ivo called, prancing in front of him. "How pretty you look with your beard all shaved off! Could I have this dance?"

"Orson!" Stephen sang out. "What is that sweet smell about you? God's nostril, even your wind smells like flowers now! Pray tell us your secret!"

"Orson! I hear you've been learning courtesies," cried Pascal. "Will you kiss my hand now? Or better yet, kiss my arse. . . ."

He started untying the leather holding up his breeches; Francine was afraid she was about to be mooned. Suddenly the door opened behind her and Nancy came out.

Pascal's fingers grew still and all the other men stopped laughing as Nancy walked up to Orson and put her hand on his arm.

"Shall we go, Orson?" she asked in her sweet voice.

The couple walked off toward the church.

The rest of the men stared after them.

Francine heard a slight cough, and turned to see Mog standing in the doorway of the cottage. "Ah, Mog!" she said loudly. "Come along, dear, we don't want to be late for church."

Francine watched from the corner of her eye as the men glanced toward Mog, then did double takes. Their mouths dropped open.

And no wonder, Francine thought with some satisfaction.

Mog, her neatly combed hair glinting golden-red in the early morning sunlight, stood there in the pretty white dress that Edith had given her, looking absolutely gorgeous. Her large brown eyes, framed with thick black lashes, looked a trifle scared, but she held her head high as she walked with Francine past the gaping men-at-arms.

From behind her, she heard Ivo say, "Was that *Mog*? Why, she's *beautiful*," and then a thud as if someone had hit him and Pascal's voice saying, "Shut up, you dunderhead."

In the church, there was a swell of whispering as they entered. No one listened to the mass that day. Everyone was too busy craning their necks to see Mog.

Afterwards, the men gathered around the girl and begged

for permission to walk her home. With a toss of her head, she said, "You may *all* walk me home."

The whole group went off, Francine smiling after them, when she heard a low voice say, "Your doing, I take it?"

She looked up to see Garrick standing beside her, gazing down at her with an odd expression on his face. Smugly, she smiled up at him. "You see, my ideas are not so crazy after all."

"Perhaps—although if all my men kill each other over her, I'll hold you responsible."

He left and she glared after him, but even Garrick couldn't destroy the pleasure of her triumph. Especially since later that day, when she was sitting in the hall spinning with Edith, the men-at-arms started to trail in.

"Uh, Lady Francine," Ivo said, combing his fingers through his dirty-blond hair. "Do you think I could attend your class?"

"Please, Lady Francine, please let me go to your class!" begged Angus, his blush making his freckles stand out.

"If you permit, my lady, I would be honored to attend your class," said Kenelm shyly.

And so it went. In the end, even Pascal, his usually animated face rather sullen, presented himself and asked to be included. She said yes to them all.

She had to move the classes back to the hall, but this time no one objected.

The pleasure of her success was short-lived.

Teaching the men-at-arms was not easy. In spite of their willingness to attend, many of them were like rambunctious schoolchildren. At times it was all she could do to keep from running screaming from the hall.

Perhaps she would have been able to be more patient with them if it hadn't been November. November, in Medieval England, it turned out, was slaughter time. Even though the hall was some distance from the field at the back of the castle where the butchering took place, she could still hear—and smell—the results. Often, while trying to speak to the men, her voice was drowned out by the squawks, squeals, and gurgles of dying animals. She found the noises very distracting. The air reeked of blood and guts, making it difficult for her to concentrate on the finer aspects of civilization.

Only by the greatest effort was she able to continue.

Entering the hall one morning, she smiled at the waiting men. "Good morning, class," she said brightly. "You'll notice I've brought a guest this morning." She nodded toward Harvey, who'd come in behind her, carrying a bucket of hot water and a razor. "I have wonderful news. Harvey has volunteered to act as the castle barber for the morning and provide all of you with a shave."

The men straightened on the benches, their hands flying protectively to their beards.

"Who will be first?" she asked.

The men hunched their shoulders and averted their gazes.

Her gaze traveled over them. "Angus? No? Then Kenelm, maybe you would like to be the first to be rid of that dirty, disgusting hair on your chin."

"No, my lady," Kenelm said. "I am very attached to my beard. It took a long time to grow it."

Francine looked at the other men. "John? Ivo? Surely *one* of you would be willing at least to try it. Just look at how nice Orson looks. Stephen?"

Six heads shook in unison.

Pascal, sitting in the third row of benches, raised his hand.

"Have you heard the story of the bearded pussy who visited the king?" he asked.

"No, I haven't," Francine said sternly. "And I don't want to, either." Seeing that they were not cooperating and fearing that the snickering men would start telling dirty jokes, she hastily dismissed the class.

They bounded out of the hall like puppies released from a kennel.

Francine glared after them. "They are impossible!" she said to Harvey.

"Men that age are usually very fond of their beards," Harvey said.

"Hmmph," was Francine's only reply. But actually, now that she thought about it, the men were fairly young—most of them under twenty, and several with that lean whipcord look that growing teenagers have. They looked like they were half starving, which they probably were—they only got two meals a day, after all. Really, they needed breakfast, too. . . .

Impulsively she turned to Harvey and kissed his cheek.

He blushed ten shades of red. "What was that for?" he asked.

"For giving me a wonderful idea. . . ."

"I can't cook another whole meal!" Gunilda exclaimed when Francine asked. "I don't have enough help as it is!"

Francine frowned. "Won't Garrick let you have more help?"

Gunilda snorted, her perpetually sour expression growing even more so. "Oh, he's authorized me to hire more, but it's impossible. Boys are pretty much useless, men don't want to work under a woman, and none of the village women will work here."

"Why not?" Francine asked.

"The men are too rough," Gunilda said.

Francine remembered that Edith had mentioned the same thing once. "But Nancy and Mog come," she said slowly.

"Nancy's father is well-respected—no one would dare tangle with him. As for Mog . . . her family needs the money, and . . . well, you know how she is."

Francine nodded, thinking of Mog's sharp tongue and the way she used it like a weapon. She gave as good as she got whenever one of the men insulted her.

Francine considered the situation, not ready to give up on her idea of bribing the men with food to shave their beards. The plan had the added bonus of giving her the opportunity to show them how to eat properly at the same time. But how could she get Gunilda the help she needed?

Perhaps it was time to give a lesson on the proper way to treat women.

"You must be polite and considerate at all times," she told them the next day. "No wolf whistles, no lewd comments, no groping . . ."

"Not even a little touch?" Angus complained.

"No," Francine said sternly. "The good news is that if you all behave yourselves, then there will be a lot more women at the castle. And if you shave, you'll get an extra meal. . . ."

The men appeared to struggle with their decisions for a while, but ultimately, none of them could resist the combined lure of women and food.

Unfortunately, Francine was only able to convince a few of the older women to come to the castle. But they were enough for the newly shaven men to get their breakfast. The men grumbled a bit that none of the younger women came, but she managed to soothe them by promising that once word spread of their improved manners, the girls would come, too.

In the meantime, Francine decided to go for the next item on her list—forks.

This, of course, involved one huge hurdle—Hugo, the blacksmith.

He was as intimidating as ever, with his big body and small head and eyes, and her throat grew dry, partly from fear, partly from the stifling heat of his hut. But this time she didn't slink away under his glare.

"I . . . I was wondering," she said, feeling the perspiration bead on her brow. "If you could make some forks for me. . . ."

"FORKS?" he yelled as he shoveled coal into the roaring furnace. "WHAT ARE FORKS?"

"They . . . they are pronged utensils used for eating food."

The ridge of his brows lowered over his eyes. "DO I LOOK LIKE I HAVE TIME TO MAKE PRONGED UTENSILS?" He pulled a piece of red-hot iron out of the fire and laid it on his anvil. "I MUST MAKE TOOLS FOR THE MASONS AND CARPENTERS, AND HIS LORDSHIP IS NOT A PATIENT MAN."

He began pounding the metal rod with a hammer, the noise making her flinch. The snarl on his lips as he applied the hammer nearly sent her scurrying off. But remembering what was at stake—forks for the men—she put her hands over her ears and stood her ground.

The noise he was making with the hammer was too great

to permit conversation, so she looked around the hut as she waited patiently.

What she saw surprised her. Vases and goblets, inlaid with copper in exquisite patterns, lined a shelf. Flower-shaped hinges and fancifully decorated keys were piled on a table. And on one wall hung a delicate ironwork grille, the elaborate design a work of art. She stepped over to inspect one sun-burst pattern in awe.

"Did you make this?" she asked when there was a pause in the hammer strokes.

Hugo's brow lowered even more. "Yes."

"I didn't realize iron could be so finely worked," she said. "It's beautiful."

The eyebrow ridge lifted and Hugo's small eyes looked less mean. "It's not easy to achieve such detail. It takes great concentration. I had to throw twenty pieces in the scrap pile before I finally completed that particular grille."

"That's amazing! When do you find the time?"

"Once I am finished with my work, I make these. I did replacement grillework at Canterbury Cathedral; it was exceedingly difficult."

"I'm sure it was. Garrick is extremely fortunate to have you."

Hugo's massive chest expanded at least another three feet. "True, my lady, true."

He was positively beaming at her now. At least, that was how Francine interpreted the grimace that bared all twelve of his teeth.

"You know," she said tentatively, "making forks takes great skill also. The prongs are very delicate and set very close together. Not many blacksmiths could make them."

"Ha! I can make anything!" Hugo boasted. "You tell me how these forks look—I will make them."

Francine did so, hiding her delight, and within a few days she had her forks. She couldn't wait to show the men-at-arms how to use them.

Chapter 10

GARRICK GLANCED OVER the household accounts, then frowned up at his steward. "Five new women in the kitchen?"

"You did tell Gunilda she could hire additional help. Lady Francine convinced some of the village women to take the positions," Clifford said, his eye twitching in his bony face.

Garrick looked at the totals by the various items. "Why has the amount of meat and bread consumed increased?"

"Gunilda has been preparing a small extra meal for the men-at-arms in the morning. Breakfast, Lady Francine calls it."

"Oh, does she?" Garrick looked farther down the scroll, his gaze stopping at one item in particular. He looked up at Clifford. "Forks?"

"Hugo made them for Lady Francine. She said she needed them for her class."

"Lady Francine has been very busy," Garrick said. His gaze narrowed on the steward. "The only question is, can I afford it?"

"I . . . I believe so, my lord."

"You *believe* so?"

Clifford swallowed, his Adam's apple bobbing in his

throat. "I am terribly sorry, my lord. I have been working hard at it—but I just cannot seem to get the numbers to balance. Your last steward left the accounts in a mess—"

"You assured me that you would be able to correct the problem."

"And I shall, I swear, my lord. If you will allow me a short while longer—"

"I've already given you nearly two months. The accounts should have been finished within a few days of Michaelmas. I am out of patience."

"My lord! I promise! I shall have the accounts balanced by St. Nicholas's Day!"

"Very well," Garrick said. "You have until then—but no longer."

"Thank you, my lord. It shall be done, I promise you."

Garrick left the storeroom and strode across the courtyard, a frown on his face. Clifford had come highly recommended; Garrick would not like having to let him go. But the situation with the accounts was intolerable. He needed to know where he stood financially. He needed to know whether he could afford additional expenditures—and whether he could afford frivolities like forks.

Forks!

Francine had certainly been busy. He'd noticed subtle changes in the castle recently. Everyone seemed . . . more polite. The men-at-arms had shaved their beards. There were more women. Fewer bugs. And he constantly seemed to hear one name mentioned over and over.

Lady Francine said this. Lady Francine said that.

What spell had she cast over the castle? He was almost beginning to believe that she was indeed a fairy—a fairy come to torment him.

He had vowed not to become entangled in her wiles—and Anne's. He knew that disaster lay in that direction. But he'd never expected to find himself growing more and more attracted to her. He hadn't expected that her presence would permeate every aspect of his life. While he worked, he could hear the sound of her melodic laughter as she gossiped and talked with the castle women. While he ate, he could see her face glow with soft smiles as the men-at-arms fought to capture her attention. While in his chamber, he smelled the lingering scent of peach soap.

He'd never expected to have his body battling his brain every step of the way. . . .

He stopped at the entrance to the hall. He stared at the door. Francine was inside, he knew, teaching her silly class to the men. He should go find Thomas, find out how the work on the battlements was progressing. . . .

Silently he opened the door and slipped inside, concealing himself in the shadows.

Over by the window, Francine sat at a table with the men-at-arms.

"You spear the meat with the fork—no, Ivo, you don't pick up the whole slab of meat. You cut off a bite-sized piece and eat it . . . with your mouth closed, Kenelm . . . ah, better . . . and it's generally considered polite to carry on a conversation with your neighbor. . . . No, no, Orson! Wait until you're finished chewing before you speak!"

A shaft of sunlight shone through the window directly onto Francine. In the dim light of the hall, with her oval face framed by her wimple, she almost appeared to glow. Gracefully she picked up her fork and demonstrated the correct way to hold it. She placed a morsel of food between her full lips.

"Like this, my lady?" the men all clamored, clutching their forks in their fists and trying to imitate her dainty gestures.

Garrick watched her, disliking the way she smiled at the men, her friendliness toward them. She was friendly with everyone—except him—it seemed. The genealogist was a perfect example. The memory of the way the other man had touched her legs still had the power to enrage him. . . .

"Lady Francine," Pascal beseeched her. "I cannot seem to get the hang of it. Could you please help me?"

"Of course, Pascal," Francine said, rising to her feet and moving behind him. She reached forward and held his hand in hers to show him the proper grip. "This is how—do you see?"

Garrick could see very well indeed—even through the red mist that rose before his eyes as he watched the sly smile on Pascal's face as he looked around the table. His smile faded, however, when his eyes met Garrick's.

"Thank you, my lady," he said abruptly, pulling his hand away from hers. "I have it now."

"Are you sure?" Francine asked. "I can show you again, if you need me to . . ." She paused, looking around the table at the suddenly silent men. "Is something wrong . . . oh!"

Her expression changed as she caught sight of Garrick.

He breathed deeply for a moment until the red mist dissipated and he had himself under control again. He stepped out of the shadows.

"Sir Garrick . . ." Her blue eyes darted nervously about as if seeking some escape. She took a deep breath. She smiled brightly.

"Would you like to learn how to use a fork?"

As soon as she said the inane words, Francine regretted them. What an idiot he must think her! Still, what else could he expect when he snuck up on her like this? The man was a menace.

He made no response to her question, but she forced herself to keep smiling at him. "Actually, I'm glad you're here. There's something I've been wanting to ask you."

"Yes?" he said.

"I wanted to talk to you about building a steam bath. I spoke to Thomas yesterday and he thinks it's a wonderful idea. He's willing to build it—"

"No."

"Why not?" she asked, used to his abrupt negatives by now.

"Because it would take time away from work on the castle."

"Only a week, no more!"

"It would also be expensive," he said, frowning. "The fuel costs alone would be exorbitant, and I cannot spare any money for frivolities. Speaking of which . . ." He looked at the men-at-arms, who all sat frozen in their seats, their forks clutched in their fists. "I notice the men all have their own personal forks."

"Oh, oh, yes," Francine said. "The blacksmith made them for me. For my class."

Garrick frowned. "I'm surprised he had time. He is always complaining he doesn't have enough time to make the tools."

"I think he made them in his spare time. Really, you should give your employees a little latitude. Hugo would be much happier and more fulfilled if you allowed him to make some decorative grillework."

"I do not care whether the blacksmith is 'fulfilled.' I only care that he makes the tools necessary for building." He looked her up and down. "Lady Francine, I would love to stand here and discuss baths and forks with you, but I have a castle to build and protect. Gentlemen"—he looked at the men-at-arms with hard eyes—"I believe Captain Fletcher is waiting for you."

The men scrambled to their feet.

"Pascal. . . ."

Pascal, a look of dread on his face, stopped in his flight toward the door and turned reluctantly to face Garrick.

"You will come with me. I have a special task for you today."

Within a few seconds, they were all gone, leaving Francine staring after them in disbelief.

"Well!" she huffed, annoyed at the way Garrick had demolished her class. Why had he come? And how long had he been standing in the shadows watching them?

She shivered a little, suddenly aware of the coldness of the hall. Today wasn't the first time she'd caught him looking at her. He was still rude to her and ignored her for the most part, but every once in a while, she would look up from her meal, or turn suddenly in the courtyard and find him staring at her.

He always looked away immediately. Usually, at least. Today he'd stared at her quite openly, with an expression in his eyes that she couldn't quite identify. . . .

She took a deep breath. She was being ridiculous. She

shouldn't be worrying about Garrick and his nonexistent emotions. She should be thinking about the steam bath and how to get the money to pay for it.

She didn't believe for a second that there wasn't enough money. She'd made a career of finding money, after all, and she'd done enough creative bookkeeping to feel certain that she could find the cash somehow.

"There is no money," Clifford averred when she found him in the storeroom, seated at a table. He was in his late twenties and had a bony, honest face that right now was scrunched into a frown as he hunched further over a set of scrolls. He'd been totalling a column of figures when she entered, and she noticed an air of desperation about him.

"At home, I had a job as steward," she said. "Perhaps I can help you."

"A woman steward?" he sneered. But the sneer was half-hearted. "Can you work an abacus?" he asked.

Francine blinked. "No, but I'm very good with numbers. Let me see your books."

Reluctantly, he passed them to her. She looked at the numbers and notations with a frown. "These are in Latin."

"Of course," he said.

"I can't read Latin," she said.

His shoulders slumped a little. "Then you are of no use to me."

"I think I can still help. We will just have to work together. It will help, though, if you switch to Arabic instead of Roman numerals."

"Arabic numerals?"

"Yes. Let me show you how they work."

She wrote them out, although it took her several tries with the quill and ink.

An awed look came over his face. "These are the new Hindu numbers—I saw them once before in London, but the man who showed them to me could not explain their meaning. You understand how to use them?"

"Yes," she said, and went on to explain about ones, tens, and hundreds. He caught on very quickly, and she showed him how to add and subtract.

"These numbers are truly wonderful," Clifford exclaimed. But then the light in his eyes died. "I'm afraid it's too late for them to do me any good, though. Sir Garrick told me to balance the accounts by St. Nicholas's Day or seek work elsewhere. I didn't dare tell him, but it's hopeless. The previous steward left the accounts in a mess. I told Sir Garrick I could fix them, but I don't think I can. I am doomed."

"Don't worry. I'll help you. He wants it by Christmas? That's almost six weeks from now. I'm sure that between the two of us, we can straighten the accounts out by then."

He shook his head. "Not Christmas. St. Nicholas's Day. Three weeks from now."

"Oh." Inwardly Francine blanched, but she kept a positive smile on her face for Clifford's sake. "Well, I'm sure we can do that. But we'd better not waste any time."

The problem was indeed complicated. The "accounts" were not ledgers at all—they were rolls of parchment, and they were all in Latin. She had to have Clifford translate each entry and write it herself in English on her own scroll to be able to make sense of the numbers.

There were scrolls detailing the crops the tenants raised, the average yield per acre, whether the crops were sold, paid out as wages, or malted for ale; and listing the servants and laborers employed, and by whom and for what amount of money. There were scrolls recording legislation enacted and fines and taxes levied and other legal matters. And there were scrolls listing the number of oxen, sheep, calves, and pigs used by Gunilda, and the quantities of eggs, butter, cheese, and milk consumed each day.

After just two days, she was remembering her job in the future with all the nostalgic affection of a widow remembering her first date. Computers, spreadsheets, accounting programs, ledgers, calculators, pens—real ones. How she missed them all as with cramped fingers, her back aching, she bent over the parchment scrolls, scratching numbers with a quill and ink.

On the third day, she arrived at the storeroom before Clifford. She started working, and was deeply engrossed in a column of figures when the steward, looking pale, entered with Mog at his side.

"I thought we could use some help," Clifford muttered, not quite meeting Francine's surprised gaze.

"An excellent idea," Francine said. "Mog, can you read and write?"

"No," Mog replied. "But I can learn."

Francine blinked. If Mog couldn't read or write, then why had Clifford asked her to help?

She glanced at him. He had such a guilty expression on his face, she knew he must have an ulterior motive. Perhaps he was attracted to Mog.

To Mog's credit, she did catch on quickly. She was also able to add long columns of figures in her head without a pen and paper.

The days began to pass more quickly. Clifford treated Mog with great respect, walking her to and from the castle every day. The expression on his face when he looked at the girl convinced Francine that she'd been right about his reasons for asking the girl to help.

Francine was happy for them, but their relationship made her think longingly of Stuart. Stuart was such a wonderful man. He never stared rudely at her. He never grabbed her legs or made suggestive remarks. Stuart *respected* her.

She continued to go to the fairy circle every day, hoping against hope that she would suddenly be transported home, but to no avail. She had another period—it was as bad as the first one, although at least she knew what to expect this time—and the Advent season started. Everyone "fasted," which meant that they only ate one evening meal of fish and not much else. Fish was acceptable because it "wasn't of the earth," and ale was tolerated because "fish must swim." The constant diet of fish grew old quickly; the only good thing about it was that it gave Francine an idea.

"When I first arrived here," she said to Clifford and Mog one day at the end of the third week, "Edith said fish were expensive during a fast. Could the tenants who had bad harvests or are in arrears be allowed to fish in the lake and rivers and pay what they owe in that way?"

Clifford nodded thoughtfully. "That might work, Lady Francine. If we dry the fish, then sell it right before Lent, it should bring an excellent price." He glanced at the neatly totalled columns of numbers on the scroll before him. "The situation is not nearly so dire as I thought. Even without the extra income there is definitely enough for a steam bath."

"And more, besides!" Francine said excitedly. "There's enough to build two! Or maybe even three!"

"Let us not get carried away," Clifford said cautiously. "Sir Garrick must keep a healthy reserve. A few years of bad crops or a siege could wipe him out."

Francine had no time for such pessimism. "Thomas should be able to start work immediately."

"If Sir Garrick will authorize it," Mog reminded her.

Francine's smile faded. He'd already rejected her request once. But how could he object when she told him how much money there was? Still, if she'd learned anything about him it was that he was impossible to predict.

She rose to her feet. There was no point putting it off. She would go and ask him right now—

A blast from a trumpet cut off her thoughts.

Clifford jumped, splattering ink on his long, thin fingers. "We must have visitors." He put the quill in its stand and rinsed his fingers in the bowl of water he kept just for that purpose. "I must go greet them and find out if they will be spending the night. Let us hope they won't be. Guests and their servants always eat their heads off, and it's not easy to accommodate them while the castle is still so ill-furnished."

He hastened away.

Francine stood up also. "I think I'll go stretch my legs," she told Mog.

The girl nodded and returned her attention to a scroll, her face scrunching up as she tried to read the words.

Outside, Francine stood in the shadows of the tower doorway and watched as a party of three riders along with a train of five wagons and armed outriders entered through the courtyard gate. They approached the spot where Garrick and Clifford were waiting to greet them.

Two of the riders wore chain mail, and one of them

looked familiar—catching a glimpse of his red beard, Francine realized he was the man Garrick had been talking to at the market. Garrick nodded to the two men, then turned to the third rider, a heavily cloaked figure. Francine watched as a slim arm lifted and pushed back the hood of the cloak to reveal a heart-shaped face with braided black hair covered only by a sheer veil and circlet.

The woman smiled at Garrick.

He smiled back and raised his arms to swing her down off her horse.

The woman's cloak parted to reveal her long braids hanging down to the waist of her red velvet gown. She laughed at whatever Garrick said to her. She was utterly gorgeous.

Hidden in the shadows, Francine watched the couple, a bleakness growing inside her. She recognized the feeling well. It was the same one she'd had whenever she was around Susie Howlick. The same one she'd had in high school when Patsy White, a cheerleader, had asked Michael Avila, the boy who sat and talked to Francine after school every day, to the prom.

Francine hated the woman on sight.

The brunette glanced around the courtyard, as if calculating the worth of the castle, and her sharp gaze fell on Francine. For a moment Francine almost ducked her head, as she always did to the Susie Howlicks and Patsy Whites of the world. But then, for some inexplicable reason, instead of lowering her chin, she raised it, meeting the woman's gaze directly.

The woman stared at her, then turned to speak to Garrick. He turned and looked in Francine's direction.

Now Francine averted her gaze. Quickly. Oh, Lord. What had the woman said to him?

A few seconds later, Clifford was at her side. "Do you speak French?" he asked anxiously.

Francine hesitated, remembering the second language she'd learned in the dream with Mrs. Rappaport. "Yes," she said rather cautiously.

"Thank heaven. Come quickly. Sir Garrick wishes to introduce you to his guests," he said.

Not likely, Francine thought as she reluctantly followed Clifford to where the visitors waited. She had no doubt that it was the lady who was curious.

Her guess was more or less confirmed when Garrick curtly introduced her.

The short, red-bearded man, introduced to Francine as Gilbert de Gant, nodded briefly and looked away. Ranulf of Chester, a few inches taller than she, with brown hair and flirtatious hazel eyes, was more enthusiastic.

"Ah, Sir Garrick, how do you always manage to find the beauties? Lady Francine, 'tis a pleasure to meet you."

Francine smiled at him and turned to the last of the riders.

Lady Ingrid, de Gant's wife, stared at her, making Francine burningly aware of her own simple dark-blue gown with the skirts knotted up and her slightly askew wimple. "Garrick, you didn't tell me there was another lady at the castle."

"She's a friend of Lady Anne's," Garrick said.

"A friend of Lady Anne's!" Ranulf interjected. "Then most certainly you are a friend of mine."

Ingrid gave a tight little smile that didn't show her teeth. "Lady Anne has great influence." She turned to Garrick. "Your guest must come hunting with us."

Hunting? Yuck. Francine opened her mouth to refuse, but before she could speak, Garrick said, "Lady Francine is busy with other matters."

"Those other matters can surely wait," Lady Ingrid said. "I want her to come."

"She doesn't ride."

"But I must have another lady along." Lady Ingrid pouted prettily. "Surely you have some horse that is calm enough for her."

"There's old Bessie," Clifford said. "She wouldn't hurt a fly, let alone a lady."

"There, you see! It's all settled." Lady Ingrid's pout disappeared and she smiled at Garrick. "Now you must show me to my chamber so that I may change into more appropriate attire."

Before Francine could object to the scheme, Garrick and

the visitors were strolling toward the hall. Francine started after them, planning to tell Garrick in no uncertain terms that she wouldn't be caught dead hunting, but Clifford detained her.

"Be careful," he warned. "Lady Ingrid can be vicious, and she will not like having competition for the men's attention."

"She has nothing to worry about," Francine said. "I have no intention of trying to gain anyone's attention."

Clifford raised his eyebrows, but only said, "Be careful anyway."

"I won't need to be careful," Francine said. "I'm not going with them."

"You cannot refuse!" Clifford looked horrified. "It would be a terrible insult to Sir Garrick's guests. He would be greatly displeased."

Francine opened her mouth to say she didn't care if Garrick was displeased, but then she remembered that she needed to ask him to approve the steam bath.

This might not be the best time to annoy him, she thought reluctantly. But how could she participate in something so barbaric as a hunt?

She swallowed. She knew Clifford was right. This wasn't the time to enrage Garrick. No matter how unpleasant it was, she had to think of her greater goal.

Francine straightened her spine. Very well, she would go. But she would ditch them at the first opportunity. Then she would return to the castle and claim she'd gotten lost.

There was absolutely no reason why she had to be present when one of these vicious killers shot some poor defenseless animal.

Chapter 11

AN HOUR OR SO later, the hunting party set off, someone called the "keeper of the hounds" leading the way, a pack of dogs leaping and straining at the leashes he held. Behind the keeper came the huntsman and then the hunters themselves.

Francine clutched Bessie's reins. "Nice horse, nice horse," she murmured over and over again. The animal was enormous, and when she dared look down, it seemed an awfully long way to the ground.

But after a while, she grew accustomed to the horse's smooth gait. She even relaxed enough to glance around at the others.

Lady Ingrid wore an emerald-green cape lined with ermine. On her back she carried a silver-chased quiver full of arrows, and a delicate bow hung from her saddle. She looked absolutely gorgeous, of course. Francine, who had changed into the silk wimple she'd purchased at the fair and the rosy gown Anne had given her to wear to church, felt pale and insignificant in comparison.

The men wore fur-lined capes also, although the colors of theirs were duller greens or browns. Francine's gaze lingered on Garrick, who rode a short distance in front of her.

He also carried a bow and arrows, and a spear as well. The hunter-green cape he wore emphasized the breadth of his shoulders and the straightness of his spine. From this angle, when she didn't have to see his scowling face, he actually looked quite handsome. He rode gracefully, as if he were part of the horse, his movements fluid.

Francine wished she could ride like that, but she'd always been afraid of horses. Although actually, Bessie seemed very nice. The horse was much more comfortable to ride than the donkey had been. . . .

Francine's gaze narrowed as she stared at Garrick's back. Why hadn't he suggested she ride Bessie instead of the donkey when they'd gone to town?

Before she could consider the question more fully, the hunting party stopped. Francine looked ahead to see the huntsman scratching at a tree. Then he knelt down and inspected the ground. He scooped something into his hunting horn and carried it over to show to Garrick.

Francine inched her horse forward next to Ingrid's to try to see what it was, but she couldn't tell.

"What are they looking at?" she asked the other woman.

"Deer droppings. The men are trying to decide whether to go after it or not. It's late in the season for deer." Ingrid gave her a pitying look. "You know absolutely nothing about hunting, do you?"

Francine shook her head. "We don't hunt much in my village."

"How quaint." Ingrid's look turned assessing. "How long have you been at Pelsworth Castle?"

"About two months," Francine replied.

"Two months living in the same castle as Garrick—how very exciting for you."

"Not really," Francine said. "I don't see him very often."

"No matter how much you try, I'll wager," Lady Ingrid said.

Francine stiffened. "I have no interest in Garrick, I assure you."

The lady gave a genteel snort. "A woman would have to

be dead to have no interest in Garrick. Do not take me for a fool."

"I don't," Francine said.

"I have every intention of becoming Garrick's lover. And I cannot abide competition."

Francine looked at her in surprise. "But what about your husband—" She stopped abruptly.

Lady Ingrid laughed. "Gilbert despises me as much as I despise him. He cares for nothing but politics and his silly rebellions."

"Why did you marry him, then?"

A shadow passed across the woman's face. "The king had the gift of my marriage. The alliance suited his purposes well."

Francine was shocked. "Couldn't you have refused?"

"Yes, but then the king would have retained control of my property—and of me. At least Gilbert allows me to do as I like."

"But . . . but that's outrageous!" Francine exclaimed. "Couldn't you have married without the king's consent?"

"Only if I paid a large fee—which I could not possibly afford at the time."

"How terrible," Francine said. King John sounded like a tyrant. She wished she weren't so ignorant about the Middle Ages. She'd taken World History in college, but she didn't remember much of it. All she knew about Medieval England she'd learned from Robin Hood movies.

She frowned a little, trying to remember when that particular story had taken place. "Is King John related to Prince John, the brother of Richard the Lionhearted?"

Ingrid looked at her strangely. "They are one and the same."

Francine's eyes widened. "But where is King Richard?" Was he languishing in some foreign prison, waiting for the ransom money?

Ingrid looked at her as if she were insane. "Richard died fifteen years ago."

"Oh," Francine said. She hastily changed the subject. "Well, I'm sorry you had to marry a man you don't love."

"Love?" Ingrid repeated scornfully. "You *are* a little fool. I had merely hoped for a more advantageous match. Lord de Vane was eighty years old and he died the next year—I would only have had to tolerate him for a short while before I was a widow again."

Francine was shocked by Ingrid's mercenary attitude. Although Garrick had expressed much the same opinion, Francine had thought that a woman would have been more enlightened. Francine's dislike of Ingrid faded a little as pity took its place. How terrible to be so greedy and never know about love. . . .

"Why are you looking at me like that, you little mouse?" Ingrid suddenly demanded. "How dare you be so impertinent?"

"I'm sorry," Francine said, taken aback by the woman's fury. "I didn't mean to—"

Her apology was interrupted by the huntsman blowing his horn. The keeper of the hounds released the dogs, which set off with wild yelps. The men followed in pursuit. With a final sneering glance at Francine that revealed stained, yellowish teeth, Lady Ingrid wheeled her horse around and took off after them at a gallop.

Francine stared after her, wondering what had enraged the woman so. She puzzled over the question as she turned her horse around and headed back toward the castle, but she couldn't come up with an answer.

The woman was strange, she finally decided. Witness her plan to seduce Garrick. What woman in her right mind would attempt that?

Francine frowned, wondering if he knew about Ingrid's plans for him. Perhaps she should warn him. As much as she disliked him, she would hate to see him caught in that harpy's clutches.

A noise distracted her from her thoughts. She looked around, seeking the source, but she could see nothing except trees and thick brush. Turning her attention back to the path, she continued on her way, her senses more alert.

Crr-rr-rrackkk!

What was that? Francine gripped the reins tightly. It had

sounded like wood breaking. Like someone stepping on a branch.

But maybe it was just an animal, she told herself, glancing around uneasily.

What if there was a robber hiding behind one of these trees right now? If only the forest wasn't so dark. And if only she wasn't all alone. And if only she didn't have an uneasy feeling that she was completely and totally lost. What if robbers like the ones who'd attacked her before popped out just as she was riding past. . . .

"Lady Francine?"

Francine jumped and gave a little scream before she recognized the voice—and the man riding toward her.

"Sir Garrick!" she said crossly. "Don't you know better than to sneak up on a person?"

"I beg your pardon," he said coolly. "Lady Ingrid was concerned you might lose your way in the forest."

"She was?" Francine stared at him in disbelief, but his expression revealed nothing. "How, er, kind of her."

"Yes, and perceptive, too. You're headed in the wrong direction."

"I decided to return to the castle. I'm not much of a hunter. Unlike Lady Ingrid." She glanced at him from the corner of her eye. "Tell me, what do you think of her?"

"She's a very fine lady."

"Yes, yes." That wasn't what Francine wanted to know at all. "But do you find her . . . well, attractive?"

He was silent a moment. Then, "Of course. She's very beautiful."

Men! Francine thought in disgust. Couldn't they see beyond mere beauty? She took a deep breath. "I think I should warn you . . . I believe she has, um, designs on your person."

Garrick turned to look at her, one heavy black brow arching in a way that made her flush. "Oh? How do you know this?"

"Well . . . she told me."

"Ah, I see." He frowned. "Hmm. This puts me in a very awkward position."

"What do you mean?"

"I cannot refuse a lady—it would be most impolite, I'm sure you will agree."

"Um, well . . ."

"So, I suppose I must resign myself to my fate—"

"Resign yourself to your fate!" Francine snapped. "Oh, *puh-LEEZE*!"

Too late, she saw the gleam in his eyes. Realizing he was making a fool of her, she scowled at him. "Oh! You—! Oh, go away! I can't stand to be around you!"

His laughter echoing through the forest, he obeyed.

Francine stared after him for a moment, unable to believe that he'd gone off and left her like that. But she supposed she shouldn't be surprised. He was nothing but a barbarian, after all.

She rode along the path, brooding over his many faults and misdeeds. He was rude and stubborn. He'd made her ride that donkey. He refused to listen to her suggestions. He'd torn off her clothes—

A bush rustled.

Francine yanked back on the reins and stared into the forest, wondering if Garrick had returned. "Garrick?" she said.

There was no response.

She saw something move. Its shadow glided along the trees.

A frisson of fear snaked along her spine. The shadow wasn't big enough to be a man on a horse. It looked like a man holding some sort of clawlike weapon aloft. And it was coming closer. . . .

She opened her mouth to scream, but before she could do so, the shadow moved out into a small clearing and became a deer.

Her fear vanished, and she sighed, half in relief, half in awe. A deer! A real, live deer! How beautiful it was. She held herself very still, watching it. The animal stared back with gentle, liquid brown eyes.

Once, when she'd been a child, her grandmother had taken her to the zoo, and there'd been an area where children could pet the animals. There had been a deer there, and she had touched it, enchanted by its soft fur and friendly snuffling for the corn in her hand.

But she'd never seen one like this, in the wild, so beautiful and proud-looking with its antlers and white-swathed neck. She wished she had a camera. Would it let her pet it?

Slowly, carefully, she dismounted and approached the deer with her hand held out.

"Hello, deer," she crooned softly. "Don't be afraid, I just want to pet you. . . ."

The deer watched her approach, perhaps a trifle warily, but with something like friendly curiosity in its eyes.

"Oh, aren't you a beauty," Francine whispered. She was almost close enough to touch it now. Just a few more feet . . .

Suddenly the deer began pawing the ground.

"It's okay, deer," Francine said. "I won't hurt you."

The deer lowered its head and shook its antlers at her. The pronged horns suddenly didn't look so cute. In fact, they looked downright dangerous.

"Deer," Francine said, taking a step back. "Oh, dear. Deer . . ."

The deer charged.

Panic-stricken, Francine ran like an Olympic sprinter toward a tree and dived behind it. Behind her, she heard antlers crashing against the trunk, the sound echoing throughout the forest. Francine scrambled to her feet and darted around the tree, the deer on her heels.

Her wimple caught on a branch. She tugged at it, but the branch wouldn't release its hold on her. The deer reared up.

Pulling frantically at her wimple, Francine screamed, only one thought clear in her terror-stricken mind—she was going to be killed by Bambi.

She lifted her arm to protect her face. But instead of sharp hooves stomping her to death, she heard a whistling noise and felt a brush of air on her cheek.

The deer dropped suddenly to the ground, its antlered head only inches from her feet.

She blinked down at it in confusion, not quite able to

grasp what had happened—until she saw the feathered arrow sticking out from its chest.

Yanking loose from her wimple, she turned and saw Garrick standing at the edge of the clearing, a bow in hand.

"You killed it," she whispered, rather stupidly.

"Yes." He walked to the deer and removed the arrow from it.

She watched as, grunting a little, he lifted the deer, carried it to Francine's horse, and slung the carcass across the mare's back. "Would you like to tell me what the hell you were doing?"

"I . . . I wanted to pet it." Francine stared transfixed at the deer, its eyes now glassy and still in the antlered head flopping against the mare's side. "It looked so cute. . . ."

"Cute? Are you insane?"

"I didn't realize . . ." Francine bit her lip. "How did you find me?"

"I was only a short distance behind you."

"Oh. I thought you'd left."

He looked up from tying the deer's hooves together beneath the mare's stomach. "Did you truly think I would leave you alone, unprotected, in this forest?"

"I . . . thank you," she said, lowering her eyes, unable to meet the intensity of his gaze. She looked at the deer and the blood dripping from the wound in its throat. "The poor thing. It must have thought I was trying to hurt it. How sad that it's dead now."

"There's nothing sad about it," he said callously. "We'll have venison to eat."

She hugged her arms across her chest. "Don't you feel the least bit guilty?"

He stared at her incredulously. "For what?"

"For killing such a magnificent animal."

He gave her a look similar to the one Lady Ingrid had given her earlier. "No. I think about having food on my plate and in my belly. I think about what it's like to go without, to be starving at the end of winter when our food runs out and another storm hits, wiping out the spring crops. I think about survival."

Survival. Francine stared at the deer on her horse, its blood draining onto the ground. She'd never had to worry about survival. Survival was a given in her world.

Garrick retrieved her torn wimple and stuffed it in his saddlebag. He gave her a leg up onto his horse, then swung up behind her. Holding Bessie's reins, he wrapped one arm around Francine and nudged his horse forward.

"In any case," he said. "I haven't noticed guilt preventing you from eating meat."

Francine flushed, partly from his words, partly from the feel of his arm around her waist. She supposed she *had* sounded rather hypocritical. "I don't object to eating meat," she attempted to explain. "I object to the way it was obtained. It seems so cruel to hunt an animal down."

"Ah, but you don't realize the pleasure you're missing." His voice was close to her ear. "It takes great skill to track a prey. A truly clever huntsman never lets on that he is there. The prey is completely unaware. Unsuspecting."

Prickles flittered down her spine. "Why go to all that trouble?"

"Because it might take fright and flee, of course. You have to wait until the last possible moment before you alert it to your presence." He shifted his arm slightly, causing it to just brush against the underside of her breast.

An accident, surely, Francine thought. She straightened her back, trying to eliminate the contact without success. Her throat grew dry. Her lips felt parched. "And then?"

"And then you go after it. There's nothing to equal the feeling, Francine." His voice was low, his breath whispering across the nape of her neck. "The wind in your face as you race across meadows, over fences, and through streams. The pounding of your heart as the horns blow and the dogs yelp. The thrill in your blood as you catch sight of the prey. . . ."

His arm tightened, pressing against her chest and the turbulent beating of her heart beneath.

"And then you destroy it." Her voice, a cracked thread of sound, hung in the air.

She felt him tense behind her; then his shoulders moved

in a shrug. "As I said, it's a matter of survival. 'Tis the way of the world."

"Your world, perhaps."

He laughed, but he didn't sound amused. "Your world, too, Francine. Your world, too."

She couldn't sleep.

She lay in bed, shifting in the narrow space between Edith and the edge of the mattress, thoughts of Garrick intruding on her like an annoying jingle from some television commercial.

She disliked him intensely. Whenever they were together, all they did was argue. He could make her angrier than any man she'd ever known. The way he had talked about hunting still made her shiver deep inside.

But at times . . . at times he could actually be almost considerate—in a rude, primitive, barbaric way. If he hadn't returned when he had, that deer might have killed her.

She should be grateful to him. She should be nicer to him. If she was nicer to him, he would probably be nicer to her. And then . . . and then . . . what? Her shivering increased. She didn't know. She didn't *want* to know. She wanted to keep him at a distance. A nice, safe, healthy distance.

Francine hugged the blanket more tightly, but the shivering did not go away. It nagged at her all the way to the pit of her stomach. Probably because she was hungry. Starving, in fact.

She should have gone to supper, she thought. But after making such a fuss about hunting, she felt that she should make some protest. She had her pride, after all. Refusing to eat the venison had seemed like a good way to make a statement. She'd realized too late that supper wouldn't include deer meat because of the Advent fasting.

If only pride could somehow fill her stomach.

She listened for a few moments to Edith's soft snores, then carefully, quietly, pushed back the curtain and slipped out of the bed.

The hall was dark, only a faint glow provided by the fire in the middle of the room. Blindly, she put on her dress and shoes, and made her way across the floor. Hands out-stretched before her, she searched with her foot before each step to make sure she didn't trip over a sleeping body.

Outside, a light rain was falling. Francine felt her way along the wall until she came to a corner. Then, estimating the direction of the kitchen, she set out across the courtyard.

A minute later she bumped into a wall. Feeling the rough wattle-and-daub construction, she breathed a sigh of relief, and made her way to the door.

To her surprise, the kitchen was deserted. She'd expected that Gunilda or some of the cookboys might be sleeping in there, or even the dogs, and that she would have to beg or bribe someone for food.

Tiptoeing anyway, Francine went over to the pantry and tried to open it. It was locked.

Frustrated, she looked around and saw a large platter covered by a cloth on the worktable. She lifted the cover, and in the glow from the banked fire, peered down at a dish of smoked herrings.

She was hungry enough that even the fish smelled good.

She'd polished off a quarter of the plate when she heard footsteps approaching.

Panicked, she covered the herrings back up and glanced around. She dived into a corner by the oven just as the door opened and three men entered.

"We will have privacy here," Francine heard a low voice say.

She recognized the voice immediately, of course. She peeked around the corner of the oven to see a dark figure bending over the hearth to light a candle stub. Its light illuminated the faces of the men—Gilbert de Gant and Ranulf of Chester. And Garrick.

Garrick turned from the hearth and the light from the candle sent a dim arc across the floor toward the corner where Francine was hiding. She quickly ducked into the shadows.

Garrick and Ranulf sat down at the kitchen table, but de Gant paced back and forth across the room.

"The time to attack is now," he said, his face as red as his beard. "The war in France is lost and the unrest in the kingdom has never been greater. Most of the north is with me, as well as Robert Fitzwalter, de Vesci, Geoffrey de Mandeville, and Roger Bigod. Join us and we shall soon have the king at our mercy."

"We must consider carefully." Ranulf's hazel eyes, no longer flirtatious, were calm and steady. "Do not be so hasty."

"Hasty! We should have attacked while John was still out of the country. He would not have stood a chance against us. Besides, he has brought it on himself with his incompetence."

"The problems of England are not all the fault of King John," Garrick said. "If the barons rise, it could mean complete anarchy."

"Bah," said de Gant. "You've let the king's promises addle your wits, Garrick. He will not keep his word and let you marry his ward. He will find someone willing to pay a higher price for her and forget all about his agreement with you."

"My marriage prospects have nothing to do with this discussion," Garrick said coldly. "Let us concentrate on the issue at hand—which is whether open rebellion will benefit England. I say it will not."

"I must agree with Garrick," Ranulf said. "It would be better to find some peaceable way to settle our complaints with the king."

"You two are nothing but a pair of old women," de Gant snarled, thumping his fist on the table. "The honorable way to settle this is through battle, and I'm ready to fight. I'm fed up with the king and his incompetence and his never-ending taxes. There is no other solution. . . ."

Something brushed against Francine's leg. Looking down, she saw two tiny bright red eyes gleaming up at her. She choked back a scream, but a small gasping noise escaped her. Chairs crashing to the floor, the men at the table rose to their feet and turned toward her corner.

"What the devil?" de Gant exclaimed. Before Francine could move, he strode across the room and grabbed her, dragging her from the shadows. "It looks as though you've been harboring a spy, Garrick."

Francine pulled at her arm, but de Gant refused to release it. "Let go of me," she said indignantly. "I'm not a spy. I was, um, just looking for the garderobe. . . ."

De Gant pulled a knife from his belt. His cold, blue eyes glared directly into hers. "You won't need a garderobe where you're going."

Francine's voice stuck in her throat as she stared at the upraised knife.

He wasn't . . . he couldn't mean . . .

Her breath came in gasps. Fear, shock, and a sense of déjà vu held her motionless as she watched the knife begin its descent. . . .

"Wait."

Garrick grabbed the man's wrist. De Gant looked up in surprise.

Garrick shook his head. "There's no reason to kill the wench. She is a woman, of no interest to us."

De Gant's eyes narrowed. "Women are dangerous. They do not know how to hold their tongues."

"This one does. She's as silent as a little lamb, aren't you, Lady Francine?"

She nodded faintly, her knees trembling.

Still de Gant hesitated. "It's foolish to take chances. She could have us all executed."

Garrick moved forward and removed her from the man's hold. "I will personally guarantee that she won't betray us."

De Gant looked back and forth between them. Understanding dawned in his eyes, but he still frowned. "Like that, is it? But I still don't like it. . . ."

"You don't need to like it," Garrick said. "Come, Lady Francine, I will escort you back to bed."

Ranulf, looking amused, said, "Wait—let the poor lady sit down a moment. She appears frightened out of her wits. Are you all right, Lady Francine?" He smiled kindly at her as if his friend hadn't just tried to kill her.

"I . . . I'm fine," she gasped.

"I'm certain she will recover quickly once she's in her bed," Garrick said. He took a step toward the door.

"Come, now, Garrick," Ranulf cried. "You hid her away at supper, you selfish boor. It's only fair to let the rest of us have a chance with her."

"I hardly think this is the time or place."

Ranulf's gaze lingered on her uncovered hair. "I cannot agree. 'Tis always the time and place to enjoy the company of a beautiful woman. Besides, I would like to know her opinion on the subject. Ladies often have great insights into these matters, I've found. So what say you, Lady Francine? Should we fight?"

"Oh, no!" she exclaimed.

De Gant glared at Ranulf. "She's a woman! Of course she would say not to fight."

"Oh, I don't know. Some women enjoy a good battle. Wouldn't you say, Sir Garrick?" Ranulf winked slyly.

Francine stiffened, sensing a sexist male joke. "Fighting is stupid," she said more firmly. "Why don't you talk to the king?"

"Bah!" de Gant snarled. "I'm through talking with the king. I say we fight."

Ranulf shrugged and glanced at Francine. "You see, Lady Francine, we have already tried to talk to the king. Unfortunately, he refuses to listen to reason."

"Aren't there any laws?" she asked. "Surely he can't just do whatever he wants."

"Yes, he can," said de Gant. "And when he goes too far, the only solution is combat!"

"Wait, she may have a point," said Ranulf. "If I remember correctly, Henry—the old Henry—guaranteed certain rights to all Englishmen. If we could find a record of those guarantees, we could use it as a basis for our demands."

De Gant snorted. "A list of our demands? Why would John care for such a thing? He would laugh in our faces!"

"Not if we could show legal precedent. We could get the archbishop to present the demands—he's been looking for a peaceful solution, too. It would also give us a cause to rally the men around."

"Be sure to ask for the right to a trial by jury," Francine said. Remembering Lady Ingrid's bitter words, she added, "And include some rights for women—like allowing them to marry whom they please. . . ."

Garrick's arm tightened around her. "I believe you've given us enough of your expert advice for one night. Excuse me, gentlemen, while I escort Lady Francine back to her bed. The cook left out a platter of herrings if you are hungry. Please help yourselves."

The men nodded, de Gant with a suspicious frown on his face, Ranulf looking amused again.

Garrick swept her out of the kitchen in spite of her protests.

"Hey, wait a minute." She stumbled after him in the pitch-black courtyard. In spite of the darkness, he didn't hesitate. "There are some other things that are really important—"

"If you are wise," Garrick said through gritted teeth, "you will hold your tongue. God's breath, what were you doing in there?"

"Nothing," she said. "That is, I told you—I was looking for the garderobe."

He stopped and turned her so that she could feel his warm breath on her face. "I hope you weren't trying to steal anything. The penalty for stealing is a day in the stocks—"

"I wasn't stealing! I was, um, just a bit hungry," she finally admitted.

"Ah."

She hated the suddenly amused tone in his voice. Shrugging off his hold on her shoulders, she peered through the blackness, trying to see which way the hall was. She took a step forward.

He grabbed her hand and led her slightly to the right. "Don't tell me you overcame your scruples and were looking for some of that venison. Step up."

"Certainly not," she said as she climbed the two hall steps to the hall door. Reaching out, she fumbled with the handle.

His hand closed over hers. "Next time, wait until morning to sate your hunger. Otherwise, you may end up dead. Or worse."

His hand was big and rough with calluses. She stood still, aware of the oblique threat radiating from him. She knew he was just trying to scare her. Not wanting to admit it was working, she said brashly, "Is that a threat?"

"No, it's friendly advice."

"It sounds like a threat to me—"

With a sound of frustration, he swept her up in his arms and strode into the hall with her.

"What are you doing?" she squeaked. "Put me down this instant!"

Ignoring her, he kept walking, somehow managing to avoid stepping on any of the people on the floor. A flutter of unease curled in Francine's stomach. "Garrick," she hissed, "put me down or I'll scream and wake everybody up!"

"Go right ahead," he said. "It will prove my point."

"And your point is?" she asked stiffly.

He stopped. From the light of one small candle in a wall sconce by the foot of the stairs, she saw him look down at her. His jaw was tight, his eyes dark.

"You will learn that I am lord and master here, that I can do whatever I want, whenever I want, and no one will stop me."

Her lips parted, but no sound came out. She stared up at him, her heart pounding.

She cleared her throat. "Garrick . . ."

His mouth closed over hers, cutting off the rest of her words. She gasped and tried to push him away, but his arms only tightened and his lips pressed harder against hers.

It should have been repulsive. And it was, Francine thought dazedly. Only . . . it wasn't *quite* as repulsive as she would have expected. His beard was soft against her skin, his mouth hard on hers. His breath, surprisingly, was pleasant. True, there was still a slight scent of sweat about him, but somehow, along with the strength of his arms and the broadness of his shoulders, that only contributed to the . . . the sheer *maleness* of him.

Something sparked within her. It spread through her veins, tingling and expanding as it went. Warmth flared, growing hotter and hotter, burning her skin and gathering in the pit of her stomach and melting her insides. She became fluid, contained only by his arms, his chest, his mouth. . . .

Then, suddenly, she was flying through the air to land with a thump on a prickly straw mattress. She heard someone grumble.

"You're like a moose," Edith mumbled, before she started snoring again.

Barely hearing her, Francine stared up at Garrick.

"Remember what I said," he growled, then turned on his heel and strode back through the hall. He was soon out of sight of the dim glow of the candle. Francine heard a yelp and Garrick's snarled "Pardon" as he stepped on someone.

Reaching up, Francine pulled the bed-curtain closed, then lay back down. Her skin was prickling, her heart pounding. She was wide awake. Edith turned over, digging skinny elbows into her side, but Francine didn't move or complain.

For once, she was grateful for the old woman's presence.

Chapter 12

GARRICK RODE BESIDE the departing caravan of wagons and horses the next morning, escorting them through the castle gate. Lady Ingrid, not wishing her velvet cloak to be ruined by the rain, traveled in a litter borne by four lackeys, while Gilbert de Gant and Ranulf of Chester rode alongside. Garrick waited until the last wagon was through the gate, then cantered forward to the head of the caravan.

"An excellent visit," Ranulf said as Garrick joined him. "I think it is possible a compromise with the king may be reached."

"Perhaps," Garrick replied, although in truth, he doubted anything would come of the negotiations. De Gant was spoiling for a fight, and he would do his best to incite his comrades to take up arms. The hot-tempered baron was always inclined to shed blood first and ask questions later— witness his attempt last night to silence Francine.

As if that were possible.

The woman caused more turmoil than any female Garrick had ever met. She also had a remarkable talent for putting herself in danger. He still could not quite believe she'd tried to pet a wild stag—had she no sense at all? She was fortunate she hadn't been gored.

Of course, that piece of foolishness paled in comparison to last night's escapade. If he hadn't intervened, her bleeding corpse would be floating down the river this very moment. Even after almost having a knife stuck through her, she'd seemed oblivious to her danger. Her tongue had flapped like a pennon in the breeze—or at least it had until he kissed her.

Garrick tightened his hands on the reins. Kissing Francine had been a mistake. He had only meant to warn her. Instead, he'd been inundated with a thousand pleasurable sensations. Her hair, soft, tickling, brushing against his cheek like the silkiest down feathers. Her skin, redolent, tantalizing, scented with peaches and cream. And her mouth . . . oh, dear God, her mouth. All warm, moist heat and honey-sweet taste, enticing him to delve deeper and deeper and deeper.

Holding her aloft in his arms, he'd been aware of her small hands clasped behind his neck; the delicate bones of her shoulders encircled by his left arm while the softness of her thighs pressed against his right; and the roundness of her hips wedged low against the increasing hardness of his loins. . . .

God's breath, he wanted her. In spite of the trouble she'd caused him, in spite of Anne and her plotting, in spite of his plans for the future, he wanted her. And last night, somewhere in the middle of that kiss, he'd reached a decision. He was going to have her.

In truth, if he hadn't given his chamber to de Gant and his wife, Garrick would have taken her last night. But it was just as well that he hadn't. That kiss had affected him more than he would have believed possible. If he had proceeded, he might have made promises to her he'd sworn never to make.

No, 'twas much better that he be in control when he bedded Francine. After a night of reflection, he'd realized that there was no reason he couldn't continue forward with his plans to strengthen his position and have Francine also. She might protest, but he was certain he could convince her without too much trouble—because he knew now that she wanted him, too. She hadn't been able to hide her response to his kiss. Who would have thought that underneath her prissy exterior lay all that passion?

Still, that prissiness might present an obstacle. He would have to plan very carefully. . . .

"Court should be interesting this year," Ranulf mused, interrupting Garrick's thoughts on how to seduce Francine. "Do you plan to attend?"

In two weeks, the king would be holding court at Winchester. It would be the perfect opportunity for Garrick to pin John down on the vague promise he'd made.

"Yes, I will be there." With a nod to Ranulf, Garrick spurred his horse and cantered forward.

His mind was made up. Within a month, he would have the king's written agreement to allow him to marry Lady Odelia.

And within a fortnight he would have Francine in his bed.

Francine lurked in the kitchen all morning to avoid Garrick and his guests, but as soon as the last wagon rolled through the gate, she hurried up to the battlements to watch the caravan go. Half the castle residents had the same idea, and the narrow ledge was crowded. In spite of the light rain, a few daring souls—kitchen and stableboys mostly—had climbed the slippery stone to sit on top of the merlons, the raised segments. Most of the people, however, were content with the view from the embrasures—the low sections—and were clustered there. Francine joined one of these groups, managing to squeeze in between Harvey and Edith.

The procession traveled along the path toward the misty forest. Francine saw a litter borne by four stout young men, and although the curtains were drawn, she knew the occupant must be Lady Ingrid. Gilbert de Gant and Ranulf of Chester rode beside the litter, along with another man—Garrick.

Unable to help herself, Francine stared at him, noticing how tall and straight he sat in the saddle. She saw a small hand part the curtains of the litter, and Garrick bend toward it as if to hear better what its owner said.

"Is Garrick going with them?" she heard herself ask.

Edith shook her head. "He is merely accompanying them to the edge of his property."

"Oh." Francine forced herself to look away, not liking the twinge of relief she felt. She didn't care if Garrick stayed or left. In fact, she would prefer it if he left. Then she wouldn't be subjected to indignities like the one last night.

She still couldn't believe that he'd kissed her. Even worse, she couldn't believe that she'd kept absolutely still and allowed it. She should have fought him. She should have screamed. But for a moment—a millisecond, no more—she had forgotten who and where she was, and who he was, and she'd felt . . . she didn't know what, exactly. She hadn't liked the feeling at all. She'd never felt like that with Stuart. With Stuart, she always knew exactly where she was and what was happening. She could think when Stuart kissed her. Stuart's face was clean-shaven, he used a strong mouthwash, and he smelled discreetly of cologne. He always kept his kisses short and respectful.

Garrick's kiss had not been respectful at all. And he had that terrible beard. She *hated* beards. His kiss had been to demonstrate his authority over her, to threaten her. How like a primitive male!

And Garrick was primitive, no doubt about it. She doubted he'd ever felt a flicker of embarrassment or a single inhibition.

Unbidden, images of the "101 Different Positions" chapter of the *Sex for Dummies* book flashed through Francine's head. Garrick probably wouldn't find them offensive at all, she thought. In fact, he'd probably want to try every single one. . . .

But not with her. Never with her. She was fairly sure he'd just been trying to scare her. Certainly he couldn't *want* to have sex with her. He'd made his dislike of her very plain. Almost as plain as she'd made her dislike of him.

"Lady Francine!"

Francine leaned forward to see Clifford, about twenty feet away in the next embrasure, waving to get her attention.

"Good morning, Clifford," she said.

"Have you heard the news?"

"What news?" she asked.

"Sir Garrick has agreed to build the steam bath!"

"He has?" Francine grasped the edge of the smooth stone in front of her.

Clifford nodded, a smile lighting his bony face. "Work starts tomorrow. Whatever did you do to convince him, Lady Francine?"

"Nothing."

All the people in the two embrasures who heard this exchange nudged each other with their elbows and looked at each other knowingly.

Francine was surprised and irritated by their sly smiles. "I didn't do anything," she reiterated. "Garrick pays no attention to what I say or do."

Several people laughed. Even Harvey and Edith snickered.

"I wish a man would pay no attention to me like that," Edith said.

"What do you mean?" Francine asked.

"He escorted you home from the hunt yesterday. No man gives up his sport unless he has some interest in the lady."

Harvey nodded in agreement. "Look how he nearly slit my throat when I, ahem"—he lowered his voice discreetly—"had my hands on your legs."

"You make it sound as though he were jealous," Francine said. "Nothing could be further from the truth. He was only upset because I was using the solar without his permission."

"Why was he so angry at Clifford for being closeted alone with you in the storeroom, then?" Edith said. "I was in the hall when Sir Garrick found out. And I saw Clifford after Sir Garrick spoke to him. Clifford was as pale and pasty as boiled linen. That's when Mog was ordered to attend you in the storeroom."

Shocked and disturbed by their words, Francine struggled to maintain a calm facade. "I'm certain you are misinterpreting his motives completely," she said as firmly as she could. "But his reasons are irrelevant as long as he's agreed to build the steam bath. In fact, if that's really true, I must go talk to Thomas about it."

With as much dignity as possible, she left the battlements, ignoring the whispers and laughter behind her.

They were wrong, she told herself firmly. Completely, absolutely, 100 percent wrong.

Francine watched the construction of the steam bath over the next several days with mixed emotions. She was glad it was being built, but she was still disturbed by what Edith and Harvey had said. The implications frightened her.

She had plenty to be frightened about. Garrick had torn the clothes off her back, after all. In the forest, he'd hinted that he would enjoy stalking her like some poor woodland creature. And just a few nights ago, in no uncertain terms, he'd told her that he could do what he wanted to her and no one would stop him.

She was worried enough, that one day she asked Gunilda for a knife.

"A knife?" Gunilda, her big spoon in hand, stared at Francine. "Why do you want a knife?"

"To protect myself," Francine replied in a low voice so Nancy and Mog and the milling kitchen boys wouldn't hear her. "In case one of the men tries to force himself on me."

"Bah," Gunilda snorted. "No one would dare. Everyone knows you are Sir Garrick's woman."

"I am *not* Garrick's woman," Francine denied hotly, forgetting to keep her voice down. "And that's why I need the knife—to make sure I won't become so."

Nancy and Mog exchanged glances; Tony, Nat, and Lars snickered; and Gunilda gave a great barking laugh. "He would never force you."

Francine flushed at the laughter, but she still managed to infuse skepticism into her voice as she said, "No?"

"No." With three quick whacks, Gunilda rapped the boys' knuckles with her spoon. The boys quickly returned their attention to their work. "He is very good at charming a woman when he sets his mind to it. If he wants you in his bed, he will wait until the perfect moment when you are in charity with him, then find some way to beguile himself into your heart and into your bed. Although, to be perfectly honest, I would be surprised if that is his intention. I'd thought . . ."

The kitchen suddenly grew silent. Tony, by the fireplace, stopped turning the spit; Nancy and Mog ceased chopping onions; Nat and Lars, in the act of removing bread from the ovens on wooden paddles, froze. Even the dogs stopped chewing on their bones to hear what the cook had thought.

"You thought what?" Francine prompted her.

"Nothing," Gunilda said abruptly.

Nancy and Mog resumed chopping; Tony turned the spit; Nat and Lars set the loaves of bread on a rack to cool. The dogs chewed on their bones.

"I would still like to have the knife," Francine said, wondering what the cook had been going to say. "Just in case."

Gunilda shook her head. "I can't spare any of my kitchen knives. You may have a spoon if you like, though."

Somehow, Francine couldn't quite envision Garrick being deterred by a wooden spoon, even if she wielded it as fiercely as Gunilda did. "No, thank you," she said.

She left the kitchen, more nervous than ever; and she watched Garrick warily every time he came near. But as the days passed and he made no overtures toward her, she became distracted by other matters—namely, the steam bath.

The workers finished it at the end of the week. Unfortunately, none of the men-at-arms would use it.

"It's perfectly safe," she urged them.

"It's not healthy," one of them muttered.

Even Orson wouldn't budge on the issue. "If God had meant us to be clean, He wouldn't have created dirt."

Finally, realizing how desperate the situation was, Francine put Plan B into action.

The next day, to the gaping amazement of the men working in the inner ward, a long line of cloaked women walked across the cold, rainy courtyard and into the bathhouse.

Francine, cloaked herself, was at the end of the line. She walked into the vestibule of the building and shut the door firmly in the faces of the goggling men. Pressing her ear to the wood, she listened to the chatter of the men outside.

"Did you see . . . ?"

"All those women . . ."

"Do you think they're naked under those cloaks?"

Smiling, Francine turned away from the door, only to stop as the women dropped their cloaks and kicked off their boots.

They *were* naked. Completely so.

They all tromped through the door on the opposite side, into the steam room.

Francine hesitated. She had her chemise on under her cloak. She'd intended to wear it in the steam bath. But now she was worried that she'd look totally ridiculous sitting there in her chemise when everyone else was naked.

She went over and opened the door a crack. Warm steam billowed in her face. Peering through it, she saw the women sitting in the bath without the least sign of self-consciousness, giggling and chattering.

Francine couldn't help noticing that the women's figures were less than perfect—nothing like the women in swimsuit magazines and on TV back home. Every kind of body flaw was represented here—heavy thighs, rounded stomachs, scars, little breasts, big breasts, sagging breasts.

Frowning, Francine shut the door. How could these women expose themselves so?

On the other hand, how wonderful to be so totally unembarrassed.

She took off her cloak and boots. She put the emerald necklace into a cloth pouch. She glanced down at her chemise.

Then, with a sudden burst of courage, she stripped off the chemise, grabbed her towel, and walked into the bath.

The women all looked at her as she entered.

Francine froze. She groped for the door latch behind her, mortified beyond words, wanting nothing except the concealment of her chemise, her dress, and any other clothes she could find.

But before she could find the latch, the women all glanced away and continued their conversations.

Francine hesitated a moment, unsure whether to stay or

leave. Now that they weren't staring at her, she didn't feel so uncomfortable. Taking a deep breath, she walked over and put her towel on a bench. She sat down on it, relief flowing through her.

She still felt self-conscious, but after a while, she realized something—these women didn't care what her body looked like. They didn't care whether she had a twenty-four- or a sixty-four-inch waist. They accepted the contours of her body just as they accepted the features of her face.

Slowly, Francine relaxed, and she felt a heady sense of freedom. She closed her eyes and basked in the pleasure of the warm, wet heat.

When she left the bathhouse some time later, there was a line of women waiting to get in. A peculiarly large number of men appeared to have business in the courtyard. They all stared at the women as they went in and out and put their hands out to feel the warm vapor escaping from the vents and the door. Over the slight hiss of the steam and the rain, bursts of laughter could be heard inside.

A group of men approached Francine—the men-at-arms.

"We have decided to accept your offer to try out the steam bath," Pascal said heroically.

Francine smiled. "Excellent! You may use it any time after dinner."

The men's faces fell. "But . . . we feel very much in need of a bath right *now*," Ivo said.

"You'll have to wait," Francine said. "Only women can use the bath before dinner."

The men left, grumbling.

Hiding another smile, Francine turned toward the hall, only to stop as she saw the man standing there against the wall near the side entrance.

He had freshly washed black hair that hung in a straight shining fall to his shoulders. His angled jaw sloped down to a knobby chin with a thin white scar on one side. He had a finely chiselled mouth with a sensual lower lip and a nose that, although it was still larger than she liked, seemed to fit his face perfectly.

He was watching her steadily, and she could see his eyes—gray beneath straight black brows.

Francine stared at him, her stomach muscles clenching and unclenching.

She never would have believed that the Barbarian of Pelsworth Castle could look so devastatingly handsome.

As if pulled by some invisible force, she walked forward.

"You shaved your beard." She stared at him, amazed at the difference a beard could make.

Rubbing his jaw, he nodded toward the stone hut a short distance away. "It would appear the steam bath is a great success."

"Yes. I . . . thank you for allowing it to be built."

"You're welcome." His gaze roved over her face and down her cloaked figure. Suddenly she was burningly aware of the fact that she had only her chemise on underneath. She gripped the edges of the soft, wool cloak.

His gaze moved back up to meet hers—his eyes were dark. Slowly, carefully, he reached out and cupped her cheek with his hand, his thumb brushing the cold raindrops from her flushed cheeks. He continued to stroke her cheek, and she stood immobile, staring up at him, unable to move, her skin growing warmer and warmer under his touch. His thumb brushed against her full lower lip. Involuntarily, she parted her lips.

His eyes grew darker. He pulled her into the partial shelter of the doorway, hemming her in against the wooden boards. "Come up to the solar with me."

His words barely penetrated her strange stupor. "Why?"

"You know why," he said, his voice rough. "I want you, Francine. I have ever since you came here. I tried to fight it . . . but it's like a fever. I ache with wanting you. Come upstairs with me where we may be private. Come upstairs now."

She stared at him, shock roiling through her. "No," she said automatically.

He leaned forward until his body was lightly touching hers from chest to thigh. His voice murmured in her ear. "Yes, Francine. Say yes. Come upstairs and share my bed with me. Let me kiss your lips, your breasts, your belly. Let me part your sweet thighs and come inside you and give you the greatest pleasure imaginable. . . ."

His mouth closed over hers. His tongue teased her lips, then slipped between them, causing heat to rush through her veins. She couldn't breathe. Her heart pounded inside her chest, and her breath came in uneven spurts. Her skin felt flushed. His words, shocking, unthinkable, unimaginable, spun inside her brain. No one had ever said such things to her before. No one had ever made her feel like this before. Not even Stuart. . . .

Stuart. Dear God.

"Stop," she said, her voice sounding appallingly weak and breathless. "I'm engaged. To Stuart."

Garrick, nuzzling the sweetness of her neck, barely comprehended her words. "Forget Stuart," he muttered, tugging gently to push her cloak aside. "Come upstairs with me, Francine."

She grasped her cloak more tightly. "No, I can't."

It took Garrick a moment to realize what she was saying. Slowly, reluctantly, he stepped back from her. What was she babbling about? Stuart?

Stuart?

That weakling that spoke of numbers to his betrothed? That half-man who'd never even taken her to his bed? How could she even think of that dunderhead at this moment?

"That dolt doesn't even know what to do with a woman," he said without thinking.

Francine stiffened. "He knows how to treat a woman with kindness and consideration. He knows not to attack her in a doorway in full view of a hundred people."

Realizing his mistake, Garrick tried to backtrack. "I'm sorry, Francine. You're right. Come, let us go up to my chamber where we may discuss this in private."

She shook her head violently.

"Francine . . . you want me. You know you do. And I want you. Please, Francine. Come upstairs."

The soft coaxing in his voice made Francine quiver deep

inside. But she managed to keep her tone steady as she spoke. "No."

He grew very still. She could feel a tension pulsing through him, as if he were debating with himself whether to accept her refusal, or to sweep her into his arms, carry her up to his room, and take what he wanted. . . .

He stepped back suddenly, his expression difficult to read. "Very well. If that is what you wish. Let me know if you change your mind."

"I won't," she said.

He just stared at her.

"I won't," she repeated.

"I believe you, Francine." He pushed a loose strand of hair behind her ear, his fingers lingering on her cheek for a moment. Then, with a cool nod, he turned on his heel and strode off across the courtyard toward the stables.

She leaned back against the door, shaking. She stood there for several long moments, but the trembling didn't subside. Clutching her cloak, she went inside the hall and up to the tower chamber where her clothes were. She dressed quickly, glancing nervously at the door all the while. Once she was finished, she fled down the stairs, out of the hall, out of the castle, and down the path to the forest. Ignoring the branches scratching at her hands and cheeks, she pushed her way through the bushes until she reached the clearing by the lake.

She stopped, panting, at the edge of the fairy circle and stared down at the mushrooms. She closed her eyes and tried to picture Stuart's face.

He had blue eyes, she remembered. But the exact shade was concealed by his glasses. He had sandy-brown hair . . . but she couldn't recall precisely how it was cut. He always dressed neatly in a suit and polka-dot bow tie . . . but the exact color and style escaped her.

Her stomach churned. How had this happened? How could she not remember what the man she loved looked like? How could the shape of his face, the timbre of his voice, and the scent of his cologne elude her?

Her hands clenched into fists. She had to go home. Surely,

with all she had accomplished, with the men minding their manners and the steam bath built, she would be able to return now.

She entered the fairy circle and sat on the rock under the willow tree. She fingered the emerald at her throat. If everything worked according to plan, she would be home in a few minutes. She would be back with Stuart and Grandma Peabody and Bentley. She would never have to see this hateful place again. Or Garrick.

Garrick . . . who had saved her life not once, not twice, but three times. Garrick, who looked so incredibly handsome without his beard. Garrick who, when he'd kissed her, had made her want to forget about everyone and everything in the future and go upstairs to his bed and let him make love to her. . . .

Was she going insane?

She didn't care about Garrick. All she cared about was going home. To Stuart. Their wedding was barely three weeks away. Once she was with him, everything would be normal again. *She* would be normal. . . .

She closed her fingers tightly around the emerald and shut her eyes.

"Take me home."

She waited for the flash of light, the dizzying pull, the icy coldness.

Nothing happened.

She sat on the rock, waiting, silently willing the emerald to take her home.

Soft mist brushed her cheeks, the birds twittered in the trees, the rock under her stayed hard and damp and immobile. She knew, even before she opened her eyes, what she would find.

She looked at the lake and the forest and the circle of mushrooms. She closed her eyes again, tightly.

What was wrong? What else did she need to do? What else *could* she do?

Opening her eyes, Francine stood up. She walked back through the forest, and up the path to Pelsworth Castle.

*   *   *

The weather grew wetter and colder, and the steam bath more popular. Slowly, gradually, layers of encrusted dirt began to disappear from the men. They came to supper with their hair combed, their chins clean-shaven.

One day before dinner, Clifford and Mog approached her and told her that they were going to get married.

"That's wonderful!" Impulsively, Francine hugged Mog.

The girl hugged her back. "We wanted to thank you for all you've done." She nudged Clifford, who flushed a little and held out a small bouquet of holly berries. Clearing his throat, he said, "Thank you, Lady Francine."

Francine stared at the bright-red berries and waxy green leaves, touched beyond words.

"This never would have happened if it weren't for you," Mog said, her beautiful brown eyes earnest. "We can never repay you."

"You don't need to repay me. . . ."

"I know we don't. But we paid to have the priest light a candle for you. He will bless you every day for a year." Mog smiled again. "Oh, and one more thing—we would be greatly honored if you would be a witness to our marriage after Twelfth Night."

"I would love to. Is Twelfth Night in January—" Suddenly, Francine remembered. "I'm sorry. I'm going home soon—I'm getting married also."

For a moment, Mog's face resumed its old scowl. "I don't want you to go!" she said.

Clifford squeezed her arm, and the scowl disappeared, replaced by a penitent look. "I'm sorry, Lady Francine. I didn't mean to be impertinent. But . . . oh, everyone wants you to stay! Couldn't you stay and marry Sir Garrick?"

"Sir Garrick!" Francine stiffened. "There's no question of my marrying Sir Garrick."

"Couldn't you at least consider it? I know he cares about you—why else would he have shaved off his beard?"

Before she could say any more, Clifford was tugging her away. "We have to go now. Thank you again, Lady Francine." In a lower voice, Francine heard him say to Mog, "Will you never learn to hold your tongue?"

Francine stood where she was, staring down at the holly. She felt . . . odd. She'd never had so many people she cared about. People who cared about *her*. She would miss them when she went home.

If she ever went home.

She'd been puzzling over the problem all week, and she still hadn't come up with any answer. She had decided, however, that she must talk to Lady Anne.

After thinking over the events of the last few months, Francine had realized several strange and inexplicable things about Anne. The woman had been a friend of Garrick's mother—yet according to Edith, no one knew who Garrick's mother had been. Or his father, either. Or anything about his childhood. There was also the fact that Garrick believed that Anne was somehow responsible for Francine's presence at the castle. Francine had dismissed the idea at first, but now she wondered. Anne certainly had seemed like she was trying to throw Garrick and Francine together.

Yes, she would really like to have a little talk with Anne, Francine thought. The only problem was . . . where was she? She'd left weeks ago, and no one had heard from her.

Unless Garrick had.

Francine drew in a deep breath. After their confrontation by the hall, she hadn't been sure how he would treat her. But in the last week, he'd behaved as though nothing had happened. He seemed mainly occupied with the castle—the wet mortar had started cracking due to the cold, so he'd halted construction and ordered that the unfinished walls be covered with straw and dung—and she rarely saw him. On the few occasions when she did, he was cool and polite and made no reference to his proposition or her refusal. In every way, he behaved as though he'd taken her seriously when she'd told him she wouldn't change her mind.

Except that he continued to shave.

The sight of those clean-shaven cheeks unsettled her. Whenever she saw them, an odd restlessness seized her, a sort of curiosity. What would it be like to . . .

No.

She thrust the traitorous thoughts away and concentrated

on thinking of Stuart. Stuart who was everything that was kind and faithful and *modern*.

She kept Stuart in mind as she approached Garrick near the castle gate one day.

She tried to act naturally. "Good afternoon, Garrick. I'm sorry to bother you, but I need to talk to Anne—do you have any idea when she'll return?"

"No, I don't," he said.

"Do you have any idea where she is? Where I could write her?"

He shook his head.

Her shoulders slumped. She gave him a strained smile and started to turn away.

"I'm leaving tomorrow," he said abruptly.

Francine turned back to stare at him. He was leaving? Her heart dipped in an uncomfortable manner.

"The king has summoned me to court at Westminster for the Christmas festivities," he continued. "By the time I return, you will be gone."

"Gone? What do you mean?"

"The day you arrived, Anne promised she would let you go home in three months. A few days after the New Year that time will have passed."

A few days after the New Year! Her wedding was on January third. But . . . "What does Anne have to do with my going home?"

He laughed, rather harshly. "Everything."

He turned to leave, but Francine, her mind spinning at his words, grabbed his arm. "Wait . . ."

He looked back at her, his brows lifted.

"Take me with you," she blurted out.

"Ahhh." The frown between his brows smoothed out; the tightness of his muscles relaxed. "So you've finally come to your senses. You waited long enough, Francine. I cannot take you to court with me, but I can delay my departure a few days. And then we can resume the relationship when I return. I must be honest with you, however—I will never leave here, and I cannot marry you, but I swear you'll never regret becoming my mistress—"

"Your mistress!" Francine, listening in shocked silence to his torrent of words, felt her face grow warm. "I wasn't offering to be your mistress."

The corners of his mouth turned down. "You weren't?"

"No," she said stiffly. "I'm marrying Stuart as soon as I get back home. But I need to talk to Anne. And it is logical to assume that she would go to court also."

Without warning, he grabbed her upper arms and swung her into a shadowed corner of the gatehouse. Eyes burning, he stared down at her.

"Do you intentionally try to torment me? Do not make a game of me, Francine. Do not blow hot, then cold, and expect me to stand tamely by. This is your last chance. I will not ask you again. Come up to the tower room with me right now or say goodbye forever."

Her lips felt stiff. "Goodbye."

His hands tightened on her shoulders and his eyes darkened. He pulled her hard up against him, and kissed her until her senses swam.

Then, just as suddenly, he released her. With a swirl of his cape, he strode away.

Shaken, Francine watched him go, telling herself it was for the best.

Yet she couldn't quite banish the odd, aching regret in her heart.

Anne arrived two days later.

Dressed in a black velvet dress and white satin wimple, she entered the castle with a procession ten times as magnificent as Lady Ingrid's had been.

She gave Francine a warm hug and bid her to come to her cottage to see the gifts she'd brought.

"Oh, Anne, you shouldn't have!" Francine said, looking at the fine gowns and veils.

"Of course I should have," Anne said. "You've accomplished wonders since I left. The men actually look like human beings instead of animals, the hall and the kitchen are clean, and Garrick . . . where *is* Garrick?"

"He left for court yesterday."

"He did?" Anne frowned. "And he didn't take you with him?"

"No." Francine felt her cheeks heat as she remembered how he'd interpreted her impulsive request that he take her along—and the hard kiss that had left her lips tingling for hours. "But I don't need to go now that you're here. I have to get back home." She looked at Anne. "Garrick said that *you* could help me."

"Did he?" Anne rummaged through her trunk. "I wonder what he could have meant."

"He said you promised that I could go home in three months. I do remember you saying something like that, although I didn't really pay much attention at the time. *Can* you help me get home, Lady Anne?"

Anne looked up rather reluctantly. "Perhaps. But do you really and truly wish to leave here?"

"Of *course* I do!" Francine said rather too emphatically. Seeing Anne's stare, Francine took a deep breath. "I'm sorry, I don't mean to sound rude. But I really must go home."

"I see." Anne's ebony eyes were inscrutable. "But didn't you have some task that you had to accomplish first?"

"Yes," Francine admitted reluctantly. "To civilize mankind. But I've done everything I can, honestly. I've taught the men-at-arms manners, and gotten help for Gunilda to clean up the kitchen, and Thomas and his men built a steam bath—"

"All very admirable, I'm sure," Anne interrupted. "But it sounds to me as if you're going about your task in the wrong way. If you are trying to civilize mankind, you need to teach the leader, not the followers."

"The leader?" Francine's heart sank. "You mean Garrick?"

Anne nodded. "He is the one everyone looks to as an example. He is the one who has the power to carry on your work after you leave the castle."

"But . . . he's impossible! He's too stubborn. He will never listen to me—"

"Then you must find some way to make him listen."

"But . . ." Francine stopped and took a deep breath. "But he's gone. He went to court." She blanched. "And he said he would not return until after the date of my wedding."

"Hmm. That is a problem. But perhaps you could go to court, too."

Francine shook her head. "I don't think so. When I asked him if I could, he said no."

"You asked to go with him?"

The heat returned to Francine's cheeks. "Only because I thought you might be there. But it's too late anyway. He's gone."

"It's never too late."

Francine stared at Anne. "You mean follow him? I don't know if I should. He would be furious."

"How can he object? It's none of his business." Anne smiled. "I have been summoned to court also. I merely stopped here on my way. If I choose to take along a female companion, what can Garrick say?"

Francine hesitated. She was afraid that if she suddenly turned up at court, he might think that she had changed her mind about being his mistress. But then again, perhaps he wouldn't think that at all. He *had* told her before he left that it was her last chance to go to bed with him. She would just have to explain that she'd had to come in order to get home in time for her wedding.

"Very well," Francine said slowly. "I will go with you to court.

But inwardly, she was still a trifle worried.

What *would* Garrick say?

Chapter 13

"YOU STUBBORN, MULE-headed, disobedient, troublemaking wench!" Garrick said through clenched teeth.
"Do you know what you have done?"

Francine, waiting in line to be presented to the king, stuck
her nose up in the air. "Yes, I know," she hissed under cover
of the herald's announcements. "I have come to court for a
short visit before I leave. Lady Anne was kind enough—unlike some people—to bring me along."

Garrick cast an exasperated look at Anne who stood several feet in front of them, whispering to an acquaintance.
"You stupid little innocent," he said. "Did you never ask
yourself why I wouldn't take you?"

"You mean besides your ridiculous idea that I might force
my way into your bed?"

"Obviously you know nothing of King John's reputation,"
he said, ignoring her facetious question. "He possesses the
worst faults of all the Plantagenet kings—an unpredictable
temper, overweening arrogance, and an insatiable appetite
for women. And he has no scruples about taking what he
wants."

Involuntarily, Francine glanced toward the head of the
line. It was very late in the evening—the court apparently

kept late hours—and the light was dim, but through the crowd of people, she could see the king sitting in a large chair on a dais about fifty feet away. From this distance, he looked short, fat, and old.

A laugh bubbled up in Francine's throat as she turned back to Garrick. "You can't be serious. He looks perfectly harmless. Besides, I'm hardly the kind of woman that's going to excite him into a frenzy of lust."

Garrick's gaze swept over her, his gaze lingering at her breasts and hips, before coming up to meet her eyes. "You underestimate yourself."

Heat rose in her cheeks. She was no femme fatale—but Garrick certainly seemed to think she was. What was it he'd said? That he ached with wanting her?

"Oh, what nonsense," she said, whether to him or herself, she wasn't sure. He probably said that to every woman he was trying to get into his bed. "John is a king. Why would he have to take an unwilling woman? There must be women lining up to sleep with him."

Garrick snorted. "Willing, unwilling—females are all the same to John. Prudent men keep their women out of view of the king."

"I'm not your woman."

"You're under my protection."

"I assure you, I can take care of myself as far as the king is concerned. Now will you please go away? People are looking at us."

With one final glare, Garrick did as she requested. From the corner of her eye, she watched him stalk over to the side of the room and stand there, arms folded across his chest, along with the other spectators.

Francine turned her shoulder and looked around the room, pretending to be absorbed in the hall's interior decoration. About twice as large as Pelsworth's hall, the room was also much more richly decorated. Vivid tapestries hung on the walls—much brighter than she would have expected with their red, gold, blue, green, and purple hues unfaded by time. Painted into the plaster on the wall above the king's chair was a huge map of what Francine supposed was the world—

although it showed only Europe, Africa, and Asia and was
wildly inaccurate.

"Lady Anne of Pelsworth and Lady Francine Peabody,"
the herald intoned in French.

Aware of Garrick's malevolent stare, Francine accompanied Anne up the steps and copied the curtsey the older
woman made.

"Lady Anne, what a pleasure to see you again."

The king also spoke in French, Francine noticed. At
Pelsworth, everyone spoke what she guessed was some early
form of English. But here at the English court, everyone
spoke French, apparently.

How weird.

"You are as beautiful as ever," the king continued.

"And you are as charming as always, sire," Anne replied.

Anne continued to chat with the king, giving Francine a
chance to study him more closely. He was more impressive
than she'd thought at first. His gray hair had a few streaks of
red left; his pale, green eyes were sharp and calculating; and
he was richly dressed in a scarlet robe lined with white fur,
jewels studding his belt and shoes, and rings on every finger,
including his thumbs.

"And now, sire, may I present my companion, Lady
Francine Peabody."

Suddenly, she found herself the target of that cold, green
gaze.

In spite of herself, Francine shivered, noticing the ruth-
lessness of those eyes. Perhaps Garrick's warning had not
been so foolish after all. . . .

"Lady Francine Peabody," John said, frowning slightly. "I
have not heard of her before. Who were her parents and
where is she from?"

"She was reared in Wales, sire, before I took her into my
care." Anne lowered her voice. "Her mother was a dear
friend of mine. Lady Francine is the result of a liaison between my friend and her lover. Her husband was insanely
jealous so she sent the child to me for safekeeping and swore
me to secrecy."

"Such a promise cannot apply to your sovereign. Tell me who her parents are."

Anne hesitated, then leaned forward and whispered in John's ear.

His eyes widened. "Ahhh. I see. A romantic tale. And very fitting that such a lovely young woman should be the result. Come closer, child, and kiss my hand."

Francine, distracted from wondering what Anne had told the king, almost grimaced. Did she really have to kiss this old man's hand? She glanced at Anne, who gave her a faint nod. Reluctantly, Francine moved forward and knelt before the king. Taking his cold, white hand in hers, she kissed the air above it. She was about to back away when she felt a slight pressure on her palm. The king was squeezing her hand! Snatching her fingers from his, she retreated quickly.

Something sparked in those cold green eyes. He observed her for a moment more before turning to a courtier standing at his side. "Where is Lady Francine lodged?"

"With the queen's ladies, your majesty."

"Hmm, that will never do. A lady of such extraordinary birth should have a private chamber. Put her in the Rose Chamber."

The courtier hesitated. "Your pardon, sire, but you arranged for Lady Alice to take that room when she arrives tomorrow."

"Find another place for her," John said carelessly. "Oh, and make certain Lady Anne and Lady Francine are seated at my table at the feast tomorrow."

"And Sir Garrick," Lady Anne inserted, rather boldly, Francine thought.

But John only nodded and dismissed them with a little wave of his hand.

The courtier, his face expressionless, bowed to Francine. "This way, my lady."

Francine followed him willingly, relieved to be away from the king and looking forward to getting some sleep.

Her new room was a small antechamber off of a much larger room. The walls were painted in red-and-white squares resembling masonry blocks, and in the middle of each one was a painted rose. The bed had a feather mattress, and there was a fire in the hearth.

Compared with the sleeping arrangements at Pelsworth, this was the height of luxury.

She should have been delighted with the room, but instead, she felt strangely . . . bereft.

She undressed slowly, trying to pinpoint the source of the feeling. Maybe it was just that Winchester Castle was a new place, with new people and unfamiliar things. She'd grown used to Pelsworth Castle.

Or maybe it was because the room was so quiet. She'd grown used to the grunts and snores—and various other noises—of the dormitory-style hall at Pelsworth.

Or maybe it was because she felt so isolated. Somehow, in the time she'd spent at Pelsworth, she'd grown used to being constantly surrounded by people, as if she were part of a large family.

Or maybe it was because she couldn't forget Garrick's warning about John, or the way the king had squeezed her hand. . . .

Oh, how silly, she scolded herself. Garrick was a worry-wart, and the king was a harmless old man. She wasn't going to think any more about either one of them.

In spite of the fire, the room was cold. There were no mats or rushes on the floor, and by the time Francine was ready for bed, her feet felt like ice cubes. Wishing she had house slippers, she hurried across the cold stones to lock the door. Just to be on the safe side, she told herself. Leaving the candle on the mantel lit—in case she needed to use the chamber pot in the middle of the night—she rushed over to the bed and climbed in.

Unlike her bed at Pelsworth, this mattress was supported by ropes that sagged in the middle. As a result, when she lay down, she was pulled to the center where she immediately sank into the depths of the mattress. It was like being swallowed whole by the Pillsbury Doughboy.

But at least it was warm, she thought, thrusting her toes into the feathery billows. She closed her eyes.

The room really was quiet, she thought. Everyone must

still be in the hall. She could have gone back there, but she found it a little intimidating. Everyone seemed to know everyone else. They stood in small groups, laughing and whispering, and staring at various individuals—at *her*. In spite of Anne's presence, she'd felt awkward and self-conscious. She'd actually been glad when she first saw Garrick approaching.

His appearance had caught her off guard. After what had passed between them, she hadn't been sure how she would react to seeing him again. The reality was a shock. Dressed in a deep-green robe that made his eyes seem less gray, with his black hair neatly combed and his jaw still clean-shaven, he'd been stunningly handsome—enough so that her heart had actually beat a little bit faster.

His first words had quickly brought her to her senses, however. Under his attractive exterior, he was still the Barbarian of Pelsworth Castle. It was just like him to try to scare her with lurid stories of the king. She doubted there was any truth to them. No way would the king, with a bevy of beautiful maidens at his disposal, be interested in her.

Although, there *had* been that squeeze on her hand. And the way he'd looked at her when she backed away. But he probably squeezed everyone's fingers and gazed lustfully at all the women. That didn't mean he was going to come knocking at her door—

A knock sounded on the door.

She froze in terror. Dear heaven. Could it be the king? Had Garrick been right after all?

She clutched the edge of the sheet, tempted to pull it over her head and pretend she wasn't there. But what if he had a key?

"Francine!" a familiar voice hissed. "Open the door!"

She released the sheet and turned to stare at the door.

"Francine!"

She gripped the sheet again—only this time, her hands formed fists. What was *he* doing here, knocking on her door at this time of night? He'd scared her half to death, the big goon.

"Francine, open this door at once or we'll both be in trouble!"

Scowling, she struggled her way out of the feather mattress, stomped over to the door, and opened it. Before she could say a word, Garrick brushed by her, pushed the door shut, and marched into the room.

"What are you doing?" she demanded. "Get out of here!"

"No," he said flatly. "I must protect you from the king."

Francine put her hands on her hips. "The king is not here. I doubt he will be, either."

Garrick's gaze fell to her breasts. Belatedly aware that she was wearing only her chemise, she quickly folded her arms over her chest. The chemise covered her from neck to wrist to knee, and she was sure he couldn't see anything in the flickering candlelight, but still . . .

"John's chambers are only a short distance from here," Garrick said coldly, as if she hadn't just caught him ogling her. "Which is no doubt the reason he put you in this room."

"I don't believe you. I think you made the whole thing up to scare me."

"I assure you, I made nothing up." His eyes were like flinty chips. "If you weren't so stupidly stubborn you would see that I am but trying to help you."

"Help me—ha! Ever since I came to Pelsworth Castle, you've been trying to get rid of me. You've been rude, obnoxious and . . . and obnoxious!"

"I would say 'tis more rude and obnoxious to invite people to a bunch of silly classes and tell them how to think and act."

"My classes were *not* silly—and everyone who attended benefited from them. It's just a shame that the one person who needed them the most didn't attend—*you*."

"I would say 'tis a greater shame that you didn't learn from them yourself. Never in my life have I met such a shrew. . . ."

"Oh? Well, that certainly didn't stop you from trying to get me into your bed!"

"A mistake on my part—and one that will not be repeated, I assure you. I would rather bed Medusa of Greek legend than a vixen like you."

"Medusa is probably the only woman you could get to sleep with you, you big, overgrown—"

A soft tapping at the door interrupted her tirade.

"Lady Francine? Little dove! Open the door!"

Francine froze. She darted a glance at Garrick who was looking at her with grim triumph. "Now do you believe me?" he whispered harshly.

"What should I do?" she asked, panic-stricken.

Garrick folded his arms across his chest. "Answer the door. You cannot ignore the king."

In great trepidation, Francine opened the door a crack. John stood outside. As she'd suspected, he was at eye level with her, although the crown he wore made him appear taller. He also wore a red velvet robe and matching slippers.

She curled her frozen toes against the cold stone floor. "Oh, Your Majesty! What a surprise! Is something wrong?"

"No, nothing, my dove," he said, smiling at her. "But I feel it is my duty to, er, know all of my subjects well. Let me in."

"Um, I was just about to go to bed. Couldn't this wait until tomorrow?"

"No, my dear, it can't. Open the door."

John might be short and fat and old, but he wasn't a king for nothing. The absolute authority in his voice made Francine fall back. Before she could stop him, he stepped into the room and shut the door. "Now, little dove, as I was saying—"

"Ahem."

With a whirl that parted his robe and revealed a glimpse of naked white flesh underneath, John turned to where Garrick was standing on the other side of the bed.

"Garrick!" the king exclaimed, quickly adjusting his robe. "What are you doing here?"

"Visiting my mistress."

Francine stiffened. Why, the dirty dog! After calling her a vixen and a shrew and saying he'd rather sleep with Medusa than her, he now tried to claim they were lovers?

The king looked astonished. "She is? But I thought—"

"You should know better than to listen to court gossip, sire."

John frowned. "That is true." He glanced at Francine and his gaze turned lustful again. "Surely you have no objection to sharing—"

"I don't think it would be wise, sire. The woman has the pox."

John drew back. "God's toenail!" But then a hint of suspicion flashed in his eyes. "I wonder that you would couple with her, if that is true."

"Alas," Francine interjected sweetly. "He is the one who gave it to me."

It was Garrick's turn to stiffen. He bared his white teeth in a wolflike imitation of a smile. "No, no, sweeting, you are confused. What I gave you has another name entirely, my sweet innocent." To the king, he said, "Because of my journey to Jerusalem and fighting against the infidels, I am immune to the pox."

John retreated to the door, his face inscrutable. "Perhaps I will wait until later to have our little conversation, Lady Francine. I just remembered some matters of state I must attend to."

As soon as he was gone, Francine turned to glare at Garrick. "Was that really necessary?"

Garrick was frowning thoughtfully at the door through which the king had just passed. But at her words, he turned to her. "I believe so. Although I'm not certain he believed me. John is no fool." He began removing his surcote. "I will have to spend the night here."

"What?!" Francine exclaimed. "There's no way I'm going to let you sleep in here with me."

"You'd rather face the king?" Garrick demanded.

"Well . . ." Darn, he had her there. "You'll have to sleep on the floor."

He gave her a hard look. "I have no intention of sleeping on the floor."

She glared at him. "Then I will."

"If that is what you wish to do." He yawned. "Although if the king comes in and finds you there, he will know that we lied."

She increased the velocity of her glare to no effect. She

was tempted to sleep on the floor anyway, but she was afraid he was right about the king. Not to mention that her toes were in danger of getting frostbite. But she decided she'd better set the ground rules right up front.

"If you try to touch me, I'll . . . I'll Bobbitize you, I swear."

"I have no idea what that means, but I assure you, Lady Francine, you have nothing to worry about," he said, his voice ice cold as he removed his robe and shirt. "Whatever desire I had for you is completely dead."

Francine averted her gaze from his bare chest. She wasn't sure whether to be insulted or relieved at his words. With a flounce, she turned her back and climbed into bed.

A moment later he blew out the candle and slid in next to her. He immediately rolled on top of her.

"You lecher! Get off me! Get off!" Arms flailing, she tried to dislodge his suffocating weight.

The weight lifted. He climbed out of the bed. "For God's sake, calm yourself. 'Tis the mattress that caused me to roll to the middle."

Reaching out, she grabbed the edge of the bed frame and pulled herself toward the side of the mattress. He got back into the bed, and she felt the mattress shift as the dip in the middle inexorably pulled him down. She clutched the side of the bed more tightly to prevent herself being sucked in after him.

She clung there, not daring to let go, mentally preparing herself for the least suggestion of impropriety on his part.

But he was silent, and after a while, when he made no move toward her in the dark, she was fairly certain he'd fallen asleep.

She relaxed a little, although she still had to hold on tightly to the bed frame. Sharing a bed with Garrick was very different from sharing one with Edith. For one thing, he did not move around like Edith. For another, he was much warmer. Even though he wasn't touching her, she could feel the heat radiating from his body.

She could smell him, too. He must have taken a bath sometime today, because he didn't smell as sweaty as usual.

In fact, he'd apparently washed with some kind of scented soap, because he smelled faintly of bay leaves.

His presence was vaguely comforting—because she felt safe from the king, she hastily assured herself. And maybe because she'd grown used to sharing a bed. . . .

He rolled over and the bare flesh of his back came in contact with her shoulder.

She stiffened. Had he done that on purpose? He seemed to be asleep. She bit her lip, trying to decide whether she should wake him up and warn him not to do that again.

But he was still.

She stayed awake for a long time to make certain he didn't try anything.

He didn't.

He was a very quiet sleeper, his breathing only slightly louder than when he was awake.

It was very late when she finally fell asleep.

Francine woke the next morning to find herself alone in the middle of the bed. Blinking, she looked around the room for a moment before slowly pushing back the covers and rising to her feet.

In daylight, it seemed unbelievable that the king had actually come to her room last night. It was even more mind-boggling to think that she'd shared a bed with Garrick—and nothing had happened.

She supposed she would have to thank him for being such a perfect gentleman. If he had been her brother, he could not have been more respectful.

A tiny frown knit her brow as she dressed. Actually, now that she thought about it, wasn't it a bit odd for a barbarian to be *such* a gentleman? Even a modern man would probably at least have attempted a pass. With his brutish instincts, she would have thought Garrick wouldn't be able to control himself. Especially since he'd claimed to ache with wanting her.

Francine sank onto the edge of the bed, her shoes in her hands. Obviously, he didn't feel that way anymore. He must have really meant it when he told her that any desire he'd felt for her was dead. It certainly hadn't taken much to kill it off. He now apparently found her completely undesirable.

An old shriveling worry took possession of her. Was there something wrong with her? Was there some flaw in her looks or personality that made men avoid her?

You're an attractive, desirable woman, she told herself silently, repeating the mantra she'd learned from an affirmations tape she'd bought once when Stuart had been urging her to lose weight and she'd been feeling particularly fat and ugly. The king of England had just tried to get into her bed— what further proof did she need of her sex appeal?

But somehow, in spite of repeating the affirmation several times, she still felt uncertain. The king didn't seem to count—from what Garrick had said, John didn't sound too picky. Besides, she really didn't care about the king. She only cared about normal males, like . . . like the boys in high school. None of them had found her attractive. She'd never even had a serious relationship until she met Stuart.

Stuart—thank heaven for Stuart. *He* found her attractive. To prove it, he'd even asked her to marry him. She shouldn't be worrying about anyone else. Everyone else was unimportant.

Especially Garrick. She didn't care what he thought of her. Nor did she care whether he found her desirable or not. The only person she cared about was Stuart.

Although, come to think of it, *he* had never tried to get her to go to bed with him, either. . . .

Oh, she was being ridiculous. Impatient with herself for her melancholy thoughts, Francine yanked on her shoes and stood up. Of course Stuart loved and desired her. He was just waiting until after the wedding.

And speaking of the wedding . . . there wouldn't be one if she didn't civilize Garrick in the next week or so.

Oh, dear heaven.

She sank back down on the bed. She'd thought it difficult to polish the manners of the men-at-arms, to get the kitchen cleaned up and the steam bath built.

But what was she supposed to do with Garrick?

Garrick was impossible—not so much because of his manners or habits, but because of who and what he was. The men-at-arms were boys by comparison—easily influenced by promises of food and women. Garrick, on the other hand, was a Medieval warrior: a man who'd grown up in a harsh, violent world and managed to survive. How was she supposed to influence him? The idea that she might be able to seemed laughable.

Francine rose to her feet. She needed help, no doubt about it. Perhaps the time had come for her to confide in Anne fully. She didn't quite trust the older woman; she was pretty sure Garrick was right when he said Anne knew more than she let on. But at this point, Francine had few options. She had to speak to Anne.

She went out into the large chamber that led to her room. Rafael was there, dressed in his scarlet-and-yellow minstrel's outfit and playing his lute for several women who listened while they sewed.

"Merry Christmas, Lady Francine!" one of the ladies called. "Come sit next to me!"

Francine had forgotten that today was Christmas. In spite of the holly and ivy decorating all the rooms in the castle, it didn't feel like Christmas. She wasn't in the mood for festivities.

She needed to talk to Anne, but she didn't want to be rude to the ladies, either. Hiding her reluctance, she sat next to a woman who introduced herself as Lady Violet and named the others present. The women all trained laserlike gazes on Francine.

"Everyone is talking about you," said Lady Violet. She was blond, her face round and innocent—until one looked into the calculating blue eyes. "Is it true you're the daughter of the archbishop of Canterbury and a Welsh princess?"

Francine choked. "It's impossible for me to say," she temporized.

"It must be true if Lady Anne says so," Lady Alice said, not looking up from the gold thread she was embroidering onto an altar cloth. She had sallow skin and heavily rouged cheeks. "Lady Anne knows everything that has gone on in this kingdom for the last twenty years. She has the ear of the king—and every other powerful man in the realm. You are very fortunate to have her as your mentor, Lady Francine."

"Uh, yes," Francine said. "She's been very kind to me."

"Although I hear she was not too pleased by the king's interest in you," said Lady Rowena, a woman with a prominent jaw and sharp teeth. She reminded Francine of a piranha. "I must say, I think it a trifle treacherous of you to steal the king's . . . ear away from her."

The ladies laughed.

Francine clasped her hands in her lap. "I haven't stolen the king's ear—or any other part of him, either. He has no interest in me."

The ladies snickered in disbelief.

"I don't understand it." A slight pout around her mouth, Lady Violet looked Francine up and down. "How can someone so unremarkable have intrigued not just the king, but Sir Garrick as well?"

Lady Rowena leaned forward. "Tell us, Lady Francine, is it true that you're *intimately* acquainted with Sir Garrick?"

Francine, looking around the circle of avid, curious faces, felt uneasy. She couldn't deny their insinuation without risking the king hearing of it. "I suppose you could say we are . . . friends."

The women burst into laughter. "Friends . . . ha, ha!" Lady Alice chortled. "I've never heard it called *that* before."

"How amusing," Lady Violet said, her smile a trifle sour.

"And how delightful to have both Garrick *and* the king panting for you," Lady Alice said, wiping her eyes.

Flushing, Francine rose to her feet. "Excuse me, ladies, but I'm afraid I must go. I must find Lady Anne."

She left the room, burningly aware of the titters behind her.

"Lady Francine, wait!" Rafael called.

She stopped, keeping her face averted as he approached. Once he'd reached her side, he said quietly, "Don't pay any attention to those silly women. They have nothing better to do than sit and gossip all day."

She smiled a little weakly. "Thank you, Rafael. I don't

care about them. I . . . I was just a little taken off guard. They seemed so friendly at first."

"Beware false friends." His bright-blue eyes were kind. "You are looking for Lady Anne?"

"Yes, I am. Do you know where she is?"

"I believe she is closeted with the queen for the day."

Francine's shoulders slumped a little at this news. "Oh, I see. Thank you, Rafael."

She started to turn away, but Rafael stopped her. "Is there some way I could be of service?"

Francine hesitated. She didn't know Rafael very well. But maybe he *could* help her. Maybe he could give her a man's perspective.

"Rafael, what would you say is the true hallmark of civilization?"

"Government," he said without hesitation.

Francine frowned. "But how can a single person influence the government?"

"Through politics, of course."

"Of course," Francine echoed. But she didn't think politics could help her in this situation. "I'm thinking of something on a more personal level—what distinguishes a civilized man from an uncivilized one? Apart from manners, that is."

Rafael stroked his chin. "Education, doubtlessly. Education gives a man the ability to reason, to discuss an issue logically, without resorting to violence."

Violence. Yes, that was the problem, Francine thought. Garrick had been exposed to violence his entire life. It had hardened him, desensitized him. She couldn't give him an entire education in one week—but could she make him see the evil of violence?

"Do you know where Garrick is?" she asked.

Rafael picked at a lute string. "I believe some of the lords and knights are having a practice joust in preparation for the tournament later this week. Doubtless you will find him in the lists."

Francine frowned. "Jousting! Isn't that dangerous—and violent?"

"Yes, indeed," Rafael agreed. "Men are often hurt, maimed, or even killed."

A sudden tightness squeezed at her heart. She remembered the scars on Garrick's body, the injury to his leg. How could he be so reckless? She had to stop him—in fact, that might be the answer—to get him to see the senselessness of tournaments and other dangerous sports. . . .

Impulsively she put her hand on the minstrel's arm. "Thank you, Rafael. You've been a great help to me."

Rafael patted her hand.

" 'Tis always a pleasure to serve you, Lady Francine."

Outside a cold wind was blowing and the field was full of icy puddles, but the men jousting in the lists didn't seem to care. Covered with mud, yelling and howling like banshees, they rode past each other with their swords drawn, swinging viciously at their opponents. Men fell to the ground with appalling regularity.

Francine scanned the men standing in clusters at the perimeter of the field, searching for Garrick. There was no sign of him and she was about to give up when a tall, helmeted knight carrying a blue shield with a gold dragon and a white castle painted on it mounted an ebony horse and whirled around to face the opposite end of the field.

A knight on an enormous white horse waited there. He held a black shield, painted with a picture of a huge fist squeezing a heart.

A trumpet blew.

The two knights took off, heading directly toward each other. For one terrible moment, Francine thought they would crash. Her heart in her throat, she watched in horror as the two knights met at the center of the field. A horse shrieked, metal clashed, and clumps of mud flew through the air. The blue-shielded knight seemed to waver in his saddle.

But then, he struck another blow, catching the black-shielded knight off guard. The unfortunate knight tilted then toppled backwards, hitting the ground with a crash.

The man on the ground lay stunned for a moment. Then he sat up and took off his helmet. Legs spraddled, he glared up at the man who'd knocked him down. "Damn you, Garrick! Have you ever in your life lost a joust?"

Garrick flipped back the visor of his helmet and grinned down at the man. "Not since I was fifteen, Robert. I would think you would have learned your lesson by now and quit challenging me."

"Someday I will get the better of you," Robert grumbled, rising to his feet.

"Perhaps when we are doddering old men playing chess by the fire."

They spoke during a lull in the wind, and the words carried clearly to Francine. She could hardly believe her ears. The two had just tried their best to kill each other, and now they were talking and joking as if they were the best of friends!

More convinced than ever that she was right, that she needed to stop Garrick from participating in this type of careless violence, she waved at him, trying to catch his attention.

"Garrick! Garrick!"

The wind whipped up again, pushing her against the rail of the fence. Although Garrick didn't hear her, Robert apparently did. He glanced toward her, then spoke to Garrick. She couldn't hear what he said this time since the wind carried his voice in the opposite direction. She could see the way Garrick tensed, however.

He glanced toward her, his hesitation plain. But then he nudged his horse and rode toward her. The great black animal stopped a short distance away, snorting and pawing the ground.

Francine drew back a little from the fearsome beast. "I must speak to you," she said to Garrick.

He held the impatient horse's reins tightly. "Later, Francine. I am to face Geoffrey de Mandeville in a moment."

"But it's important," she insisted.

"Then tell me now. Quickly."

She bit her lip. She knew she had little chance of convincing him to quit the joust on the spot. But she at least had to try.

"Garrick," she said in a low voice. "You must stop this madness right now."

He frowned. "What madness?"

"This juvenile jousting madness! Can't you see how dangerous it is? You could be killed!"

"You are concerned for my safety? I am touched, Francine."

"I . . . I am concerned for the safety of everyone involved. I'm appalled by the violence. Will you please stop, Garrick?"

He stared at her, an odd look in his eyes. "You are very persuasive when you ask so prettily."

Hope sprouted within her. "Then you'll stop?"

"No. But if you ask me to wear your favor I might accept."

"My favor!" Francine scowled, the faint hope burned to a crisp by her anger. "You can take my favor and stuff it up your—"

"Now, now." Laughter gleamed in his eyes. "Do not forget how violence appalls you."

The trumpet blew before she could think of a sufficiently scathing response. With a smile and a nod, he wheeled his horse around and rode back to the end of the field.

His horse's hooves kicked up mud, spattering a few specks on Francine's cheek. Silently cursing both Garrick and his horse, she took out her handkerchief and wiped the mud away.

Clutching the handkerchief in her fist, she watched as Garrick prepared to ride at his next opponent. Why did he insist on being so foolish? And how would she ever stop him? He didn't seem to care at all that he was risking his life.

The trumpet blew again and the two knights set off toward each other. Unable to bear it, Francine raised her hands to cover her eyes. As she did so, the wind whipped the handkerchief from her loosened grip.

She watched open-mouthed as the handkerchief flew straight toward Garrick and plastered itself across the eye slit of his visor just as he reached the center of the field.

The horses whinnied. Metal clashed. Clumps of mud flew everywhere. But this time it was Garrick who crashed to the ground.

Francine stared at the motionless figure on the ground, her hands covering her mouth. Dear God, he was dead. And it was all her fault. Oh, dear heaven, she would never forgive herself. . . .

Garrick's leg twitched.

Slowly, he rolled over, rose to his feet, and pulled off his helmet. He staggered a bit. Gaining his balance, he took a step forward, then paused, looking down at the ground. He bent over and picked up a muddy, white square of cloth. His eyes narrowed.

He turned and stared across the field directly at Francine.

If only she hadn't embroidered that stupid F on her handkerchief, Francine thought later that night as she clutched the edge of the bed to keep from rolling to the center. It had seemed like a good idea at the time, an easy project to practice the embroidery stitches Edith had taught her. Who would have guessed that one wobbly purple letter of the alphabet could cause her so much trouble?

If it hadn't been for that F, Garrick never would have known it was her handkerchief.

Francine glanced over her shoulder to where he was undressing. Firelight limned the smooth silhouette of his broad shoulders and muscled legs and arms as he pulled off a shoe. She turned her gaze back to the wall. He'd barely spoken to her at the Christmas festivities earlier, and he hadn't said a word since entering the room.

He slid into the bed, sinking into the middle. Francine held tightly to the side of the bed. She waited until he settled himself, then took a deep breath.

"I'm sorry about what happened this morning, Garrick," she whispered.

For an endless moment, there was silence. Her stomach shrivelled into a tight little knot.

But then she heard a long sigh.

"Very well. I accept your apology."

Relief flowed through her. Looking over her shoulder at his dark silhouette, she said in a rush, "I honestly didn't mean for my handkerchief to fly in your face. How could I? What are the chances of that happening? But even if I *could* have made it do that, I wouldn't have. I truly am sorry."

"I believe you, Francine. In truth, the same thought had occurred to me once my anger cooled."

"It was really weird, wasn't it? That handkerchief seemed like it was aiming for you. It almost seemed like a sign from God that you should stop jousting."

"Francine . . . ," he growled.

"Okay, okay. It was just a thought. I guess I've been listening to too many stories about omens. What did you think about that friar's story at the feast?"

"The dream he claimed was a message from God? Pure drivel."

"I thought it was very interesting—the sword-wielding stars fighting against the sun. But why did King John get so upset?"

"Dreams of omen make him uneasy. He nearly lost England because he disregarded one such prophecy. Or so many believe."

Francine shook her head at the gullibility of people in the Medieval era. But then again, such superstition seemed almost natural in a place where Christmas was celebrated by eating a boar's head, drinking wassail from a great bowl, and playing games like Hunt the Slipper and Hoodman's Blind. . . .

Her hold on the edge of the bed relaxed for a moment. Before she could prevent herself, she rolled down on top of Garrick.

"Oh!" she exclaimed as his arms automatically came up around her.

They both lay frozen.

Then, coming to her senses, she quickly extricated herself from his hold and returned to her perch at the side of the bed. "I'm sorry," she muttered.

He didn't answer her.

The room was very quiet.

It stayed that way for the rest of the night.

Chapter 14

THE NEXT FEW days was a series of entertainments—sports, games, plays called "mummeries," and feasts. Francine would have been horrified by what went on if she'd had enough energy. But nearly sleepless nights were taking their toll on her—she found it difficult to be shocked by anything.

She did manage to drum up some disgust at one feast where the men all started discussing the glories of the Crusades. Each one had to stand up and tell a story about his bravery during the fighting. To hear them talk, Francine was surprised there was a single "infidel" left anywhere. Most had witnessed a miracle of one sort or another, and told about that also.

After their argument, Francine had avoided bringing up the topic of violence with Garrick, even though she knew he was still practicing in the lists every day. She refrained partly because she'd noticed a certain savage tension in him during the last few days. She suspected he was not sleeping well, either—his eyes were red-rimmed, and once or twice she'd noticed him nodding off over the dessert at some feast or another.

But she knew she couldn't avoid the subject much

longer—the day of her wedding loomed closer and closer. Deciding that the men's boastful tales of the Crusades would be the perfect segue into the topic, she went to her room early that night and waited for Garrick.

She'd fallen asleep by the time the door finally opened, and she sat up, startled.

"Who's there?" she asked, thinking for a frightening moment that it was the king.

" 'Tis I," Garrick said in a slurred voice.

She heard his fumbling movements and curses as he struggled to remove his clothes. He stomped loudly across the floor, and then a soft glow filled the room as he lit a candle from the fire and put it on the mantel. He untied his breeches and shucked them off. Clad only in his drawers, he stumbled over to the bed and lay down on the mattress with a deep sigh. He smelled of wine.

"Garrick," she said.

He didn't respond.

"Garrick," she repeated, more loudly.

Still no response.

"Garrick!" She poked him in the shoulder with her finger.

"What do you want, Francine?" His voice was suddenly very clear and not very friendly.

She was a bit taken aback by his tone. She wondered if she should wait for a more propitious time—but knowing Garrick, she doubted there would be such an occasion.

"I want to talk to you about the Crusades."

"The Crusades," he repeated. "Could this discussion possibly wait until morning?"

"No, it can't. I really need to ask you something about the Crusades."

"Then ask it." He sounded half-asleep.

"Why do men fight like that?" she asked. "Why can't you settle your differences some other way?"

"What other way is there?"

"Sitting down and talking, for one."

" 'Tis not always feasible to sit and talk."

"Or not convenient?" she asked. "Listening to those men

tonight, I think they enjoyed going off to Jerusalem and fighting."

Garrick made a noise that was half laugh, half snort. "Most of those men never went near the Holy Land. They bought their badges in France and came home. They have no idea what it's like to fight against the Saracens."

The weary bitterness of his voice made her grow still. "And what is it like?"

" 'Tis hell," he said grimly. "Hell here on earth."

His words startled her. She stared down at his face, barely illuminated by the soft glow of the candle. "Then why did you go?"

He was silent. She heard the crackle of the fire and muffled laughter from the room next door.

" 'Tis difficult for a woman to understand," he finally said. "It's a test of one's courage. Everyone knows the risks. To die in battle is an honor. To prove oneself in war is to gain power and riches, to win the respect of man and God alike."

"I hardly think God would approve of killing other people."

Garrick sighed. "Perhaps not. But I will do whatever is necessary to protect my own. And if that means fighting, then so be it."

"But—"

"You will not change my mind on this matter. Be silent, now, and let me sleep."

She was about to argue when she saw him grimace as if in pain. He reached down and rubbed his calf, a barely discernible groan escaping him.

Francine bit her lip. Was his injury acting up? It would be no surprise if it was, after the workout he had been giving it. What an idiot he was to be straining his bad leg jousting every day!

She knew he deserved whatever pain he was in. But in spite of her disapproval, she couldn't help saying, "I know a little bit about massage therapy. It would probably be very effective for someone with your problem."

He stiffened, his hand freezing on his calf. "I thought I

told you never to mention my—" He paused. In a different voice, he repeated, "Massage therapy?"

"Yes." Realizing that there was no translation for "massage therapy," Francine explained, "It's a method where I rub the affected part. My grandmother Peabody had very poor circulation in her feet and the doctor recommended massage once a week, more often if possible. We couldn't afford a real therapist at the time, so I learned how to do it. Would you like me to try?"

"Exactly which part would you rub?" he asked.

"Why, your calf, of course. Where you have your old injury. That's where the problem is, isn't it?"

He lay back on the mattress and put his forearm across his eyes, not speaking. After several long moments of silence, he finally said, "I would be most grateful if you would."

He didn't move, so Francine sat up and scooted down the mattress. She lifted his leg onto her lap and began to rub it.

He tensed involuntarily as she dug deep into the muscles of his leg. "Ahhh," he groaned. "That feels truly wonderful."

She continued rubbing. His leg was hard, all muscle, covered with coarse hair. There was an ugly scar that distorted the skin.

She touched the scar lightly. "Where did you get this?"

"In Constantinople," he murmured. "Fighting the Saracens. It was a terrible battle. . . ."

His voice trailed off.

Francine rubbed for a few minutes more. The candle sputtered suddenly, then went out, casting the room into darkness. She became aware of a far-off voice, a sweet, clear contralto singing a psalm. She could hear the crackle of burning logs in the fireplace. One snapped, and a flame flared up, casting a streak of light across Garrick's sleeping face.

She stared at him a moment until the flame died down, casting the room back into darkness.

How odd it was, she thought, to be sharing a room with a man. To be alone with him in a small dark space while he slept. It felt so . . . intimate.

Shaking away the thought, she pushed his leg off her lap and climbed underneath the covers next to him.

Francine squinted at the handkerchief in front of her, trying to figure out where to set the next stitch in the unrecognizable animal she was embroidering. The small feat was beyond her. Sticking the needle haphazardly into the cloth, she leaned back in her chair and closed her burning eyes, resting them for just a second.

She'd barely slept at all last night. Every time she'd managed to doze off, Garrick woke, his leg cramping. Each time she'd rubbed it until he fell asleep again. It wasn't until he'd gotten up and left early in the morning that she'd been able to sleep. And that was only for an hour or two until she was roused out of bed by Anne, who wanted her to join the ladies at their sewing. Francine wouldn't have minded that too much, but as soon as she'd sat down, the older woman had flitted off somewhere else, leaving her to the tender mercies of the "ladies."

Francine's head lolled to the side, wrenching her awake.

Titters greeted her jerky movements.

Realizing she'd dozed off for a minute, Francine quickly glanced around the circle of women. They hadn't been paying much attention to her—they'd been too busy discussing court gossip—but now, to her dismay, she saw they were all staring at her.

The piranha-faced Lady Rowena smiled. "You seem tired, Lady Francine. Did you not sleep well last night?"

"With Sir Garrick in her bed, how could she sleep?" The circles of rouge on Lady Alice's cheeks seemed brighter.

Lady Violet sniffed delicately. "Very easily—if the rumors about Sir Garrick are true."

"What rumors?" Francine asked.

Lady Violet lowered her eyelashes demurely. "About Sir Garrick's . . . problem."

Francine stared at the woman's falsely innocent face. She knew that Garrick had snubbed Lady Violet a few times—but was the woman really so petty that she would spread stories when Garrick was so sensitive about his leg?

"The rumors are greatly exaggerated, I'm sure," she said coldly.

Lady Rowena's brows rose at her tone. "How exaggerated can they be? It sounds to me as though Garrick is but half a man."

Francine widened the scope of her glare to include both women. How could these women be so small-minded as to think less of someone because of one small weakness? If this was what the "ladies" of the Middle Ages were like, she didn't blame Garrick for being self-conscious about his injury.

"I haven't found him half a man at all," she told them emphatically. "His weakness makes little difference. I know a special rubbing technique that relieves the problem instantly."

Lady Violet's thread snapped; Lady Alice's altar cloth fell to the floor; Lady Rowena's needle pricked her finger.

"You've used this technique?" Lady Violet tried to rethread her needle, but failed.

"Yes. In fact, I used it four times last night—no, five times. Garrick responded . . . I mean the *muscle* responded every single time."

The women goggled at her. "Five times?" Lady Alice breathed, ignoring the altar cloth lying on the ground. "Lady Francine, would you tell us how to do it?"

"It's simple enough," Francine said. "You merely take the affected muscle in your hands and knead it as hard as you can—like bread dough."

"I would think that would hurt," Lady Rowena said, sucking her finger.

"It does at first," Francine admitted. "But Garrick was very grateful afterwards, believe me. Now if you'll excuse me, I must go."

As she closed the door, she heard a burst of chatter through the wooden panels.

"Silly women," she muttered and turned, almost bumping into Rafael.

"Ah, good morrow, Lady Francine," he said. "How goes your attempt to wean Sir Garrick from violence?"

"Not well." Realizing she held her embroidery in her clutched fist, she tried to smooth it out. "I spoke to him about quitting jousting, but he paid no attention. When my handkerchief flew in his face in the middle of his joust, I thought he might take it as a sign from God, but unfortunately, he's not the least bit superstitious."

Rafael made a slight choking noise. "It was your handkerchief that flew in his face? I had not heard that."

"I don't think anyone else knew. But anyway, then I spoke to him about not fighting, but he said there's no other way to protect what's his."

"How primitive." Rafael shook his head.

"Exactly. But now what can I do?"

"Perhaps you need to prove that other methods work better than violence."

Francine, folding her still-wrinkled sewing, gave him a doubtful glance. "That's a wonderful idea," she said as she slipped the embroidery into the pouch hanging from her belt. "But how?"

"Politics, my dear."

Before she could question him further, Rafael nodded and strolled into the room behind her.

Politics. Francine frowned. How on earth could politics help Garrick—or her?

She was still puzzling over the question later that night while sitting next to him at yet another feast. Dressed in a dark-green velvet tunic, he appeared completely at ease as he spoke to the elderly woman on his other side. Taking a bite of a pielike concoction that she thankfully didn't know the ingredients of, she wondered if she should encourage him to be more political. In spite of his meeting with Ranulf and de Gant, he seemed more interested in Pelsworth Castle and his affairs there than in anything else.

But perhaps that was the problem. Perhaps he needed to take a more active role in the government, develop a wider view of the world—

"I will never concede to these rebels," John's voice interrupted her thoughts. "They think to threaten me, to seize power for themselves—but it will never happen, I swear it!"

"Yea!" the diners around the table murmured.

"If they want to fight, let them come forward!" shouted someone down the table. "I will face them gladly!"

"Yea, yea!"

"We should hunt down the rebels and execute them!" yelled another man. "A few heads stuck on pikes above London Bridge will soon discourage this treason!"

"Yea, yea, yea. . . ."

"But, Sire." Francine's voice, sounding high and clear after the deep ones of the men, carried to every corner of the room. "Why not sit down and talk to these men first?"

There was silence around the table. Then . . .

"Ha, ha, ha!" Everyone burst into laughter.

The gentleman who'd recommended sticking the rebels' heads on pikes pounded his fist against his chest. "We are men—we fight. Talking is a woman's way."

"Actually, it is Sir Garrick's way. He agrees with me."

Silence fell again—but no one laughed this time. Everyone looked from the king to Garrick and back again. John's face was turning purple.

"You would have me treat with these rebels, Sir Garrick?"

All gazes flew to Garrick. He sat calmly in his chair, twirling the wine in his cup. "Sire, pay no attention to the woman. She has no understanding of the situation. She speaks with a simple tongue."

Everyone turned to stare at Francine. In spite of her dismay over the king's reaction to her words, she stiffened. A simple tongue? Was Garrick implying that she was an idiot? She opened her mouth.

"Sire!" Lady Anne, seated at the king's right, across the table from Francine, hastily intervened. "Is it not time for the dancing?"

John paused for a long moment, then nodded and rose to his feet. A sigh of relief seemed to go around the hall as everyone else stood and the minstrels in the gallery struck up a lively tune.

Out of the corner of his mouth, Garrick said to Francine, "Go to our chamber—and for God's sake, stay there!"

He strode off. Frowning, Francine started after him, but

Anne cornered her. Taking Francine's arm, she led her out of the hall.

"Lady Francine," Anne said in the relative quiet of an antechamber, "what on earth possessed you to speak so to the king?"

"I was hoping the idea would impress the king and cause him to think more highly of Garrick."

Francine's words surprised Anne, but pleased her enormously. "You were? That's wonderful, child. But I don't think putting words in Garrick's mouth was the best way to go about it. John is very touchy and wants to believe his men will back him without question in any fight."

"I see. I guess I really screwed things up for Garrick, then, didn't I?" Suddenly the tension of the episode she'd just caused, her worry about getting home in time to marry Stuart, and her lack of sleep for the last several days all caught up with her. She felt foolishly, dangerously on the verge of tears. "Oh, Anne! What can I do? I thought Rafael was right—that I needed to encourage Garrick to be less violent."

"Rafael!" Anne, leading Francine toward a window seat, stopped in her tracks. "What does he have to do with this?"

"He gave me a few ideas on how to civilize Garrick. First he suggested that I urge Garrick to quit jousting. . . ."

Anne's eyes narrowed. "Oh, did he? And did that work?"

"No. Garrick ignored me. Rafael explained that men often won't listen to women—"

"He's right about that," Anne muttered.

"—and that I should try to encourage Garrick to take a more active role in the government. But obviously that was a failure. Now I don't know what to do. I don't know how I can civilize Garrick."

"My dear," Anne said, "you are going about this all wrong."

"I am?"

"Yes. In the first place, you never should have asked a man for advice. Men don't understand civilization at all. They think it has to do with politics."

"Yes, that's what Rafael said."

"Ha! Politics is the surest and quickest way to lose your head. You must think like a woman. Think, Lady Francine. What is the *true* hallmark of civilization?"

Francine's brows knit in confusion for a moment, then they relaxed. "I see," she said slowly. "You're right, of course. I should have thought of it myself. Thank you, Lady Anne."

She left, a thoughtful expression on her face. Anne, smiling in satisfaction, watched her go.

"You look like the cat who ate the cream," a new voice said.

Anne turned to find that Rafael had entered the chamber silently and was standing by the door. "I'm sure I don't know what you mean," she said. She looked him up and down. "Must you always dress in such a ridiculous costume? You look like a clown. Why don't you find some better occupation? A *real* occupation, with responsibility. Maybe you should go into *politics. . . .*"

Rafael grinned. "Why, Anne! I didn't know you cared so much about me."

"Bah! You're not playing fair, Rafael, manipulating the girl like that."

"You're accusing *me* of being manipulative? I think that's a case of the pot calling the kettle black, my sweet. Besides, the advice I gave her was sound."

"Hmmph. Well, your little ploy has afforded you nothing. After tonight, you will have to admit the two of them are in love."

"After tonight?" Rafael studied her face. "What have you done, Anne?"

Anne smiled. "Nothing. Nothing at all. You'll have to excuse me now. I have an appointment with a lady who is interested in purchasing some of my herbs."

She swept away, and Rafael looked after her, stroking his chin thoughtfully. Then he set off to find Garrick.

Chapter 15

GARRICK APPROACHED THE bedchamber warily several hours later, uncertain what to expect.

After Rafael's warning that Francine was up to something and would likely try to trap him into marriage that very night, Garrick had found it difficult to concentrate on the dancing and other diversions. He'd been angry to have his long suspicion that Francine was part of Anne's matchmaking schemes confirmed. But in spite of his anger, he was also aware of a certain curiosity.

Exactly how did she plan to trap him into marriage?

No doubt she intended to seduce him into coupling with her in hope of getting herself with child. 'Twas a hoary old trick. But she'd obviously schemed long and well. Cleverly, she'd refused him several times, knowing that her elusiveness would only make him want her more. Then, by flirting with the king, she'd made it necessary for Garrick to share her bed—all the while protesting her innocence, of course—thus inflaming his desire to ever greater heights. Now that his lust had reached a fevered pitch, she was prepared to spring her trap.

What would she do? She might try to ply him with drink and alluring words. If that were the case, she would be sorely

disappointed—he could hold his liquor well and he was immune to sweet nothings. She would also be disappointed if
she thought anointing herself with some heady perfume, designed to drive him wild, would break his resolve to have
nothing to do with her.

No, likely she would realize those methods would be in-
sufficient. 'Twas more probable that she would make some
excuse about her chemise being soiled and would be waiting
in bed, stark naked, the sheet discreetly draped to reveal the
curves of her breasts and hips and thighs. . . .

He stopped at the bedchamber door, staring at the rough-
hewn wooden planks.

The last several nights, actually sleeping with her in her
bed, had been pure torture. In truth, he hadn't slept at all.
He'd lain awake night after night, fighting the nearly overwhelming demands of his body, trying to ignore the alluring
sweetness of her. Only by thinking of how she had spurned
him had he been able to restrain his desire. He would not
allow her to entrap him at this late date.

Grasping the knob, he silently eased open the door.

She was in bed, the covers drawn up around her neck, her
gaze fixed on the canopy above. Her hair had grown a few
inches since her arrival, and the candlelight cast a soft glow
on golden strands spread across the pillow. Her full, red lips
moved as she murmured to herself.

In spite of himself, Garrick felt his pulse quicken. She
must have prepared some seductive speech. And 'twas apparent she had nothing on under those blankets.

He closed the door with a *click*.

She jumped a little at the sound and looked toward the
door. Seeing him, she sat up and said in a welcoming voice,
"Garrick!"

As she sat up, the covers fell away, revealing her plain
chemise. Garrick looked from her slightly parted lips to her
pointed nipples, visible even through the sensible linen, and
back up to the smiling dark blue of her eyes. Ah. So she
planned to play the tease. His muscles tensed. He would have
to resist all her wiles.

"Come to bed, Garrick." She patted the mattress beside her. "I would like to . . . talk to you."

He hesitated a moment, then quickly stripped off his clothes. Although she discreetly averted her gaze, he saw her peek a time or two.

He got in bed, rolling to the middle of the mattress. He expected her to release her grip on the side board of the bed and roll on top of him, but she didn't. He waited for her to make her first move.

Before she could, however, there was a loud masculine yowl from the room next door.

She jumped a little and looked at the wall. "What was that?"

"I have no idea," Garrick said. "Go on."

She glanced doubtfully toward the wall where the sounds of shouting and crying and some thumping noises emerged, then turned her attention back to Garrick.

"Garrick," she said softly. "Have you ever heard the phrase, 'Do unto others as you would have them do unto you'?"

Garrick blinked. Yes, he'd heard the phrase. Although never in quite this context. Did she mean to imply that it was permissible to couple with her because she wanted it, too?

"Have you heard the phrase, 'Love thy neighbor'?"

Ah. Now this made more sense. His gaze traveled down to where the linen lay flat against her stomach and then rose a little at the mound between her thighs. "Yes," he answered, his voice a gruff whisper.

"Do you know what God said to Leviticus? He said, 'And he that is to be cleansed shall wash his clothes, and shave off all his hair, and wash himself in water, that he may be clean; and after that he shall come into the camp.'"

Garrick frowned. He'd already shaved his beard. Surely she didn't expect him to wash his clothes now? Her words were most odd. . . .

"And Amos 4:6: 'And the Lord God saith, "I have given you cleanness of teeth in all your cities.' "

"Lady Francine . . ."

"And Corinthians: 'Be not deceived . . . evil communications corrupt good manners . . .'"

"Lady Francine . . ."

"And 1 Samuel: 'Yet they had a file for the mattocks, and for the coulters, and for the forks—'"

"Lady Francine!"

Francine, concentrating intently on remembering all the verses she'd learned, looked up in surprise at his tone.

"Lady Francine," he said softly, grimly, "what is the point of all this?"

"I, um, I am trying to . . . help you."

"You are trying to help me," he repeated flatly. "How?"

She shifted uneasily. "Well, first I tried talking to you about jousting and fighting, but that didn't work," she said, not very cogently. "And then the politics, but that didn't help, either. Then Anne told me to ignore Rafael—"

"Rafael told you to talk to me about fighting and politics?"

"Uh . . . yes."

"I see." His voice frightened her a little. "And Anne told you not to listen to him?"

"Yes. She said I should think like a woman, not a man, and asked me to think of the great civilizing force of mankind, and then I realized what she meant. . . ."

"Forgive me for being dense, but could you please enlighten me?"

"Religion, of course. Although it took me a moment, too, to think of it."

"Religion," he repeated. "Hence the Bible verses."

"Yes. I spoke to the priest this evening, and there are lots of them that pertain to cleanliness and manners. Did I mention 1 Corinthians, 15:33? It says—"

"Lady Francine," he interrupted. His teeth came together in an audible snap. "If you do not wish to be beaten within an inch of your life, I suggest you quote no more Bible verses at me."

With that, he got up, dressed, and stalked out of the room, slamming the door behind him.

Francine gaped after him.

Outside the room, Garrick headed toward the hall where

Rafael was likely to be sleeping. Garrick had every intention of venting his anger on the minstrel, and sleeping there in the hall afterwards . . . as far away from Francine as possible.

Francine.

How could he have thought her capable of plotting to seduce him? The woman had no more idea of seduction than a newborn kitten. She was as maddeningly innocent as a lamb. She was lucky that some big gray wolf hadn't gobbled her up. . . .

He stopped in his tracks, remembering the king and his interest in Francine.

Garrick groaned. He couldn't leave her unprotected. Reluctantly, he retraced his steps and looked at the stone floor in front of her chamber. Resigned to his fate for the moment, he wrapped his cloak around himself and laid down on the hard, cold stones.

The situation had become intolerable. Having Francine around was like being stretched on the rack. Instead of thinking of his plans and his ambitions, his thoughts were constantly filled with the image of this troublesome woman. He couldn't endure this torture any longer.

He shifted his shoulders into a slightly less uncomfortable position.

Tomorrow, he would do what he should have done long ago.

The next morning, Garrick went searching for Rafael. He nodded as he passed several men standing in an awkward, knock-kneed manner, but they turned a cold shoulder to him. One said with direful intent, "Ah, Sir Garrick. I look forward to seeing you in the joust tomorrow afternoon."

Garrick made the appropriate response, frowning inwardly a little at their odd behavior. But he thought no more about it when he found Rafael playing his lute in the queen's antechamber for an audience of unhappy-looking ladies.

"Rafael," Garrick said when the song was finished. "Might I have a word with you?"

Rafael studied him a moment, then excused himself to the women.

"Yes?" Rafael said after they'd moved to an isolated corner of the chamber.

"I wanted to express my thanks for your warning of yesterday."

"Ahhh." Rafael fingered a lute string idly. "So I was right—she did try something."

"Yes, indeed, she certainly did. Something completely beyond my experience. 'Twas incredible. 'Twas amazing. 'Twas beyond belief."

Rafael raised his brows. "It would seem I underestimated the Lady Francine."

"Yes, you did. When I came to the chamber she was waiting for me in bed. Once I joined her there, she plied her seductive wiles. If it hadn't been for your warning, I doubt I would have been able to resist. It was incomparable."

Rafael's eyes widened. "Er . . . what exactly did she do?"

"She quoted Bible verses."

Rafael's fingers grew still on the lute strings. "Bible verses?"

"Yes. She informed me that religion is the hallmark of civilization. I particularly enjoyed the verse about evil communications corrupting good manners."

"Good manners?" Rafael choked a little before bursting into laughter.

"I'm glad you find it so amusing."

Rafael stopped laughing, alerted by a particular note in Garrick's voice. He looked at the other man warily.

Garrick's smile was not pleasant. "Rafael, it's time you found somewhere else to live besides Pelsworth Castle. Perhaps the king needs another minstrel."

Rafael stared at Garrick in disbelief. "You're banishing me from Pelsworth Castle?"

"Your quickness of mind is admirable," Garrick said.

"May I ask why?" Rafael asked, his voice equally as cold as Garrick's now.

"Over the years I've noticed that you and Anne seem to be engaged in some sort of game."

Rafael's gaze shifted. "I do not think—"

"I've endured the two of you," Garrick said, ignoring the

interruption, "trying to manipulate me for some mysterious purpose of your own for the last five years. I do not intend to do so any longer. To be blunt—I am fed up with it."

"Very blunt," Rafael said, his lips tight. "And will Anne be joining me in my exile?"

"That will be up to her. Oh, and Rafael—I suggest you don't even visit Pelsworth Castle for the next twenty years or so—if you want to keep your neck intact."

With that little pleasantry, Garrick walked away.

Rafael was standing like a column of marble when Anne entered the chamber a short while later and saw him. She was surprised by the expression on his face—she'd never seen him look so stunned.

"Rafael, what is wrong?" she asked.

"That . . . that foolish pet knight of yours actually had the effrontery to threaten me. 'Tis unbelievable. . . ."

"He threatened you?" Anne frowned. "Why would he do that?"

"Because . . ." Rafael paused for a fraction of a second, then continued smoothly, "he is a mortal. Who knows what goes on in their puny brains." He looked at Anne, and a smile curled his lips. "Have you talked to your other pet this morning, Anne?"

"Don't call them my pets. And no, I haven't spoken to Lady Francine. Why?"

"It would seem that she's found a new method to seduce Garrick—Bible verses."

"Bible verses?" Anne echoed blankly.

Rafael's grin widened. "Yes, apparently Lady Francine is convinced that religion is the sure way to civilize Garrick."

"Religion! Good heavens, surely she couldn't be so fool—" Anne stopped short and bit her lip. "Perhaps I should talk to her."

Rafael laughed. "Perhaps you should."

Anne glared at him, then left the antechamber. She passed through the hall and turned a corner, only to bump into someone. Looking up, she saw Garrick.

"Lady Anne," he said grimly. "How fortunate. The very person I wished to see."

"Oh?" She swallowed a little. She had never seen Garrick look so . . . so *forbidding*.

"Yes. I want you to return Lady Francine to wherever she came from."

"But . . . but . . ."

"No buts, Lady Anne. After all you've done for me, I would hate to have to tell you what I told Rafael—that you are no longer welcome at Pelsworth Castle."

"Rafael is not returning to Pelsworth Castle?"

"No."

"But what happened?"

"What happened is that I'm fed up with his and your interference in my private life. I will no longer tolerate your matchmaking efforts. I want you to send Francine home."

"But I can't send her home—she has to finish her task—"

"Her task to civilize me? I think not."

Anne averted her gaze. "At the very least, she has to be in the fairy circle and have the emerald."

"That is easily arranged. And one more thing—I want you to remove the spell."

"What spell?"

"You know what spell. The one you cast two years ago to prevent me from being aroused by a woman."

"Oh, that one. But you're mistaken. That spell only prevented you from being aroused by a woman you didn't love."

"Don't try to cloud the issue with your talk of foolish emotions."

"They're not foolish! And I had to do something. At the rate you were going, you would have bedded every woman in the kingdom by the time you were thirty—"

"No more prevarications, Lady Anne. Remove the spell."

Pinching her lips together, she waved a careless hand over him.

He frowned. "That's it?"

"What did you expect—a magic wand?"

"I want your word that you've lifted any and all spells you've cast upon me—"

"Yes, yes," she said crossly.

"—and that when Francine goes to the fairy circle you won't somehow prevent her from going home."

"I . . . I . . ."

"Lady Anne . . ."

"Oh, very well!" she snapped. "I give you my word."

"Excellent." He took her arm and began pulling her toward a door.

"Wait!" she cried. "Where are you taking me?"

"To Lady Francine. I want you to tell her that she's finished whatever task she needed to do and that she'll be able to go home."

"Garrick, be reasonable. . . ."

But it was like talking to a block of stone.

Francine looked up in surprise when the door of her chamber burst open. Garrick and Lady Anne stood there.

"Tell her," Garrick said.

Anne glared at him.

"Tell me what?" Francine asked.

Anne forced herself to smile. "I have good news, my dear. You have accomplished your task. You may return home as soon as we get back to Pelsworth Castle and you go to the fairy circle."

Francine's face lit up. "That's wonderful! Oh, thank you, Lady Anne! When can we leave?"

"Not until the morning after tomorrow's tournament," Anne said, trying not to sound as sour as she felt.

Anne left them and went to her room. Sitting down with her spindle, she twisted the thread and seethed over Garrick's behavior. Why, he was becoming almost as bad as Rafael! Ordering her about in that manner! *Her!* And to forbid Rafael to return to Pelsworth Castle! Not that she cared a fig where Rafael went or what he did, but it was very rude of Garrick.

She was beginning to wonder if she'd made an error in judgment when she'd chosen him for this task all those years ago. When she'd first seen him in her bowl, a thirteen-year-old boy, she'd caught a glimpse of something in his eyes. Yes, he'd been wild. Yes, he'd been rebellious. But there had been that look of vulnerability, too. That longing to love and be loved.

At least, that's how she'd interpreted his expressions. Could she possibly have been mistaken? She'd expected him to fall in love with one of the Medieval maidens and marry long ago. She'd thought that minstrels—hired by her, naturally—would be traveling around Europe, singing about the great love of Garrick for his wife, and that the whole world would know about the true meaning of love by now.

But Garrick had not adjusted the way she'd expected. Or rather, he'd adjusted too well. He was just as bad as the other louts living here in Medieval times.

He would be well served if she did as he'd ordered and abandoned him to his own devices. Fortunately for him, she wasn't so easily dissuaded. She would figure out some way to make him see sense. But she would have to do it quickly. Before he ruined everything she had worked so long and so hard to achieve.

Glad of an excuse to avoid attending the tournament, Francine stayed in her room and packed her possessions slowly. Anne had said they would leave in the morning, so Francine needed to be ready. If they got an early start, they might get home before dark on the second day. Then she could immediately walk to the fairy circle and go home.

But her first flare of excitement had faded. Now, instead of feeling happy, she felt oddly . . . dissatisfied. As if she'd somehow failed. Which was ridiculous, because Anne had said she'd done what she was supposed to do. Still, Francine didn't quite understand how that could be, since Garrick had not changed at all. But whenever she tried to ask Anne about it, the older woman shrugged and changed the subject.

It didn't matter, Francine told herself. All that mattered was that she was going home. Home to Bentley and Grandma Peabody and Stuart. By this time the day after tomorrow, she and Stuart would be married. . . .

The room was close and stuffy. She went over to the window and opened the shutters so she could look out. There wasn't much to see—gray skies, gray river, and gray trees. She sniffed the cold air, smelling meat cooking and fresh bread and pies, no doubt part of the feast that would be presented to everyone after the tournament. In the distance, she could hear a roar of shouts and laughter. And trumpets and drums and clashing metal. How unfair, she thought, that barbarity should sound like so much fun.

She wondered how Garrick was doing. Probably very well. She'd heard the servants placing bets, and Garrick was heavily favored to win numerous prizes. She almost wished she was out there, too, watching him ride about the field on his great black horse. But then she would also have to watch if he fell and hurt himself.

She might not even see him again. Actually, she was almost sorry. He really wasn't as bad as she'd first thought. In spite of the disadvantage of being born in the Middle Ages, he had a few qualities that she liked: he was strong and brave. And he could be kind, upon occasion. She'd even sort of enjoyed arguing with him. It was almost a relief not to have to restrain her emotions all the time, the way she did with—

That is, what she really meant was that she wished Garrick well. She hoped he won all the prizes. She hoped he married some little medieval maiden and lived happily ever after. . . .

The door burst open. Francine turned to see Garrick limp in, his chain mail covered with mud, an ugly scratch starting high on his cheek and disappearing under the edge of the mail coif covering his chin.

"Oh!" she exclaimed involuntarily. "What happened to you?"

His gaze fastened on her and narrowed. "That's what I would like to know."

Francine, heading for the wash basin, paused. "What do you mean? What happened?"

"I mean that every knight on the other side decided to attack me and me alone. I managed to fight off about twenty of them, but then my own side joined with our opponents and beat me to a pulp."

"How horrible!" Francine ran her gaze over him anxiously, wondering how seriously he was hurt. Was he holding his arm a trifle stiffly? "Surely ganging up on one person like that is against the rules?"

"There are no rules." He watched her through slitted eyes

as she poured water from the ewer into the basin and dipped a rag into it. "Robert Fitzwalter made an odd comment. He said to tell my mistress not to give any more advice to his wife."

"He called me your mistress! Did you tell him I was no such thing?"

Garrick ignored her question. He spoke softly, almost gently. "What advice did you give his wife, Francine?"

"Advice?" She wrung out the cloth and handed it to him. "I haven't given anyone any advice. Although I did tell some of the women about massage therapy. They seemed very interested."

"What exactly did you tell them?" He made no move to clean the scratch on his face.

Francine tried to remember. "I don't know, exactly. I was mad at them because they were mocking you for your leg injury. I think I mentioned that you'd experienced trouble with it four or five times the night before, and that kneading the affected muscle as hard as possible had alleviated your problem. . . ."

"My problem." Garrick closed his eyes. "God's breath."

His face twisted as though he were in pain. Francine watched him worriedly, wondering whether the scratch hurt, or his leg was bothering him, or if it was some other injury. Her alarm increased when his shoulders started shaking.

"Garrick," she said anxiously, "do you need to lie down?"

To her astonishment, he burst out laughing. Bent nearly double at the waist, he roared with laughter, gasping helplessly as he did so.

She stared at him in confusion, uncertain whether to calm him or call for help.

Her dilemma was solved, however, when he stopped as abruptly as he'd begun, his gaze fastened on the bag resting on the bed.

"What is that?" he asked.

"My things," she responded. "Anne and I are leaving in the morning."

His expression grew shuttered. "Ah, yes. I had almost forgotten."

He looked at her for a long moment, standing very still and quiet. Then, without a word, he turned and left the room.

Francine stared after him, wondering what on earth was the matter with him. He'd looked at her so strangely. She wished he hadn't left. She still wanted to talk to him.

No matter, she told herself. She could talk to him later when he came to bed.

But he didn't come to bed that night.

She waited, shivering, as the air seemed to grow colder and colder. Finally, when the bells of the abbey tolled the hour of midnight, she climbed into bed and lay down alone.

She touched the empty pillow next to her, wondering where he was. Were the parties still going on? Was he talking to the men about the tournament? Or was he with some woman, kissing her, stroking her, making love to her . . . ?

Restlessly, Francine rolled over. She didn't care what Garrick did with other women. She shouldn't be thinking about him at all. She should be thinking about Stuart—the man she loved, the man she was going to marry in two days' time. What would he say when she returned? How surprised he would be. And how happy. She couldn't wait to see him and tell him everything that had happened to her.

She would tell him the truth, of course. She could do no less. But what would he think of her story? Would he believe her? Of course he would. Just as she would him if the situations were reversed.

She paused a moment, trying to imagine what she would have thought if Stuart had disappeared for three months, then returned and said he'd been transported back in time.

She frowned.

But then she shook the uneasiness away. Stuart would stand by her. She was sure of it. . . .

Her thoughts drifted, and she fell asleep. She dreamed that she'd returned home and that she was going to meet Stuart. The whole scene unraveled before her eyes as if she were watching a movie. She stood on a beautiful beach, the sun shining, the sky blue. She saw Stuart. She ran through the glistening white sand toward him as he ran toward her, his arms held out, a joyful smile on his face. Foamy white waves crashed in the background. The music soared. Francine, her heart bursting with joy, ran into his arms. He bent to kiss her. . . .

"Pee-ewww," he said. "You stink."

She turned red. "I'm sorry, but I've been living in the Middle Ages."

He stepped back, shaking his head. "That's no excuse. . . ."

She woke up suddenly. It was still dark, and the room was freezing cold. Instinctively, she reached out toward Garrick. His side of the bed was empty.

An odd pang squeezed her heart. Had he come to bed at all last night? Had he spent the whole night with another woman, even knowing that Francine was leaving this morning?

Annoyed at herself for her foolish thoughts, Francine got up, shivering in the chill air. She lit a candle and dressed quickly, then hurried off to find Garrick.

To say goodbye, she told herself.

He was in the hall, involved in some deep discussion, his face intent, his head bent toward a man who said, "He has summoned the barons to New Temple in London to hear their demands . . . ," but Francine focused her attention on Garrick. There were shadows beneath his eyes, testimony to his lack of sleep. He glanced at her and frowned impatiently when she asked him to step aside.

"What is it, Lady Francine?" he asked, his tone harsh.

"I'm going," she said. "I wanted to say goodbye."

"Going?" he repeated. "Going where?"

"Back to Pelsworth Castle, of course."

He frowned down at her. "Didn't you look outside?"

"No. Why?"

"There is a blizzard. The roads are impassable."

She felt dizzy for a moment, as if all the blood in her head had drained out. She went over to the window and unlatched the shutters. They sprang open, allowing a cold, swirling mass of snow to sweep over her. Icy pellets drove against her face, blinding her. The cold wetness soaked through her dress within seconds.

She heard an exclamation, then the sound of the shutters being slammed and relatched.

Hugging her arms around herself, she peered blearily up at Garrick.

"Satisfied?" he asked.

"It d-d-doesn't look so bad," she said, her teeth chattering. "I'm sure Anne and I can m-m-make it back to the castle."

"Are you insane? There's no way anyone is going to leave anytime soon."

"B-b-but I must! I must get back to the castle by tomorrow!"

He shook his head. "No one can travel this day."

"You don't understand." She reached out and grasped his sleeve. "I *must* go today. Or . . . or it will be too late."

"Too late for what?"

"For my wedding," she whispered. "I am getting married tomorrow."

His lip curled. "Oh, yes. To your precious Stuart. Will he not wait for you?"

"No! You don't understand! He probably thinks I'm dead!"

He removed her grasping fingers from his sleeve. His voice was a bit gentler as he said, "I'm sorry, Francine."

Choking back a sob, she turned and hurried away. She went to the chamber where the other ladies were sitting about. She didn't join in the conversation; she sat by a round, little window, one of the few in the king's castle that had glass. Although the glass was stained, there was one small area that was clear. She stared through it, praying that the snow would stop.

But it didn't. The hours passed; everyone left to attend another feast, but still Francine sat by the window, her heart sinking lower and lower along with the sun. The sky darkened and tears came to her eyes. She was too late. She would never get home in time. But what did it matter? She'd been deceiving herself all along. It had probably been too late that very first day. By now Bentley was probably gone, caught by the animal shelter and euthanized. Everyone at work probably thought she was dead. Poor Grandma Peabody must be overwrought with worry. And Stuart. Dear, beloved Stuart. What was he doing right now? Sitting in his apartment, thinking of her as she was thinking of him?

The tears overflowed and ran down her cheeks.

"Francine?"

Francine looked around to see Anne standing behind her, concern written on her face.

"Is something wrong?" the older woman asked.

Francine wiped her cheeks with the back of her hand. "Everything's wrong. I want to go home. Everyone must be so worried about me. And Stuart . . ."

Fresh tears welled up in her eyes.

Anne hesitated a moment, then said, "Come with me."

Francine obeyed listlessly.

Anne led her to a small closet of a room with a table and two chairs. She placed an earthen bowl of water on the table and sprinkled some herbs in it, mumbling a few strange words.

"Look, child," Anne said, her voice vibrating oddly. "Look into the bowl."

Francine approached the table and looked down into the bowl of water. She gasped.

There, reflected in the surface, was a slightly blurry picture. As she watched, the scene cleared. She sank into the chair, her gaze glued to the images.

"It's Bentley!" she cried out. The cat, purring blissfully, lay curled up on a chair next to a pink crystal. As the scene grew sharper, Francine could see the faces of two women. Mrs. Rappaport and . . . Grandma Peabody!

"Ah, this tea is delicious, Mrs. Rappaport," Grandma Peabody said.

"Thank you." Mrs. Rappaport smiled sweetly.

"Have you had any more trouble with the police?" Grandma Peabody asked.

"They asked me to come to the station, but they still don't believe that Francine traveled through time."

"Policemen just don't understand about things like time travel," Grandma Peabody agreed.

Francine blinked. Grandma Peabody *believed* that story?

Well, at least she didn't think Francine was dead—that was a relief.

"I'm just glad they don't think I murdered her anymore," Mrs. Rappaport said.

Francine gasped. The police had thought Mrs. Rappaport murdered her? Oh, the poor woman. . . .

"But they've arrested Stuart on Murder One."

Stuart! Francine half started from her chair. Oh, dear heaven! This was terrible!

"They found out he's been sleeping with some woman he works with—a redheaded floozy—and they think he got rid of Francine because she found out about this girl. Poor Stuart," Mrs. Rappaport continued. "He swears he was going to tell Francine about the floozy the night she disappeared, but the police are skeptical."

"What will happen to him?" Grandma Peabody asked.

"Nothing," said Mrs. Rappaport. "With no body and no real evidence, the police will have to release him."

Francine sank back in the chair, stunned. A redheaded floozy? Stuart and *Susie*? "I don't believe it," she whispered.

Anne's eyes were compassionate. "The bowl never lies."

"I . . . I see." Francine stood up. "Please excuse me, Lady Anne. I need to be alone for a while."

She went to her room, undressed in the dark, and lay down on the bed. Stuart and that . . . that *tart*? How could he? How *could* he?

Stuart—the man she'd loved and planned to marry. The one she'd always felt safe with, the one person she'd thought she could depend on, the one who would never betray her. What a fool she'd been. What a stupid, blind fool. . . .

And now—dear God!—what would she do? She dreaded the thought of facing all the pitying looks and whispers when she went home. She felt exposed, vulnerable, the way she had when she'd been eight years old and her mother died.

She pressed her fingers against her closed eyelids, the memory of that time flashing through her mind. Death had been difficult for her to comprehend at that age. It had seemed so unreal. After the funeral, Grandma Peabody had taken her by the hand and driven her back to the old, gabled house and the room that had so frightened her as a toddler.

"This will be your room now," Grandma Peabody had said.

And Francine had realized at that moment that her home was gone forever. . . .

The door opened, but Francine didn't look around. "Please go away, Anne. . . ."

"It's not Anne. 'Tis I."

Francine didn't look around. "Well, you go away, too. I don't want to talk right now."

There was a moment of silence, then footsteps crossed the room to the fireplace. She heard the sound of a log being thrown on the fire and saw the dim glow of a candle being lit. The footsteps approached the side of the bed. She felt the mattress give as Garrick sat down, causing her to sink in his direction.

Sitting up, she scooted away, glaring at him.

"Why are you crying?" he asked.

"Because I feel like it," she snapped. "Will you please go away?"

"Not until you tell me why you are crying." His gray eyes were implacable.

"If you must know—I just found out that my fiancé was cheating on me with another woman."

"Ah."

"I suppose you think it is a perfectly acceptable thing for a man to do."

He shook his head slowly. "I am sorry," he said simply. "It is not pleasant to be betrayed."

The unexpected sympathy made the tears come to her eyes again. "How could he do that to me?" she whispered. "How could he?"

Garrick moved his arms around her. "Obviously he is a fool. You are better off without him."

"I know I am. But . . . it hurts so much." Francine turned her face into the soft velvet of his robe. "I loved him. I met him when he first started working in accounting. Most of the women made fun of him because he had pimples and wasn't athletic. But I felt a connection with him . . . I suppose because I wasn't athletic, either. But one day we had an intense conversation. He talked about how much he hated Jimmy Pearson, the jock in marketing; and I told him how much I hated Susie, the redhead in accounting who could never balance her books. After that, I felt bonded to him somehow."

She sniffled. "When he asked me to marry him, it was the happiest day of my life. He was my first and only love."

Garrick's hand moved in a circle on her back. His touch comforted her somehow. The motion of his hand soothed her, warmed her. His palm swept from her shoulder blade, down to her waist, and up to her other shoulder blade. Down, up, and around. Down, up—

Abruptly, he pushed her away and rose to his feet. Without his arms supporting her, she floundered a little in the mattress.

"Love is a foolish emotion," he said. "You're better off without it."

He moved around the room, preparing for bed, and Francine watched him, thinking about his words. Love, foolish? She could never believe that. All her life, it seemed, she'd been searching for love, and with Stuart, she'd thought she'd found it. Obviously, she'd been mistaken. How could he love her and have sex with Susie? Francine had never thought sex was important to Stuart. Why hadn't he asked her if he wanted sex? She would have been open to discussing it.

She might have even let him do it with her. If he'd really insisted, she might have allowed it. But he never had. She'd thought it was because he respected her. But maybe he just hadn't wanted her.

Garrick blew out the candle and climbed into bed. She listened to his steady breathing, smelled the scent of him. They'd shared a bed for over a week now and he hadn't made the slightest move toward her. Apparently he didn't want her, either.

There must be something wrong with her. Her fiancé didn't want her. The man she shared a bed with didn't want her. Tears stung her eyes again. Was she really that unattractive?

Did men only like women with big breasts and small hips? Surely not. Then what? What was wrong with her?

Was it the way she behaved around men? She'd been accused before of being standoffish. Perhaps men needed a little encouragement. . . .

Without thinking, she reached out. Her fingers fell on Garrick's shoulder. He stiffened at her touch.

"What do you want?" he growled.

"Nothing," she said, hastily withdrawing her hand.

She gripped the side of the bed tightly. Oh, dear God, it was true.

She was completely undesirable to men.

What was wrong with her?

A layer of snow lay thick and deep on the ground the next morning, but the blizzard had stopped. Francine felt no urgency to return to Pelsworth Castle, however. Her emotions were as frozen as the world around her.

The castle seemed deserted. She went outside and saw people gathered in clumps around a snowy clearing where two men were fighting with sticks. Bursts of laughter rang out whenever one of the men managed to land a blow.

To one side, she saw Anne, standing alone by some bushes. Wrapping her cloak around herself, Francine tromped through the snow to the older woman's side.

"Good morning, Lady Anne."

Anne smiled and nodded absently. "Good morning," she said, before turning her attention back to the men in the clearing.

Francine followed her gaze, tensing a little as she realized that Garrick was one of the combatants. He struck a blow to his opponent's shin that made the other man grab his leg and hop around on one foot. Guffaws rose from the crowd.

His face reddening at the laughter, the man turned suddenly and swung at Garrick's head.

Garrick ducked and quickly spun around, swinging his stick like a bat into his opponent's stomach. The man doubled over. With another swing, Garrick whacked him across the buttocks, sending him sprawling into the snow.

Gales of laughter, cheers, and applause erupted from the crowd.

"How can he be so stupid?" Francine murmured as another challenger took the place of the first. "He's going to get hurt sooner or later."

Anne didn't answer.

The sound of sighing made Francine look over. Nearly invisible through the leaves, three ladies had stopped on the other side of the bush, just a few feet away. Francine, peering through the leaves, didn't recognize any of them.

None of the three appeared to have seen Francine or Anne—their complete attention was focused on Garrick.

"He is so magnificent," said the first lady, a redhead. "I remember York—" Sighing, she broke off her sentence.

"So manly," said the second, a blonde. "I remember London. . . ."

"So virile," said the third, a brunette. "I remember Paris. . . ."

Cold air seared into Francine's lungs. For a moment, she couldn't breathe as an odd mix of emotions roiled through her—jealousy, envy . . . and despair.

She turned away and headed back to the castle. She wasn't aware that Anne had followed until she felt a hand on her arm.

"Don't listen to those women," Anne said, a worried frown on her face. "Garrick has no interest in any of them."

"It's a matter of complete indifference to me who he sleeps with." Francine put her gloved hands under her arms and hugged herself tightly in an effort to control her shivering. "It's what I would expect of a barbarian like him. I just can't understand why anyone would find him attractive. He probably has some horrible disease."

"Oh, no, he doesn't."

Francine looked at her in surprise. "How do you know? Unless . . ." She blanched.

"Heavens above, certainly not!" Anne said, blanching also. She pulled Francine off the path and toward a leafless orchard where no one could overhear them. "Garrick is much too young for me. You mustn't think ill of him because of his past. And don't judge him by the words of those silly women."

"Why not?"

"Because they are lying."

"How do you know?"

"Because . . . because Garrick is a virgin."

"A virgin!" Francine leaned back against a tree for support. "How can that be?"

"For all his bravado, he is really a very shy man. He is afraid of not measuring up. His private parts are . . . not as large as most men's. He's terribly embarrassed about his lack."

"Oh, poor Garrick!" Francine said involuntarily.

Anne shrugged. "He has become very adept at disguising his inexperience. I'm hoping that some day, a very kind woman will show him that he's not inadequate." Snow fell from a branch above, sprinkling across Anne's cloak. Brushing at it with her fingers, she said, "My dear, I trust I need not tell you *never* to mention this to anyone."

"Oh, no. Of course I wouldn't," Francine automatically agreed, her brain whirling. A virgin! Of course. It all made sense now. The whispers. His lack of interest in her last night. But wait . . . what about back at Pelsworth? He'd been serious about his efforts to get her into bed with him there.

Or had he?

He must have been bluffing. To disguise the fact that he had a problem. His problem! First his leg, now this!

Oh, the poor man. How terrible. How utterly awful, to be a virgin in this day and age when men were judged by their virility on the battlefield and in the bedchamber. Her heart went out to him. After everyone's reaction to his leg injury, he must know that if his lack of sexual experience became common knowledge, he would be the laughingstock of the kingdom.

She straightened from the tree, her gloved hands forming fists. No one would find out the truth from her. Personally, knowing the truth made her like him much better. He was actually a lot like her. She'd been nervous about sex, too. At least she'd been able to get some information from the library. What avenues were open to the people of this time?

She wished she could help him somehow. She wished there was something she could do. . . .

Wait. Maybe there was something she could do. Something she never would have dreamed of a few days ago.

It was an insane idea. Stuart would be shocked if he knew what she was contemplating. But she didn't care what Stuart thought anymore. She was tired of always being the "good" girl, of always doing the sensible thing. She wasn't going to live like that any longer. She was a different person now. She intended to take a lesson from the people here. They didn't think about tomorrow. They lived only for the day.

She stomped her boots in the snow.

She was going to be a wild woman now.

But no, wait, she couldn't. She couldn't risk getting pregnant. Even if she was a wild woman now, living only for today, that didn't mean she was going to be stupid.

"My dear."

Francine jumped. She'd forgotten Anne was there.

"Could you possibly do me a favor?" Anne asked. "I promised these herbs to Lady Rowena. Would you give them to her for me? Tell her that she need only mix them with a cup of hot water and drink the entire infusion. The herbs will be effective for a week."

Francine took the packet. "Of course, Lady Anne," she said automatically.

Anne smiled and left, her footsteps muffled by the snow. Once she was gone, Francine looked down at the packet of herbs. Slowly, she lifted it to her nose and sniffed.

Sure enough, the herbs had the familiar fish odor like the ones she'd bought at the market, the ones that Riva Arber said prevented birth.

It was a sign.

Not that she was superstitious, but the coincidence was just too great. She felt a sense of fate, of karma, of destiny.

She *knew* she was meant to teach Garrick how to make love.

Chapter 16

GARRICK NOTICED SOMETHING odd about Francine at the feast that evening. She was . . . *friendly*. She didn't warn him about the evils of fighting, or quote Bible verses at him, or take offense at any of his remarks. She just looked at him with an expression akin to pity in her eyes.

Throughout the rest of the meal, she behaved the same way, her manner so overly solicitous that it actually made him nervous. It was a relief when she murmured goodnight and went to their bedchamber early.

He tried to distract himself from thoughts of Francine by flirting with a beautiful blonde. Now that Anne had broken the spell, he could take any woman to bed, and Lady Violet was exactly the type he found attractive: demure, quiet, and shy, her conversation charmingly trivial.

A touch *too* trivial, perhaps, he thought as he stood at her side listening to her twitter on and on about clothes and fashion and what lord was visiting which lady in her chamber. He found it difficult to concentrate on what she was saying. He wondered if Francine was asleep yet. Probably not. She had not looked particularly tired when she'd bid him goodnight. She appeared completely recovered from her distress of yesterday. She didn't have that lost, hurt look in her eyes anymore. He hadn't liked seeing that. It had made him want to take her in his arms and hold her. . . .

Abruptly, Garrick asked Lady Violet to dance.

The lady, cut off in mid-sentence, appeared surprised, but then smiled widely. Garrick danced with her, but found that the idea of bedding her was not particularly appealing. He danced with several others, hoping to find someone more to his taste, but without success.

Finally, when it was very late, and he was very tired and certain that Francine must be asleep by then, he returned to their room—only to find her still awake.

"Good evening, Garrick."

She lay in the center of the mattress, smiling at him. She had lit several candles, and they cast a soft glow over her shining golden curls, her smooth flawless skin, her dark-blue eyes and soft, moist lips. . . .

"Good evening," he replied. Something was wrong here, but he couldn't figure out what precisely.

Knowing that if he looked at her any longer he would become a solid mass of desire, he quickly snuffed the candles. He undressed in the dark and moved to the edge of the bed, listening for the slight mushing sound the mattress made whenever she moved to her side.

The mattress was perfectly quiet.

He climbed into the bed and held on to the frame so he wouldn't roll to the center. He lay there, his senses alert, painfully aware of her soft, slim body only inches away. And of her sweet peaches-and-honey scent. And of the complete privacy of the chamber as they lay together on the soft, yielding mattress. . . .

Gritting his teeth, he closed his eyes and thought of Pelsworth, of John's promise to him, of the barons' complaints against the king, of the rumors of war flying about Winchester. . . .

"Garrick . . ." A soft hand touched his thigh, just below his drawers, causing him nearly to jump out of his skin.

"What?" he asked.

Her hand, incredibly soft and warm, rested on his leg, just

inches from his erect manhood. "I just wanted you to know that you don't have to pretend with me."

"Pretend what?" Her fingers spread out, the tip of each one burning like an ember into his skin.

"I know the truth," she said, her voice full of tender sympathy. "I know that you're a virgin."

He forgot about her hand on his thigh. "You know *what*?"

"That you're a virgin. Anne told me."

"Anne," he groaned. "I should have known. . . ."

"So you see, you don't have to put on this macho act for me anymore."

He shook his head. This was beyond belief—even for Francine. "I assure you, I am *not*—"

"Please, Garrick, don't lie. Listen to me. I've been thinking about this all day, and I've come to a decision. It doesn't matter if you know nothing about sex—"

"Francine, I assure you—"

"Don't be embarrassed. I will show you what to do."

"—I am not . . ." He paused. "What did you say?"

"I will show you what to do."

He froze. "You will?"

"If you want me to."

He didn't speak, desire and caution at war within him. Another of Anne's traps. He should get out of the bed and leave the room immediately. But . . . it had been so long since he'd known the pleasure of a woman's body. And Francine—dear God, how he wanted her. He'd wanted her forever, it seemed. He'd sworn to himself that he would not ask her to be his mistress again. But now *she* was asking *him*. How could he possibly resist?

"You know a lot about this?" he finally asked.

"Yes," she assured him. "I read a sex manual—a book about coupling—before I came here. It explained everything."

"You learned . . . from a book?"

His voice sounded a trifle choked. Francine knew he must be surprised. She doubted there was anything like *Sex for Dummies* in the Middle Ages. She also knew she was exaggerating a bit—she hadn't actually read the book—but she had to make him as comfortable as possible to overcome his fear. "Yes."

He was quiet for another long moment. She shrank a little inside as it suddenly occurred to her that maybe she'd been wrong. Maybe it wasn't his virginity that was causing his restraint, but her undesirability. . . .

She started to remove her hand from his thigh and retreat to her side of the bed, when he spoke.

"How can I refuse such a generous offer? Show me, Francine."

His voice sounded oddly muffled—shy almost. Relief flowed through her. He sounded so nervous. She could hear his breathing, faster than normal. Yes, she thought, he was definitely nervous. She could sense the tension in him. Did he think she would laugh at him?

A wave of tenderness washed over her. She would never laugh at him, no matter how tiny his private part or how awkward he was in bed.

"Francine . . . what should I do first?" he asked.

"First . . ." She hesitated. She supposed they should take off their clothes. But the idea of being naked was daunting.

"Don't we take off our undergarments?" he asked.

Some of her courage fled. "Um, no, it's not necessary. First we kiss."

She leaned over and kissed him lightly on the lips.

He seemed tense, the line of his mouth hard; but as she applied more pressure, he relaxed and his mouth softened. He released his hold on the side of the bed, causing them to roll to the center, with him on top.

The weight of his body pressed down against her. She couldn't breathe.

She opened her mouth to ask him to get off her, but he mimicked her action, his tongue slipping between her lips. He stroked and caressed the inside of her mouth. Her blood coursed through her veins; a strange light-headedness made her tingle all over.

She turned her head to one side, gasping for air. "You kiss very well." Extremely well, in fact. Where had he learned to kiss like that? It seemed very advanced for a beginner. "You kissed me like that before?" she said, a slight question in her voice.

He must have heard it because he said, "Kissing is not so hard." He rolled to one side, his arm underneath her shoulders. "Francine . . . may I . . . touch you?"

Her heart sank. He wanted to touch her. Probably her breasts. She really wished he wouldn't. Lying on her back like this, her breasts flattened out to near nonexistence. What would he think?

Somehow, when she'd offered to do this with him, she hadn't quite thought about the reality of it. She'd pictured it more as a dreamy sort of event, tender and romantic. She hadn't thought so much about actual physical contact.

She couldn't refuse him, though. Men had a thing about breasts, she knew, and she wanted him to enjoy this experience.

"Yes, of course," she said.

She braced herself, expecting him to grab her breasts immediately. But instead, he lifted her hand and carried it to his mouth.

"Have I told you what beautiful hands you have?" he murmured.

"N-no."

"You do. They're so soft." He pressed his mouth against her palm, making it tingle. He kissed her fingers and gently nipped at each one. He sucked on the pad below her thumb.

She was surprised at how . . . erotic it felt.

He kissed her wrist and the inside curve of her elbow. "Francine . . . this is very difficult for me . . . you must tell me if where I'm touching you feels good. Do you like it when I touch you here?" He stroked the inside of her arm where his mouth had just been.

"Yes," she whispered. "That's very nice. . . ."

He put his hand on her jaw and turned her mouth to his. He kissed her mouth, his hand stroking down her waist and up the curve of her hip. "Here?"

She tensed a little, wondering if he would make some joking comment about her overabundant curves. He didn't, though. He just kept stroking until she relaxed.

"Yes . . . ," she murmured.

He caught the hem of her chemise and started to pull it up, but she caught his wrist, preventing him. He released the linen immediately and moved his hand up over the cloth to her breast. "Here?"

She held her breath, torn between embarrassment and an unwilling excitement. He palmed the slight curve, his thumb brushing her nipple. Burying his face in the curve of her neck and shoulder, he lapped at her skin with his tongue while continuing to play with her breast.

Tremors ebbed and flowed through her. Part of her reveled in the fiery heat spreading across her skin and the warmth rushing inside her. Part of her was embarrassed by his touch. The combined intensity of his touch and her emotions made her uneasy.

His fingers traced a line down her belly, startling her from her thoughts. Instinctively she clamped her legs together. But his fingers slipped under her chemise and between her thighs, stroking her.

Her brain reeled at the intimacy of his touch. She'd never expected *this*. She could feel her wetness down there, and she knew he must feel it, too. She squirmed in mortification, trying to dislodge his fingers, but only succeeded in giving him greater access.

He slipped a finger up inside her.

Shock reverberated through her. She couldn't believe what he was doing. She couldn't believe that she was allowing it. . . .

She opened her mouth to tell him to stop, but the words wouldn't come—only slight, panting gasps.

"You feel so tight," he said huskily. "I'm afraid I'm going to hurt you."

She was afraid, too. She wished she'd never agreed to this. It felt too strange, too alien. Too intimate. Her brain seemed unable to function.

"Francine . . . Francine? Are you all right?"

"I'm fine." Her voice came out steady and calm, totally autonomous from the chaos churning inside her. She felt odd. Every part of her seemed to be humming—her breasts, her thighs, her toes, her blood, and deep inside her belly. She couldn't quite decide whether it was pleasant or unpleasant. . . .

She inhaled sharply. She couldn't take much more of this. She wanted it to be over with. "Now, you—"

"I think I can guess." Kissing her deeply, his hand caressing her breast, he moved over and into her.

He filled her, stretched her, pressed against her. Some barely functioning instinct made her try to pull away, but the mattress prevented retreat. She arched upward, in an attempt to push him off, but his weight held her down.

"Francine, slow down. I'm not sure—" She moved again and he groaned. He thrust forward, pushing through the small barrier there.

She stopped moving completely, pain eradicating the pleasant-unpleasant humming. She was acutely aware of him above her, of the embarrassing nature of their position, of the part of him that was embedded deeply inside of her— the *huge* part. This was *small*? She shuddered to think what big was like.

He groaned again. "Oh, God. I hurt you, didn't I? I'm sorry, Francine. . . ."

"No, no," she managed to say. "I'm fine. It was fine."

"It's not over yet."

"It's not? Oh. Well . . . go ahead."

He seemed to hesitate, but then he bent over her and kissed her deeply. Slowly, he thrust deep within her, and then again. And again. He touched her and stroked her, and for a moment, the humming started up again. His movements quickened, and she felt the humming grow more intense, and more so, and more so. . . .

He tensed, and she felt a slight jerking movement deep within her. A few moments later, he rolled off of her.

She lay there, her heartbeat slowing, the humming fading away, her brain cells slowly reconnecting. She'd done it. She could hardly believe it, but it was really true. She'd had sex. And it had been pretty much as she'd expected. Hot. Sweaty. And messy.

Disappointment flickered through her.

Although actually, the first part hadn't been so bad. She'd liked it when he'd kissed her hand. She just wished the end had been a little more pleasant.

But at least it was over with, and really, she had no reason to complain. She'd done this for him, not for herself. She'd wanted him to overcome his fear of making love to a woman—and he had. He didn't need to worry about being a virgin any longer. . . .

"God, I'm sorry, Francine."

"Sorry for what?"

He hesitated, as if choosing his words with care. "You didn't enjoy that, did you?"

"Oh, no. I mean, yes! Of course I enjoyed it!" she lied.

"Did you?" She felt his fingers in her hair, stroking the strands gently. "Let's do it again. It will be better this time."

"No!" she half shouted.

His fingers grew still in her hair. Realizing that she'd been less than tactful, she swallowed. "You need to rest. And to be perfectly truthful, I'm a little bit sore. Besides, there's really no reason to do it again. We both know everything there is to know about coupling now."

He was quiet a long moment. "God, I'm a selfish bastard."

Shocked by the bitter self-disgust in his voice, she reached out and touched his arm. "What are you talking about? You're no such thing."

"Yes, I am." He pulled her close against him. "But you are a generous woman, Francine Peabody. And a very kind one."

His words ignited a soft glow inside her. His arm wrapped around her waist, heavy and possessive, pressing her up against his warmth. Suddenly, the whole experience didn't seem so dismal after all. Somehow, being curled up next to him made the pain seem unimportant.

She closed her eyes. Within seconds she was fast asleep.

Garrick wasn't so fortunate.

He lay awake in the dark, cursing himself for his pitiful performance. How could he have lost control so completely and so utterly? He couldn't have made a worse showing if he'd been the virgin she thought him. He'd made several mistakes. He should have taken more time with her, eliminated her inhibitions right away. He should have coaxed her into shedding her chemise—she couldn't enjoy the experience properly with her clothes on. He should have kissed her and stroked her until she screamed with pleasure. . . .

Any other woman would have kicked him out of the bed. But not Francine. Francine was . . . dear God, she was amazing. Holding her, touching her, burying himself deep inside her had been sheer heaven. He'd forgotten the pleasure a woman could bring. He didn't remember the act of coupling being so intense, so extraordinary, so completely sublime. He was burning up with a desire to repeat it immediately.

She, however, obviously did not feel the same way.

He still didn't understand how he could have performed so inadequately. Women throughout Europe had sought him out because of his reputation as an excellent lover. To fail now, with Francine of all people, was mortifying.

Perhaps it was because of his long abstinence. Or perhaps because he'd wanted her for so long.

But truly, the reason didn't matter. All that mattered was that he make it up to her.

Which he had every intention of doing tomorrow night.

Francine was eager to leave the next morning, so she was disappointed when Garrick told her that they must delay their departure again due to the extremely cold temperatures.

A few days ago, she might have argued with him that it wasn't all that cold, but after last night, she couldn't quite bring herself to do so. She felt too self-conscious.

In the cold light of day, it was hard to believe that last night had really happened. She couldn't quite believe the things she'd allowed him to do to her.

She really would have preferred not to have to spend another night with him, but she had no choice. She went to her room early that evening, planning to pretend to be asleep when Garrick came in.

But Garrick was already there. In bed.

Candlelight bathed the room with a soft golden glow, and Garrick, dressed only in his shirt and drawers, lay on his back, his hands behind his head, staring up at the canopy above him. She must have made some sound, because he turned suddenly and looked at her.

He smiled.

Involuntarily, she smiled back. He leapt to his feet and came toward her, his hand held out. Light skittered across his shirt, rippling with the movement of the muscles underneath. He walked with the barest hint of a limp.

Half mesmerized, she put her hand in his and allowed him to lead her toward the bed.

He stopped next to it and looked down at her, his eyes dark in the dim light.

"Francine, I must ask you a question, and you must tell me the truth."

"Yes?"

"You didn't enjoy last night, did you?"

"Oh! Well, um . . ." She tried to think of a response that was truthful but that wouldn't hurt his feelings. None occurred to her.

"It doesn't matter if I enjoyed it," she finally said. "The important thing is that *you* enjoyed it."

"In truth, it didn't feel that great for me, either."

"It didn't!" Stunned, she gaped at him. What had she done wrong? She felt like a failure. "I'm sorry," she whispered. "Perhaps another woman—"

"Oh, no, it wasn't your fault," he said. "It's just that it was new for me, Francine, and I felt a little . . . embarrassed."

"Oh, I know what you mean!" Relief flowed through her. "But it will probably be better for you next time."

"You think so?"

"I'm sure of it."

"Francine . . . will you do it with me again?"

She almost recoiled. She didn't want to have to go through all that again. But . . . how could she say no? She might damage his still-fragile confidence in his newly found sexual prowess. She might damage him permanently.

She would hate for that to happen. She knew only too

well what it felt like to feel unattractive to the opposite sex. But could she really endure having sex with him again?

"Very well," she said finally, hiding her reluctance as best she could.

She heard him exhale a long sigh. "Thank you, Francine. May I help you out of your gown?"

She hesitated. She wished she could stay fully dressed. She wanted to get this over with as quickly as possible. But she couldn't very well tell him that.

She turned slightly to allow him access to the laces at the side of her gown.

He bent over slightly so he could see the strings better. His mouth was right next to her ear; the dark strands of his hair mingled with her much lighter ones. He performed his task with apparent concentration, his right hand brushing against her breast, her rib cage, and then her waist as he pulled at the strings. When the last string was loosened, he spoke in a low voice against her ear.

"Hold up your arms."

She obeyed, and he pulled the dress up over her head and tossed it on a chair.

He stood looking at her for a moment. Then he put his hands on her waist, where the cote was tightly laced. His hands pressed up her sides to her underarms, then curved inward to cover her breasts through the fabric of her dress.

Her nipples rose to prominence. She could feel his palms over the sensitive points, his hands pressing against her chest as it expanded and contracted in her efforts to get air into her lungs.

Calm down, she told herself. *It will soon be over.*

But really, it wasn't quite as unpleasant as she'd expected. His touch was less embarrassing. More exciting. So exciting, in fact, that she almost wanted to arch her back so that he would touch her again. . . .

The cote followed the surcote onto the chair. Now only her chemise separated her skin from the touch of his fingers. The odd excitement intensified. She wanted him to touch her breasts again. She wanted . . . more.

But instead of touching her breasts, his hand moved downward to the hem of her chemise.

She grasped his wrist, but this time, instead of releasing her chemise immediately as he had the night before, he continued inexorably to pull it up.

Panic washed through her. The candles were lit. She couldn't stand here in the light and let him see her.

"Garrick!"

His hand stopped. He breathed deeply for a few moments, then buried his face in the curve of her neck and shoulder. "I'm sorry, Francine. I didn't mean to do anything you found repulsive."

"Oh, no. That's not it. I . . . I just think it's better if I keep my chemise on. . . ."

Her voice trailed off as she felt him open his mouth on her throat and apply a gentle pressure. Tingling sensations raced over her skin. Her muscles grew liquid, making it difficult for her to stand.

His hands smoothed over the curves of her buttocks, then cupped her and pulled her tight up against the juncture of his thighs.

"Oh!" The exclamation escaped her before she could prevent it as she felt the bulging hardness of him pressing against her. A fleeting memory of the pain and discomfort of last night buzzed through her brain, but her body refused to listen.

In fact, her body seemed to have a will of its own.

It pressed right back against him, as if aware of something her brain was not. The contact didn't satisfy it though—it wanted more. . . .

"Francine," he murmured. "Let's get in bed."

She blinked. What was happening to her? She was having trouble thinking. She didn't like not being able to think.

She nodded, expecting him to release her and give her a moment's respite. But he didn't. Keeping his hips pressed against hers, he kissed her deeply and moved with slow, sideways steps to the bed. When they reached the side he tilted her back and they fell into the mattress, sinking into its soft depths.

"Wait," she said, struggling to regain control of herself. "The light."

"Leave it," he muttered against her throat.

"No, we can't." The idea terrified her.

Without lifting his mouth, he reached out and yanked at the bed-curtains, drawing them closed and casting the bed into darkness. "Is that better?"

"Yes . . ." she said uncertainly. It was better—and worse. The closed curtains afforded some darkness, but the space seemed smaller, more confined; more sensual, more intimate.

She jumped a little when his hand touched her bare thigh, below her bunched-up chemise.

"Francine," he murmured. "Your skin is so soft. I like how it feels." He kissed her lightly, and his hand moved up under her chemise to her hip. "And I like the way you curve here."

She'd been about to protest his touching her under her chemise, but his words stopped her. "You do?"

"Yes. You're so feminine. So rounded. And your waist . . ." His fingers moved upwards. "It curves in so nicely, so elegantly."

He stroked from her side to her belly and back. Her stomach muscles rippled under his touch. "It does?"

"Mmm-hmm. And your breasts . . ." His hand covered one. "Your breasts are perfect. Your nipples are so sensitive, they respond so instantly to my touch. . . ." Gently, his thumb rubbed back and forth across one, sending shards of sensation pulsing through her.

She'd never thought of her body in the way he described. He made it sound . . . sexy. As though the shape of it gave him enormous pleasure. . . .

He leaned over and covered her breast with his mouth.

Surprise jolted her. She'd been so intent on what he'd been saying, she'd barely noticed her chemise being pulled upward as his hand had inched toward her breast.

She noticed now.

His tongue lapped at her nipple, sending tremors rippling through her. His face and shoulders and chest pressed against her breasts and rib cage and stomach. Somehow he'd ended up between her thighs, so he pressed against her down there, too. His shirt rubbed against her bare skin, creating a slight, pleasurable friction.

His mouth trailed down her rib cage, as he traced each rib with his tongue. He moved to her navel and laved it thoroughly.

She shifted uneasily. He was uncomfortably close to the area between her legs, his shoulders pressing her thighs wide apart. She felt exposed. Vulnerable. . . .

His mouth moved down to her thighs.

"Garrick! Oh, no! No!" She grabbed his hair and pulled at him.

He ignored her tugging. His tongue stroked along the most intimate part of her.

"Garrick!" she said again, writhing against him. She pulled his hair again.

"What's wrong, Francine?" His voice sounded husky and dark and unbearably sensual. "Let me kiss you. You taste so sweet . . . so incredibly sweet. . . ." His tongue stroked her again.

A whimper escaped her throat. Tremors coursed through her. It was too intense, too frightening. She felt as though she were on the verge of exploding.

She yanked harder at his hair. "No. No. You must stop. . . ."

He moved up; his harsh breathing rasped in her ear. "Let me kiss you there, Francine. Let me kiss you all over."

"No . . . I can't."

He kissed her ear, his tongue tracing the curves. "Yes, you can, Francine." His fingers stroked between her legs, imitating his mouth. "You'll like it, I promise."

"No. . . ."

He must have heard the thread of panic in her voice, because he stopped stroking her. He lay still for several long moments.

"Is it because of my ugliness?"

"Your what?" she asked, startled.

"My ugliness. I know my body is hideous."

"What on earth are you talking about? Your body isn't hideous! It's beautiful."

"No, it's ugly. And I worry about you seeing it. And feeling it." He turned away from her.

A lightbulb went off in her head as she realized the truth—he wasn't worried about his "ugliness." He was worried about her seeing how small he was! How foolish. As if she cared about his size. She hadn't noticed any lack on his part. He certainly hadn't *felt* small.

"Garrick." She pulled away from him and pushed back the bed-curtains, allowing the candlelight to illuminate the small space again so that she could see him. Moving into a kneeling position, she put her hand on his shoulder. "You have nothing to be ashamed of, I promise you."

"You wouldn't say that if you saw it."

"Yes, I would. Come on, now, take off your shirt."

"No, I can't. I would be too embarrassed. Unless . . ."

"Unless what?"

His voice was slightly muffled. "Unless you took your clothes off also."

She pulled her hand away from his shoulder.

His words revolving in her brain, she stared down at him. She'd made love with this man. He'd just kissed the most intimate part of her. Why should she balk at letting him look at her naked body?

He'd already seen it. True, it had been a long time ago, and he probably didn't really remember how she looked, but he *had* seen her.

But that had been a completely different situation. Everything was different now. In spite of the fact that they'd had sex—or perhaps because of it—she felt more vulnerable now. If she took off her chemise, all her flaws would be there for him to see. She would be completely exposed.

She probably looked better now that she'd lost some weight; but her breasts were still too small, her hips still too wide. The plain and simple fact was her body was made that way. He would never think her "perfect" if he saw her as she really was.

She opened her mouth to refuse . . . then shut it again.

How could she turn him down? He was exposing himself, too. He was vulnerable, too. Couldn't she put aside her own fears for his sake?

Reaching down, she took hold of the hem of her chemise.

She paused, her heart pounding. She felt slightly sick. She didn't know if she could go through with this.

She'd sat naked in the steam bath with the village women, she reminded herself. Why should being naked in front of Garrick be any different?

She took a deep breath. "Come on, Garrick, I've always been embarrassed by my body, too. Look, I'll take my clothes off, too. If I can do it, so can you." Quickly, before she could think too much about it, she pulled her chemise over her head and threw it onto the floor. "There. See? I'm naked."

He turned and looked.

Something shivered through her as his gaze wandered over her. She felt an instinctive urge to cover herself, but she forced herself to sit up straight with her arms hanging loosely at her sides.

This *wasn't* the same as the village women. They had not been interested in her nudity at all. Garrick definitely *was*.

He looked at each part of her—her breasts; her arms; her navel; her stomach; and the juncture of her legs, half hidden by her kneeling position. Everywhere his gaze settled was like a palpable touch on her skin. She could feel her flesh tingling and growing warm.

He rose from the bed and stood on the other side. He pulled off his shirt and drawers and tossed them aside.

And then . . . and *then* she could understand why he stared at her so, because she was doing the same to him. He looked so . . . different from her. All big and muscled and flat and angled and. . . .

"Oh, my," she whispered, her gaze irresistibly drawn to his groin. She thought of the pain she'd experienced last night. Now she could see why. If he'd been any bigger, he would have ripped her apart.

His eyes dark, he took a step toward her.

"Oh, Garrick," she whispered. "I'm glad you're so small."

He stopped. "I beg your pardon?"

She bit her lip. "I hope you don't mind . . . Anne mentioned that you were embarrassed about the smallness of your . . . private parts. But I just wanted you to know I don't find you inadequate in any way."

He made a strange gasping sound.

"Is something wrong?" she asked.

"No," he said, his voice still sounding odd. "I am glad you are pleased." His voice grew husky. "I, too, am pleased. You are beautiful, Francine."

Instinctively, Francine opened her mouth to protest and point out her too-wide hips, her too-small breasts, the light fuzz of hair on her upper lip, and all the other flaws. But then, seeing the look in his eyes, she realized that none of it mattered. To him, she *was* beautiful. He wasn't comparing her to anorexic models or *Playboy* centerfolds. He truly thought she was beautiful.

A tightness in her stomach, something she hadn't even been aware of, relaxed. A glow spread outward, growing and expanding until it enveloped her.

And for the first time in her life, she truly *felt* beautiful.

He reached out and touched the emerald hanging between her breasts. A jolt of electricity passed through the jewel and hummed through her body.

"This is how I saw you that first time," he murmured. "With nothing but the emerald. You made me ache with wanting you. Now you make me ache even more."

He lay back down, and in a motion as natural and easy as breathing, she lay down beside him. He began kissing her again—all over, as he'd wanted to do earlier. But this time she didn't protest. Because this time, every place his mouth touched felt beautiful.

The humming she'd felt last night returned, only stronger.

Urgently, but gently, he nudged her knees apart. Slowly, carefully, he eased into her.

She felt the same stretching fullness she had last night—

but it didn't seem alien this time, and it didn't hurt. He began to move in rhythmic strokes.

She tried to match his rhythm, but she moved a little awkwardly, breaking the motion and interrupting the sensations building inside her. She tried again, but couldn't seem to get it quite right.

"Francine . . . ," he said, stroking her breasts and kissing them. "Relax."

She stared up at him—at his knobby chin; his strong jaw and nose; his fierce, gray eyes. This was Garrick. Garrick who in the last three months had somehow worked his way into her heart. In some ways she didn't know him very well—but in others, she felt as though she'd known him all her life.

He touched her all over. There was no self-consciousness, no awkwardness, just the two of them touching each other, moving together, giving to each other. He kissed her again, more deeply, and she felt the humming increasing. The rhythm came to her as if she'd always known it, and the humming turned into music . . . she gasped.

"Oh, Garrick. Oh, Garrick! Oh . . . Ahhhhhhhhhhhhh!"

Chapter 17

GARRICK WAS GONE, as usual, when Francine woke up the next morning. She looked at the empty pillow for a moment, then impulsively buried her face in it.

How wonderful, how extraordinary, how *magical* last night had been.

She wished Garrick had woken her up. She was anxious to see him, talk to him. She wanted to find out if the previous night had been as wonderful for him as it had been for her.

The door opened, and she looked up eagerly. But instead of Garrick, Anne stood there.

The older woman studied her a moment, then smiled. "You look well-satisfied this morning."

Francine felt her face grow warm. But she couldn't help smiling, either. "Have you seen Garrick?"

"He's in council with the king. He gave me a message for you. We are to leave this morning, and he will follow shortly. He should catch up to us by the time we reach Pelsworth."

Francine was disappointed to have to wait to see him— but she was glad to be returning to Pelsworth. Winchester,

with all its courtiers and intrigues, was not a very friendly
place.

The journey back to Pelsworth seemed long and tedious.
Francine spent most of it listening for the jingling of harness
and galloping hooves that would signal Garrick's approach.
She tried to concentrate on the scenery, but more often than
not, she found her gaze wandering from the snow-covered
fields and trees to back over her shoulder, hoping to catch a
glimpse of a tall, dark-haired horseman.

But to her dismay, they arrived at the castle without Garrick appearing.

It was late, and Francine entered the darkened hall to find
everyone already asleep. Uncertainty washed over her.
Where should she sleep? Garrick's bed seemed the obvious
choice, but she was afraid to presume so much. He might not
want her there. He might not want *her*, period. He had
wanted to overcome his shyness about making love—he'd
done that. As far as he was concerned, their relationship
could be over and done with.

And it was probably for the best if it was. She really
should go home tomorrow. Anne had said she could. How
wonderful it would be to see Grandma Peabody and tell her
everything that had happened. How pleasant it would be to
hold Bentley in her arms and stroke him. . . .

She dallied over her preparations for bed as long as possible, but finally, with a wistful glance at the stairs that led
up to Garrick's room, she climbed into bed with Edith.

She must have fallen asleep, because she woke up suddenly to find strong arms lifting her from the bed.

"Garrick?" she asked, instantly wide awake.

"Yes," he growled, carrying her up the stairs. "Why aren't
you in my bed?"

"I wasn't sure . . . I thought maybe you'd learned
enough."

He entered his room, put her on his bed, and lay down
next to her, his hands lifting her chemise. "I haven't learned
nearly enough. I'm a very slow learner. It will likely take me
months to get it right."

Relief and happiness surged through her. But then his

mouth closed over her breast, and another emotion swept through her.

"I . . . I, oh, I will do my best to teach you," she gasped.

And then she could talk no more.

Some time later, Garrick lay in the bed thinking how good it was to be back at Pelsworth and how *right* it felt to hold Francine in his arms. He wished the rest of his life could be as perfect as this moment.

He closed his eyes and was about to fall asleep when he heard a sleepy whisper.

"What took you so long?"

"I thought you preferred it longer, madam," he teased.

He felt her smile against his cheek. "Not *that*, you wretch. Why did it take so long for you to return?"

His own smile faded, and he stared through the darkness at the canopy above him. "The council meeting went on longer than I expected."

"Oh? Was there a problem?"

"No, not exactly." He smoothed her hair behind her ear. "The king is removing to London. He intends to summon the barons there to hear their demands."

"But that's wonderful! Perhaps they will be able to settle their differences without fighting."

"Perhaps. Francine . . ."

"Yes?"

Garrick hesitated, wondering if he should tell her the other business he'd discussed with the king—the matter of Garrick's marriage. At long last, John had given him a written agreement—that in exchange for Garrick's promised support against the barons, the king would permit a betrothal between Garrick and Lady Odelia. . . .

Francine lifted her head from his chest and moved slightly away. "Are you trying to tell me you don't want to continue this relationship?" Her voice sounded stiff. "That's okay, Garrick. I have to leave tomorrow anyway. . . ."

"Leave?" Instinctively he tightened his arm around her waist. "What in God's name are you talking about?"

"I have to go sometime. I can't stay here forever."

"You promised to teach me everything you know."

"Oh. Well, that won't take too long."

It would take forever, he vowed silently. He needed Lady Odelia for the power she would bring him. But he needed Francine for the pleasure she gave him.

He bent over her, seeking her mouth in the dark. "You forget what I told you—that I'm a very slow learner."

"I wouldn't describe you that way—"

His mouth found hers, cutting off the rest of her words. All thought of telling her about his agreement with the king disappeared as he kissed her deeply, thoroughly, possessively, until she clung tightly to him.

"Perhaps I can stay a little bit longer," she gasped as he moved his hand between her thighs. "Perhaps a week or two. . . ."

Living by bells and festivals instead of clocks and calendars made it difficult to keep track of time.

Francine slipped back into life at the castle almost as if she'd never left. Edith, Mog, Nancy, and even Gunilda were eager to hear about her two weeks at court. She had to tell about the king, the queen—whom she'd never even seen— the courtiers, and their ladies. In crowded steam-bath sessions and afternoon sewing circles, she described the feasts, the entertainments, the clothes, and every other detail she could remember.

Garrick gave her free rein over household matters, something she'd been itching—literally—to have control of. She instituted a cleaning program—clothes, linens, mattresses were all washed and aired. All the old rushes were thrown out, walls and floors scrubbed, livestock banished to outlying fields and pens. Everyone was checked regularly for lice. She even hired some men to clean out the cesspool beneath the castle, a job long overdue.

She found that days could slip into weeks and weeks into months with astonishing speed.

She carried candles on Candlemas, ate hard-boiled eggs and played games on Shrove Tuesday, and ate fish during

Lent. She even learned how to disguise the taste of herring with a large dollop of mustard.

Messengers came from London with increasing frequency. The barons, in full chain mail, had approached the king in London and demanded that he confirm the good laws of Edward the Confessor and the reissue of the charter of liberties granted by Henry I. John requested a truce until Easter—then proceeded to hire an army of mercenaries and ordered all his and his allies' castles to prepare for war.

Garrick prepared to defend Pelsworth, "merely as a precaution," he assured Francine. She had to discontinue her classes as the men-at-arms were busy at various tasks: guard duty; sorties into the countryside to scout for possible attackers; and inventorying swords, pikes, crossbows, arrows, and other weapons.

But in spite of the war preparations, there was an air of optimism at Pelsworth. Or perhaps it was just romance in the air. With all the women working at the castle now, romance was blooming between various couples—including several of the men-at-arms and the new servant girls, Captain Fletcher and Sarah the Spinster, and Harvey and Edith. Francine even saw Hugo and Gunilda holding hands.

But nowhere did romance bloom so strongly as in the lord's bedchamber.

Francine spent her nights in absolute bliss. Garrick was a wonderful lover. She'd soon exhausted her small supply of knowledge about sex, but Garrick insisted that he still needed her so that he could ask her questions. Since he had lots of questions and they almost always began with, "Is it possible to . . . ," she was kept very busy.

The masons and mortarmen had trickled back after December and resumed work on the castle. With startling speed, battlements, towers, and walls went up. New structures still needed to be built inside the walls, but the main edifice was complete.

On the day it was finished, Francine stood by Garrick's side on the path near the forest's edge and watched his face as he stared up at the castle. "Five years," he murmured.

" 'Tis strange how much stone and mortar can come to mean to one."

She followed his gaze, and for an instant she could see it as he did—the result of five years of persistence, determination, toil, and self-sacrifice. He had created this place. It was a part of him as surely as if he'd mixed his blood into the mortar.

At times like this, and when she lay in his arms at night, she thought she could stay there forever.

But then at other times—when she went to Mog's and Clifford's wedding and saw the happiness on their faces, and when she saw women fussing and cooing over their babies, a deep uneasiness washed over her—a panic almost. Garrick never talked about marriage or the future, and neither did she. She knew she couldn't stay here. Not forever. But she also knew that the longer she stayed, the harder it would be to leave him when the time finally came.

Whenever she had one of these episodes, she promised herself she would go home at the end of the week.

The only problem was that, somehow, the end of the week never came.

Chapter 18

A SE'NNIGHT BEFORE Easter, Anne left the castle and hurried down the path to the budding forest. She made her way through the thick, new-leafed brush. None of the bushes scratched her or caught at her clothes, and when she entered the clearing by the lake, she looked as fresh and pristine as if she'd just dressed.

Rafael, sitting on a rock outside the fairy circle, looked up as she approached.

"Ah, Anne," he said appreciatively, admiring the contrast of her scarlet cloak against her ebony hair. "Beautiful as always."

Anne waved her hand impatiently. "Never mind that, Rafael. What do you think?"

"Think of what?"

"Of Garrick and Francine." Exasperation filled her voice. "Haven't you been watching in the bowl I gave you? They're in love. Will you admit now that I was right?"

He arched a brow. "That's what you call love? Enjoying each other in bed? If that is what love is, then we've been arguing for nothing, Anne. I love you—come, let's go to bed."

"Oh, you!" She scowled at him. "It's more than that, you fool. Can't you see?"

"I only see two people who can barely keep their hands off each other. It's a common enough condition. Besides, I don't see Garrick rushing out to marry the girl."

"These things take time. He'll realize soon enough that he can't live without her."

"You always were the eternal optimist, Anne."

"And you always were impossible! I don't blame Garrick one bit for banishing you."

"Don't be cruel, Anne. Have you convinced him to allow me back?"

She studied the thin silver ring on her finger. "No, I'm afraid not. He *is* very stubborn, I must admit."

Rafael snorted. "You always did have a talent for understatement." He strummed the strings of his lute, the notes jarring and angry. "I don't know why I let you talk me into staying away. I ought to go up to that pitiful hovel he calls a castle and—"

"Now, Rafael," Anne said. "Don't be rash. Your temper is what got us banished to this place and time in the first place."

"*My* temper. What about yours?"

"My temper has always been what it should be." Ignoring his look of disbelief, she continued. "I'm sure I can convince Garrick. You must be patient." She paused a moment, then said, "Or you could admit that I'm right, Rafael. We would be home in an instant."

His fingers slowed on the strings. "Or *you* could admit that *I'm* right."

She glared at him. "You are unbelievably stubborn. I will leave you to enjoy your solitude."

She stomped off.

Rafael smiled after her, but then his smile faded and he stroked his chin thoughtfully. Tucking his lute under his arm, he strolled through the forest after Anne, but instead of heading for the castle, he turned in the direction of the village.

A short while later he was in a small thatched cottage, greeting Joan the Weaver, Sarah the Spinster, and Francine. The door and windows were open to let in the fresh spring air and to provide light for their sewing.

Francine looked up from a piece of black leather on her lap. "Rafael! How nice to see you again. How was London?"

"London?"

"Anne said you'd decided to go to London with the king."

"Ah, yes. In truth, I only stayed there a short while. I've been visiting friends." Rafael studied her a moment. By this time in the Lent fasting, most women had taken on a gray pallor and lethargic air. Not Francine. Her cheeks were rosy and her golden hair had lost none of its shine, nor her dark-blue eyes their sparkle. Of course, a thorough bedding had that effect on a woman. He doubted there was any more to it.

"What are you making, Lady Francine?" he asked.

"A present for Garrick." She held up a half-finished black leather jerkin. Her stitches were uneven and some of the seams a bit crooked, but it was obvious she'd put a lot of care and work into it.

A tiny frown knit Rafael's brow. But then he smiled. "Shall I entertain you ladies while you sew?"

"Oh, yes!" Sarah's thin face lit up.

"'Tis always pleasant to have music," Joan agreed comfortably.

Rafael strummed a few notes. "I understand Sir Garrick has made a remarkable recovery from his sad affliction," he said to no one in particular.

Francine frowned. "What affliction?"

The other two women exchanged glances. Sarah pressed her lips together and focused her attention on the dress she was hemming.

"Hmmph." Joan shrugged. "I suppose it doesn't hurt to talk about it now. 'Twas said he was impotent."

"Impotent!" Francine exclaimed. "Oh, no, that's not what was wrong with him."

Sarah looked doubtful. "There were many who tried to rouse him. They all failed."

"What *was* his problem, then?" Joan asked bluntly.

Francine hesitated, searching for a tactful way to explain the truth. "Actually, I think he was just a trifle . . . inexperienced."

The two women stared at her for a long moment. Then they burst into howls of laughter.

"Inexperienced?" Joan hooted. "Why, Garrick was known as the randiest buck in Christendom until two years ago."

" 'Twas said there wasn't a woman in England that he hadn't bedded," Sarah chortled. "Some thought the priest had imposed celibacy upon him as penance for his licentious ways."

Francine sat as if turned to stone. Memories, like her Grandma Peabody's old slide photographs, clicked through her brain.

Francine . . . this is very difficult for me.

Francine . . . may I . . . touch you?

Francine . . . what should I do first?

A bright-red mist rose before her eyes.

She was vaguely aware that Rafael left the cottage, a smile on his face. And that the two women were staring at her oddly.

"Lady Francine," Joan said rather hesitantly. "Is something wrong?"

"Shall I summon Sir Garrick?" Sarah laid aside her sewing and half rose to her feet.

"No!" Francine burst out. She struggled to regain her composure. "No, nothing's wrong." *He's a dead man,* she said to herself.

Taking deep breaths, she stared down at the black leather on her lap—the gift she'd been making for *him,* the lying, cheating dog. . . .

She looked up at the women and smiled with superhuman calm.

"But I was wondering if you could help me with this gift I'm making for Garrick. . . ."

Garrick strode into the courtyard, his feet crunching on the oyster shells tossed there by the night guards. He'd toured the castle with Captain Fletcher, inspecting the war preparations, and he was looking forward to seeing Francine at supper.

He'd always hated Lent and the dull ache in his belly from lack of food. It always reminded him of the lean, hungry times he'd endured—and his determination never to experience them again. The gloomy days of Lent were usually marked by surly tempers and frequent fights.

But this year everything was different. Francine made the long, cold days bearable. At the single evening meal, it was a pleasure to pick out tender morsels of food and place them between her soft red lips, to watch her chew daintily, to share a cup of wine with her. Sometimes he could barely restrain himself from dragging her off before the final course.

He worried a trifle, though, about the effect of the fasting on her—he knew she wasn't used to it. He bought her candied violets and crystalized ginger, deemed by the church too small to be considered a meal, but enough to help stave off the constant hunger. The sweets were costly, but any expense would have been worth the soft glow of appreciation he saw in her eyes when he offered them to her.

He was heading for the hall when he caught sight of Francine in one corner of the courtyard near the stables. She had a whip and she was slashing at a post.

He stopped and stared. She missed the post a couple of times, but on the third try she managed to wrap the thing around it.

"Nutekin," he called to a passing boy. "What is Lady Francine doing?"

The boy shrugged. "I don't know, exactly. She's been out there almost all day. She's improved, too—at first, she couldn't even hit the post."

The boy hurried on his way. Garrick watched Francine, tempted to go over to her. But he wanted to use the steam bath before supper, and he didn't have much time. He decided to talk to her later.

But later, at supper, she only shrugged and smiled mysteriously when he asked about the whip.

"Garrick," she said, licking her lips sensuously after drinking some wine, "I have a surprise for you. Slip away and come up to our room after the last course."

She left the table and headed for the stairs. He watched her go, half mesmerized by the sway of her hips.

A fever of impatience seized him. "Bring forth the oysters," he called out, even though he hadn't finished his smoked herrings.

The command echoed down the line of servants toward the kitchen.

"Bring forth the oysters!"

"Bring forth the oysters!"

"Bring forth the oysters!"

They came. Garrick swallowed a few, then rose to his feet. "Please excuse me," he said. "I feel an urgent call of nature."

Ignoring the snickers that followed him, Garrick took the stairs three at a time up to the tower room. It *was* a call of nature—even if it wasn't the usual kind.

He reached the door. Blood coursing through his veins, he pushed it open.

The room was shadowed, with only a few candles lit in their sconces. Francine stood in a dark corner, making it difficult for him to see her.

"Take off your clothes," she whispered.

He complied, almost ripping his shirt in his haste.

When he was completely naked, she stepped out of the shadows.

His jaw dropped.

She was dressed in a black leather bodice, laced up the front. A triangle of black leather clung to the juncture of her thighs; she wore black hose, attached by garters to the thong, and shoes with a narrow piece of wood attached to each heel. Coiled in her hand was the whip she'd been practicing with all afternoon.

"I've decided that you're ready to learn a new method of lovemaking," she said. "It involves pleasure—and pain."

He stared at her, his lips twitching. He'd learned about the principles of pleasure and pain in Constantinople. He'd never found the exercise of it very appealing. But looking at Francine, he was half tempted to play along with whatever crazy game she intended. She stood with her breasts and hips thrust forward, the black leather contrasting with the milky-white skin of her belly and chest. She pouted and tossed her hair and wobbled on the ridiculous shoes.

But her aim with that whip had looked none too steady.

"I don't think I'm ready for anything so advanced," he said.

"Tough," she answered. "Go lie down on the bed."

Garrick could hardly keep from laughing. "I think this has gone far enough. Give me the whip."

"No. Lie down on the bed. Or else . . ." She uncoiled the whip.

He smiled disbelievingly. "Go ahead then, because I'm coming to get that whip."

He took a step forward. Suddenly, the thong lashed out and struck him across the thigh.

He stared at the welt on his leg—only inches from a much more important part—then at her. "You hit me," he said, all desire to laugh disappearing.

"Oh! I . . . I'm sorry!" A horrified look on her face, she dropped the whip. "I didn't mean to—it's just that I'm not too proficient with the whip yet."

"You're not too proficient with the whip yet?" he repeated grimly. "Allow me to give you a few lessons."

He advanced on her.

She retreated.

He feinted to the left.

She darted behind a chair.

He knocked it aside, picked her up, and slung her over his shoulder.

"Stop!" she screamed. "What are you doing?"

"You'll see." He threw her on the bed and lay on top of her thrashing, wriggling body.

"You deserved it!" she screamed. "You lying, cheating bastard."

He grabbed her wrists in his hand. "What the hell are you talking about?"

"I'm talking about Sir randy-romps-in-every-bed-in-England Garrick!"

"Oh." His grip on her wrists loosened. "You found out about that, did you?"

"Yes, and you deserved that lash and one hundred more! You deserve to be boiled in oil, burned at the stake, hanged and quartered—"

"All right. I get the idea." He pushed her hair back from her damp, flushed face. "I admit it, I deserve all that. And more."

"You do?" Her lips parted in surprise.

"Yes. I shouldn't have lied to you, Francine. I'm sorry. 'Twas only that I wanted you so much that when you offered, I could not resist."

"Oh." She chewed on her lip. "But did you have to say all those silly things about being embarrassed and shy?"

"I said them in the hope of making you more comfortable. It was wrong of me, I know. Will you forgive me?"

"I suppose." If she were honest she would admit that she'd deceived him as well. She'd pretended to be making love to him for his benefit, when in truth she'd done it for her own. After Stuart's desertion, she'd desperately wanted to feel desirable. Garrick had certainly obliged her in that respect. She'd liked the idea of him being a virgin so he couldn't compare her with other women. "I must have seemed pitiful compared to all those other women you've slept with," she said in a small voice.

He kissed her forehead. "Not at all. In fact, *you* made *them* seem pitiful."

His words made her feel a little better, although she wasn't quite sure she believed him. "Why did you stop sleeping with them?"

He didn't answer immediately, and Francine felt her throat constrict. "Did you contract a venereal disease? Anne said you hadn't, but—"

Garrick laughed shortly. "No, I have no disease. Something almost as bad. Anne put a spell on me to prevent me coupling with any woman. She is a witch and Rafael . . . I don't know what Rafael is."

A witch. As ridiculous as it sounded, it made sense. Magic bowls, impotency spells . . . what other powers did Anne have? Francine wondered. "I still don't understand. Why would she do such a thing? And why would she take such extreme measures?"

"'Tis some game between her and Rafael. I don't understand it, either. I only know that for five years she has tried to marry me off to some eligible maiden."

"That's why you were so suspicious of me when I first arrived," Francine said slowly. "But what broke the spell?"

"I had her remove it when we were at Winchester."

She frowned a little. "But you wanted me to sleep with you before that."

His eyes flickered. "I believe the spell was already wearing off. I cannot be certain. I am just glad the spell is gone."

"So am I." She fixed her gaze on his chest. "I'm sorry about the whip."

"You should be."

She glanced up at his stern tone, then quickly back down again. "I really am sorry. It would have been terrible if I'd accidentally—"

"Do not say it," he said. "Do not even think it."

"Very well," she said meekly. She drew a finger down his bare chest. "Do you forgive me?"

He took her hand and lightly nipped her fingers. "How can I not, when you are wearing such a very fetching outfit?" He tugged at the knot on her hip that held the triangle of leather in place. "Where did you get it?"

"Joan and Sarah helped me make it. They thought it was very strange. I'm afraid I used the leather that I was making your jerkin out of."

"Do not apologize. I consider this a much better use. Where did you learn about such things?"

"From that book I told you about."

"Ah, yes, the infamous book. I shall have to read it. What is the name?"

"Um, well . . ." She translated the title in her head. *"Coupling for Blockheads."*

Garrick choked.

"I don't think it's available around here, though," she told him.

"You will have to tell me more about it—some other time. Right now I am going to have to punish you for your impudence."

"Punish me? What do you mean?"

"I mean that before this night is over you will be begging for mercy. . . ."

Chapter 19

FRANCINE HUMMED SOFTLY as she walked back toward the castle from the village. She had just visited Mog to give the girl a piece of finely woven pale-yellow linen as a bride gift. Mog had been so excited, she'd practically danced with joy.

She rounded a bend in the path and saw Rafael lounging against a tree, tuning his lute.

"Good morning, Rafael," she said. "Are you going up to the castle? Everyone will be very glad to see you—especially Anne."

"Sweet Anne. How I would love to see her also. Alas, I'm afraid Sir Garrick would not appreciate my visit. We had a small disagreement when last I saw him."

"I'm sure he's forgotten all about it. He's been in an excellent mood lately."

"I'll wager he has been," Rafael murmured. Then in a louder voice, he said, "I still think it would be wise to wait a while longer before I visit. I must confess that Sir Garrick is exceedingly angry with me."

"But why?"

"The reason is of little import. What is truly troublesome to me is not being able to see Anne and everyone else at the

castle." He sighed. "You must know how I feel. You, too,
know what it is like to be away from your home—from your
friends and family. The longing to see them is nigh overwhelming. Have you not found it so, Lady Francine?"

She thought of Bentley, her friends at work, and Grandma
Peabody. Dear Grandma Peabody. She'd been like a mother
to Francine since she was eight years old. Grandma was almost seventy now, independent and active, but Francine had
still called her almost every week. Grandma always listened,
always cheered her up, was always excited over Francine's
triumphs. How she missed that complete, unquestioning
love, trust, and support. "Yes," she whispered.

"The worst part," Rafael continued, "is that I know they
miss me, too. I feel guilty for not being there with them.
Does that sound foolish?"

"No, not at all."

Rafael smiled bravely. "But here, what am I about, plagu-
ing you with my problems? Let us speak of something more
cheerful. Your home, for instance. You're returning there
soon, aren't you?"

An incoherent noise came from her mouth.

"I beg your pardon, Lady Francine?"

She cleared her throat. "Yes," she said. "Yes, I am. In fact,
I . . . I'm planning to go at the end of the week. Right after
Easter."

"How fortunate you are." He hoisted his lute over his
shoulder. "I must be off, now. Please give my regards to
Anne. Good day, Lady Francine."

"Good day." She continued up the path, no longer humming.

That night Francine listened to the rain pattering against the
wooden shutters. The room was cold in spite of the crackling fire, but lying curled up in the cocoon of Garrick's arms,
Francine felt warm, safe, and more content than she ever
had in her life. She didn't want to do or say anything to disturb that pleasant feeling, but she knew she must.

She took a deep breath. "I need to talk to you."

"Mmm?"

"I've been thinking about this all day, and I decided I must tell you everything so you will understand. I know you may not believe me. You may even think I'm insane. But it's the truth, I swear it."

"Oh?"

His voice was not encouraging, but she ignored his lack of response. She took a deep breath. "I'm not really from around here."

He was silent.

"I'm not a fairy or anything," she assured him hastily. "But . . . I am from a different place. A different time. I'm from the future."

His arm tightened around her, but still he said nothing.

"Garrick? Did you hear what I said?"

"Yes, Francine. I heard you."

She waited for him to say more, but he didn't.

That's it? She'd prepared herself for different responses— disbelief, scorn, even anger. But she'd never expected this . . . this nonresponse.

"Do you believe me?" she prodded.

"Yes."

"You do?" Was he telling her the truth? He must be—why would he lie? But how could he accept what she said without a single question, without even a hint of skepticism?

But perhaps in a time where people believed in fairies and witches, time travel didn't seem so remarkable.

"All right," she said. "You believe me. Then you must realize I had a life there. People I care about and who care about me. People I miss."

She felt him tense, but still he said nothing.

"So you see . . ." She took another deep breath and finished in a rush. "That's why I can't stay here. That's why I must go home—"

"No."

"No? What do you mean, no?"

"You can't go home. I won't let you."

She stiffened. He was doing his caveman act. She hated when he did that. "You can't stop me."

"By the cross, don't argue with me." He finally looked at

her, and what she saw in his eyes startled her. "Please, don't go." His voice sounded choppy. "I want you here with me. I need you, Francine."

"You . . . you do?"

He held her tightly. "Yes. Desperately."

Francine hesitated, torn between wanting to stay with him and wanting to go back to everyone in the future. But in the end, there really was no choice.

How could she possibly leave when Garrick needed her so much?

Standing in the darkened church on Good Friday, Francine watched as the last of the villagers approached the cross lying on the altar, knelt, and kissed it. The man backed away and the priest approached, murmuring prayers. He lifted the cross and carried it to an opening in the church wall. After placing it inside, he covered the space with a veil and lit the shelf of candles beneath it. He walked out of the church, the hushed congregation following.

Francine lingered a moment, strangely moved by the odd creeping-to-the-cross ceremony. She lit another candle, and said a prayer for Grandma Peabody and Bentley.

She left the church, stopping when she heard her name called. Looking around, she saw Rafael standing by the gate to the graveyard.

"Lady Francine!" he said. "I'm so glad I saw you. I wanted to say goodbye in case I don't see you again. It's truly been a pleasure knowing you."

"Thank you—but I'm not leaving after all." She blushed a little. "Garrick asked me to stay a while longer, and I agreed."

Annoyance flashed across his face, startling Francine. But it disappeared so quickly, she thought she must have imagined it.

"Did he?" Rafael said smoothly. "In truth, I cannot say I blame him. I only hope for your sake that Lady Odelia is the understanding sort."

"Lady who?"

"Odelia. The king's ward. Garrick's betrothed. Did he not tell you her name?"

"No." Francine's lips suddenly felt very stiff and dry. "He didn't."

"It's a very good match for Garrick. Lady Odelia has been thrice widowed and is very wealthy. She will bring Garrick an excellent dowry."

"How nice for Garrick." She licked her parched lips. "How long have they been betrothed?"

"It's not a formal betrothal yet. Garrick asked the king to agree to a preliminary betrothal agreement, promising Lady Odelia's hand in exchange for Garrick's support in the upcoming clash with the barons. The king signed the agreement and gave it to Garrick several months ago. That last day at Winchester, in fact."

The last day at Winchester. The morning after they'd experienced such glorious lovemaking. While she'd been lying in bed, glowing from the memories of the previous night, he'd been with the king, negotiating a betrothal agreement.

Only half aware of what she was doing, she mumbled a farewell to Rafael and stumbled up the path toward the castle.

She remembered Garrick's words that first night when they'd returned to Pelsworth Castle. *The council meeting went on longer than I expected.*

She hadn't even questioned him too much about it. She'd been too worried about whether or not she should return home. Whether or not he wanted her in his bed. . . .

She reached the castle gate and went inside, heading toward the tower room, wanting nothing so much as to be alone and think about what Rafael had told her. She paused, however, when she caught sight of Garrick across the courtyard with some of the workmen near the new, half-built kitchen.

The men were working steadily, smiles on their faces. As she approached, she heard Matthew of Stourhead telling a joke. Garrick joined in the laughter.

For a moment, her heart leapt at the sight of him—his gray eyes lit up with laughter, the fierce lines of his face smoothed out and curving upwards, the welcoming smile on his lips as he saw her.

But just as quickly, her heart sank back down, aching all the more. "May I speak to you?" she said.

His smile faded at her tone. He glanced around the crowded courtyard. "Come in here."

He led her into the well tower. Cool and dim, it smelled of wet stone. Taking both her hands in his, he studied her face. "Is something wrong?"

She didn't answer him directly. "I need to ask you a question, and I need you to tell me the truth." She looked up at his face. "Are you going to marry someone named Odelia?"

A steady *drip, drip, drip* of water falling to the floor filled the silence that followed her question.

"Where did you hear that name?" he asked.

"Rafael told me at the creeping ceremony. Is it true? Are you going to marry her?"

He met her gaze, a hard expression on his face. "Yes," he answered with brutal honesty.

"I see." She pulled her hands away from his. "Do you love her?"

He frowned. "Love—what is that, Francine? What a mother feels for her child? What a man feels for his horse? Or perhaps you speak of that foolish emotion sung about by troubadours—that of a chivalrous knight for a lady he can never take to his bed."

"I'm talking about the feeling that exists between a man and a woman where they care about each other more than anyone else. Regardless of status or wealth, they express that love by marrying and promising to love each other for the rest of their lives."

"Then love doesn't exist here. Marriage is a business arrangement, nothing more."

"I see."

He put his hands on her stiff shoulders and turned her to face him. "Francine, you have to understand—power and wealth are necessary here. They make all the difference when the crops fail, or when a renegade baron decides to go pillaging. They mean the difference between death and survival. Love, as you define it, is a luxury—no, a *weakness*, that I cannot afford."

"I understand," she said quietly. "I have to go now, Garrick. I believe Edith is waiting for me." She hurried out of the well tower.

Garrick stood staring after her for a long moment. Then, with a muttered curse, he strode outside.

By the waist-high kitchen wall, two of the men had stopped working for a moment to exchange a word.

"Digby! Rufus!" Garrick snarled. "What in God's name are you two doing? There's work to be done, and by the cross, you'd better do it or you're fired."

The men stopped smiling. Hunching their shoulders, they lowered their gazes to the ground and went back to work.

A scowl on his face, Garrick strode across the courtyard toward the stables.

Up in the tower chamber, Francine lay on the bed she'd shared with Garrick, her face buried in her pillow. Her heart was breaking, but she knew what she had to do.

She might have been able to live in a world without modern conveniences.

But she could never live in a world where love didn't exist.

$\mathscr{C}hapter$ 20

RAFAEL WAS SITTING on the rock by the fairy circle, idly strumming his lute and waiting for Anne, when he heard the thunder of horses' hooves. A group of horsemen in chain mail and helmets burst from the forest and rode directly toward him. His eyes narrowed. Slowly he rose to his feet.

Swords drawn, the men circled around him, their horses pawing the ground and snorting loudly. "Good morrow, Sir Garrick," Rafael said to the knight who stopped in front of him.

Garrick pushed back the visor of his helmet and stared down at the minstrel, his face hard and cold. "I warned you, Rafael, not to return here."

Rafael arched a brow. "So you did."

Garrick nodded curtly to Orson. "Tie him up."

Orson, his face impassive, dismounted and approached the minstrel.

"I really don't think it would be wise of you to try to tie me up," Rafael said softly.

Frowning, Garrick looked from Rafael to Orson and back to Rafael. Rafael was several inches taller than Orson, but slender and languid-looking in his brightly colored minstrel's outfit. Orson was brawny and muscular and could wrestle a bear to the ground with ease.

Garrick tightened his grip on the reins as his big black mount sidestepped nervously. "Do I have your word you will not attempt to escape?"

Rafael cast him a haughty glance. "Certainly."

The small cavalcade set off for the castle, Rafael walking alongside Garrick's horse, the men-at-arms following.

Rafael strummed his lute as he strolled up the path. "I must say, I'm a trifle surprised by your antagonism, Sir Garrick." Rafael's voice, with the bell-like tones required by his profession, carried clearly, even over the clip-clopping of hooves and the creak of armor and leather. "I thought to do you a service by encouraging the woman to return home."

Garrick made no response.

Rafael continued smoothly. "I would hate for Lady Odelia to refuse the betrothal because you're keeping a mistress. And, truth to tell, I doubt Lady Francine will be agreeable to the situation, either. She strikes me as a bit naive—the sort of woman that expects constancy from a man."

Garrick's brows drew together, but he didn't respond to the minstrel's provocative comments. He didn't speak until they arrived at the castle.

"Lock him in the gatehouse storeroom until I decide what to do with him," he said in a hard voice to the men-at-arms. "Post a guard. He is to have no visitors." He spurred his horse toward the stables, leaving the men-at-arms to glance at each other uneasily before complying with Garrick's orders.

Angus and Ivo escorted him into the small, barrel-filled room with two narrow, barred windows—one in the door and one looking out into the courtyard. The two men backed out quickly. Orson closed the door and turned the key in the lock.

Rafael laughed.

The Easter procession, the feast, the games, and the dancing had been over for many hours when Garrick finally ascended the stairs to the chamber where Francine lay sleeping. Or pretending to sleep, rather.

He looked down at her, at the gold of her hair spread out across the pillow, the curve of her breasts and hips below the counterpane.

He wanted nothing so much as to take her in his arms and make love to her, but he knew she was still upset about Lady Odelia. She hadn't spoken to him since their confrontation yesterday, and last night, when he'd come to bed, she'd also been pretending to be asleep. He'd been able to tell she was awake, then as now, by the cadence of her breathing—slightly quicker than was normal for sleep.

Quietly, he undressed and lay down beside her. He traced her nose with his finger.

Her nose wrinkled and she turned away.

He drew his fingers up her shoulder, slipping the chemise over and down her arm.

Still pretending to be asleep, she batted his hand away.

He reached inside her chemise and cupped her breast.

She stiffened. She turned on her back, her arm pushing his hand away. Her lashes fluttered. "Garrick?"

"Yes, 'tis I."

"I was asleep."

"Oh, did I wake you?"

"Well . . . yes."

"I'm sorry, but there's something I must tell you."

She feigned a yawn. "What?"

"I'm leaving tomorrow."

Her hand dropped away from her mouth; she stared at him. "You are? Why?"

"The messenger that came during the feast—he brought a summons from the king. I must go to London."

All her pretense of tiredness was gone. "Will you go alone?"

He shook his head. "My men go with me. Although I will leave Orson and Ivo and some of the villagers to protect the castle."

She folded the edge of the counterpane with her fingers. "Will there be a battle?"

"It's highly unlikely. The king would prefer to negotiate. He cannot afford a civil war. But he will want to make a show of strength."

"How long will you be gone?"

He hesitated. "No more than a month or two, I believe."

"Oh." She looked up at him, her eyes solemn.

He bent over and kissed her fiercely.

He sensed her holding back at first, but he wouldn't allow it. He kissed her more deeply, and slipped his hand under her chemise to touch and caress her breasts until she was kissing him back. He made love to her until he'd demolished all the barriers she'd tried to erect between them, until they were no longer two separate people, but one, united together for the rest of eternity.

Gasping in the aftermath, he rolled over on his back, weary with satiation and satisfaction. Her body had spoken—she was bound to him forever. She would not leave him now.

He fell asleep, a smile curving his mouth.

Next to him, Francine listened to his breathing grow slow and steady. She'd never experienced such closeness. She wondered if he'd understood the words she'd tried to convey with her body.

She rolled over and pressed her lips against his.

"Goodbye," she whispered.

Chapter 21

FRANCINE WATCHED HIM leave from the chamber window. As if he knew she was there, he stopped at the gate and looked back toward her. Even though she knew he couldn't see her, she stepped into the shadows.

He looked back down at Orson and spoke to him for a few minutes. Then he left. She watched him go, trying to memorize the straight line of his back, the broad shoulders, the effortless way he controlled his horse.

Francine felt an ache in her heart. She would miss him. But she had to go home.

She was surprised to see Orson blocking her path when she approached the outer wall an hour later.

"Is something wrong?" she asked him.

"Sir Garrick has ordered that no one is to leave the safety of the outer wall unless accompanied by an armed guard. There are reports of robbers."

"Oh!" Francine said rather anxiously. "Has anyone been hurt?"

"I wouldn't know, my lady," Orson said, staring straight ahead.

Francine was surprised by his curtness. "Would it be possible for one of the guards to escort me sometime today to the forest?"

"I'm afraid not. What few men are available are busy searching for the robbers."

"When do you think someone will be available?"

"Perhaps in a se'nnight, my lady."

"That long!" Frustrated, Francine turned away. It had been extremely difficult for her to work up the willpower to leave—the delay was irksome and disheartening.

She hoped the men would capture the robbers soon.

But they didn't.

A week went by and then another. Orson and Ivo, who shared guard duty, always told the same story—robbers in the forest. No men available to escort her. No other information available.

She went to the kitchen one day to try to find out more from Nancy.

"Has Orson told you anything about these robbers?" Francine asked.

Nancy kept her eyes on the pot she was scrubbing. "No, he hasn't."

"Has anyone in the village been robbed?"

"No, I don't believe so."

"This is ridiculous!" Francine exclaimed. "Where are these invisible robbers? They must have moved somewhere else. I'm ready to take my chances."

"Oh, no, my lady, you mustn't," Nancy said. "Just think of those thieves that set upon you once before. Sir Garrick isn't here to rescue you now."

The memory of the two thieves was enough to deter Francine for another few days. But on the third day, she marched up to the gate.

"Lady Francine," Orson said before she could speak. "I have good news—the robbers have been caught!"

"They have? That's wonderful!"

"Unfortunately, I have bad news also." He looked at her solemnly. "There is an army encamped five miles away from here."

Francine grew pale. "Do you think they will attack the castle?"

"I doubt it. But the men are foraging in the area. A woman was raped by several of the soldiers in the forest near the lake."

"Dear heaven! Who was the woman? Was she from the village?"

"No, I believe not."

"Then who?"

"I don't know, my lady."

"Who told you the story? I will ask him."

"He is gone. 'Twas the messenger that brought the news of the robbers being captured."

Francine's eyes narrowed on Orson. "Why would an army be encamped five miles from here? I thought the king was in London."

"The army is probably on its way to join him."

"Then it should be gone within a day or two."

"Um, I would think a week—"

"A week. Very well. I will be back then."

But a week later, when she asked Orson about the army, he said, "Yes, my lady. It has moved on. However—"

"However?" she repeated dangerously.

"However, there are now reports of wolves in the forest."

"Wolves. What kind of wolves?"

"Why, er, gray ones, I suppose."

"How many?"

"Um, I don't know."

"Who saw these wolves?"

"Um, I—"

"You don't know," she said in unison with him. "Orson, is there something you would like to tell me?"

He swallowed nervously. "I'm sorry, my lady, but Sir Garrick gave strict orders that you . . . that no one was to be allowed to leave the castle. Unless it's perfectly safe," he added almost as an afterthought.

Francine stared at him, her heart suddenly pounding. "Garrick said *I* wasn't to be allowed to leave the castle? Why not?"

Orson flushed. His eyes darted to each side nervously, as if hoping someone would come rescue him. "I . . . um . . ."

"What exactly did he say to you?" she demanded.

"For God's sake, Lady Francine! I have no choice! It will be my life if I let you through these gates."

Francine stared at him incredulously. Then she turned and stomped away. That bastard. That low-down, conniving bastard. . . .

She heard lute music coming from the gatehouse. Almost involuntarily, her footsteps slowed and turned in that direction.

She looked in the small, barred window and saw Rafael plucking idly at the strings of the lute.

"Greetings, Lady Francine," he said. "You look upset."

"I just found out that Garrick is keeping me a prisoner in this castle!" she said.

"Hmm. 'Tis not pleasant to be a prisoner," Rafael said. "Would you like to escape?"

"Yes . . . but how? Orson won't let me through the gate."

"Perhaps I could be of aid," he said. Languidly he rose to his feet, walked to the door of his prison, and opened it.

Francine blinked. "How did you do that?" she asked, as he joined her in the courtyard.

"The guard forgot to lock it last night. Come, Lady Francine, we must hurry."

Francine felt uneasy, but she obeyed. She followed him to the gate, where Orson stared at Rafael in astonishment. "What the devil—"

"Lady Francine and I would like to leave," Rafael said.

Orson frowned. "I can't do that . . . and how did you get out of the storeroom? I'm taking you back immediately. . . ."

Rafael started playing his lute. Francine listened in astonishment. She had never heard Rafael play like this before. The music was indescribably beautiful. It had a haunting quality like music heard in a dream that you could never quite remember when you woke up. It was almost hypnotic. . . .

"Come along," Rafael said.

With a start, Francine came out of her near-trance. She

glanced at Orson and saw that he had nodded off where he stood, a smile on his lips.

Almost warily, she turned her gaze to Rafael. "How did you—"

"He's been on watch all night. 'Twas a simple matter. Now come. We must hurry."

She followed him out the gate and down the path to the woods. Keeping up a quick pace, he plunged in amongst the trees, Francine half running behind him. She was panting when they came out of the woods to the fairy circle by the lake.

She stepped inside the circle and sat down on the stone. She hesitated.

"Hurry," Rafael urged.

"Orson will be in trouble," she said. "Garrick said he would hang him."

"I will tell Garrick it was my fault."

Francine bit her lip. "But what if he doesn't believe you?"

"He will. You must go, Lady Francine."

But still Francine hesitated. This felt wrong. She felt as though she were making a terrible mistake.

"I can't do this," she said to Rafael. "I have to talk to Garrick first."

Rafael frowned. "Don't be a little fool. Go now while you have the chance, before the battle."

Francine grew pale. "What battle?"

Rafael looked impatient. "The barons laid siege to Northampton Castle a fortnight ago. It failed, but they advanced on London and took the city. Now their army is gathering at Stamford and the king has summoned his men to Oxford. There's bound to be fighting sooner or later."

Francine rose to her feet. "Garrick could get killed! I can't leave now. I must make sure he's all right."

"There's nothing you can do." Rafael's voice was sharp, and she looked at him in surprise. He laughed a little, and spoke again, this time in a light tone. "Don't be a fool, Lady Francine. You mean nothing to him—look at how he's treated you, how he's deceived you."

"Deceived me? What are you talking about?"

He laughed. "Garrick is from the future, too."

Francine stared at him in disbelief. "I don't believe you. He would have told me."

Rafael, his eyes bright, shrugged. "Obviously you don't know him as well as you think you do."

She stood still. She remembered his lack of interest when she'd told him she was from the future, the way he'd torn her clothes off her when she first arrived.

Her eyes narrowed. That no-good, dirty, rotten scoundrel. . . .

"Are you ready to go now, Lady Francine?"

She shook her head. "I'm not leaving until I know the truth—the whole truth."

"But he may not be home for months!"

"I'm certainly not going to wait that long," she said.

Rafael relaxed a trifle. But then Francine spoke again.

"Which is why I'm going to have to go find him—wherever he is."

Chapter 22

Anne, in spite of her close-lipped refusal to answer any questions about Garrick's origins, insisted on going with Francine—and somehow convinced Rafael to escort them. He looked quite surly, but Francine paid little attention to him. Her thoughts were focused completely on Garrick, anger and confusion dominating her emotions. But underneath there was something else—a deep and despairing fear that he might have been killed.

They rode for several days, spending the nights in whatever lodgings they could find. Francine didn't care about the discomfort—she only wanted to find Garrick as soon as possible. A sense of urgency drove her, a premonition that if she didn't find him soon, it might be too late. . . .

On the afternoon of the fifth day they came across unmistakable signs that an army had passed this way—deep ruts in the grass from carts, hoofprints, bushes trampled alongside the path. Several sullen farmers nodded when asked about the army—the soldiers had taken most of their food.

They rode into a forest and followed a narrow trail. Dusk was falling on the forest path when a voice suddenly called out, "Halt! Who goes there?"

Rafael answered, "'Tis the ladies Anne and Francine of Pelsworth, friends to King John and England."

A dirty, bearded soldier stepped out from behind a tree, his crossbow aimed directly at Rafael. "And who are you, my fine fellow?"

"He is but a lowly minstrel," Anne said, riding her horse forward before Rafael could answer. "We are here to see Sir Garrick of Pelsworth. 'Tis urgent. You must take us to him at once."

The man lowered his bow, whether because of the authority in Anne's voice or because of some magical influence, Francine wasn't sure.

"I believe Sir Garrick was in a skirmish a few days ago and was wounded," the soldier said. "He might be dead."

Francine reeled in the saddle, her hands going slack on the reins. *Dead?* Oh, dear God, *no*, he couldn't be.

"Where would he be if he is still alive?" Anne asked.

The soldier nodded to the right. "At the king's camp. I will escort you there."

The soldier tied the horses in a single-file line and led them through the trees. It was dark now, and Francine leaned her head on Bessie's mane for a moment, feeling sick. Fear greater than any she'd ever known clawed at her heart. He couldn't be dead—he just couldn't be.

They came out of the trees. Visible in the light of a hundred campfires, a half-circle of tents stood between the forest and meadow. The soldier continued forward through the camp. Ignoring the stares and whispers that followed them, Francine searched the firelit faces, searching for one in particular, one that had come to mean more to her than she could ever have imagined.

She didn't find it.

The sick feeling grew stronger. She wouldn't be able to bear it if he was dead. She would die, too. . . .

A flap to one of the tents lifted and a man bent double came out, frowning over a scroll in his hands. Not breaking his stride, he straightened and continued forward.

"Garrick!"

Her voice came out a strangled squawk, but he heard her.

He stopped and turned to stare at her. "Francine? What the devil . . . ?"

Francine barely heard him. Giddy with relief, she slid off her horse, ran to him, and threw her arms around his shoulders, hugging him tightly. "I thought you were dead!" She burst into tears.

He smoothed her hair, and glared at the men smirking around him. "Why on earth would you think that?"

"The . . . soldier . . . said . . . you'd been injured," she said in between sobs.

"He was mistaken—don't cry, Francine. Please don't cry. Come into the tent and tell me what you're doing here."

"I . . . I . . . oh!" The tears stopped flowing. She stepped back and slapped him as hard as she could.

The watching men burst out laughing.

His eyes narrowing, Garrick picked her up, slung her over his shoulder like a sack of potatoes, and strode into the tent.

The men outside roared louder.

Garrick flung her onto a bed of soft furs and said grimly, "*Now* would you like to tell me what the hell you're doing here?"

Francine, the breath knocked out of her, couldn't answer. She lay mutely, staring up at him, trying to regain her tongue.

Garrick's eyes narrowed. "I'm going to skin Orson alive. . . ."

Francine regained her breath and her tongue at the same moment. "Don't you dare!" she screeched. "Don't you dare lay a finger on him. It's not his fault you gave that ridiculous order to keep me prisoner. How could you do that?" Her voice rose as she repeated, "How *could* you?"

He looked away from her accusing gaze. "It was for your own safety. The robbers . . ."

"Ha! There weren't any robbers—or soldiers or wolves, either. Did you think I wouldn't discover the truth?"

For a moment she thought he wasn't going to answer her. But then he looked at her with dark eyes. "I couldn't bear for you to leave."

Francine stared at him, fury and some other emotion warring within her. His words didn't excuse him. He'd lied to her—repeatedly! She should never speak to him again. She should tell him that she was going home now and would never see him again.

But how could she leave when he looked at her like that?

He must have sensed her weakening, because he stepped closer, his hand coming up to cup her cheek. "Stay with me, Francine," he whispered. "Forget about that other world."

"*Your* world, too."

His hand dropped to his side, and he looked at her warily. "What do you mean?"

"Rafael told me you are from the future, also."

"Rafael—that damned troublemaker."

"Is it true?"

"Yes."

Francine released the breath she hadn't even been aware she was holding. Although she hadn't doubted Rafael, she hadn't quite been able to believe it until this moment. It made no sense. "How?" she asked, bewildered. "Why?"

"I ran away from home when I was fourteen," he said. "My mother had died several years before, and my father and I didn't get along, to say the least. I lived on the streets for a month, surviving by shoplifting, until I ran afoul of a gang. One of them cornered me in an alley and was about to shoot me, when an old woman appeared." He shook his head. "I thought she was going to be killed, too. I shouted at her to get the hell out of there, but she ignored me and started talking to the gang member. I couldn't hear what she said, but a few minutes later he left. Then she turned to me and made me an offer."

"An offer?"

"To transform the world. I was just young and arrogant enough to think that I could do it. I accepted. Next thing I knew, I was in 1202 England."

"Oh, you poor boy!" she exclaimed. It had been bad enough for her, a grown woman. She couldn't imagine how traumatic it must have been for a young boy. "Was it terrible?"

His mouth curved upward. "It was the most exciting experience of my life."

She gaped at him. "But didn't you hate how primitive everything was?"

He shrugged. "I didn't mind at all. I reveled in every aspect of this place. Oh, I was scared at first, but Anne found me at the side of the road and took me in. A year later she sent me to foster with William Marshal. I was here for some great purpose, and I thought I knew what it was—to become a knight, go on Crusades, and fight against evil." He smiled bleakly. "I became a knight. I went on a Crusade. But the evil was me."

Francine shivered. She couldn't imagine what terrible things he'd seen and done. She couldn't imagine how they'd affected him. She hated to think of how much he must have endured. Although she'd discovered that life here could be fairly pleasant, life in the Middle Ages on the whole would always be difficult, violent, and uncertain.

She reached out and grasped his hand. "Garrick, you don't need to stay in this terrible place any longer. You can come back to the future with me. I'm sure the emerald will take both of us."

He pulled away and stood, staring down at her, his face harsh in the shadowed light. "You still don't understand, do you? I'm not going back, Francine. That war was wrong, but it changed me. After that, I was no longer a boy. I knew what I wanted and how I was going to get it. With the ransom money I'd won in Constantinople, I bribed John into granting me land and license to build Pelsworth Castle. That is my home now. It is who I am."

She stared at him in shock, hardly able to comprehend what he was saying. "You can't mean that you want to stay here?"

"This is where I belong. That place in the future is like a distant dream. I have almost no memory of it. I'm not Rick Sinclair any more." He looked at her with a hard expression. "I'm not going back there, Francine."

He was deadly serious, she realized. He had no intention of returning to the future. If she were honest, she would have to admit that he was right—he didn't belong there. She would hate to see him change into a twentieth-century man, a man in a suit and tie, sitting in an office all day, living in a small box of a house or apartment, surrounded by streets and buildings and masses of people. In a way, it almost seemed obscene to think of him there.

"So what does that mean for us?" she asked.

He cupped her face between his hands, holding her so she couldn't look away. "It means that you will stay here with me. You cannot leave, Francine. You care about me. You know you do."

She stared at him, everything inside her trembling. She wanted to tell him he was wrong, that she didn't care about him at all, that she felt absolutely nothing for him. But she couldn't. Because it wasn't true. She loved him. She loved him so much she ached. The emotion she'd felt for Stuart was pallid by comparison, limited by her perceptions and inhibitions, and perhaps by his as well. Her love for Garrick, on the other hand, was deep and rich and full. She loved him with her mind, her heart, her body, and her soul. . . .

He was watching her closely, and must have read her answer in her face, because he smiled and lowered his mouth toward hers.

But before he could kiss her, she put her hand to his lips, preventing him. "If I stay, will you give up Odelia?"

His smile vanished. His hands dropped from her face and he stepped back. "Francine, I already explained to you about Odelia. I must marry her."

She took a deep breath. "It's true. I do care about you. And I would willingly give up the twentieth century, my job, my friends, even my family."

His expression softened, and he took a step forward. "Francine . . ."

She shook her head. "I would do all of that—but only if you were willing to do the same for me. If you loved me as much as I love you." She tried to smile, but her mouth trembled. "It's clear that you don't."

He scowled. "Francine, you don't understand—"

"Yes, I do," she said. "I understand the way things are here. And maybe someone else could accept that. But I can't."

She took a deep breath. "I'm willing to sacrifice a lot for you, Garrick. But not my self-respect."

Chapter 23

GARRICK DID NOT like what he was hearing. In one breath she claimed to be willing to sacrifice all for him. In the next, she said she would leave him because of some foolish idea of self-respect. She was not making sense.

He opened his mouth to argue with her, but before he could speak, a guard spoke through the flap of the tent.

"The king has summoned you, Sir Garrick. He requests that you appear at once."

"Very well," Garrick called, before turning his attention back to Francine. Resolution was written across her face. He frowned. "Stay here. We'll finish this discussion later."

He followed the guard to the king's tent, where John, in a foul humor, was threatening to fight to the death before signing the onerous charter the barons had presented. His two advisors, Stephen Langton and William Marshal, were trying, as tactfully as possible, to make him reconsider.

"The barons do have control of London," Garrick reminded the king when asked his opinion.

This set the king off again on a long, vindictive tirade about the disloyalty of the barons. Garrick tried to listen, but his thoughts kept drifting to Francine.

If you loved me as much as I do you . . .

Love. What did that mean, exactly? He remembered vaguely talk of love when he'd been in her world, that place that seemed so foreign to him now. He remembered his father stone-faced at his mother's funeral and two weeping women telling him that his father had loved her very, very much.

Perhaps if he'd stayed there, he would have learned about a different kind of love, a love that meant marrying a woman and living with her happily forever after. Love like that didn't exist here.

Or did it?

Why exactly was Francine important to him?

She was a tenuous link to his childhood—the only person here who'd known and experienced that different world. From the moment she'd arrived, in spite of all his resistance to her, her presence had lessened his sense of isolation.

But he'd lived with that isolation for a long time. He could do so again.

She provided incredible, mind-blowing, blood-singing sex that he could never get enough of. Sometimes he wanted to take her to bed and keep her there for days, weeks, and years. . . .

But he could have sex with other women. Now that Anne's spell was broken, he could sleep with an endless variety of women, in an endless variety of ways.

No, there was something else about Francine. Something unique just to her. Her odd notions that so often made him smile. The kindness that seemed to have been bred into her bones. The generosity of heart and spirit and soul that sometimes awed him, sometimes humbled him.

She had expanded his world in some mysterious way, made it richer, brighter, more meaningful. It was as if she'd added a whole new dimension to his life, a dimension whose existence he'd been completely unaware of. As if he'd only seen black and white before and now he could see every color of the rainbow.

Sunbursting awareness flashed through him.

Dear God.

Why hadn't he realized it before?

* * *

Francine was pacing about the tent when Anne entered.

"What happened?" the older woman asked. "Did he tell you he loves you?"

Francine tried to smile. "No, I'm afraid not. I'm going to return home as soon as possible."

Anne frowned. "You can't leave now. Not when there's about to be a battle."

"A battle?" Francine repeated. "What do you mean? I thought the king was going to sign some sort of peace treaty."

"That's what everyone thought. But everyone within fifty feet of his tent can hear him yelling that he won't sign, that he's going to order the attack."

"Oh, no!" Francine clasped her hands. "This is terrible! Isn't there anything you can do, Lady Anne?"

Anne shook her head. "No, I'm afraid not. But perhaps you could."

"Me! What could I do?"

"You could talk to him, convince him that he's taking the wrong course. He's always had a weakness for a pretty girl. Perhaps he'll listen to you."

If anyone else had made such a suggestion to Francine, she would have laughed. But with Anne anything, no matter how far-fetched, seemed possible. "But I wouldn't know what to say."

Anne ignored her weak excuse. "I'll tell you what to say. Now, listen. . . ."

The guard was surprisingly willing to let Francine in the tent—although perhaps it wasn't so surprising, Francine thought, watching the way Anne spoke to him in a hypnotic voice.

Francine entered the tent where a small group of men sat around a small table. They were bent over a diagram of some sort.

The king looked up impatiently. "Well? What is it?"

The guard cleared his throat. "The Lady Francine to see you, sire."

Francine was aware of Garrick's gaze on her, but she didn't look at him as she curtsied to the king.

"Lady Francine?" The king arched his brows. "To what do we owe this honor?"

She took a deep breath and said, "Sire, I came to warn you."

"Warn me?" He frowned. "Of what?"

"Last night I had a dream," she said. "I dreamed that night and day were one and that the sun and the stars lived together in harmony. But then the stars became angry at the sun and turned against him. They raised an army of stars and fought him. The sun had an army of meteors, and the meteors lifted their swords to fight the stars, but at the moment of victory, a terrible thing happened—the meteors' swords turned into jelly."

"Soft swords!" murmured one of the men.

John stiffened and glared at the man, before looking back at Francine. "And then what happened?"

"The sun lifted his mighty sword, but it, too, turned soft. The enormous blade started shrinking. It shrank and shrank until it was the size of a lady's pin. The stars laughed at him. They filled the sky and the sun was no more."

A mutter rose from the men—except for Garrick, whose face was completely expressionless.

King John looked pale, but he said, "A dream . . . it could mean anything—or nothing."

"It might be wise to heed Lady Francine, sire," Garrick said. "Her dreams usually prove most accurate."

"Sire," Langton said in a low voice. "I ask you once again to consider signing the demands of the barons. If we fight and lose, the crown will be lost forever."

For a long moment there was silence in the tent. Frowning deeply, John stroked his beard.

Finally he said, "Bring me paper."

Langton hurriedly complied. Everyone watched with bated breath as the king wrote something then attached his seal. "There," he scowled. "That should make them happy. Langton, Marshal, take this to the barons. I will sign the charter in the morning."

The two men bowed and retreated.

Garrick bowed also. "If you will excuse me, sire, I will take Lady Francine to my tent."

John waved his hand. "Very well, Sir Garrick. You may go."

Garrick hesitated a moment, then removed a small square of parchment from inside his doublet. "If it pleases you, sire, I will return this to you."

John looked at the parchment, then scowled up at Garrick. "Does this mean you are withdrawing your support?"

"No. It merely means that I no longer desire a match with Lady Odelia."

John turned his attention to Francine. "So be it. Good morrow, Lady Francine."

"Good morrow, sire," she said. She hesitated a moment, then said, "And may I say I think you're doing a very wise and noble thing? I'm certain people will speak of your generosity for years to come."

John snorted. "I have no intention of honoring this charter. I intend to write the pope immediately and ask him to dismiss it."

Francine stared at him. "But—"

"Excuse us, sire," Garrick interrupted. "I believe Lady Francine needs to lie down for a few moments after all the excitement."

John, his brow creased as if in thought, dismissed them with a lazy wave of his hand.

Francine looked over her shoulder as Garrick dragged her away from the king's tent. "Can you believe that? He's going to renege on the charter—"

"God's throat, Francine. For once in your life, hold your tongue!"

"Yes, Garrick," she said meekly.

He looked at her suspiciously. "How could you tell that ridiculous story about a dream of soft swords? Don't you know 'Softsword' is the name the barons call the king? To jeer at him for his lack of military prowess? You're fortunate he didn't hang you on the spot for your impertinence."

"Well, he didn't," she said.

He dragged her into the tent. Anne and Rafael were there, but except for one hard look at Rafael, Garrick ignored them, intent on Francine.

To her he said, "I was a fool to think I could marry Odelia. Can you ever forgive me?"

A flush of happiness spread over Francine. "I think so. But are you sure, Garrick?"

"I'm sure."

Tears came to her eyes. "I don't want you to regret this."

"I won't. Francine, I lo—"

"Take care what you say," Rafael said sharply. "Do not subjugate man to the domination of woman."

"Be quiet, Rafael," Anne snapped. To Garrick she said, "Go on, Garrick. What were you about to say?"

Garrick turned back to Francine. "Francine," he said in a low voice. "I love you. Will you marry me?"

Francine was vaguely aware of a groan from Rafael and a brilliant smile from Anne. She could barely see through the tears in her eyes. "Oh, Garrick. I love you, too. And yes, I'll marry you."

He swept her into his arms and kissed her.

With a snort of disgust, Rafael left the tent. Anne glanced at the fluttering flap, then turned back to Francine and Garrick. She cleared her throat.

The two lovers broke apart. Garrick smiled rather ruefully. "Are you satisfied now, Anne?"

"Oh, yes. Although I was never in any doubt as to the outcome."

Francine laughed. "How could you be so sure? I certainly wasn't."

Anne smiled smugly. "Oh, I knew Garrick would never let you leave. Especially not once he discovered you were carrying his child."

Garrick and Francine froze. Slowly, Garrick turned to Francine, a dazed expression in his eyes. "Is this true?"

Francine, looking equally dazed, said, "I don't know . . . I'm not sure. I suppose it *could* be true." She turned to Anne. "But what about the herbs you've been giving me? I thought they prevented conception."

"What made you think that?" Anne asked innocently.

Francine was too stunned to explain.

"A baby," Francine sighed, a smile lighting up her face. But then, just as quickly, it disappeared. She looked at Garrick. His expression was grim.

They stared at each other for several long moments in silence.

Finally, Garrick spoke. "You must return to the future."

"What?" Anne gasped.

Francine didn't move her gaze from Garrick's face. "I don't want to leave you."

He hesitated a moment, then said slowly, "You were willing to leave your world for mine. I can do no less for you."

Francine felt sick inside. Deep within her she knew that he belonged here, no matter where he'd come from originally—she'd always known that. "I'd hate to leave here."

"What is the matter with you two?" Anne interrupted. "What are you talking about?"

Garrick looked at her grimly. "I will not allow Francine to stay here and put her own life as well as the life of our child at risk."

"Oh, what nonsense," Anne said. "Many women have delivered children and survived."

"Only to see those babies die," Francine said quietly. "From illness. From accidents." Her voice lowered to a whisper. "From starvation. I couldn't bear it."

"Women have borne it for centuries," Anne said. "So can you."

Garrick and Francine ignored her. He turned and lifted the tent flap to allow her to go through. Francine took a step—

"Wait! You can't do this!"

Anne's screech jarred Francine out of her misery. She looked at the woman who was watching her and Garrick with an expression of disbelief, disgust . . . and dismay.

Francine's brain began to function again. "Why not?" she asked, watching Anne closely.

"Because, don't you see? Unless you stay, the world will continue to marry for power and land, and will continue to fight and kill."

Garrick's eyebrows rose. "We cannot change that."

"Yes, you can. It's of the utmost importance that you both stay here. So the world will know about love."

A gleam entered Garrick's eyes. "Perhaps we can make a bargain."

"A bargain?" Anne repeated warily.

Francine, meeting Garrick's gaze, caught on quickly. "Yes, a bargain. I will stay if you guarantee that Garrick and I and all our descendants will lead happy and healthy lives."

"What?!" Anne screeched again. "I can't do that! There are certain rules . . ."

"Then Francine and I go," Garrick said. "I will not risk her life or our child's."

"All right, all right, let me think," Anne said. She looked back and forth between the two of them. "I suppose I can guarantee health and happiness for the two of you. And for your descendants . . . but only if they marry for love. Otherwise, they take their chances like everybody else."

"I also want you to get a message to my grandmother and let her know I am well and happy; and to Garrick's family also. *And* I want you to make sure my overdue library book gets returned."

"How am I supposed to do that?" Anne expostulated, but then she subsided under Garrick's stare. "Very well," she conceded sourly. "I will do as you ask. Is that all?"

Garrick grinned at Francine. "Is that all, sweeting?"

She smiled back. "I think so, darling. Unless you can think of anything else."

"No, I think you've covered it. Except . . ." He fingered the emerald at her throat. "We'll keep the emerald as a guarantee of your promise."

Anne opened her mouth to protest, but seeing the uncompromising expression on his face, she pressed her lips tightly together. Vexed, she left the tent and stomped through the camp to the edge of the woods. She stopped when she saw Rafael staring at a point behind her. She moved to his side and turned to see the sun rising over the meadow.

Bright banners and pennons danced in the breeze. The barons' and earls' pavilions, hung with cloth of silk and gold, shimmered in the brilliant sunlight. Row upon row of knights stood in their mail hauberks and belted swords, while behind them, a ragged army of soldiers lounged and diced.

Trumpets blaring, King John slowly and haughtily left his tent and walked over to his own pavilion where Stephen Langton and William Marshal were waiting. John ascended the steps and sat in a chair. With a bored expression on his face, he listened while Langton read the charter aloud.

When Langton finished, he brought the vellum to the king and placed it before him. John rose, looked down his nose at the charter, then stared around the meadow. There was a collective inhalation of air.

With a contemptuous gesture, John affixed the royal seal to the charter.

A loud cheer rang out.

Anne, who'd been holding her breath as well, let out a sigh of relief and turned to Rafael. "At least that's over with."

"Hmm." He glanced at her sideways. "So, it would seem your plot succeeded."

Anne shrugged. "She's staying."

Rafael raised his eyebrows. "You don't sound too happy about it."

"I had to make several concessions. Garrick insisted on keeping the emerald as a guarantee. That was my best crystal."

"You gave him the emerald?" Rafael frowned. "That was not wise, Anne."

"I'll get it back—sooner or later. But in the meantime, it will take me weeks to work out the necessary spells without it."

"Poor Anne." He fell into step beside her. "You should have left well enough alone."

"Bah." She tossed her head. "Will you at least concede now that I am right?"

He shrugged. "I concede that two fools fancy themselves in love. It will not change the world. They will soon be forgotten."

Anne glared at him. "You are a stubborn mule, Rafael. Stubborn and *blind*."

He stumbled suddenly, putting his hand up to cover his eyes. "Anne, what have you done? Anne . . . !"

Back in their tent, Garrick bent over and kissed Francine. He kissed her again, then said in a serious tone, "Are you certain you wish to stay here?"

She smiled. "I can't imagine living anywhere else."

"Francine . . ."

"Yes?"

"Tell me more about that book, *Coupling for Blockheads*. Is it possible to . . ." He whispered in her ear.

A flush rose in her cheeks.

"I believe so. Did I tell you about the one hundred and one positions? There's one in particular I want to try. Only, it may take some practice. . . ."

Author's Note

King John did indeed try to renege on his agreement with the barons. Pope Innocent III agreed with him that the charter was illegal and declared it void. However, the barons would not put up with this treachery, and continued to fight the king. John died of dysentery a year later, in 1216. The barons renegotiated the charter with his heir, Henry III. Eventually it became known as the Great Charter, or Magna Carta—and some five hundred years later formed a partial basis for our own Bill of Rights.

If you would like a free bookmark and a copy of *The Secret Diary of Angie Ray: Researching* A Knight to Cherish, please send a self-addressed stamped envelope to: Angie Ray, P.O. Box 4672, Orange, CA 92863-4672. Also, please visit my website at: http://members.aol.com/occauthor/angieray.

If you enjoyed
A KNIGHT TO CHERISH
you won't want to miss

The More I
See You

by LYNN KURLAND

Coming in October from Berkley Books

One

Jessica Blakely didn't believe in Fate.

Yet as she stood at the top of a medieval circular staircase and peered down into its gloomy depths, she had to wonder if someone other than herself might be at the helm of her ship, as it were. Things were not progressing as she had planned. Surely Fate had known she wasn't at all interested in stark, bare castles or knights in rusting armor.

Surely.

She took a deep breath and forced herself to examine the turns of events that had brought her to her present perch. Things had seemed so logical at the time. She'd gone on a blind date, accepted said blind date's invitation to go to England as part of his university department's faculty sabbatical, then hopped cheerfully on a plane with him two weeks later.

Their host was Lord Henry de Galtres, possessor of a beautifully maintained Victorian manor house. Jessica had taken one look and fallen instantly in love—with the house, that is. The appointments were luxurious, the food heavenly, and the surrounding countryside idyllic. The only downside was that for some unfathomable reason, Lord Henry had decided that the crumbling castle attached to his house was something that needed to remain undemolished. Just the sight of it had sent chills down Jessica's spine. She couldn't say why, and she hadn't wanted to dig around to find the answer.

Instead, she'd availed herself of all the modern comforts Lord Henry's house could provide. And she'd been certain that when she could tear herself away from her temporary home-away-from-home, she might even venture to London for a little savings-account-reducing shopping at Harrods. Yet before she could find herself facing a cash register, she'd been driven to seek sanctuary in the crumbling castle attached to Lord Henry's house.

There was something seriously amiss in her life.

A draft hit her square in the face, loaded with the smell of seven centuries of mustiness. She coughed and flapped her hand in front of her nose. Maybe she should have kept her big mouth shut and avoided expressing any disbelief in Providence.

Then again, it probably would have been best if she'd remained silent a long time ago, maybe before she'd agreed to that blind date. She gave that some thought, then shook her head. Her troubles had begun long before her outing with Archibald Stafford III. In fact, she could lay her finger on the precise moment when she had lost control and Fate had taken over.

Piano lessons. At age five.

You wouldn't think that something so innocuous, so innocent and child-friendly would have led a woman where she never had any intention of having gone, but Jessica couldn't find any evidence to contradict the results.

Piano lessons had led to music scholarships that had led to a career in music that had somehow demolished her social life, leaving her no choice but to sink to accepting the latest in a series of hopeless blind dates: Archie Stafford and his shiny penny loafers. Archie was the one who had invited her to England for a month with all expenses paid. He had scored the trip thanks to a great deal of sucking up to the dean of his department. He didn't exactly fit in with the rest of the good old boys who clustered with the dean and Lord

Henry every night smoking cigars into the wee hours, but maybe that's what Archie aspired to.

Jessica wondered now how hard up he must have been for a date to have asked her to come along. At the time he'd invited her, though, she'd been too busy thinking about tea and crumpets to let the invitation worry her. It had been a university-sponsored outing. She'd felt perfectly safe.

Unfortunately, being Archie's guest also meant that she had to speak to him, and *that* was something she wished she could avoid for the next three weeks. It was only on the flight over that she'd discovered the depth of his swininess. She made a mental note never to pull out her passport for anyone she'd known less than a month if such an occasion should arise again.

But like it or not, she was stuck with him for this trip, which meant at the very least polite conversation, and if nothing else, her mother had instilled in her a deep compulsion to be polite.

Of course, being civil didn't mean she couldn't escape now and then, which was precisely what she was doing at present. And escape had meant finding the one place where Archie would never think to look for her.

The depths of Henry's medieval castle.

She wondered if an alarm would sound if she disconnected the rope that barred her way. She looked to her left and saw that there were a great many people who would hear such an alarm if it sounded, but then again, maybe she wouldn't be noticed in the ensuing panic. Apparently Lord Henry funded some of his house upkeep by conducting tours of his castle. Those tours were seemingly well attended, if the one in progress was any indication.

Jessica eyed the sightseers. They were moving in a herd-like fashion and it was possible they might set up a stampede if she startled them. They were uncomfortably nestled together, gaping at cordoned-off family heirlooms, also uncomfortably nestled together. Lord Henry of Marcham's home was a prime destination spot and Jessica seemed to have placed herself in the midst of the latest crowd at the precise moment she needed the most peace and quiet. She had already done the castle tour and learned more than she wanted to know about Burwyck-on-the-Sea and its accompanying history. Another lesson on the intricacies of medieval happenings was the last thing she needed.

"—Of course the castle here at Marcham, or Merceham, as it was known in the 1300s, was one of the family's minor holdings. Even though it has been added to during the years and extensively remodeled during the Victorian period, it is not the more impressive of the family's possessions. The true gem of the de Galtres crown lies one-hundred-fifty kilometers away on the eastern coast. If we move further along here, you'll find a painting of the keep."

The crowd shuffled to the left obediently as the tour guide continued with his speech.

"As you can see here in this rendering of Burwyck-on-the-Sea—aptly named, if I might offer an opinion—the most remarkable feature of the family's original seat is the round tower built not into the center of the bailey as we find in Pembroke Castle, but rather into the outer seawall. I would imagine the third lord of the de Galtres family fancied having his ocean view unobstructed—"

So could Jessica and she heartily agreed with the sentiment, but for now an ocean view was not what she was interested in. If the basement was roped off it could only mean that it was free of tourists and tour guides. It was also possible that below was where the castle kept all its resident spiders and ghosts, but it was a chance she would have to take. Archie would never think to look for her there. Ghosts could be ignored. Spiders could be squashed.

She put her shoulders back, unhooked the rope, and descended.

She stopped at the foot of the steps and looked for someplace appropriate. Suits of armor stood at silent attention along both walls. Lighting was minimal and creature comforts nonexistent, but that didn't deter her. She walked over the flagstones until she found a likely spot, then eased her way between a fierce-looking knight brandishing a sword and another grimly holding a pike. She did a quick cobweb check before she settled down with her back against the stone wall. It was the first time that day she'd been grateful for the heavy gown she wore. A medieval costume might suit her surroundings, but it seemed like a very silly thing to wear to an afternoon tea—and said afternoon tea was precisely what she'd planned to avoid by fleeing to the basement.

Well, that and Archie.

She reached into her bag and pulled out what she needed for complete relaxation. Reverently, she set a package of two chilled peanut-butter cups on the stone floor. Those she would save for later. A can of pop followed. The floor was cold enough to keep it at a perfect temperature as well. Then she pulled out her portable CD player, put the headphones on her head, made herself more comfortable and, finally closing her eyes with a sigh, pushed the play button. A chill went down her spine that had nothing to do with the cold stone.

Bruckner's Seventh could do that to a girl, given the right circumstances.

Jessica took a deep breath and prepared for what she knew was to come. The symphony started out simply. She knew eventually it would increase in strength and magnitude until it came crashing down on her with such force that she wouldn't be able to catch her breath.

She felt her breathing begin to quicken and had to wipe her palms on her dress. It was every bit as good as it had been the past 139 times she had listened to the same piece. It was music straight from the vaults of heav—

Squeak.

Jessica froze. She was tempted to open her eyes, but she was almost certain what she would see would be a big, fat rat sitting right next to her, and then where would she be? Her snack was still wrapped, and since it really didn't count as food anyway, what could a rat want with it? She returned her attention to the symphony. It was the London Philharmonic, one of her favorite orchestras—

Wreek, wreek, wreeeeeek.

Rusty shutters? Were there shutters in the basement? Hard to say. She wasn't about to open her eyes and find out. There was probably some kind of gate nearby and it was moving thanks to a stiff breeze set up by all the tourists tromping around upstairs. Or maybe it was a trapdoor to the dungeon. She immediately turned away from that thought, as it wasn't a place she wanted to go. She closed her eyes even more firmly. It was a good thing she was so adept at shutting out distractions. The noise might have ruined the afternoon for her otherwise.

Wreeka, wreeka, wreeeeeeka.

All right, that was too much. It was probably some stray kid fiddling with one of the suits of armor. She'd give him an earful, send him on his way, and get back to her business.

She opened her eyes—then shrieked.

There, looming over her with obviously evil intent, was a knight in full battle gear. She pushed herself back against the stone wall, pulling her feet under her and wondering just what she could possibly do to defend herself. The knight, however, seemed to dismiss her upper person because he bent his helmeted head to look at her feet. By the alacrity with which he suddenly leaned over in that direction, she knew what was to come.

The armor creaked as the mailed hand reached out. Then, without any hesitation, the fingers closed around her peanut-butter cups. The visor was flipped up with enthusiasm, the candy's covering ripped aside with more dexterity than any gloved hand should have possessed, and Jessica's last vestige of American junk food disappeared with two great chomps.

The chomper burped.

"Hey, Jess," he said, licking his chops, "thought you might be down here hiding. Got any more of those?" He pointed at the empty space near her feet, his arm producing another mighty squeak.

Rule number one: No one interrupted her during Bruckner.

Rule number two: No one ate her peanut-butter cups, *especially* when she found herself stranded in England for a month without the benefit of a Mini Mart down the street. She had yet to see any peanut-butter cups in England and she'd been saving her last two for a quiet moment alone. Well, at least the thief hadn't absconded with her drink as of yet—

"Geez, Jess," he said, reaching for her can of pop, popping the top, and draining the contents, "why are you hiding?"

She could hardly think straight. "I was listening to Bruckner."

He burped loudly. "Never understood a girl who could get all sweaty over a bunch of fairies playing the violin." He squashed the can, then grinned widely at the results a mailed glove could generate. Then he looked at her and winked. "How'd you like to come here and give your knight in shining armor a big ol' kiss?"

I'd rather kiss a rat was on the tip of her tongue, but Archibald Stafford III didn't wait for that to make it past her lips. He hauled her up from between her guardians—and of good two empty suits of armor had done her—sending her CD player and headphones crashing to the ground, pulled her against him, and gave her the wettest, slobberiest kiss that had ever been given an unwilling maiden fair.

She would have clobbered him, but she was trapped in a mailed embrace and powerless to rescue herself.

"Let me go," she squeaked.

"What's the matter? Aren't you interested in my strong, manly arms?" he said, giving her a squeeze to show just how strong and manly his arms were.

"Not when they're squeezing the life from me," she gasped. "Archie, let me go!"

"It'll be good for research purposes."

"I'm a musician, for heaven's sake. I don't need to do this kind of research. And you are a . . ." and she had to pause before she said it because she still couldn't believe such a thing was possible, given the new insights she'd had into the man currently crushing the life from her, "a . . . philosopher," she managed. "A tenured philosopher at a major university, not a knight."

Archibald sighed with exaggerated patience. "The costume party, remember?"

As if she could forget, especially since she was already dressed à la medieval, complete with headgear and lousy shoes. And it was an afternoon tea for the vacationing faculty of Archie's university. Why they had chosen to dress themselves up as knights and ladies fair she couldn't have said. It had to have been the brainchild of that nutty history professor who hadn't been able to clear his sword through airport security. She'd known just by looking at him that he was trouble.

If only she'd been as observant with Archie. And now here she was, staring at what had, at first blush, seemed to be one of her more successful blind dates. She could hardly reconcile his current self with his philosophy self. Either he'd gotten chivalry confused with chauvinism, or wearing that suit of armor too long had allowed metal to leach into his brain and alter his personality.

"I'll carry you up," Archie said suddenly. "It'll be a nice touch."

But instead of being swept up into his arms, which would have been bad enough, she found herself hoisted and dumped over his shoulder like a sack of potatoes.

"My CD player," she protested.

"Get it later," he said, trudging off toward the stairs.

She struggled, but it was futile. She thought about name-calling, but that, she decided, was beneath her. He'd have to put her down eventually and then she would really let him have it. For the moment, however, it was all she could do to avoid having her head make contact with the stairwell as Archie huffed up the steps. He paused and Jessica heard a cacophony of startled gasps. Fortunately she was hanging mostly upside down, so her face couldn't get any redder.

"I love this medieval stuff," Archie announced to whatever assembly there was there, "don't you?"

And with that, he slapped her happily on the rump—to the accompaniment of more horrified gasps—and continued on his way.

Jessica wondered if that sword she'd seen with the armor in the basement was sharp. Then again, maybe it would be just as effective if it were dull. Either way, she had the feeling she was going to have to use it on the man who chortled happily as he carried her, minus her dignity, on down the hallway to where she was certain she would be humiliated even further.